The Idea of Him

·y Peterson is the author of the *New York Times* bestseller *Manny*. She was a contributing editor for *Newsweek* and ·or-at-large for *Talk* magazine. She was also an Emmy ·ard-winning producer for *ABC News* for more than a ·ade, where she covered global politics. Her writing has ·n published in the *New York Times*, *Newsweek*, *Talk*, the ·*ly Beast*, *Vogue*, *Harper's Bazaar*, and other publications.

BY THE SAME AUTHOR

The Manny

The Idea of Him

Holly Peterson

HARPER

Harper
An imprint of HarperCollins*Publishers*
77–85 Fulham Palace Road,
Hammersmith, London W6 8JB

www.harpercollins.co.uk

This paperback edition 2014
1

Holly Peterson asserts the moral right to
be identified as the author of this work

A catalogue record for this book
is available from the British Library

ISBN: 978-0-00-723305-2

Printed and bound in Great Britain by
Clays Ltd, St Ives plc

FSC
www.fsc.org
MIX
Paper from
responsible sources
FSC® C007454

FSC™ is a non-profit international organization established to promote
the responsible management of the world's forests. Products carrying the
FSC label are independently certified to assure consumers that they come
from forests that are managed to meet the social, economic and
ecological needs of present and future generations,
and other controlled sources.

Find out more about HarperCollins and the environment at
www.harpercollins.co.uk/green

To my four parents in their starring roles as role models: Sally for teaching empathy, Pete for personifying drive, Joan for dispensing wisdom at every turn, and Michael for setting a high intellectual bar for all of us.

1

Memory Lane

The taxi driver took off down Seventh Avenue as if he'd just mainlined a pound of crystal meth. This guy was on a kamikaze mission, reckless even by New York standards where taxi drivers charge down the streets with no regard for their passengers' lives.

"Slow down, sir, please!" I yelled through the opening in the glass partition as I contemplated ditching this driver at the next corner.

He slammed on his brakes. "Okay, lady! I'll slow it down a little. Yeah." But when the light turned green, he began weaving between cars and playing chicken to blow past the giant city buses. We brushed a bike messenger who retaliated with a fisted punch on the trunk. I again waffled about getting out, but it was that bustling time of early rush hour just before the taxi shift change, when I wouldn't be able to get another, so I stayed put and latched my seat belt. Besides, my kids were waiting for me at home, and I was already half an hour late leaving the office.

I sat strapped in the ratty backseat, tossed back and forth down the length of Manhattan's Seventh Avenue like a Ping-Pong ball.

This car is going to crash.

The lethal night of the plane accident came back to me in waves, starting with the instinctual pangs telling me not to step up from the tarmac onto the slippery, rickety staircase of the little six-seater. *This plane is not made for all this stormy snow,* I had said to myself that night. And I was right.

So much of my life had gone according to plan since then, much of it mapped out in a two-decades'-long fit to fix wrongs—the most evil happening on the eve of my sixteenth birthday that winter night, eighteen-years and four-months ago.

MY FATHER HAD been planning the trip all year. He had told Mom it was his chance to spend a few days one-on-one with his only child, teaching me the secrets of ice fishing at his favorite spot on Diamond Lake up north. He'd been talking about this as long as I could remember, and, finally, a week before my sixteenth birthday, Mom said I was old enough to go.

Dad had handed in his boarding pass outside, and he came onto the small commuter plane in Montreal, dusting snow off his beard and shoulders once he managed to jam his huge frame into the seat. I knew Dad saw the fear in my face and tried his best to reassure me. All I could think about was how small and fragile that plane seemed against the howling winds outside. Deep down that voice was telling me this was a bad idea, but I kept my mouth shut at first. I didn't want to look like a frightened little girl.

Dad smelled of metal and cold air, a scent that further unsettled me because it was so far from his usual salty warmth. I rubbed his arm to chase away the odor and he smiled down at me.

On the plane, I thought danger was nearby but I didn't want to scare anybody. Others have certainly had that same feeling before they board a plane with severe weather forecast in the flight path, wondering if they should resist getting on because this could be the one that goes down. A moment's hesitation before they step over that little gap and feel the rush of cold outside air between the boarding ramp and the aircraft front galley. *Is my mind playing tricks or do I somehow* know *this plane is going down? Am I having some kind of psychic experience? Am I going to be on the local news as the one person who survived only because I didn't get on at the last minute?*

The whole body stiffens on the ramp for a moment to stall and consider the possibility.

But then, *No. That's ridiculous. Screw it. I'm getting on. Statistics say it is more dangerous to drive to the airport than to get on this plane.*

At least most often it goes like that. I guess you don't need to be clairvoyant to know that during a blizzard, when a lumberjack pilot in a plaid shirt working for a low-budget commuter airline in Canada's outback says, "It's just a little snow," you get out of the twin-engine Cessna and run for your life.

MY PLAN SINCE then *has* been to run for my life. Run away from a boyfriend who kept traveling too far, run into a marriage that I thought would work. Rush to have kids to cement the union. Rush home to them today. This plan means I've tried to solve everything quickly before all hell descended on me again. Trauma is like that. It smashes into your life out of the blue and just lingers, dripping like a broken egg.

The kamikaze taxi lurched me back into the New York present, and the frayed seat belt snapped into place, jerking me hard. "Please slow down, sir," I yelled again at the driver. "That light was clearly turning red, and you were never going to make it, so you don't need to speed up just to slam the brakes."

"Okay, lady. Thanks for the driving tip. All I need at the end of my shift." This time he took off two full seconds before the light even turned green. I clenched my teeth and again started to feel that old tingle I'd felt in my bones as the pilot had swung the plane out of the boarding area some eighteen years earlier.

THE ENGINES HAD revved up as he made a ninety-degree tight turn at the end of the snowy runway. I gripped my armrests, imagining how my funeral would be. Matching father-daughter coffins. That's what it would look like. I blinked hard against the image.

Dad seemed oblivious to my fears. "You don't actually sit outside and fish all day. You can leave the lines in and then go check them," Dad went on. "You're gonna love it, Allie Lamb. No trout tastes like this anywhere in the world. This lake is crystal clear in the winter; beneath five feet of ice those damn fish still manage to . . ."

"Dad," I rasped. "The snow, it's just . . ."

He held my hand and kissed my forehead. "It's okay, honey.

A dozen guys I know have flown to this paradise in weather like this. All good."

The plane made a high-pitched whine as we sped down the runway into a cloudy, billowy, late-afternoon haze. The takeoff was absolutely normal, save a few little bumps when we made the initial ascent, and I let out a small breath. Dad patted my thigh. "You see, honey. It's all fine. We'll be above the clouds soon and see the sun." Our craft coasted up toward the sky.

OUTSIDE THE WINDOW of the taxi, I could see we were now speeding west across Forty-Second Street, past a seedy commercial section of town, heading toward the flashing lights of Times Square and standstill traffic. I said through the glass, "You might want to loop over to Ninth . . ."

The guy slammed on the brakes and turned around. "Look, lady, I'm gonna get you there." Two blocks later, we were parked in traffic. I did the math: it would take me about twenty minutes to walk, but if this traffic jam broke after five minutes, then it would only take fifteen more to reach home. Same difference. Same exploding anxiety over something with the same result that I couldn't change. I sat back against the seat again, frustrated and sweaty, my hands clammy from the plane ride down memory lane.

"YOU'RE NEVER GOING to forget the first time the fish bite, it's so exciting out there, the nature so delicate," Dad yelled over the whirl of the propellers, still gaining altitude. He cradled me in the crook of his elbow and kissed the top of my head.

My dad couldn't contain his excitement about introducing me to his greatest joy, and I couldn't spoil everything for him, so intoxicating was his commitment to seek that thrill with his own daughter. I wanted to warn the pilot that I *felt* we were in serious trouble, but I kept silent. I *felt* we shouldn't even take off in this weather. Maybe I was too young to protest, to be taken seriously. And I loved my dad too much to drag him through my worries. Downers were anathema to everything he stood for.

But there was that unmistakable ice on the wing. I'd seen something on TV about ice buildup that doomed a big plane, and I wasn't sure if it was the same thing. Or was it just beads of water pooled out there that would slide off somehow? Or was my mind conjuring up troubles? It sure looked like little bubbles of ice were popping up. Maybe the lights on the wing were just reflecting off beads of water. But would there be water at this altitude and at this temperature? I had reminded myself the takeoff was absolutely normal. Surely my mind was playing tricks.

It was getting dark and the lights on the wings were flashing intermittently so I couldn't tell how bad the storm was. The snow socked us in with zero visibility. We did not see one ray of that sun Dad had promised me.

"Dad. It's, like, pouring snow. Are you sure . . ."

"Allie. Don't worry, we are doing just fine."

Ten minutes passed, and the plane dipped into a mini wind pocket and then jerked up again. It felt like we just dropped fifteen feet, hit something hard, and bounced right back up. The metal on the wings rattled. I gasped.

"Hey, pull those belts extra-tight back there; it's getting pretty damn windy," the pilot yelled to us. "We're beginning our descent, but it's gonna be bumpy."

The wings now alternated up and down like a seesaw with our passenger capsule in the middle. Dad tried to get my mind off things. "What about the summer? I don't want you selling T-shirts at that ratty shop downtown. Scooping ice cream just off my dock will be easier to get to and . . ."

He paused and looked out the window; the last bump was so big he had to rest his arm on his head for protection. "Now I know teenagers veer toward doing whatever their friends are doing downtown, but . . ." Dad's chatter went on, with him talking faster and faster, while the teeny cabin shook so much his words came out all jumpy.

I think he might have been scared too and wanted to distract us both. He kept looking out the window, pausing, then talking again quickly. "I sure don't want you in cars of any teenagers, so I'd have to drive you, and that won't work for my early morning work schedule . . ." I don't know what was really going on for him. God, the number of times I've wondered. How I wish to have been able to ask him. I'll never know if he *knew* what I *felt* at that point.

My father grabbed my hand. The plane seemed to fall twenty feet and then lunge forward.

The pilot yelled. "We're descending fast. Hold on!" Dad's eyes grew large. He then knew what I knew. For a millisecond, part of me felt relief that my fears were justified, but then seeing him anxious did anything but quell them.

"Hold on, honey!!!" he screamed at me.

I'd never seen fear in his eyes before. Ever. I screamed. I think everyone did, but I'm not sure. Seconds later, metal crunched everywhere around me.

I remember every jolt of force throwing me forward as we bumped along the icy grass. They say I must have blacked out for a while after the crash, but I know I remember it. Blood sloshed around my mouth. I smelled the burned fibers of the synthetic royal blue seat fabric.

After we slowed to a deceiving, gentle stop: total silence.

"Dad!" I screamed. "Dad!"

Wind whistled through the cracks in the metal, and snow started whirling into the now shattered front windshield. It was way too calm inside. And next I knew, maybe three full minutes later, the skidding sound of vehicles outside the craft penetrated the eeriness inside. A man in a yellow suit with reflective silver stripes started coaxing me through the wreckage, the gusts of snowfall obscuring the beam of his flashlight. I couldn't see my father or the pilot. I knew they were hurt. I didn't hear them and they weren't taking care of me, the child, in the wreckage. And I had the sudden sense they were dead.

Once they pried open the window, the men asked if we could move. I was curled upside down and waited for my father to answer.

"Dad?"

That was the worst moment of all: the silence after I asked again. I would have actually been relieved to hear him screaming in pain at that point.

Freezing wind was now howling through the front window and the sides of the open plane. The men asked again if we could move, if anyone heard them. I finally said out loud, "I'm okay."

"Good. That's good. Can you try to get through this window?"

"I don't know if anyone else is okay."

"C'mon, sweetie, we'll get them; you just get yourself through the window. Undo your seat belt if you can. There's room for you to get out from under the seat. Crawl through right here." The top of my hand was cut badly and my bones felt rattled, but, as far as I could tell, nothing was broken. The red light of the ambulance siren reflected off the snow and metal, blinding me every time it whipped around like a lighthouse beam. I did not want to leave that plane.

I shook my head. "I gotta get my father. I gotta get my dad!"

"We're going to get him for you. We have to get you out first; you are next to the exit." He grabbed my upper arm with one hand and supported my lower arm with the other. "Can you get out this way?" I thought that metal had somehow gotten lodged in my mouth. My tongue felt jagged, shattered teeth on the right side. I remember worrying the edges were going to cut my tongue.

"Where's my dad! Where's my dad!" I screamed, the taste of iron from the blood in my mouth now thick and soupy. My head filled with pounding wrath.

How dare Dad let us take off.

And how dare he let two other people from back home get on the plane with us.

*

"HEY, LADY, YOU gonna pay or what? What are you doin' so quietly back there, knitting an entire sweater? I don't got all day. We're here already," the taxi driver said, knocking on the partition to stir me out of my trance. In a flash, I was back in the taxi, shaking with a rage I hadn't felt in years.

How dare he die on me so young.

I had to wipe my trembling hand on my jeans before I could open my wallet and pay for the sickening ride.

2

Homefront

When I walked through my front door, I had to push every memory from that taxi ride out of my head. Lucy, in particular, would need me to focus on the excitement she'd had wearing the caterpillar costume made out of foam and pipe cleaners we'd worked on for days. Even after dinner, Lucy wouldn't let me take off her green face paint from the caterpillar role until her daddy got to see her.

"Wade. You have to make a big deal about Lucy's face," I whispered. My husband arrived home about an hour after I had that night, work forcing him to miss Lucy's kindergarten staging of *Alice in Wonderland*.

"Where's my superstar?" Wade said to Lucy on cue, as he rushed into our bedroom with a bouquet of purple tulips he had picked up at the corner market for her. "I hate that I had to be at boring meetings at the magazine all day and miss your show!"

Lucy jumped up onto the bed to see him at eye level. "Daddy! I didn't forget anything this time."

He hugged her hard and then held her at arm's length. "You have a little something green on your face," he said in a mock-serious way that made Lucy first furrow her brow and then break into a giant smile once she got the joke. Wade released her, and she snuggled back up beside me as he pulled off his work shirt and tie in one big motion, throwing both into the hamper.

That's when a very strange thing happened. A casino chip with Five Thousand Dollars written on it fell out of his shirt pocket. I wouldn't necessarily have noticed had Wade not dove for the chip like a linebacker. I didn't let on that I'd seen it or the more alarming amount; instead I made a mental note of his unusually athletic attempt to hide it. Something inside made my heart break for no concrete reason except that it felt suspicious.

Once he got up off the floor and surreptitiously stuffed the chip into his khaki pants, I looked at my husband like I didn't even know him. He grabbed Lucy and carried her back to her room sack-of-potatoes style.

I stood in the doorway of the bedroom in our cramped New York apartment mulling over that chip. We didn't have five thousand dollars to throw around or to keep in our pants' pockets. Wade was the editor of a flashy newsmagazine, but that didn't mean we had a comfortable amount of savings. New York is like that. Everyone here except the Wall Street, one-percenter crowd is living on a financial edge where close to nothing is left over. My PR firm salary combined with his editor salary didn't pay for much beyond a small apartment and two private-school tuitions. Five thousand dollars really mattered to our bottom line.

And Wade wasn't a gambler. He didn't hide things from me. We were opposites, but we came together at a safe place in the middle where I harbored a notion that trust was key. When I first met Wade, he had six people glued onto him like a snake charmer and still had enough juice to lure me across a room and into his comforting spell. And despite the distraction of a persistent flame from my past, and to be honest, partially because of that flame, I leaped into a frenetic New York City life with Wade, covering my eyes and holding my breath.

I heard Lucy screaming from the bedroom, "Daddy, air lift!" I entered and saw Wade hoisting her skyward, missing the light fixture by mere inches.

"Wade. Please! You're going to hurt her on the light! And make sure you give Blake some attention before bedtime; he's upset over . . ."

"Who gets every joy of the earth?" he asked as he threw Lucy up again, giving me the eye.

"Lucy!" she shrieked, falling back into his strong hands.

"And who was the best caterpillar in the show?"

"Daddy, there's only ONE caterpillar!"

"And what girl does Daddy love best in the world?"

"Lucy!" They collapsed onto the bed, and Wade tickled her until she yelled out for him to stop, happy tears streaming down her face. Wade cradled her in his arms for a few more moments, singing a little song he had made up when she was a baby, then turned to me and held my face in his hands, dispelling any residual wifely annoyance over the casino chip I preferred to ask him about later.

"Allie, I know all you do to make the kids happy—making her costume so intensely the night before and keeping all your work pressures out of the kids' lives—and I love you for it." He kissed my nose. "And don't worry about Blake; I know you're worrying about him too. I see that concern in your face."

"Yes, I'm worried about him. They don't include him in so many of the little things his group does all day. All because of one kid who loves the power to exclude. I want so badly to call Jeremy's mom again and—"

"You cannot do that again. No way. She is going to tell the kid exactly what you said on the call even though she promises to handle it discreetly. And that'll just make Jeremy ostracize Blake more, and then you get busted for interfering. Fourth grade is rough, but he's got to learn to handle his friendships on his own."

"Wade, I know you are right, but his circle is edging him out again, and I don't know how a nine-year-old is supposed to figure that out. They went to get snacks at the vending machine again at recess and told him he couldn't come."

"Well, I'm going to help him man up a little, and then he'll work this out for himself."

Another thing I loved about Wade: he knew exactly what our kids needed when they were down. What woman doesn't love a man for that? But that casino chip would pop up again and, in time, signal a transgression no wife could ignore.

3

Power Jaunt

The next morning, I rushed to see my boss for fifteen minutes before a client meeting at New York's famed Tudor Room. It didn't help my mood that I was meeting him at a restaurant that operated more like a private club for high-octane achievers than a pleasant place for lunch. Absolutely nothing in my makeup or past experiences prepared me to hold my own in the ring with the wealthy gladiators who lunched there regularly; I just happened to be employed by one of them. I walked into the restaurant lobby with a confident stride, wondering if the people watching my entrance pegged me as an imposter.

My boss, Murray Hillsinger, a toadlike man, had already positioned his large bottom smack in the middle of a coveted corner banquette, twisting his jowls left and right to survey the scene from his primo lily pad. He was very proud to have his square corner banquette (even though it wasn't as prestigious as the center round tables—those went to higher rollers with huger titles, companies, and net worths). I took a deep breath and walked over, smoothing my hair as I did so, trying to exude professional acumen, the only attribute I could for sure hold on to.

"Allie, come here. Glad you came before my lunch partner shows up." He patted the leather next to him. "You're going to do fine, kid."

Like so many guys named Murray, it seems, he grew up poor on the backstreets—in this case, Long Island City, Queens. His nose was crooked from one too many fistfights, and his large forehead was now crowned with an unfortunate shoe-polish comb-over. The expensive loafers he sported were not designed for feet that caused the leather to crack in a fault line next to his big fat pinkie toe.

I moved my way around the seat on Murray's right. "Relax. It's going to go fine," he told me as he chomped on a large cauliflower cluster drenched in green dip and roughed up the back of my hair like I was his kid sister. I *was* a kid when I started this job a decade ago in my early twenties, and neither he, nor I, to my dismay, ever got past that initial dynamic.

Georges—the famous-in-his-own-right maître d' of the Tudor Room—rushed to the table, an invisible cloud of his cologne preceding him. Georges ladled more dip into the ramekin dish as he asked, "Would you rather I pour the sauce on your tie directly, or should I allow you to stain it yourself?"

The very French Georges knew that the powerful always favor those employees willing to show jocular insubordination. I watched as he moved off into the room, slipping from table to table making clever, and often hilarious, asides to the assembled men and women who pretty much ran every major hedge fund, real estate empire, and media conglomerate in Manhattan.

Murray sat at the helm of the biggest public relations firm in New York, Hillsinger Consulting, hell-bent on saving the reputations of most of the people in this very room, many of them guilty as charged for causing the recurring economic downturns that trickled down and crippled the rest of us. The Tudor Room was a new hotspot for these powerful warriors who dined in packs, many having migrated from the more clubby Four Seasons Grill Room. The new place was part lunch spot and part womblike secret society where they all felt cozy in their amniotic bubble—this protective coating thickening ever since they had been targeted by America for causing the biggest economic downfall since the Great Depression.

"Order something, Allie!" Murray barked, always solicitous in his own special way.

"Thanks, no food, my meeting is soon," I said. "Besides, I'm too on edge."

"About what? You're tough. That's why you got the big job," Murray said, trying to prop me up for my meeting in fifteen minutes at the Tudor Room bar to placate the unreasonable newswoman Delsie Arceneaux. If I didn't always have the keen sense that Murray believed in me, and if I hadn't always witnessed him doing the mensch-y thing, like promoting all the smartest women in the office, I would have quit doing crazy things for him long ago.

Sitting at the bar, Delsie Arceneaux glanced over and winked at Murray through her signature large tortoiseshell glasses as she barked into her phone before our meeting started. She was the impetuous, African American news anchor of the "all Delsie all the time" cable news network, most famous for draping her fortysomething, voluptuous body over an army tank while she interviewed the commander of the U.S. forces in Kabul. The perennial glasses had been Murray's idea to disguise her beauty queen looks and highlight her legitimate cerebral side.

"No," I replied. "You got the big job. I service your requests and put your crazy notions on paper." Today's particular request was to placate a news anchor, known for alienating her staff by overriding their every decision and action. "Does she even know we are also representing the people who are asking her to speak . . ."

"Order some broth, Allie." Conflict of interest was a concept that Murray Hillsinger found utterly tiresome. "Calm the fuck down. Nothing wrong with us booking our own clients for our other clients and taking a little cut on both sides." He pushed the tan parchment paper menu too close to my face and pointed at the appetizers.

Georges came over to hover and pour two thousand more calories of dill cream into the dip ramekin.

"I don't want any soup, Murray."

"Give her the soup, Georges. She works too damn hard and deserves a little pleasure once in a while. You know the good one I mean. The light one, the brothy one. With those duck balls."

"Foie gras wontons, sir." Georges wrote the request down with his dainty fingers wrapped around the tip of a miniature gold pen.

"Really, Murray?" I pleaded. "Thirty-eight dollars for consommé I don't even want?"

"She'll have the consommé." Murray looked at the maître d' and then back at me. "You got some time before your meeting. It'll settle you down. Gimme the lobster salad before my guest arrives as a little preappetizer. Double order." Georges nodded and left the table.

"Why are the most famous people also the most neurotic about public speaking gigs? She looks into a camera and speaks to four million viewers and she can't give a speech to two hundred people?"

He patted my hand. "All the news anchors do this. The camera is her guardian and her barrier. Without it, the live audience terrifies her. Just go handle her nerves for me. And have some soup."

Next to me, a glamorous newspaper publisher in a sunny yellow Oscar de la Renta spring dress and matching bolero sweater raised her index finger in the air at Georges and mouthed *Charge it to my account* as she sashayed toward the door.

I leaned toward Murray, whispering, "I don't need the soup because I don't like to throw money away like all your friends in here."

"It's not about the money in this room. It's about what you've accomplished." He stole my nose with his finger like I was five years old. "M-E-R-I-T-O-C-R-A-C-Y, kid. 'Tis the beauty of this room. Money gives you power in here, but only if it's 'fuck you' money you earned. There's no one with Daddy's inherited cash in here. Self-made or get the hell out." Murray's voice was thick, more truck driver yelling at someone to get out of the way than genius spinmeister. As Murray turned his head to wave with feigned friendliness to a rival, two little curls of hair behind his ears bounced out from the hair gel meant to smooth them down, making the flat part of his comb-over seem that much more incongruous.

I looked at my watch. Five more minutes before my meeting. Across the room, I saw Delsie throw the long end of her spring, lime-green cashmere scarf around her neck and behind her shoulder. "What about Delsie with her four-point-five-million-dollar annual salary you worked so hard to leak?" I asked. "It's not about the money in here?"

"That broad's got raw star power and black and white viewer appeal no one can touch. Delsie took over that cable network and got the ratings they'd coveted for years. No one can say she didn't do that on her own."

"On her own? Really? You believe everything you peddle, Murray? Delsie secretly pays us to doctor her appearances and often her scripts. Did you forget you have me fixing her lame copy at all hours?"

He smiled at me. "Even a fuckin' genius like me can't spin something out of nothing. Everyone in here has to deliver the goods."

I didn't try to argue. I knew he was right on some level: Manhattan did harvest a huge crop of people who came to this city from small towns across the land and rose to become the lead players in their fields of art, fashion, publishing, or banking.

Most of those tried-and-tested winners were in this very room.

The consommé arrived, and I know Murray made me order it just to prove his point: that a foie gras wonton floating in a small bowl of duck broth could actually command a $38 price tag. I tried the broth first. It went down smoky, gamey, with a big hint of honey. Even though it was a clear soup, it was so rich that just two sips made me thirsty. Like their patrons, the chefs had also overachieved to create something outstanding: they must have roasted three hundred duck carcasses to produce the heft of this broth.

I smiled. "You're right. I mean, it's not worth thirty-eight dollars of my money for a small cup of soup, but if you can afford it, I guess, yes, it's very special."

Murray splashed his big spoon in my broth, spilled a little on the table, and slurped up some for himself. "No. It is worth that money!" He was almost yelling at me. "It's supply and demand and the effort to . . ."

There were supersized personalities back home in Squanto, Massachusetts, for sure—many of them in fact. My own father had led the pack. He had had no money to speak of, but I remember so much about how he behaved around the house: he always had his fellow fishermen over after they'd all chartered their boats out or had come in from a day on the sea. Everyone would bring burger patties or beer and they'd sit around pontificating just as loudly and confidently as the men and women in this restaurant. My father was one of the loudest and most charming ones—boisterous and charismatic—but he didn't think everyone had to agree with his every opinion just because he walked into a room.

"And don't forget to tell Delsie I want her covering the Fulton Film Festival I've worked so fuckin' hard to put on the map. Art films. Science. Action. Whatever. Fuck Sundance!" Murray picked up an entire lobster claw from his salad with his fingers, put it on half a roll, and mashed both into his mouth. "Mark my words, Allie, maybe you'll never have big money or pick up the check. But you're going to be respected 'cause you did something great. You saved people. You invented people. Your PR helped them reach their greatest potential."

Creating illusions had never actually been my plan. My plan had been to write novels or long magazine essays, not use my MFA creative writing degree to craft press releases that got people out of trouble or made them appear to be something they weren't.

"Take that guy over there for starters," Murray yelled as he glanced over to the podium at the entryway of the restaurant where Wade stood to have lunch with a potential interview subject. My husband came to the Tudor Room as a way to network with important people he needed to put in the magazine or to entertain potential advertisers. He was able to play in the power brokers' sandbox by charging every lunch to his parent company.

"Maybe," I allowed. Across the room, Wade smacked Georges's shoulder while whispering some delicious bit of gossip into his ear. I adored my husband's ability to get everyone on his side, but his arrival also made me feel even more out of place here, like everyone but me had a code and language and sense of humor I could never quite grasp.

When I first met Wade, I was instantly drawn to the symmetrical, thick, blondish-gray waves in his hair that neatly rolled down the back of his head, ending about a quarter inch below his collar. As I watched him walk up the movie aisle that first night, he flashed his smile back at me, having noticed me a few seats down. I felt my stomach churn because the long hair reminded me of brawny guys on the Squanto fishing docks I'd grown up with. When he joined a group of rapt partygoers to grab a drink beside the bar in the lobby, I instantly felt left out. That's the effect he had on a room: his circle was the one to be in—and most of us were on the outside looking in.

Murray beckoned for Wade to come over. "Well, for one thing, your husband's the only prick cocky enough to walk in here in jeans, and not even Georges stops him."

My husband did have an uncanny ability to skirt the rules without acknowledging them in the first place. A brass plaque on the coat check downstairs clearly read: *Jacket required. Please refrain from wearing blue jeans at the Tudor Room.* Wade had on very blue jeans, a white Oxford cloth shirt, a beat-up leather blazer, and black sneakers. He was a bit of a rebel in his industry by always going after people in print he seemed to be cozying up with on the social front. "Always bite the hand that feeds you" was his professional motto.

Wade glad-handed his way toward us as Murray watched him. "M-E-R-I-T-O-C-R-A-C-Y, baby, I'm telling you. Your husband isn't known for having much cash on hand, but he's a member of this crowd no doubt. That magazine he runs is still a juggernaut, despite the fact that it's a fuckload thinner than it used to be. Maybe his parent company is deep in the red right now and he's always going to be low on personal funds because what the fuck does an editor make? Peanuts in this city." Murray slammed the table so hard that the cauliflower popped out of the basket. "But he's got primitive power—he turned *Meter* magazine around from a piece of dilapidated dusty old shit into the absolute number one must-read for everyone in this room. *The ultimate media macher.*" I didn't remind Murray that my husband, ten years my senior, did all that twenty years ago—before YouTube, Facebook, Twitter, Instagram, blogs, and online anything. People who still worked on real glossy paper in 2013 had far more uncertain futures than anyone in the room, even if Wade did everything he could to dispel that. "And he had the sense to marry you!" Then Murray added, "*And if he ever doesn't treat you right, I swear I'll kill him.*"

Wade walked up to our corner, kissed me behind my ear, whispering, "You look *hot,*" and slapped Murray's back. I didn't feel hot and I doubt he meant that. He said it because he always did want me to do well and didn't like to see me stressed. I quickly sipped my last fourteen dollars of broth, eager to get out of the booth and over to the bar before Wade and Murray got into their exclusionary boys' club banter.

"Thanks for the soup, Murray. I'll see you tonight, Wade," I said to them, as I stood and smoothed my knee-length black skirt. "Wish me luck making an insanely insecure woman feel satisfied."

"Knock her dead," Murray answered.

Wade raised an eyebrow at my tight skirt and looked at me tenderly. "You look gorgeous. You always knock 'em out."

I whispered to him, "Thanks, honey. But I don't. You're blind."

"You do." He brushed my cheek. "And I'm going to go to my grave making you believe that."

I crossed the room to go meet Delsie at the red-paneled bar wondering why both my boss and my husband were being so awfully nice to me. It was only when I had a clearer view of that bar that I noticed at first a spectacular pair of bare legs belonging to a beautiful young woman. Her snakeskin sandals wrapped around her ankles, mimicking the reptile that had been gouged to make them. She was sitting alone and scarfing down the famous Tudor Room line-caught tuna tartare served in a martini glass before her, when Georges whispered something *amusant* into her ear. She tossed her shimmering blond curls over her sexy belted white Ralph Lauren jacket, where they flowed down into a V-shaped back and brushed against the top of a very round bottom.

Without even saying hello, Delsie started in with this: "I can't do a speech for Murray one more time at another one of his charity ventures. I know I agreed, but now I want to back out. He wants me to whore myself out for every goddamn cause he's attached to."

"Whoring yourself out?" I asked.

"Yes." She was now extra pissy because no one was allowed to challenge her opinions either—a charming trait apparently shared by every patron in the room. "Whoring out. That's what I said and, funny as it may seem to you, that's what I meant."

I breathed in a slow breath. "Delsie. Let's just review why you agreed to do the speech, because 'whoring out' has the connotation of maybe you're being used or maybe this wasn't your choice. You hired us for more visibility, so we got you the keynote speaker at the Fulton Film Festival media lunch, which is a very prestigious affair. Yes, it raises money for journalism schools but . . ."

She looked at me sternly, as though she was considering whether to call Murray over to reprimand me.

I went on, giving her a pitch I'd given so many times. "You're getting paid a large speaker's fee as a professional to MC the event, Delsie. And it's an important celebration that will only bring you recognition in a media spotlight I know you care about. You will be impressive, don't worry about that."

She backed down a tad. "Who's coming? Anyone important?"

"Who isn't coming?" I responded. "Anyone important who cares about the future of this city. The Fulton Film Festival brings a bunch of first-class films here over the next month, so you are boosting New York's culture and getting a lot of good press while doing so." I may have successfully delivered the gist of this very pitch, but I was not anywhere close to present during it. My mind and eyes were drawn to the young woman down the bar. She was looking right at us—something in her eyes made me shudder.

Her bare legs glistened like the maroon curtains that draped the front windows, filtering the harsh noonday light now bursting through the storm clouds. The soaring height of the glass walls made it feel like we were on top of the world, looking out over all Manhattan, even though we were at street level. This young woman took a long, slow sip of her iced tea, no hint that she was secretly uncovering the madness that would detonate around all of us in due time.

I glanced over at Wade, who gave me an encouraging little wave, the kind he gave Lucy when she went blank last fall on her three Carrot Number One lines for the *Vegetable Play*.

I pressed ahead, bolstered by all the times I had to push powerful clients onto a stage. "I'm not sure there's a downside, unless you don't like hanging out with movie stars." I then stared into Delsie's needy eyes. "You need more culture in your portfolio if you're going to crack Manhattan, be somebody in this room. I assure you this is good old-fashioned PR for a nice Carolina woman like you."

I couldn't help but remain half in, half out of my pitch as my gaze locked once again on the man-eater down the mahogany bar. She looked like she was maybe twenty-eight, but I figured she was really a poised twenty-five-year-old. I stealthily neatened up my blouse and the belt around my waist. My outfit was much like hers—a pencil skirt, no stockings, high Stuart Weitzman sandal heels, and a Tory Burch white blouse—but the sex appeal differential was enormous. My five-foot-four-inch height didn't exactly make for sexy, lanky legs. I did have nice, thick dark hair that fell a little below my shoulders and a passable pretty thirty-four-year-old face, but more because of my unusual blue eyes and dark hair combination than actual head-turning beauty.

The woman down the bar then bit her thick, tomato-red lips, which matched the red lacquer walls, and walked over to us with great purpose.

She interrupted. "Excuse me for overhearing. I'd just like to say that Allie Crawford is known to have more innate PR business sense than anyone in this room." She brushed her body ever so slightly against Delsie's shoulder, whispering, "*Including her boss, Murray Hillsinger.* If you're interested in doing something high profile, then I'd follow her advice and do whatever she wants."

"Um, thank you . . ." This was all I could get out as she strode back to her barstool perch. At this point, I didn't even know her name or have any idea why she wanted to help me.

Georges came over to address the beauty once again, her brown eyes sparkling back at him. He whispered something into her ear. At first, I assumed he might be having a little fling with her, but then I sensed that they were going over something. Out of his left blazer pocket, he took a casino chip and placed it discreetly in her purse. I saw a tiny piece of the chip, the top of a section with "Five" written on it, as in Five Thousand Dollars.

Also, as in the same goddamn chip that fell out of my husband's shirt pocket the evening before.

4

Party in the House

The next night's cocktail party had started like any other, with me determined to perform my wife and mother roles as best I could given the impending frenzy about to descend on my apartment. Wade liked to throw little get-togethers every month at our place to coddle *Meter* magazine advertisers and potential story subjects. Each party featured a brand-new cast of wannabes, has-beens, and already-ares. Our small apartment couldn't accommodate a large crowd, so guests were on some lists, off others—every one of them anxiously trying to figure out the invite formula. Very smooth, very smart, very manipulative, very Wade Crawford.

I wanted to spend the whole night in bed with my kids and find time to be alone with my Blake and decipher why his friends were still excluding him. I had no desire to face this party and people who cared nothing about me, a hostess who couldn't facilitate their upward mobility. All heads would be turned toward the glow of Wade the Sun King who might put them in his magazine. I grew up with people who might have had less money and power, but they certainly had better manners and knew to say hello and thank you to the wife.

Before the party even started, I thought about asking Wade if he knew the beauty at the Tudor Room who had helped me. He'd say he'd never seen her before, but when I would ask why she had the same casino chip he had tried to hide from me, he would refuse even to understand my question. I knew him so well this way. He'd walk down the hall and make it seem like nothing, when I sensed it was definitely something. He would then say his crowd often went to Atlantic City with Murray and various clients. First, I had to comprehend more on my own in order to be armed with a comeback for his denial.

Wade rummaged through his color-coordinated closet to find just the proper outfit to telegraph that he was festive, but relaxed. He brought out a hip lavender tie with a sky-blue shirt and asked, "Does this look inviting?" He pulled me into him. "Will it get me laid with my beautiful bride?"

"Yes, Wade. Exactly that," I answered, noting that he seemed more desperate these days to get his look right. "Your purple tie is what does it for me." Was he trying too hard to act solicitous or was I imagining things?

"Purple's my favorite," Lucy said, as she entered the room and hugged his thigh.

"Mine too, kiddo," he said as he ruffled her hair, dragging her along with him to the mirror. For the finishing touch, Wade slipped on his black, "downtown" blazer with the little antique gold buttons. "Now come here and kiss me good night."

I saw my chance and raced back to the kids' room, where I found Blake punching his thumbs into his Nintendo DS with extra hostility.

"What's with Jeremy today, honey? Did he respond or did you even explain to him you wanted to go this time? Did you use the money I gave you for your snack?"

"Mom. They went to get Doritos in the machines without me. I'm not going to ask why. It's obvious. They didn't want me to come."

"Well, honey, I . . ."

"Mom. They didn't want me to come. You can't say anything that is going to make me feel better. After social studies, when I ask them to wait before going to playstreet and when I'm packing my bag, they always run out."

"That is just so mean, honey." I kissed my hurt little boy's nine-year-old forehead and wished with all my heart I could take this blow for him.

"And don't call his mom and tell him to be nicer to me like you did last time."

"I won't, I . . ." Of course that is exactly what I wanted to do.

"It makes me look like a snitch. She told him to play nicer and he told everyone I told on him, so don't do it again. For real, Mom. Don't."

"I love you, honey. I'm here to talk if you want."

"I said I don't want to."

I gently closed his door, mumbling to myself, "A mother's only as happy as her unhappiest child." Pained but resigned to let him stew, I ran into the kitchen to place thirty Trader Joe's hors d'oeuvres on cookie sheets and into a warm oven. With the downturn having hit ad revenues hard, Wade's magazine company had slashed his budget for home cocktail parties to almost nothing. They would only pay for a scant two college students, a mediocre bar, and the cheapest hors d'oeuvres from the frozen section. For every event, I had to fork out for flowers and a few extras with our own money. When I protested that these parties didn't quite fit into our tight monthly budget in expensive New York City, Wade countered that he couldn't make *Meter* successful if he couldn't continue to network as he wished, and any and every time he wished.

The cut-rate bartender and server from the Columbia University Bartending service were late, and the wine and club soda cases were stacked in the cramped kitchen hallway untouched. Six thirty. It was getting awfully close to the seven o'clock game time and I realized the guests might actually arrive before the two servers did. I struggled to push the cartons a few inches across the floor so that I could maneuver around them and open the oven door.

In the oven, dozens of frozen miniquiches and spinach phyllo pies started to sweat off freezer burn as I pulled a chair up to the cupboard so I could reach above the fridge and get down two bottles of vodka. This being a New York apartment, table and shelf space in the living room were too valuable to use for cumbersome bar bottles when company wasn't around.

Why I was the one about to break my neck reaching for a vodka bottle and stressing that our tonic and limes were low for *his work party* while Wade was lying around oblivious in bed tickling Lucy at 6:49 was a question most wives know the answer to.

My red silk blouse had started to show lovely little sweat stains around my armpits with all the aerobic activity I was performing in the kitchen. At 6:53, the server and bartender finally arrived from the Columbia campus, apologizing and blaming the poor subway service.

Back in my closet to select another shirt, I heard Lucy screaming with laughter and jumping high on the bed. Wade was trying to swing a pillow into her legs midjump so she'd flip down on the bed sideways. This always ended in tears. No matter how many times I begged them not to play this game, Lucy always wanted more.

"Wade, can you talk to Blake before the party? Jeremy and those mean kids are . . ."

Wade wasn't listening. He was counting the timing of Lucy's jump so he could slam her with the huge pillow as she pulled her feet up in midair.

"Wade. Are you listening?"

"Got you!" he yelled.

Lucy went flying ninety degrees sideways with the force of the pillow and was in full hysterics now. "Again, Daddy!"

Wade turned to me. "I got her. I told her we'd do it until I got her. Now I'll go talk to Blake, but he's not going to want to discuss it, I promise."

"He could use some boosting from his father, so please go talk to him quick. I'm running around here like the Tasmanian Devil. I'm sweating, I look like hell . . ." I tore my shirt off and rummaged through my closet for another blouse that, by some miracle, wasn't creased.

As I threw on a tight black sweater, Wade the design guru peeked back in and made this unwelcome suggestion: "That traditional red blouse was good with those spiky shoes. If you change to that more contemporary black look, you're going to need a clunkier heel."

When I shook my head at him, he walked over to me and kissed my forehead gingerly. "Sorry, honey, I know you try, but the outfit's just not working. But I love you and if I wanted to marry a clothes designer, I guess I could have. Tonight, though, I need you to cope on the outfit because there's a ton of fashion advertisers coming."

Where I grew up, everyone wore shoes that sensibly confronted the environment, not the Fashion Nazis of Manhattan. What the hell did my crappy little hometown of Squanto on the Atlantic teach anyone about decor and style? My family resided in a small colonial home about five blocks from the docks where salt water and sand pervaded every room. We lived in winter boots or sneakers or flip-flops. I didn't have a pair of heels until I went to Middlebury College, and I think I wore them five times total before I hit the judgmental shores of Manhattan.

"Which heel did you mean?" I yelled back at him. "And do you mean a sling-back sandal or a real shoe? Could you just come back here and show me? I've got to get Lucy settled now that you wound her up. If Blake won't talk, make sure he's doing his homework." I was sure Blake was still on his Nintendo, and not ready to study at all, but I couldn't really blame him, what with the students from Columbia now furiously clanging in the kitchen outside of the kids' room.

"Which shoe exactly?"

But Wade was long gone.

"I wish Daddy would stay," Lucy whimpered, with a whiplash mood swing to the dark side. This was the downside of their lovefest: she always craved more. I flashed momentarily on an image of my father walking out the door to his two prized fishing boats to cater to some wealthy summer tourists, past my outstretched five-year-old arms, off and gone, leaving me for days. When he came home and flashed that smile framed by his salty beard, it was as if he'd never left me with a mother who spent much of her day passed out from drinking in front of the blue glow of her television game shows.

My father's charm, much like my husband's, was so irresistible that I couldn't help but forgive him the instant he reappeared at my bedroom door. No wonder Wade got whatever he wanted from me: I had had no practice staying angry with the man I adored most in the world.

"Blake's just fine," he announced. "Like I said, he doesn't want us micromanaging all his friendships. Fourth grade is time to handle some stuff on his own."

As always just before the parties started, Wade stood in front of the mirror once last time to admire his sporty frame. He flipped his tie over his shoulder while he smoothed down the front of his shirt. Working intently on his cool media master aura, he delicately brushed a piece of hair up over his brow.

Wade came from a small eastern town too, but, as an upper-middle-class accountant's son, and an arrogant one at that, Wade's lofty career aspirations seemed to be met anytime he damn well felt like it. His self-assuredness was another one of those interlocking parts of our relationship. Watching him in action helped inspire the part of me that feared I couldn't achieve anything quite well enough.

"You know everyone's name on the list, right, Allie?"

"I don't know, Wade. I hope so."

"This is important." He rubbed my ear. "C'mon, babe. I know you're freaking out about Blake's bruised feelings and Lucy's caterpillar costumes and that you are juggling a ton at work, but I rely on your uncanny ability to execute. Do me this little favor? I'll owe you one."

"Sure, Wade. I got it handled." I wanted to help him out, but I was so fatigued that night. I gritted my teeth and carried on anyway, oblivious to the tsunami rolling my way.

"That's my other best girl." He kissed me quickly on the lips. "Now, Lucy, be a good girl, and I'll sneak away to read you a book at bedtime." She held out her pinkie and he looped his around it, beaming his love into her little face. Then he went into the living room to make sure the candles and music were setting the proper cool mood to match his look. I stood up and went down the hall to overcoddle and infantilize Blake some more—anything to delay my entry into the hordes of guests who would soon be shamelessly clamoring all over my husband.

5

That Woman Again

I maneuvered around the crush of people, placing small glass bowls of cashews and wasabi peas on every little table and windowsill to give the illusion that food was abundant. When I came back from checking on the latest batch of Trader Joe's party treats, I almost tripped over Delsie Arceneaux's gorgeous, cappuccino gams outstretched in the alcove corner. She nodded a lame attempt at hello to me, the woman who worked so hard to make her words clear and precise in every speech she'd given for the past two years.

I hovered around the cocktail bar and dropped some ice into a small glass while studying Delsie's pounce technique with the still very horny seventy-two-year-old Max Rowland, freshly sprung from nine months in the white-collar division of Allenwood prison. He was one of our highest-paying (and highest-maintenance) clients. Murray had him invested in our film festival to diminish Max's image as a tax-evading, greedy corporate criminal—one of those twofer conflicts of interest that Murray lived for.

"Tell me, Max," Delsie purred, as she smoothed out her sky-blue Chanel knit suit with a short tight jacket and miniskirt. "How did you fare in there? Everyone was so damned worried about you and I kept telling them, 'Puhleese. It's Max. He's what my daddy would call a high-stepper. He's built an empire of parking lots with his own hands. He's going to whip that prison population into . . .' "

Max, a heavyset Texan who started out in New York City at age twenty-one to make his equally outsized fortune, sank into the soft white corduroy couch. He placed his feet on one of the zebra-skinned Ralph Lauren ottomans that Wade had swiped from one of his photo shoots. "You're rahhht," he chuckled. "The food was crap, but the prison guys weren't so dahmn bad. Have to admit, they kinda hung on my evereh word."

"As we all do, Max." Delsie's librarian glasses only heightened the sexual potency that emanated from her every raspy, semi-out-of-breath word. She was positioned as if she were about to screw this old man's brains out, hips arched back, chest thrust heavenward: her way of trying to score the first postprison interview. He hadn't talked to the press since his release, and this was another win-win in the making if Murray could get him to talk to Delsie, since they were both clients.

The party was bursting with exclusivity, even though our apartment was situated on a busy block in the commercial West Twenties and not in a pricey location. We'd knocked out the wall between the dining alcove and living room, making a larger space that could accommodate a squished-up crowd. There was also a corner window off the green alcove that featured a giant beige couch and Wade's home office desk, where the kinds of people who like to be cliquish tended to congregate.

Wade cared far more about the "stage" than I ever did, and he'd go to great lengths to get it just right on our tight budget: the exact shade of the red anemones, the black lacquer party trays he'd coveted enough to trek down to Chinatown to buy, the outfits the student servers wore (black shirts, black jackets, never ties, to exude the same Chelsea hipness as their host), the hors d'oeuvres (never crab cakes or smoked salmon—Mrs. Vincent Astor once told him a decade ago they gave the guests bad breath), and even the cocktail napkins (always in the same synergistic color as the cover subject's dress, in this case a supermodel named simply "Angel"). High-gloss posters of the latest cover and photo spread hung like art on a blank white wall in our front entry. Angel's dress was fuchsia, so was the *Meter* logo on the cover, as was the bold cover line YOU WANT ACTION?. And so were our cocktail napkins.

As I put ice-cold vodka to my lips, a shot of green in Wade's general vicinity caught my eye, and I nearly dropped my glass. It was the gorgeous girl who had helped me at the Tudor Room bar the day before, all done up in a tight olive dress. She was talking in a highly animated fashion to a wealthy hedge funder sporting the facial expression of someone getting a lap dance. As I stared at her, she noticed, but then looked at Wade—whose back was to me—and nodded in the direction of the kitchen. She drifted down the hall. I found this strange. A woman I didn't know was signaling to me in no uncertain terms that she was headed to my back kitchen . . . and what was she referring to about Wade exactly?

"It's all okay, right, my love?" Wade shouted over the din, relishing that he controlled every last detail of the party turf and I didn't care to. Even more guests had poured in and filled the loft space in what felt like seconds. "I checked on Blake. He's fine, like he forgot all about Jeremy being mean. The party—going well so far, right?"

Yes, I mouthed without sound as I bit into a miniquiche that was warm to the touch, but cold on the inside. I took a deep breath and looked for the nineteen-year-old stoned-out server across the room so I could remind him to leave the next batch in the oven a bit longer.

"You sure?" Wade's eyes searched the room. They moved toward the girl in green.

"Positive." In that instant, with that one glance in her direction, I knew my instincts over that past year were correct and that I had to stop glossing over problems; while on the surface we were status quo, something beneath had changed for Wade. Warm on the outside, cold on the inside.

There had been a discreet but seismic shift in his smallest gestures: he used to let his eyes linger on mine, but tonight he broke the stare so he could steal a glance at this woman. I found his telling me I was so hot all the time inauthentic because he wasn't acting on it. He used to want to make out in our elevator, even after the kids were born, last year even. Now his compliments were more frequent, but his kisses more like bird pecks.

"I'm going to check on the food. We seem to be running low." Wade gave me another one of those hard-lip kisses, spun on his heel, and buzzed off after the impossibly hot woman, not even noticing me noticing him.

6

Bizarre Behavior

Mouth agape in a silent scream, I searched the crowd for Caitlin, my office right hand and friend, half hoping she had, and half praying she hadn't, witnessed my husband chase after the gorgeous girl who'd helped me at the bar of the Tudor Room. I finally caught Caitlin's eye, and she hopscotched over Delsie's caramel, daddy longlegs to reach me.

"What's wrong—other than this party, that is," she said out of the side of her mouth. Her curly blond, 1920s bob slanted across her cheek as she smirked. "All the requisite douche bags are here. Wade must be very happy."

"Yeah," I said, trying to remain calm as I watched the hallway for the return of either my husband or that woman. "He's happy with everything."

Caitlin squinted at my creased brow. "But you're not. What's up?"

I couldn't stop myself. "He just disappeared down the hall

with a lovely young thing who actually was very kind and generous to me during my Delsie meeting. I'm sure it's nothing. He wouldn't . . . he's just all hyper tonight with the . . ."

"Oh, he wouldn't in his own home." Caitlin crossed her arms. She looked intensely angry. "Aren't the kids back that way?"

I certainly wasn't expecting to have my fears of a cheating husband reignited that night. When Wade strayed *that one time,* he claimed he was "ignored and lonely" and that he'd made a monumental mistake with a photo assistant for *Meter* magazine while I was breast-feeding Lucy. It almost derailed our marriage. *A onetime thing,* he had promised. Not a day went by that I didn't remember my pain when I figured it out. I had heard him talking to her one night about the sexy things he wanted to do to her—whispering in the bathroom with the door slightly ajar. He didn't realize I was home and had overheard the entire conversation. I had crumpled my mushy postpregnancy body onto the bed, waiting for the call to end. And there was nothing he could say to refute it when he saw me minutes afterward. It took me a very long time even to sit next to him on a couch.

For months after that, he came home directly after work every night to assure me it was a "mistake" and that he understood he had nearly destroyed everything between us. I had chosen to believe that it was out of his system and in the past. Now I wasn't so sure.

"Hold on. I'll be right back. I've got to check on the food," I lied. Why would that woman approach me at the Tudor Room, help me, connect with me so brazenly and out of the blue if she were fooling around with Wade? She'd even just hinted a minute ago with that nod in the direction of the kitchen that they were headed together somewhere back there.

What the hell?

I pretended to waltz into my kitchen, no big deal, just checking on the food, and found the college server frantically filling black lacquer trays with hot-outside, frozen-inside hors d'oeuvres. No sign of Wade. "Jim. Have you seen my husband?"

"Sorry, I'm really too busy to . . ." Jim shook his head, clearly exasperated trying to feed sixty people with one small oven and too few goodies coming out of it and too much pregig marijuana slowing down his executive functioning.

The laundry room door was shut, but I could see the light under the crack. *Couldn't be.* I nervously checked our back bedroom. No sign of two adults, just my two kids on our king bed, hypnotized by the television.

"Ten more minutes and you have to get into your own bunks. I love you both!"

My heart in pieces, I marched back to the front of the apartment to where Caitlin stood, arms on her hips, ready to help me in any way she could.

"Where are they?" She had urged me countless times to stop letting Wade go out late so often when he'd already strayed once. "And don't tell me you were checking on the food. I am going to help you figure this out." She seemed almost more determined to uncover his behavior than I did, which I thought a little bizarre.

"I think they are in the laundry room," I said, squeezing my hands while tears pooled in my eyes. I blinked them away. "It's the only room I haven't checked."

"No way."

"He's not at the party. He's not in the kitchen. They didn't jump out the window or tuck in the kids. It's the only room that makes any sense—there's a light on in there."

"You sure she isn't some writer?" Caitlin asked. "Maybe she's helping him write a toast?"

"She's definitely not from *Meter.* She's hot enough to be on the cover. Besides, I already wrote his friggin' toast."

"When are you going to stop doing that, by the way; he's a grown man with dozens of writers at his disposal . . ."

"In the laundry room, Caitlin. *Where I wash his children's clothes.*"

"If I were you, I'd try to catch him in the act." She forced the words out of her mouth with spit flying. "We should go back there and fling that door open."

"Not we, me. You're too rash; you'll screw it up," I said. She started to protest, but she knew what I meant. "Keep people from going into the back of the apartment. I need to sort this out myself."

I walked down the hall and sat on a kitchen stool while my eyes burned with humiliation over something too crazy to be true. As the student waiter took out the latest batch of crumbly phyllo hors d'oeuvres, they went sliding onto the floor.

"The floor is clean," I said. "Pick them up, place them on the lovely lacquer trays, and serve them to the guests, Jim."

"Really, Mrs. Crawford? I would never . . ."

"Really. Do it."

I was so tense I couldn't breathe, so I waited down the hall in a hidden corner and stared at the light under the laundry room door. If my husband and the girl came out together, I couldn't yell at him in front of *her* and all the guests. Or could I? I had to think of some approach that would give me the advantage and find an unflappable new personality inside me to fuel it. If I didn't persevere, I would never be able to maintain that I "had the goods" on him. It would only be hearsay and innuendo that could be easily refuted. Then I wondered: Why should I be waffling if I'm catching *him* in the act? Easy answer: because I didn't want it to be true.

Just when I'd decided (correctly) that nothing else would do but to knock, the knuckles on my tightly clenched hand mere inches from the laundry room door, a groggy Lucy appeared in the kitchen in the lint-balled, pink Disney princess nightgown she'd insisted, going on two years now, she could not fall asleep without. "Where's Daddy?" she murmured while rubbing her left eye. "I'm ready for my story."

"Honey, you need to get back in bed. If you walk around and get all excited, you're going to get overtired and . . ." And witness me catching your father in flagrante.

Blake suddenly appeared behind his sister. This was getting dangerous. "Mom," he said. "I *tried* to tell her to get into her bunk, but she wouldn't listen. She *had* to find Dad."

"It's okay, Blake. Tell you what. If you read her the *Angelina Ballerina,* that will count as the rest of the reading you need to do." I kissed the top of Lucy's head, turned her around, and watched Blake shepherd her back to their room. If this laundry room situation was as bad as it looked, I worried, how would I mitigate the damage on them?

"Allie!" Murray yelled next, gesticulating with his muscular arms in huge circles around my kitchen. I noticed a gold watch the size of a hockey puck on his trunklike limb. I looked past him to give Caitlin the "WTF" for letting him back here, but she was nowhere to be found.

Murray's thinning comb-over looked slightly askew as he stopped to catch his breath. "Allie," he wheezed, picking up a cheese stick and pointing it at my heart before he mashed it down his throat with the center of his palm. "Where the fuck is your husband?"

I shrugged. Murray rested his elbow on the island counter, displaying sweat stains across the creases of his dark blue shirt. The Columbia server couldn't place the last phyllo spinach pies or the new fried wontons on the tray in front of him fast enough to beat Murray's rapid-fire arm movements from tray to mouth, tray to mouth, quicker than a real toad would catch a fly with his tongue.

Murray spat the following in my ear as he scarfed down a few more. "Delsie thinks you're fantastic! Your pitch worked and she is so happy to have you handling her writing for the big media pitch we'd put—"

"Thanks, Murray, but I need to deal with the party." At that I left and hid down the hall to witness how Wade would exit the room now.

Then the unimaginable happened. My boss eyed the laundry

room door, saw the light on underneath, and strode over to the room where my husband was possibly shagging his mistress. He banged on the door with the back of his fist. Murray made my day, and my soft spot for him grew.

"Wade, you crazy schmuck! You in there?! You got me wanting to toast your fabulous ass." He rattled the locked doorknob.

"Right out, Murray. Just gotta finish one, more, thing, here . . ." Wade yelled nonchalantly from the inside as if he wasn't about to explode into a young woman's voluptuous mouth.

A full, long twenty-two seconds later—I know, because I counted—Wade appeared with his nose high, as if he wasn't ever going to be accountable to Murray, or his ball-and-chain, for his bizarre shenanigans. Only I detected a hint of anger in his posture. It couldn't have thrilled him to find the irascible Murray on the other side of the door—or to have to rush his eruption in there.

"You good?" Murray then smacked his back even harder, leaving flecks of phyllo and finger grease stains on Wade's shirt.

From twenty feet down the hall, I tried to peek around them into the laundry room, but Wade gingerly closed the door and steered Murray in the direction of the party.

Wade didn't see me watching him. "Yeah, just a loose . . . I had to go get a . . . ah, doesn't matter, what the hell's going on with you, Murray?" He turned to the waiter a lot more aggressively than appropriate. "How does a guy get a drink around here?" I could see beads of sweat forming on his slightly receded hairline. He was definitely pissed off.

"Right on it, sir," Jim answered, straightening the bottom

hem of his rumpled black jacket. That's what was missing: Wade's jacket.

Without waiting for his drink, or witnessing my presence, Wade put his arm around Murray's shoulder and started recounting one of his half-fictional exploits. Murray guffawed as Wade turned on his conversational charm amid the adjacent living room chatter, which had reached a thousand-decibel pitch.

7

Wifely Conundrums

I was left drumming the wall behind me with my fingers while waiting for Ms. Reptile Shoes to exit my laundry room. Bile inched up in my throat as I tried to decide how to handle this. What was I supposed to do, march into our living room and ask Wade right then and there what it all meant? Was his telling me I was *so hot* all the time when we barely had sex anymore a clear sign that he loved someone else?

I got up the guts to walk back down to the laundry room door, but she opened it herself just as I arrived. There stood the Tudor Room woman with her hair perfectly coiffed, and her full lips smothered with gloss, lavishly but accurately, without the remotest hint that she'd been performing sexual tongue gymnastics minutes before. She returned my stare with simple, elegant composure.

Though fuming, I was also heartbroken by her beauty and what it must mean to my husband. "What the hell was going on in here?!"

She then did the unthinkable—she held out her hand. "Jackie Malone."

"What the . . ." My eyes darted to the vacant scene behind her.

"Look, he's all yours." She stared straight at me. "It's not what you think. You may not believe me now, but I was in there on your behalf. I was looking for something and he caught me."

I studied her clothes for signs they'd just had mad groping sex. I had to admit that she did look completely unruffled. All I could see behind her was laundry neatly folded, and all I could smell was powder detergent—no scent of lust, no mess. "You're telling me you were alone, locked in a room with my husband, and I'm supposed to believe nothing was going on in here?!!"

"Yes. Nothing. And more important . . ." She paused and held my arm. Then she said, "This is going to sound extremely improbable, but you are actually going to need to trust me."

I yanked out of her grasp and whispered through clenched teeth. "Trust you? You just spent the last ten minutes locked in the laundry room with my husband who just walked out of here."

"I told you. I was looking for something having to do with the men in your living room that you know nothing about. What they are doing is going to sap your finances, any stability you have, probably deplete everything you have saved. It's not safe in any way. Nothing sexual was going on here. He came in and caught me looking for something in his jacket." She pulled me into the laundry room.

"What were you looking for? And tell me about the casino chips you both seem to have," I demanded, keeping one eye on the hall in case Wade returned.

"The casino chips mean nothing." Jackie looked vulnerable for a moment and I took it as a sign that those chips were not an innocent prop in whatever game she was playing. "We've been to Atlantic City is all. Earlier, from the hall, I saw him take off his jacket back here, so I came back and I thought I might be able to find—"

"Allie?" I heard Caitlin before I saw her walking furiously in our direction, her miniskirt stretched to the gills over her tight little gymnast form, and her thick platforms loudly stomping on my floors. She was my close friend, but far too nosy to be invited into this scene. I walked farther into the kitchen and slammed the laundry room door behind Jackie so fast I wondered if I'd clipped her nose.

"Not now, Caitlin."

She was inches from me. "All okay? Wade's in the living room with all the men drooling over the hot fashionistas, and he looks pissed. Did you fight?"

"Can you go back to the party, please?"

Caitlin crossed her arms and planted her feet Mexican-standoff style. "I know you, and I know you're not telling me something." She looked at the closed door. "Did you find her?"

"I was mistaken," I said, turning her around and pushing her in the direction of the party. "Go make sure Wade doesn't have his palm on anyone's ass, please."

"Happy to," Caitlin said, relishing the chance to catch my husband in another sticky situation.

With Caitlin gone, I opened the door and snuck inside to continue my line of questioning.

"Look, I need to know a few things besides the obvious question of why you were back here with Wade: Who are you? Why did you help me with Delsie? What was it you were looking for? What is Wade doing with which men that is going to take away our savings, as you supposedly contend?" Despite all my suspicions, in the far reaches of my anterior lobe, I did allow for the possibility that she was telling the truth.

"Not who. *What*. Documents and photos," she answered tersely, still trying to size me up even as she scanned the floor. "Or a flash drive, that little stick that goes into the side of a computer."

"I know what a flash drive is. Who the hell are you, anyway?"

"I told you. I'm Jackie."

I leaned against the dryer, holding my throbbing head with one hand. "Stop being cute. I catch you red-handed with my husband. All this 'I'm trying to help you' shit looks like your way of getting out of the room. But I admit, it's creative." I was amazed I said that without my voice cracking. Once I feel like I might cry, my toughness evaporates instantly.

Jackie began folding the clothes that had scattered on the

floor. "I'm sorry, I know this is confusing and really hard to believe, but I swear on my life that I'm not lying to you one bit." She suddenly looked five years younger.

I stopped her manic folding with a pat on her hand and looked her in the eye. "What kind of documents and photos?" I considered the very remote possibility that she and Wade weren't doing anything "wrong"; her hair was too perfect, her blouse too unwrinkled, her lip gloss too polished.

"Meet me at the Tudor Room bar tomorrow around five," she said calmly, but with a hard glint in her eye. "You've got to keep this quiet, but if you find anything at all new in his papers and folders that seems like it wouldn't be . . ." She started scribbling down her cell-phone number and passed it to me on a gum wrapper from her purse.

I stuffed it into my pocket, glad to have some kind of way to reach her should I find proof she and Wade were together; I could use it to confront him somehow. "Wouldn't be what?" I asked in a tough and angry tone. "He's a journalist, an editor of a general interest magazine. He could have any kind of documents dealing with every story under the sun on his desk. Movie stars, legal wars, political corruption, how the hell am I supposed to know . . . what isn't safe? I pay the bills; it's all there . . ." I whispered. "What the hell do you mean? And if I found something, you wouldn't be getting it, just so you know. He's my husband. You're a total stranger."

She laid it on the line in a way I could not avoid any longer, no matter how hard I tried. "Listen carefully. This whole deal has been going on a lot longer than you know. And you're never going to understand how without my help."

Really?

And then the beauty added this:

"And just so you know, I didn't just get screwed in there, *you* did."

8

Pulled Toward the Edge

Jackie Malone knew way too much about Wade. My mind was racing. *This, their relationship—whatever that may be—must have been going on awhile now.* As she teetered back into the party showing her lean, racehorse calves and the flash of lacquered red on her high-heeled soles, I couldn't help but stare, vanquished, at the most amazing piece of ass I'd ever seen.

She didn't just get screwed in there, but somehow I did?

Wishing there was a pill to make my legs grow longer, I went to my bedroom to take a little break and figure out my next moves. After I poured enough Visine in my eyes and cold water on my flushed cheeks to return to the living room, half the guests were gone. Jackie was nowhere to be seen. Other revelers were collecting their jackets and starting to head out. Caitlin was in deep conversation with a tall stylist who was so thin she looked like a praying mantis.

When Wade finally noticed the look on my face, he excused

himself from a Russian supermodel stunner named Svetlana and hurried over. "Hey, don't think I don't know how exasperating these parties are for the wife."

I squinted at him. He actually believed I was upset over the quiche temperature. "Murray and Max Rowland want me to go to Atlantic City. I really don't want to go, but"—he shrugged his handsome shoulders, a willing pawn—"I should."

"Wade, I need to ask you something," I said, voice just unsteady enough that he'd notice if he wanted to, which he didn't.

"Wade! Get your butt in here!" Murray yelled impatiently, banging on the opening from inside the elevator.

Wade gestured to Murray that he was right there in a sec. He turned to me and said, "Hey, can we talk tomorrow? I gotta go. Murray has fifteen clients out in Atlantic City who are going to buy ad space, big buys, and I need . . ." He wasn't even looking at me.

"Who was the woman? You tell me and then you go."

"What woman?" Wade said like I'd asked about a purple giraffe in our home.

"Wade. THERE . . . WAS . . . A . . . WOMAN . . . IN . . . THE . . . LAUNDRY . . . ROOM. I saw her leave after you left."

"Oh God. She's just some woman who hangs around the Tudor Room. She had papers from some event she's trying to deal with and I had them in my jacket and I don't know, she wanted . . ."

"You were in there with the door closed."

"Wade!" Murray bellowed, now angry.

"Honey, it looks weird, I know. I just thought it best to talk to her privately not to raise suspicions because I know you get upset about beautiful women sometimes around me, and I'm just so sorry, my tactic did the opposite. She just wanted advice on how to handle one of the clients out there and I . . . I gotta go. I love you." He rushed to the door. I knew I wouldn't get anything out of him this way.

Caitlin glanced back at me and then sprinted to my side as I gathered unused little fuchsia napkins into a neat pile around the bar, anything to busy myself. "You don't mind if I go home, do you?" she asked, her eyes searching mine for yet one more clue to what had happened. "You okay?"

"I'm fine," I said, even as I pictured Jackie Malone with her legs entwined around my husband in Max Rowland's Borgata-bound Atlantic City helicopter. "False alarm."

Four minutes later, as the elevator finally banged shut for the two stoned Columbia University waiters I practically pushed out the door, I laid my head against my front door, knowing my husband would deny all of it.

With tears obscuring my vision and judgment, I walked over to Wade's work alcove and feverishly riffled through every single piece of paper my husband had ever come into contact with. I encountered nothing unusual, except this fresh ache in my heart signaling we were headed nowhere good fast.

A FULL HOUR later, I slumped onto my corner sofa, feeling defeated and sucker punched, with a wrinkled-up photo in my hand of Wade and me taken from the night we met. When I found it, I'd crumpled it into a ball and thrown it into the trash can across the room. I loved that photo. It was black and white and taken in the moments after a screening. We'd been talking only about ten minutes, but he was craning his neck toward me as if he were completely transfixed by my very presence. I had retrieved the photo from the trash, and now I flattened it out on a big book in my lap. Then I just stared at it, at us.

I then watched the light beams of a dozen flickering votives meld together on the windowsill and told myself this: at the ripe age of thirty-four I did have to grow up and start facing realities I didn't want to accept. One thing would never change: I would charge Wade up and he would, in turn, charge out the door to conquer and seduce the world. Problem was this: he was just too damn good at that seduction and unable to resist its bounty.

The photo in my trembling hand had been taken the night Hillsinger Consulting was working pro bono to promote a project to benefit veterans' causes; we were launching a gorgeous little gem of a World War Two documentary and book series that would win several awards the next winter. With all the press I'd convinced to show up, the buzz in the room was radioactive.

At some point during the afterglow, Murray introduced me to my future husband, then wandered off into the movie lobby to revel in the accolades for my hard work: I'd gotten every important person in New York to the event. Wade and I fell into a deep conversation until the guy trying to sweep away the complimentary popcorn nudged us out. In our now crumpled first photo, we were in midstep, heads focused on each other, walking the aisle like we were already a done deal.

Wade had moved with an awkward charm as he escorted me out of the screening room and into the sea of guests, demonstrating a tender shyness I would never again see in him. "You must be hungry after pulling off this great event?" he asked, and I nodded. "We can get a table next door at the Gotham. Unless you would prefer the bar." I liked the way his arm felt on my back as he guided me through the room. He was a good height for me, and lanky—the complete opposite build of James, the lifelong soul mate I would leave for Wade, who at that point was on month eleven of inoculating children in East Asia.

Truth be told, I didn't really like lanky, but I thought maybe I could fall for this Wade guy anyway. The shoulders were strong and confident, which helped. His blondish long hair hinted he might be cool like the guys on the docks I grew up with; but he was also urbane: everything rolled up into one neat package I'd left my small seaside hamlet for. The city and its sophisticated inhabitants were there to save me, and I was as willing as I'd ever be. I was also trying hard to be as single as I could with James off discovering the world instead of my body.

We had walked into the bright lights of Gotham restaurant, a place bubbling with that exact sharp, pulsing New York City energy I'd grown to love. A pack of mortals waited at the bar—hedge funders, models, fabulous gay fashion editors, all looking very worthy of commandeering any table at any restaurant in New York. Yet the hostess led us swiftly past all of them to a romantic little corner complete with a lone red candle and a tasteful bouquet of purple poppies. Three people tried to get Wade's attention on the way to our seats.

"What do they want?" I asked, as if I didn't understand why on earth they would even want to talk to him. His magazine was crackling with popularity back then and I saw no need to massage his ego.

Now I'd put him in a position where this Wade Crawford I'd heard so much about would have to brag. And this was a little test: either he was going to be discreet about his placement on the New York totem pole, or he was going to be one of those insecure douche bags Caitlin and I always laughed about—the ones who felt compelled to highlight their prowess in yellow marker.

"I guess they want to be in the magazine," he said, pulling out my chair and handing me my napkin. "Maybe they think it'll help their careers. Who knows?"

That passed muster. Honest enough without showing off.

Before we could get settled into our unplanned date, a slick-looking thirtysomething in a shiny Hugo Boss suit sidled up to the table and slapped Wade on the back too hard.

"Hey, man, did you get the book? We're already shopping it in Hollywood; I'm telling you, it's *The Perfect Storm* meets *Friday Night Lights*. A race around the world that—"

"Joe. I got it. And I get it." Wade winked at Joe, a man I guessed to be an agent. "And you know what?" He tilted his head toward me. "I'm on it too, but I'm in the middle of something here." He high-fived the guy and turned around before Joe could say anything else.

During our nonstop conversation that night, Wade listened to me intently, fixing his gorgeous hazel eyes on me, nailing me with a crazy look on his chiseled face like he was completely smitten. "So I just commissioned a story on this company down in Texas that has really screwed over a lot of people," he said while attempting to loop an olive out of the bottom of his lowball. "They were manipulating energy prices all along California by—"

I placed my head on my hand in mock disgust. "Corruption for $400. And the answer is: What is Enron?"

"So you know about . . ."

My laugh was light and happy. "Wade, I'm thrilled to have dinner with you, but, really, you just laid your cards on the table big-time."

"What do you mean?" he asked, flustered, which, though I barely knew him, I surmised was a new feeling.

"You've obviously been dating women who don't understand what you do. You don't need to be surprised I've heard of Enron. It's been front page in the *New York Times* for a week now. And by the way, you're a little late jumping on the story."

"I was just trying to . . ."

"I know, you were being polite, but, like I said, you're kinda busted. You'd have to be a Victoria's Secret angel not to have heard of Enron."

He laughed out loud and looked at me like he was going to propose right then and there. "You got me," he said with a devilish half-curved smile. My smallish breasts and short legs weren't exactly the angel material he'd apparently been accustomed to, but I pressed on.

Despite his reputation for being an inveterate mover and

shaker, only twice during the meal did I notice Wade scan the room. And though this may have been a record in restraint for him, he got up only once, to say hello to a table filled with young Hollywood somethings.

"I'm sorry," he said as he returned. "I didn't think I had to do any work tonight, but I have to whore myself out sometimes. Just tried to convince a young Hollywood schmuck he's gotta do my cover instead of *People* magazine." Wade looked a little desperate, like he'd taken the shafting personally. It was clear this guy's ego was completely wrapped up in whom he could secure for his magazine, like a hostess fretting over the RSVP list for her party.

"Did he bite?"

"Not sure. The ugly truth is I now have to kiss the asses of a bunch of idiots a fair amount of the time to get what I want out of them."

"What were you doing before you were kissing idiots' asses?"

He choked a little on that one. "You know, sadly enough, that's exactly how I spend most of my day. But it wasn't always like this. I started out in my twenties working for the *Boston Globe,* which was a much more scrappy kind of journalism, and something I thought I'd always stick with. You know, not to sound too righteous, but the great stuff for any reporter—exposing politicians and corporate criminals, that stuff we thrive on."

"Why did you leave?" I asked.

"I started writing longer pieces for magazines, and then I landed my first job as an editor, and the chance to rise was too powerful to pass up."

"And that makes you melancholy for the hard news?"

All of a sudden, he sat very rigidly, as if trying to make up for something he'd just done wrong. "You know the way life pulls you away from your goals, before you know it's happening? I have a different kind of influence working at *Meter,* I guess I could say, but it isn't the same real sense of breaking news. I get to pick important people to go after and we do significant hard news pieces sometimes, but there's a lot more celebrity stuff I never thought I'd get involved with. Truth is, for those people, a *Meter* cover can make someone's career. It's a major statement. Period."

He took a sip of his drink and looked at me strangely, like I may have been the first woman he'd dated in a while with whom he could talk. He liked me. I could read it all over his face. "I'm not saying it's me, you know. It's the magazine, to be alongside more substantive pieces about movies, blue-blood scandals, and literary sensations. It's a huge opportunity for that kid across the room, pure and simple, and he's making me work for it when it's usually the other way around. Yes, I got in this business to root out the bad guys, but now that I'm the editor, the bottom line keeps my job afloat and I have to focus on what the magazine needs, which is celebrity cluster-fucks." He shook his head.

"Do you mind the 'whoring'?"

He held my gaze. "You wanna know the truth?"

"Sure." I didn't dare blink.

"Put it this way: I don't like to lose." He placed his forearms flat almost to my edge of the table. "And I like to think I'm more of a high-class courtesan than a two-bit hooker."

We talked into the night and I was amazed at my ability to hold my own with an accomplished editor ten years older than me. Yes, I felt like the imposter, as I often do even today around new people I meet in the city, but I also sensed this man before me needed to be tamed. He liked my point of view, he liked me putting him in his place, and he even liked not acting like a pretentious ass for once. I tried to make my PR work for Murray sound more serious than event planning, which was most of what I did at the beginning. Wade was interested in my job, but not as interested as he was in explaining his.

While he was coming to quick terms with the idea that he'd finally found an attractive woman who cared about his world of nonstop news and gossip, right away, I knew that I too certainly liked the idea of this Wade Crawford man before me. He fit a need, like a square peg into a square hole. His enthusiasm for life and work would soften my losses: my father in a plane to the ravages of an untimely blizzard and James to a burning obsession to save every child on the other side of the world.

New York glimmered around us that night, the way it can when spontaneity falls perfectly into place. After dinner, Wade escorted me to two downtown parties filled with cigarette smoke and writers. Someday I hoped to be like his writer friends who wrote long magazine stories and books that they'd mined from their souls. It was clear from every angle that Wade's nonstop joie de vivre was more than contagious. He was sheer fun, and full of the possibility of escape, of renewal even.

He dropped me at my stoop at dawn, kissing me tenderly on the lips and disappearing into the early morning glow. As I watched him bounce down the street, all I could think was that he had Daddy's electricity and confidence. And that suited me just fine.

NOW I THREW the photo on the side table, my heart tightening. Next I did some more sifting through his desk to look for something a young girl could categorize as "unsafe" and a clue to his affections for this same girl. No jewelry receipts, no trips to swanky hotels in South Beach, no damaging Monkey Business photos. Was it possible my wifely hunch was off? Was Jackie honestly trying to help me at the bar? *And* in my own laundry room?

Around Wade's work alcove, I only found celebrity snapshots amid journalistic projects I knew he was working on—cocaine dealers in Tijuana, photos of well-known American CEOs at an exclusive conference in the Rockies, and a draft piece about a society murder in Argentina linked to the grandson of an SS Nazi officer—but nothing seemed secret or nefarious. Or they all seemed secret and nefarious, but that was the nature of Wade's work: find twisted stories that drew people in.

And then, something hidden inside a book in his right desk drawer—an annual company report on Luxor computer chips—caught my attention. Luxor, a growing computer networking company, wasn't the kind of flashy story Wade would usually go after. It was suspicious purely because it seemed so mundane. Was he investing someone else's cash? The one thing any wife in any regular situation would think was normal to see in her husband's desk—a company annual report—I found disturbingly abnormal.

It had rattled me enough that I unfolded the gum wrapper in my back pocket and sent Jackie a text.

ME: *It's Allie. Is this Jackie?*

About thirty seconds later she texted:

Find anything?
ME: *No. Nothing at all.*
JACKIE: *Can we meet? Tudor Room tomorrow?*

Meet with a woman I'd like wiped off the face of the planet? Problem was the admonition she delivered as she exited the laundry room rang in my ears and I'd have to understand what she meant before she got whacked. Next, I froze. This was way too early. I had no business contacting her. I don't know what I was thinking by texting her so rashly.

ME: *Tomorrow no good. Just wanted to know this was you for sure.*

I googled her immediately, but I couldn't find any information on her. No digital footprints at all.

I sensed only this: Jackie Malone used her sexual appeal to drive men over the edge. What she did with that power once they were plummeting, I did not know.

9

No Choice but the Grindstone

The cold light of day sobered my brain as I sat at my desk a week later. I was doing my best to focus on the screen in front of me, open to a blank page, the cursor pulsing like an impatient suitor. At least this was something that was all *mine,* not a writing task to boost a demanding client's career or image. Two months earlier, I had gathered my courage and submitted an old script I'd left for dead to a Tuesday night screenwriting class at New York University. I'd assumed I'd get rejected, but to my surprise, I got in, and this week's assignment was in danger of being late if I couldn't concentrate and begin it.

I'd write a few sentences of dialogue, but when I couldn't find the word I was searching for, my marriage angst would cloud my head instead, and then the beaming faces of our two children would break my heart more. A week had passed, and I hadn't made a move yet to meet Jackie. I wanted to lie low, find clues, consider my actions before I jumped too fast. Asking Wade how he knew her would yield another obfuscation until I could prove something solid.

I was very tempted to text Jackie again and meet her. She might say something to use as a comeback when Wade denied doing something with her. I also had to figure out what her bizarre warnings meant, if anything.

Yet, if I contacted her, how would I be able to tell if Jackie were lying? Was she possibly just blowing my husband in there? Maybe this wild-goose chase to find documents was nothing more than a game of distract-the-wife.

One thing was certain: I had to face the fact that I'd been feeling on edge with Wade—I believe now because I felt him pulling away. Before we were in sync; now he and I weren't. He made the motions, he'd kissed my ear at a party in a sexual way like he wanted me so badly, but then when we were alone, he was too tired and spent. Part of me was used to winding him up and letting him go. Yet this clarity slowly signalled something new: he was either having an affair or just didn't feel the same about us. I felt hurt and confused and angry and more than a little aggressive toward this Jackie woman.

"Allie." Caitlin popped her blond head into my office. "Selena asked me to tell you that Murray wants you in there in ten minutes." I glanced at the clock in the corner of my screen. How had it become 9:25 so quickly? Now I'd never get any pages polished before class. "Are you okay? Why are your eyes red?"

"Nothing. I'm getting a cold."

"You sure? You need to talk?" she asked softly.

"There's no news. I left early this morning."

"Was he out again?" she asked, fuming.

"Yes, gambling I guess, or entertaining."

Caitlin snorted. "Like there's a difference?" She put her hands on her hips. "And you still haven't filled me in on the laundry room episode last week. Why was he hidden away in the middle of his own friggin' party when he's usually the guy holding court?"

"It's too long a story, Caitlin."

She walked to my desk and splayed her arms out on the other side of it, with her chin resting on my computer screen. "One thing you have to tell me. What exactly is going on or not going on with you two? You and Wade look like robots together every time I see you. Believe me, I study you guys. I keep telling you that."

I put my head in my hands. "I love what I loved about him from day one: his irreverence, his magic touch with kids, but I just feel out of sorts with him right now. It's weird, like I'm questioning some things . . . it's nothing. We'll be fine."

"Questioning what? Your love for him?"

"No, but you know Wade isn't easy to be married to; he's so all over the place all the time. The flip side of that is I love how exciting he is, but suddenly I'm thinking about things I'd shut out before."

"Like what?"

I straightened up my back. Caitlin always pushed so hard on everything, there was no use resisting. "Like way back when, even on our wedding day, maybe, perhaps, I may have seen some things I didn't really digest."

"What the hell? What did you see back then?"

"His hand on my bridesmaid's rear end for starters." I laughed slightly; somehow it seemed ridiculous in that instant of lucidity. Every few days during that spring I felt something click, like those lenses eye doctors roll down over eyes to test and then sharpen the patient's vision. With each slow click, everything comes into focus a notch better.

"No!" Caitlin walked over to my desk and crossed her arms. "Really? Back then? You never told me that."

"Well, I was putting on my veil in an anteroom and I saw him ushering Kathy Vincent down the hall and his hand was practically on her butt and I just thought, 'Oh, gee.' But then I just plowed forward into unholy matrimony. I couldn't begin to process that."

"And you think the girl from the party and he are . . . and you should be suspicious always after the cheating with the photo assistant during the breast-feeding moment?" Hard to fool Caitlin, not that the dots would be that difficult to connect for a sixth grader. Maybe I just hadn't wanted to.

"Well, kind of like maybe I've been in a blur with work and kids and now he's just distracted and not that focused on me and . . ." Click.

"Listen, Allie, when you marry an ego like Wade, there's a limit to the intimacy you are going to feel. You weren't overlooking that one. It's all about him. You had to know *that* going in."

"It's like I don't rock his world the way I used to."

"Does he rock yours?" Caitlin sounded weirdly like she hoped he didn't.

This was the seminal question of the day I wasn't ready for. It literally stung. I felt an acidic chemical shoot up my body, tighten my heart, and give me an instant headache. Caitlin laid it all on the line right then and there in a way I'd never really let myself fully consider.

How and when did he rock my world?

What did this guy actually give to me? For a horrible, terrifying, very honest moment, I thought to myself: *Was I just wanting and needing to rock his so much I don't even know the answer?*

"Caitlin, I don't know about rocking my world. Of course he has or did or does at times," I blurted out to convince both her and myself. "I'm so distracted by catering to his man-baby needs and getting the kids fed while I'm handling every Murray explosion to be able to answer that honestly right this second."

"He's fucking around again, isn't he?" she asked. "I will literally chop off his dick if he is."

"Jesus, Caitlin! You didn't listen to what I just said!"

"I certainly did, but I'm not so sure that you did. How can you say one day you love his magic touch and the next that it's so hard to be with someone like him?" She perched on the desk's edge and looked straight at me. "Are *you* fucking around?"

"Don't be crazy," I answered, rubbing the pain out of my forehead and wishing she would leave.

"There is definitely something that you're hiding from me."

She looked at me long and hard. "You have to tell me. I live for this stuff, you know that. There's none in my life, God knows."

I smiled at her. "It'll happen soon for you when you're not expecting it, Caitlin. He'll just pop out of nowhere."

"Wouldn't know it if it happened, haven't had a guy even look at me in a year," she said.

"What are you talking about? Guys like you; you just don't see it."

"No, Allie. You don't get it: guys don't like me. I'm the fun best friend, not the one they want to take home."

"Well, then we'll work on it." I glanced at her bulky shoes and thick, muscly thighs peeking through her skirt. "We'll soften your look a little or something. I promise he's just around the corner. Let me just deal with the monster down the hall first."

I grabbed a pen and paper and quickstepped down the short hall to Murray's corner office.

SELENA, A CURVACEOUS Colombian woman, and one of the only beings on the planet who didn't fear Murray Hillsinger, nodded me in with a roll of her big eyes and a pursing of her huge shiny lips lined in dark pencil. My boss was clearly not in a good mood. All I needed.

"I don't give a shit who he *thinks* he is," Murray roared into his phone as I entered. He waved me to the straight-backed chair next to the black leather couch where he tended to hold court. I crossed and recrossed my legs while his tirade continued. His yellow tie dotted with little purple crowns didn't quite cover his belly, which protruded in a horizontal glob over his belt. "You gotta say what I tell you to say publicly or you're screwed. Plain and simple. I hate to state the obvious, but the cover-up is always worse than the crime, buddy. Just admit your mistake and move on. Otherwise you're toast. Trust me, that's what you're paying me for. I'll get a good reporter to take your mea culpa. Someone important. I know: I'll get Delsie Arceneaux to do it for you. Sound good? She'll be gentle."

Arrayed on the coffee table was Bouley Bakery's freshest assortment of chocolate croissants and buttery Danish and muffins, delivered daily the minute Murray arrived. As he listened to the diminished soul on the other end of the line, he gestured toward the coffeepot for me to pour him a refill. I felt like a stewardess.

Murray suddenly threw the phone down the length of the couch, grabbed a giant blueberry crumb muffin, tore off the top, and bit a large section from it, spraying balls of sugar everywhere in the process. "I'm so happy Delsie is ready to emcee the Fulton Film Festival media lunch, and some panels. It's like some light went on for her after your pitch and she's excited. But now we gotta create even more buzz. Remember I got Max Rowland to invest in the festival, so he'll have his jail buddies break my kneecaps if we mess this up."

"Okay," I said and wrote *more buzz* on my notepad. Murray always liked people to take notes, no matter how simple his demands. He knew damn well the buzz we were going to find was already in the pipeline. The Fulton Film Festival was practically running itself.

"Whatever you have, I'm not impressed, it's not enough for Delsie or Max—"

"Murray," I interrupted. "Why did you get that criminal Max Rowland to invest in a do-gooder festival like ours and put extra pressure on us to please him as well? I'm managing so many projects I don't know if I have the time to . . ." My home situation was sapping so much energy out of me that I could barely listen to his commands, let alone execute them.

"Bullshit. You got spunk and intelligence." He counted these attributes on his fingers without releasing the raspberry pastry in his grip. "You like to argue. Delsie likes that. I like that. I need to be told when I'm off base."

For the past ten years, Murray had never once listened to me when I told him he was off base. I put down my pen.

"So what do you want me to do?"

"I want you to promise me everything will go okay with the festival."

"First of all, as much as you'd like me to be, Murray, I'm not your mommy. And second, why do I have to go it alone? Why can't you be more involved?"

"You are to deal alone with Max on festival business; I'm not doing it anymore. Have a pastry. You're too goddamned thin."

Why was every man in my life acting like a little child who had to have everything the way he wanted just now? Maybe I courted them. That thought depressed me as I thought about making an effort to expunge the next generation of too many man-babies. I decided I'd let Blake handle his friend issues on his own and give him praise when he did.

I turned to Murray. "You *have* to talk to me about the other business with Max Rowland; he's a felon so I deserve to know you are being careful, or I refuse . . ."

Selena peeked into the room and said, "Sorry, Mr. Hillsinger. Your mother. Line two. You know how she reacts when I say you're in a meeting so the light will be blinking until you pick up."

"Shit!" Murray slammed the table. "Never satisfied. She's working on me now to go to the Venice Film Festival at the end of summer, thinks she's a film expert because her son has a few fuckin' famous clients in Hollywood." He picked up the receiver and completely changed the tone of his voice. "Yes, Ma." He sounded like a little boy and slumped his shoulders. "Yes, sure, Ma. I'll work on it. I thought you'd like the idea of Boca with your girlfriends again, but Venice it is." He slumped deep into his sofa at her latest request. "No, Ma. You know the hotels are all booked. No, Ma. Doesn't matter what they say, the Cipriani isn't the only good one, but, yes, Ma, I'll try to get you a room, but please remember if I can't deliver for you, it's because it's been booked for celebrities for a year now."

He had to pull the phone away from his ear as she reacted to that bit of news.

"Ma, I'll try to get you in. I'll call you later." Pause. "Yes, I love you." He put down the receiver.

"How come you look like a dejected eight-year-old every time you talk to her?"

"Because she terrifies me, that's why," he admitted in total defeat. "She purposely asks for the hotel that's booked out five years in advance. They want Clooney and DiCaprio in the

Cipriani that week, not my mom in her fuckin' fanny pack and Mephisto shoes! Jesus."

I looked at the explosion of crumbs in front of me and shook my head. "Do you want me to write something specific for Delsie's speech at the festival?"

"You decide what to put in it. You wrote those great environmental speeches when I hired you. A kid out of college who writes speeches with that much impact, I want going full tilt on this."

"Okay, Murray. And there were a lot of people I wrote them with; it wasn't all me."

He dusted his hands and heaved into a standing position, getting ready to dismiss me. "I don't give a shit if all your environmental writing success back then was genetic talent from your dad's love of the sea, or dumb luck on timing with the globe going green and the fuckin' terrorists controlling all the oil. Point is, you're gonna do what I ask and you're the best writer I got . . . and I'm very indebted to you, even though I don't say it enough."

"Of course, Murray," I said, my feelings for him warming back up as they invariably did.

"Look, kid," he said. I turned at the tender sound in his voice. "Your dad would have been proud. Too bad the good die young and he never saw your work promoting a cause that championed the ocean he lived in."

"Something like that."

He put his arm around me, ushering me out. "I remember when I first heard you give a speech. I knew that instant you could coach all my clients and write all their speeches. You sounded like a senator: junior fucking Barbara Boxer or something. Just don't get all lesbo on me."

"Excuse me?" I said.

"I mean, that short hair, all tough . . ."

"I don't think Barbara Boxer is known to be gay; I think she—"

"I don't give a fuck about whether she is or isn't. Just don't start takin' yourself too fuckin' seriously." He grabbed his cordless phone, started punching numbers into it, and looked at it as though it were shouting obscenities in his ear. "Goddamn it, Selena, get in here and dial this thing."

Selena scurried in, her Kardashian ass bouncing up and down like a beach ball, and took the phone while Murray finished lecturing me. "I want you to write more press releases on each film to create more press buzz for everything we do here. You know, groundbreaking shit lesbo senators pay attention to."

Selena handed him the phone and waited to be sent back to her desk. She looked at me in solidarity. Murray wasn't finished.

"Get me every goddamn cable news screamer screaming about the high-gloss, high-fuckin'-quality festival."

Now he was just being ridiculous. "Nobody on cable news cares about art and culture. They're too busy yelling at each other. We're on the right track, Murray. We're doing fine. We're getting good coverage already this week . . ."

"Max?" he said into the phone, swatting one hand at Selena and me. "That brunette looked like she could fit your balls *and* your dick in her mouth! After your behavior last night in A.C., you fucking owe me fifty grand and two whores, you old bastard." Gales of laughter followed. I honestly had no idea if Murray was joking around or making a factual statement to the criminal client who seemed to be invading our lives more every day.

10

Necessary Reckoning

When I got back to my office, Caitlin was lounging on my couch reading a report she'd pulled out of the hot pink computer bag I'd given her for her twenty-ninth birthday last winter.

"What was so earth-shatteringly important?" she asked.

"Murray wants me to get more press for the whole film festival, since the pitch to Delsie went so well and because now he's got Max financially invested in it," I said as I sat at my desk and clicked on my computer screen. I scrolled through what looked like a hundred e-mails that had come in since I'd left. "You know, just more buzz."

"Murray always wants more attention," she pointed out. "No amount will ever satisfy him, you know that."

"Yes, I know that. That's why my job sucks."

Caitlin sat up and threw the report onto the coffee table. "That's a piece of crap. Anyway, whatever you did or didn't do right, all that matters is that what you said seemed to work for him."

I stopped what I was doing and looked at her. "Really,

Caitlin, that's all that matters?" Caitlin and I spent so much time together all day long that we often went into sister mode. I felt like picking a fight with her just because she was in front of me.

She tilted her head. "That's not what I meant." She lay back on the sofa. "You're good at what you do, but you should be concentrating your anxiety on your other talents. Maybe you'd get further, faster, and be able to leave this place."

"Why?" I asked sarcastically. "You angling for my job?"

"Jesus, Allie. Chill," she said. "Why would you say that, when all I'm doing is showing my support for your writing?"

"Sorry. I was kind of joking, or trying to," I said. It had been unfair of me; she was right.

She grinned, apology accepted. "I read your reports and speeches every day. They sing compared to everyone else's around here. You should be using your clout with Wade or Murray to move your own fiction writing career along and stop worrying about the little stuff that Murray is always going to take credit for anyway." She settled in for a little lecture. "If I had access to Murray's connections like you do, or to Wade's, I'd be working them harder is all. If I was writing a script about a surrogate mom, like you are, I'd be asking Wade to show it to Sarah Jessica Parker, poster mom for surrogates."

"Are you out of your mind? I'm not involving Wade in my writing career. I want to do it my way."

"Fine. Do it all slow and appropriate. But just remember slow and appropriate usually gets beaten at the box office by swift and shrewd." Caitlin started balancing a pillow on her feet. This woman could never sit still. "Max is meeting with the festival team and Murray again tomorrow. You could go and get Max to invest in your script."

"That's not possible," I said, meaning the Max meeting and not the immature notion that a script I hadn't even finished yet could be pitched. Murray didn't lie to me. That's one thing I could count on. "Murray isn't going to talk business with the festival people for a while. He wants me to handle it all."

"Well, it said FF on his calendar for tomorrow. They're meeting at some hotel in the West Forties. I'm sure of it."

I was shocked anew at her espionage. "How do you know FF is film festival?"

"Well, they are the initials for starters, and I asked Selena, because I'm really nosy and she told me yes, but that I shouldn't say anything."

I let that sit. Caitlin was always on my side, but a little difficult to control. I just had to channel her energy into productive areas, like this revelation that my boss had lied about not getting involved in festival business. Her skill was often valuable, but it made Caitlin seem at times much more than five years younger than she was. "You've got a package waiting for you up front," she said, bouncing toward my door. "You want me to go get it? Maybe it's Wade trying to get on your good side."

"Oh my God, Caitlin! You talk like a cattle auctioneer! Yes, go get the package. Jesus!" I sat at my desk thinking that something with my boss wasn't sitting right. He told me he wasn't doing festival business with Max Rowland anymore, then he has a private meeting about it without telling me? Was every man in my life cheating on me in one way or another?

Click.

Caitlin sped out of the room and returned just as quickly, holding a box wrapped in dark brown paper, peppered with an absurd number of crooked postage stamps, and my address written in a familiar script. I ran a finger across the handsomely scrawled *Par Avion,* and I knew instantly the provenance. I opened it up. No card, but just as I expected: a pair of black silk long johns. I hadn't heard from James since the last pair.

Caitlin peeked over my computer again. "Who the hell sends long underwear in May?"

"It's nothing."

"Oh. It's something. Just something you don't want to tell me." She smiled, completely softening up. That, and knowing she was getting nowhere. "It's okay. I still adore you. Keep your secrets. But if you want an ear, I'm here for you." She had the sense to close the door behind her and leave me alone, wry amusement written all over her face.

James again. Through the years, he would always try to make me feel protected by sending a pair of long johns like these with a note saying: *I will always keep you warm and safe.* Part of me would immediately begin to feel better just remembering his words.

James had started promising this warm and safe thing right after the accident in the horrible blizzard—that I'd never feel that fear again. He'd said it when he left for college in San Francisco. Again and again he'd send pairs of long johns every time he skipped town—like when he'd left repeatedly to work in East Asia in our twenties—or when he felt I needed some support.

Once after I received a pair, he told me he had news to deliver in the accompanying note. A sense of dread had begun to creep up my ankles and settled in my knees, immobilizing me with the realization that my first love was actually, finally, fully in love with someone else—a woman named Clementine in Paris, whom he'd met at UNESCO. I guess the long johns that time were his way of saying our deal still held, that he'd keep me safe, no matter what life brought or who he lived with, even if she was named after a piece of fruit.

And here again were the long johns from the guy who would not stop being that soul mate I couldn't ever call all mine. I still hadn't moved an inch five minutes later when Caitlin placed a cup of hot tea on my desk.

I closed my eyes and played with the black silkiness through my fingertips and decided to soften up my sister act to give her an inch. "James sends these because he worries about me, and it's always bizarre how spot-on his timing is."

"He'll always know you best. You guys met at what, thirteen?" She perched on the edge of my desk and I settled back in my chair.

It's safe to say any connection with James in any form made me queasy with what-ifs. I looked at photos of my kids on my wall and thought, *There is beauty to this plan. James was never going to be. I had Blake and Lucy instead. I have them and I don't want it any other way. (Although my kids plus James wouldn't be the worst . . .)*

"James doesn't seem to know his seasons very well," she pointed out.

I laughed. "Yeah, well, if you really want some juice, these are a reminder of a particular moment in our tortured existence." I fingered the buttery silk some more, wondering just what my life would be like if James and I had closed the deal after our brief, second-time-around affair in our twenties, rather than me and Wade. "Though the ones he peeled off me were heavy, wet wool."

Caitlin leaned so close to me, she practically sat down in my lap. "What was *he* wearing?"

"Ski pants. His senior year in high school. We'd just spent the whole day on Loon Mountain. It was so freaking cold we were the only people in the parking lot by the time we made it, frozen, to his Jeep."

"Tell me," she asked in a demanding voice. "I never get enough about James out of you."

"We're old friends with a complicated past. Simple as that. I don't like to dwell on the moments when things got weird between us. I told you that many times. It's too painful, and then I remember all the bad stuff of the plane crash. So stop." I pushed her off my desk and pointed her small but powerful body toward the door. "Go find something to do."

She backed away. "Only if you promise to tell me the whole dirty story later."

I threw a pencil in her general direction. Once she'd left, I dialed James's number, but hung up before it rang. Then I repeated that action and reaction about five times until I told myself I had to get a grip. Would there ever be a point in my life when he would cease to be *the one who got away*?

I was embarrassed by my own high school girl behavior. One guy hurt me so I was running to another? Was that supposed to happen with grown women when the hurtful guy was their husband? Couldn't I find a way to just feel stronger about what I deserved or convince myself of something self-affirming rather than feeling like my husband's interests were elsewhere and I wouldn't hold up without James telling me I was okay and still pretty? Jesus!

I swiveled in my chair to look out at the sky, holding the silk of the long johns, wondering how many women in their thirties can't fully grow up. The longing memory of the cold Jeep, James's warm hands, and the heat blasting out of the vents still made me sleepy when I thought about it.

NO QUESTION HE'D felt the pangs too. All I'd suddenly wanted was for him to run his hands up my goose-bumped thighs before he graduated and moved to the West Coast for college. *If not now, when?* kept chanting through my head. Then in the Jeep that late afternoon, out of the blue, he just reached across me and with his right hand popped my seat back flat. The gesture seemed so easy and natural for him; I had to restrain myself from thinking about how many times he'd done just this before for other girls. I'd already been with my share of other boys but that didn't deaden the thrill of fantasizing about my best friend so graphically. He suddenly pulled himself on top of me like it was the most normal thing to be doing.

First James gave me a bottomless kiss as he held on to my head with both hands. But, quickly, he reached down to open his pants, tear the snowsuit off my body, and pull my long johns down my freezing thighs. When he rolled on top of me, he was so solid and ready before I'd even touched him. Seconds later, as we moved together, the claustrophobic space of the Jeep opened up around us, and as the dark winter night settled in and flakes of snow began to swirl in the distant glow of the parking lot lights, I panicked. The dive had been too high, and now I felt more like I was drowning rather than making love. He reached his hand down to me again. The power of our bodies together scared me so much that as he made me come, I burst into tears.

"It's okay, Allie," he whispered as he finished, his voice crackly and kind as he kissed me between the words. "I'm not going anywhere. Nothing's changed."

"I know," I said too softly for him to hear. I pushed him back to his side of the Jeep and hastily pulled my ski pants on over bare legs. "We're going to be late."

He shimmied into his pants, stared out at the snow for a long time, then just slammed the steering wheel with the palm of his hand. "Why do you have to freak out over everything? You didn't seem like you didn't want that. It's not like you haven't been looking at me weird for a month now."

"I have not. And I did want that. I just want to go is all. Now." Truth be told, I was merely petrified I'd lose him with Dad gone and Mom drinking so much.

He pulled my face sideways so I had to look at him. "I thought this was what you wanted. We're still friends. Like always. This doesn't change anything."

I curled into a ball in my seat, unable to look him in the eye the entire ride home. "I don't know how to feel and I don't want to talk about it."

The pain was evident on his face as he drove us home in silence.

NOW I LOOKED down at the ripped-up brown packing paper, silky long johns, and box and threw the whole mess into the corner of my office in a fit of muted, confused fury over what perhaps should have been. Maybe I would have been so much happier with James if I hadn't been so skittish and if bad timing and his do-gooder, twentysomething globe-trotting hadn't side-tracked our chances. How dare he suddenly pierce my carefully orchestrated life with another package, just as I was having bigger troubles with Wade than I could handle. My desk phone rang, and I snatched up the receiver, telepathy telling me for certain it was James.

"Very funny," I said, a slight edge of whimsy in my hard-bitten voice.

Wade replied. "Is this a bad time?"

"Oh, it's you," I answered.

"Allie, don't be like that. I'm sorry I had the weekly all-nighter close of the magazine at work and didn't get home in time to help with the kids this morning. How 'bout I make it up to you by taking them later and you can grab a drink with Caitlin or something?"

"You already have the kids tonight. Remember?" It killed me to keep the Jackie question bottled up inside. "I have my screen-writing class. You know?"

"Oh, right! Even better. I thought I'd take the kids to the premiere of the new IMAX movie on the deep sea. I got special tickets for them to go to the whale party at the museum afterward," he said. Wade always showered them with the kinds of outings normal kids could only dream of, especially on a school night. Parenting is about knowing when to be the bad guy—something Wade the Narcissist never cared to consider.

I exhaled, exasperated, knowing his best side was his worst side. "It's a school night, Wade."

"Maybe for you! Come on, don't be a drag, Allie. They won't be little forever, and Blake could use a homework pass just this once."

"Look, do what you want with the IMAX movie, just make sure Blake finishes his homework before you go." I held myself back from suggesting he get his young girlfriend Jackie Malone to help him with Blake's work, her grade-school math skills being far more current than Wade's.

"Of course you're right." His tone mellowed, turning from petulant to repentant. "We will get the homework done, I promise."

"Before the movie?"

Wade laughed. "Okay, have it your way, Mom of the Year. We wouldn't survive without you."

"Beyond true," I said and hung up the phone, resolving to leave the question of his level of interest for Jackie Malone be until I could confirm more.

11

Crash Course

If I wanted to end this period of robotic encounters with Wade and bring things to a head, I had to reach out to Jackie. He would deny any involvement with her if I pushed him. He would even start calling me paranoid as he does when I ask about models or hot young interns who always surround him at events. Admittedly, I didn't ever catch any of them in a laundry room with him, but I knew he'd go nuts denying a dalliance with Jackie and somehow make me look stupid for even bringing it up again.

This new rationale developed: contacting Jackie might be an insane step on my part, but it might also chart my path. It could lead me to figure out why she supported me with Delsie and why she warned me about the men in my living room. At the very least, what did I have to lose? Either I'd somehow confirm proof of an affair or she'd be great material for a future screenplay.

Right then and there one afternoon in my office, I texted her.

ME: *It's Allie. I'm ready to talk to you.*
JACKIE: *Good. You want to meet for a drink soon, even today? At the Tudor Room. It'll be empty this afternoon, and everyone we know will be gone.*
ME: *Gimme two hours.*

The time passed quickly once I'd started the motions on Murray's latest requests and finished another few pages of my script (both of which I completed in a daze). Soon enough, the time to meet Jackie had arrived, and I tore my coat off the back of my office door and raced out into the street to meet her.

I WALKED INTO the inviting entry area of the Tudor Room, completely still at this precocktail hour, ten minutes early, time enough to get into the restaurant and order a drink at the bar and compose myself for this very peculiar meeting I'd thrust upon my day.

The gold art deco clock behind me clicked 4:00 P.M. I stood on the steps between the entryway and the restaurant, my eyes level with the main dining room, which was empty and silent. All the tables were set with low bouquets of hot pink peonies in sterling mint julep cups. Crystal cylinders with fresh candles circled the centerpieces, unlit for now. After a full two minutes, a waiter walked past quietly and purposefully. Then nothing. Stillness. The chieftains and priestesses of industry were long gone, keeping our meeting safe from rubbernecking. Georges the maître d' only presided over the power lunch and would surely be gone by now. Over to my right, in the red, book-lined bar, the bartender dried off the insides of champagne flutes with a crisp white napkin in preparation for the evening rush.

My mission was now clear: get Jackie's information and use it to properly confront Wade. He and I were the real players in this drama, and the secondary characters around us could no longer distract me. From the midstaircase landing, I could see Jackie's extraordinary legs wrapped around a barstool. She ordered a drink and combed her fingers through her streaked blond hair with her eyes shut. Letting out a huge breath, she looked annoyed, as if everyone and everything and every goddamn man clawing at her were one big nuisance.

I closed my eyes for a moment to gather my strength and walked over to the bar. Jackie actually smiled slightly when she saw me. She was luminous in a white Ralph Lauren sheath dress, as if Marlene Dietrich's crew had lit her perfectly. A suede tan Gucci bag with some kind of animal antler handle lay on the mahogany bar counter. Where the hell did she get the cash to look so good? I sat down next to her.

The bartender walked over to us. "I'm sorry, miss, we aren't open for an hour, but I can—"

"She's with me, Robby," Jackie said. "Give us a little break and get her a cup of tea or coffee. Or maybe even a shot of something strong. From the look on her face, she needs one."

"A cup of tea, please, and also, a glass of chardonnay, thanks." I figured I needed both an upper and a downer to deal with this confrontation.

Jackie looked at me intently. "We've got a lot of ground to cover, but before we do, you are going to have to at least attempt to trust that what I'm telling you is true," she said, putting me immediately on the defensive.

"I trust only that you helped me once here with Delsie Arceneaux." I looked at her young face, trying hard to read her. "Why did you do that? That could have been to get me conveniently on your side. What are you after?"

"I said that to Delsie because you're good at your job and you deserved it," she answered, pulling her hair into a messy bun with a clip, her blond streaks almost white with the afternoon light shining in through the paned windows behind her. All at once I thoroughly hated her and found her completely beguiling.

I shouldn't have been nervous to say the following, but I was. "Let me get straight to the point: *Are you sleeping with my husband?* Usually it would mean something that he ran off to you in our laundry room in the middle of our party. Let's just put that on the table." My voice cracked, hopefully not revealing too much about how anxious I felt inside.

"Don't forget I looked you in the eye across the room at the party and motioned to you that something would be going on in the back of the apartment and turned my head to communicate that you should go back there."

She did do that. I nodded very slightly, not wanting to give her anything, but, yes, she did warn me she'd be headed back there. And she did insinuate that Wade would be going too, which he promptly did. I had to grant her that.

"Okay," she continued. "So why would I signal to the wife if I was trying to bang her husband in the middle of her home?"

"Not sure. I do find the whole thing a little confusing, I admit. One reason you got me here."

"Glad I got you here, because nothing happened that night in the laundry room except him catching me looking for something. And I'm telling you, you need to watch out; there are things going on with these men who lunch here every day that you don't understand." Not a sign of weakness in her voice, not a quiver of her lip. I had to channel her, or copycat her at the very least.

"C'mon, Jackie. *What is going on really?* I'm not ready to say I'm going to believe that you and my husband never—"

She interrupted and threw a loose snake of hair over her shoulder. "All right then, let's cut to it: I'll never lie to you. Did you hear me just now?"

"I heard you. I'm not sure I believe you, but I heard you, yes."

She looked down for a moment and tied her straw into a loop. "I repeat: I'll never lie to you. Your instincts are right. Something did happen between Wade and me."

My entire chest cavity hurt.

She went on. "I'm not talking about the laundry room that night, I'm talking way way way before that. And while I take due responsibility for it, he was driving the train."

She admitted to an affair just like that? To the wife? I pressed her. "You're admitting outright you slept with my husband?"

She nodded, her eyes showing kindness toward me; clearly she didn't enjoy having to confirm this news. I'm not ready to say I had anything but animosity toward this woman, but she did seem to be strangely in sisterhood with where I was just then.

"How did it happen?" I managed to say. The thought of Wade in bed with this beauty felt just as painful as Wade in bed with the photo assistant years earlier. I pursed my lips, blowing out air slowly as if it would extinguish the intense hurt inside.

"It just happened. And now meeting you, I'm honestly really sorry about it. I need to say that to you." The last part she said very deliberately and slowly and I felt in that moment that I believed her.

"Are *you* in love with my husband?"

"No."

"Is he in love with you?"

"Most unfortunately, he was at some point."

I thought about his kissing the kids and me at night, acting the all chipper husband and daddy. Then I thought about him passing out before any chance of sex entered our bed. No wonder—he'd already had sex hours before. My chest tightened a notch further than I thought possible.

"And not anymore?"

"Nope."

I had to know. My voice was weaker than I wanted when I asked, "Then how did it all begin with Wade?"

"It's complicated." She placed her elbow on the edge of the bar and touched the bottom of her chin lightly with the tips of her fingers. I stared into her eyes and tried in vain to figure out where her extraordinary composure came from.

What was it that Wade saw when he looked at these same eyes and thought, *This, I can crack,* or, even, *This, I love*?

"You were having a love affair with my husband for a while?"

"I believe you need to have feelings to be having a love affair. No? Whatever happened with Wade, it's now over. You can be reassured of that at least."

"You sure of that?" That notion of it being over between them softened the body blow I'd just received. I wasn't ready to leave him, and so I felt a false, momentary comfort knowing maybe my husband was back to being all mine.

"Whatever was going on didn't end with hurt feelings or rage, because, frankly, I didn't care that much, and he moved on." She took a long, cool sip of her drink—by the smell of it, a gin and tonic—and set it down delicately. Jackie went on, changing the subject. "We both know that the country is in a financial mess because so many of the men and women in this very room running huge investment banks and huge multinational corporations think they can screw the country over for their own greedy gain."

"What are you figuring out exactly?" I asked. "Murray's finances? Surely not Wade's."

"Hello? Everyone's finances are off in these unstable times. The question is, What do you resort to when the finances are off?" she answered. "Do you pull up your bootstraps or do you skirt the law?" She placed a finger lightly on my arm. It was much hotter than I would have expected. "Did you find something on his desk? Did you look?" she asked.

"Quite a lot on his desk, as a matter of fact." I wasn't about to give up the company report to a woman who just admitted to an affair with Wade.

"Like what?" Jackie asked.

"Actresses in rehab. Mobsters in Monaco. My husband is in the storytelling business. He reads research given to him as support material for articles he publishes. If he has Pablo Escobar's Interpol case file on his desk, that doesn't mean Wade was or is dealing cocaine."

"That's it, huh?" She played with the lime on the edge of her drink.

"Not that I would give you anything anyway since he's my husband and I don't have any proof that you are for real. But, tell me, what the hell are you alluding to?"

She stopped me by placing her full hand on my arm. "I study a lot about how the people in this room interact."

"How?" I asked.

"Do you have a business degree, Allie?"

"No, do you?" I scoffed condescendingly.

"Finishing my second year at Wharton at UPenn, in Philadelphia, right now. As a matter of fact, I'll have the diploma by the end of the month. But I didn't grow up anything like the rich kids who were groomed for business. I grew up in a dump of a house with my mom, a single working mother, that's it, just us two. So don't go making assumptions about my life just because I'm in business school."

"That's a very good program, but I'm not sure . . ."

She groaned and pulled out a small Louis Vuitton wallet and

fished out a Wharton School of Business ID card. "Good enough? I'm happy to do anything to prove this to you, but I swear I will never lie to you." Then she reached again into the depths of her bag. Out came a three-subject, big wire-bound notebook with the UPenn seal on the front.

"All right. So you're in school. Maybe you understand a spreadsheet."

"Yes, I understand a spreadsheet, a capital asset pricing model, and can run a Monte Carlo simulation in my sleep."

"Really?"

She laughed at me mocking her. "Hey, don't knock my degree. I'm minoring my degree on the entertainment industry and I'll tell you, the film business you are wading into is a broken business model—something I do understand, and, by the way, that's more proof I'm actually studying it. One thing's for sure: the studios are only banking on predictable action blockbusters and the indie market is just dead. You're never going to make money off a film festival; it's all about figuring out the distribution channels with VOD, PPV—"

"Excuse me, VOD? PPV?"

"Video on Demand. Pay-Per-View. Robert Redford made cash from the Sundance Channel, not the festival. Remember that as you make your festival plans and get all these big shots to invest in it."

"Okaay," I answered, slowly accepting the veracity of her business knowledge. "And now you're working . . ." I was still trying to figure out how she was always wearing shoes Carrie Bradshaw would weep over.

"On my business degree until I graduate this month. And some research projects. I work in investment banks in the summers and make a lot of money for someone my age."

"And that salary explains all these spectacular clothes and shoes and Gucci bags you seem to have?"

"My college roommate became a stylist's assistant for fashion magazines, so she gives me used runway and photo shoot clothes from last season. I'm not as sinister as you think, Allie," she said. "All these guys and their behavior is just as weird and foreign to me as it is to you. So don't let last season's clothes intimidate you or fool you." She took another slow sip of her drink. "Look, I didn't grow up in Manhattan by a long shot and I use some strategies to fit in. Don't tell me you don't; it's a survival thing."

I thought about how some people acclimatize to New York better and faster than others. After eleven years of living in New York, I never once felt I had an outfit really nailed head to toe. Though I hated to agree with anything she said, I did say, "Point taken."

I felt dizzy from too much alcohol on an empty stomach and too much information, some of it crazy painful, coming at me so furiously. The pounding of an early evening hangover started far off in the distant corner of my head. I blinked hard to soak up the tears I felt forming.

Jackie placed her hands on my shoulders. "You have to keep disciplined in your mind. You must separate your emotions from the concrete facts here and help me help you put them together to protect yourself. Forget your philandering husband, Wade, for a second."

"Well, it's a little hard to talk girl to girl with someone who just told me she slept with my husband. And forgetting my philandering husband is easier said than done. We have a family."

"Well, then you at least need to protect yourself and the children. I need to know if you've seen any company documents, maybe something called Luxor? It's a growing computer networking company."

I remained mute, remembering that was the exact name of the company report hidden in Wade's desk, and took a huge gulp of my chardonnay.

"Has Wade ever been to Liechtenstein, that little principality in Europe where they hide accounts and . . ."

Now I needed to ask her for some of the meds she was clearly on. "You may be a fabulous business school student, but you're way off base. And I'm not disclosing anything by telling you that Wade is a business Neanderthal and doesn't have any extra money. Believe me, I pay the bills."

"He's got something better than that. He's got access to everyone. And they all want him."

"Everyone always wants him. I'm not sure I'm buying this, but I'm listening. Once again, why do you want to protect me?"

She sniffed loudly and rearranged her shoulders. "My mother got royally screwed financially by a man, and I hate to see it happen to another unsuspecting woman like yourself."

"I'm sorry about your mom, but I feel there's something more at stake," I insisted.

Her eyes told me there was indeed something more.

"And you're not telling me what that other thing is. Why

don't you fess up, Jackie? We've gotten this far. I mean, supposed ex-lover and wife are talking without the husband even knowing. We are as bare as we can be; just go all the way and tell me."

We each took a sip of our drinks and placed the glasses on the table in unison. She turned to me. "You're writing a screenplay, right?"

"Who told you?"

"And is your position with Murray Hillsinger's PR firm your main job?"

"The screenplay is a pipe dream, not income until it's done. At least not yet."

Jackie then nodded and swiveled the barstool around, preparing to leave. "I'll get back to you when I find out more myself. But watch that Luxor stock and see if Wade mentions it." With her skinny white sheath dress clinging to her, she hopped down and leaned into my ear—her breath was hot and fragrant, like the gin she'd been drinking. "Just one thing. You need to write like your life depends on it."

With that, she sauntered out of the room like she owned my world. Which, I would later find out, she basically did.

12

Left-Field Curveball

"Everyone thinks their life is a movie. That's a load of crap. Lives meander. People may be wildly adventurous, lucky or unlucky in love, but birth-life-death does not give you your three-act structure you will need in a script." At this, our screenwriting professor, the reviled and revered David Heller, New York's answer to the more famous Robert McKee, jumped from his seated position on the edge of the desk and threw his arms in the air. He circled around my desk chair and pointed at my face.

"Also, by this Friday I expect, let's see, Braden, Foster, Greenfield, and Keller to e-mail to the class their first twenty pages. If you go to the multiplex this week and look down at your watch ten minutes in, I guarantee you something's happened that throws your protagonist out of his or her comfort zone. So what if I'm an alien dirt farmer, there's a princess in danger! I'm gonna follow the old dude with the British accent and his pair of robots and join the rebel cause! If your protagonist isn't taking a risk by page twenty, you're dead in Hollywood, and dead in this class, so don't bother sending it in. You follow me, Braden?"

"Yes," I said, nodding to show just how closely I followed. I'd used my maiden name, Braden, when I applied for the screenwriting class at New York University a few months back. I didn't use that name at the job with Murray, but while taking this class, I wanted to make sure I had some independence from the well-known Wade Crawford.

Heller went back to his desk and turned to the board. "Remember the simple three acts." I wrote down every word. "Also remember hundreds of students have used my clear-cut methods to—"

The door opened and Tommy O'Malley barged in. He and I had been sitting next to each other, having coffee with the group after the class, and comparing notes after the previous sessions.

Two chairs around the circle were still open. He chose the one next to me, looked at me with his bedroom eyes, and sauntered over like Brad Pitt. Heller threw him a glare.

"Don't ever forget this is a very competitive class with a waiting list as long as my arm. See that you are all on time." He then looked at the rest of us, adding, "Now as you can see, I've already written on the board Acts I, II, and III."

After a brief explanation of said outline, Heller took a sip of water and went on, enthralled by every notion that came out of his mouth. "In the middle of Act I, by page twenty, your problem has to be set up."

Tommy scribbled something on a note and passed it to me. It read, *So what's your problem this week?*

I wrote on the back of the same piece of paper. *My new script is a mess. I'm not sure I even know. Girl loses boy over baby problems. Yours?*

He scribbled back: *Can a tight-knit summer lifeguard crew stay close when real life sets in? . . .* St. Elmo's Fire *meets bad economy.*

A few minutes later Tommy touched my elbow with his as he was taking notes. "Sorry," he said. He pulled some Twizzlers out of his backpack, peeled one off, and offered it to me. "You'll need some sugar to handle all this information," he whispered, no longer any space at all between us.

"By the second act"—Heller looked at Tommy and squinted at the candy—"your hero *must commit* to his or her adventure." He made the line between Act I and Act II on the board thicker with repeated strokes of his marker. "This is Blake Snyder's 'promise of the premise.' It's at this point that Roy Scheider, the landlubber, heads out to open sea in search of his shark, or James Bond goes after Goldfinger."

I tuned out and instead divided my real life into three acts just like the ones on the board in front of me. My first act was set in stone up until the point where the heroine's father dies tragically in a plane crash and her mother puddles into an even drunker and eventually fatal mess in the six years that follow. I thought about my second act. The heroine chooses not to close the deal with her soul mate and sometime-lover James, marries a dashing but flawed man, has two children with him, but then is forced to reevaluate her past decisions.

The problem with this premise was that it had no promise whatsoever, and I knew it. James was long gone, the push and pull of our friendship over the years having exhausted him and catapulted him to safety overseas.

Next I glanced at Tommy O'Malley. Maybe Twizzler Guy was a little spicy decoy that a screenwriter would throw into the middle of the second act to fire up the plot. For the zillionth time that week, I tried to consider moving on from my pain over Wade's newest betrayal and cheered myself up by noting that Tommy's thighs, one now unnecessarily close to mine, were actually pretty damn epic. It didn't hurt to window-shop.

Heller turned back to the board and underlined Act III. "The third act follows hard upon your 'everything is lost' moment. By an hour, an hour fifteen, thirty, your hero should be at rock bottom. Intense drama. Passionate reckoning."

Rock bottom did not sound as good as passionate reckoning. Though logic would suggest that if the heroine did gather the strength to ditch the cheating husband, then someone else might just show up to save the day and provide the happy ending that Hollywood—and the world—so adored.

If only life could be as tidy as Hollywood.

Heller added drama to his voice to deliver the moral of the story. "After everything is lost, the hero picks himself up from the ashes, dusts himself off, and saves the princess or kills the shark before being killed. Hamlet finally stops kvetching and kicks some ass," he said directly to me. "This should happen no later than page ninety, and from here it's a sprint to the finish. No more equivocating, it's payoff time. It's fine in the first act to say I'm going after the shark. It's another thing entirely to grab the gun and stare into that big jaw full of razor-sharp teeth as your boat's sinking underneath you. Then it's up to you, the writer, to decide how he fares."

Tommy raised his hand, revealing a sharp hip bone as his shirt came up enough to expose a Michelangelo muscle line that extended to his sweet spot below.

"I still can't figure out why all the professors keep hammering in that every movie has to be so formulaic. When I follow rules, my script turns into some lame Jennifer Aniston movie I never wanted to write."

Heller took offense. "Are you calling my attempts to help you structure your work a pedestrian . . ."

Tommy seemed pleased to have gotten the reaction from Heller he was after. I watched him smirk and studied his looks: short, cropped dark hair and blue Irish eyes, and a slightly square forehead. More macho than handsome. A fragrant mix of rosemary soap wafted my way. I glanced behind his chair and saw his helmet and dark black bag. Maybe my way out of Act II was on the back of a motorcycle and I should just hop on with abandon. Wade's behavior would certainly justify it.

I turned my back on Tommy just then, as if to simply shut him off like a lightbulb. I had to focus on the lesson, or at least try.

That tactic worked for about thirty seconds. "Truth is, most every movie does follow these rules; I just hate to be told what I have to do," Tommy whispered, looking down into my eyes after I couldn't help but look back at him. "It's just going to mess with my head like the last class."

Tommy then turned his entire large body toward mine with his elbows resting on his knees as the class ended. The whole class had hung out by the student coffee bar just last week to celebrate his thirty-second birthday, but tonight he acted more inquisitive and attentive. His muscular limbs were spread wide, like some kind of human male mating call. He had thick eyebrows that matched his thick, dark hair, and he had an unkempt, rugged quality that read like a neon sign blinking DANGER. When we stood at the same time, bumping heads, he straightened up to at least six feet two.

"You want to grab a coffee at a place I know down the street?" Tommy asked. "We haven't been there yet." The room had cleared out of our usual cohorts; he was not proposing coffee with the group, but a step into the outside world alone, and I wasn't sure how I felt about that.

"Sure," I said and pushed out a breath.

Tommy stood up, grabbed my jacket off the chair, and put it on me like he was already my boyfriend.

"Let's go. I think we're going to need to make sense of this teacher and to decide whether we should take his advice or tell him and his screenwriting rules to go fuck themselves."

13

Date with Destruction?

Tommy was walking toward me with two steaming cups of cappuccino—just what I needed at ten o'clock at night—in the darkly lit Hungarian pastry shop four blocks down from our class near Washington Square Park. The shop had about twenty dusty tables in it, covered in mounds of candles with wax that had dripped over and over again in different colored layers. A few older professors and students stared intently at their laptops at tables nearby.

"So tell me what it was like where you grew up," Tommy said, handing a coffee cup to me. "I only know you didn't spend much time in New York, clearly."

"How come you know that?"

"Your manner; you don't have that *I own the world,* cocky, New-York-born-and-bred thing in the way you talk—or walk, for that matter." His eyes were locked on mine like a weapons system. I bit the inside of my cheek way too hard as he rubbed his stubbly chin. I thought about bolting for the door.

"I guess," I said, and I pulled my cardigan sweater tight up against my shoulders as if to defend myself. "I didn't leave my fishing town in Squanto, Massachusetts, much. My mom was a housewife, kind of, when she wasn't drinking. And my dad owned a tourist and work boat, anything to get out to sea, something he really loved." *And anything to get away from my mom.* I wrapped the arms of the sweater once around my neck and still felt completely naked.

"Is he still around? It sounds like not . . ."

"Nope. And speaking of not, why not give Heller a break in class? Yes, he's annoying, but . . ."

"Well, I like to push his buttons, and he reacts so fast."

I was so nervous to be alone with Tommy; I had to throw questions back at him. "How come you started writing scripts? I only know you grew up here. Queens, right?"

"The Rockaways; I've been in every home Hurricane Sandy destroyed. It's a solid blue-collar area, filled with cops and firemen. Grew up a few blocks from the beach, just off the boardwalk." His blue eyes sparkled extrabright against the reflection of his light Irish skin.

"Were you thinking about writing back then?"

"I was always writing in my head. I used to go to SoHo and buy movie scripts they sold off card tables on the sidewalks to see how it was done. I must have read *Chinatown* a hundred times."

"Is writing how you earn your living?"

"Of course not. That's the dream. I make money by consulting at these high-end New York restaurants where I help buy wines cheap at auctions—I don't drink, too much of that in my family, but I learned a lot from working in my uncle's liquor store, and I'm pretty encyclopedic when it comes to good wine buys."

We fell into an awkward silence as I tried to think of a safe topic.

After a beat, he couldn't help himself. "So your dad died recently?"

"When I was sixteen, or just about."

"And your mom?"

I took a quick sip of coffee and burned my tongue. "When I was twenty-two. The bottle killed her liver."

"That's a tough break to lose both so young. What was your dad like? You've mentioned him a few times, seems you were close."

I took a more careful sip of coffee, mainly so I would have something to do with my hands, which were shaking. "He was amazing, you know? Larger than life." I shook my head and looked into the cup, pacing my thoughts. "He was a great father, always taking me places in my imagination that few fathers make the time to do. If they even can. He used to read me a story from this old book of fairy tales, and then he'd tell me to recast it, and change the ending. If it was a sad story, he'd have me help him make it come out happy." I blinked hard and rubbed a burning spot on my lower right eyelid.

"I'm sorry he's not around anymore," Tommy said in a soft tone. "He must have been a great guy. How did he die so young?"

"He was. And he died in a plane crash in the snow." I let out a deep breath. I wish people just knew and wouldn't bring it up. It still felt like a cancerous tumor inside that engendered empathy I didn't even ask for.

"I'm so sorry. I meant to focus on the good stuff in his life."

I turned to the bakery counter and read the wall menu behind a Hungarian girl who was wiping crumbs off the counters as if I didn't hear him.

Ten seconds passed, and he took a bite of his oatmeal cookie and looked right at me.

When I didn't respond at all, he took that as a sign that I wanted him to keep talking and dug deeper into the wound. "I'm sure it must have been tough, you were at such a vulnerable age."

I smiled wryly and curled my lip to fend off any show of emotion. "Then why do you keep talking about it?"

"I'm sorry again. I'm scared to fly, if you want to know the truth." He shrugged, trying to get less uncomfortable in my awkward presence.

I turned to face him. "I was on the plane."

Tommy looked at me like I'd punched him in the stomach. He took a sip of his coffee, waited another long ten seconds, and then said softly, "Jesus Christ. I had no idea."

"A lot of people don't know about that part."

"Any others you knew on the plane?"

"Yeah. Two others. One was okay; one didn't make it."

"Well," Tommy said, emboldened, "did you ever write about it?"

I looked at him blankly and shook my head.

"Look, I'm sorry," Tommy said. "It could be powerful writing, that's all."

"Thanks for the advice."

"All right." He touched my arm. "Let's talk about something else. What have you been working on since last class?"

"You really interested?" I smiled, trying to think of a way to make anything I did sound compelling.

"Unbelievably." His crooked grin was warm and adorable, and I had to keep looking down to avoid his stare. He slid his hair down with the palm of his right hand, revealing a thick scar at the hairline that I hadn't noticed before. It made me feel better thinking that his life hadn't been entirely pain-free either.

I suddenly felt like I was doing something illegal.

"Tell me about your script: girl loses boy over baby," he said, reaching across the table and brushing a crumb off my lower lip.

I blushed.

"Oh, you based this on someone you know," he added, cueing in on my red cheeks as an invitation for his hand to linger at my chin.

I looked down into my coffee. "Sort of. Other than the baby part, I guess."

"What's his name?"

I hesitated, then answered his question. "James. Kind of lifelong best friend with a few moments of complications, let's say. Technically my first love, I guess, though we never really went out as a couple for real."

Tommy made a lazy circle around the coffee cup with his finger. "Still is someone who gets to you. I have plenty of those in my life."

"No more, not really," I lied. "Moments of regret here and there, but he was just *there,* always."

"Like after your dad died."

"No, like *when* he died." My throat constricted. "He was there, in the little commuter plane with his mother."

"Sorry. Wow." He shook his head hard.

I took a long sip of my coffee as we just sat there for a long moment of silence, he surely trying to come up with something to say while I remembered too much, too fast.

JAMES AND HIS mom were buckled in the back row as a surprise when I'd finally stepped into the little Cessna.

"Hey, Allie," James had said. I could see the same fear of flying behind his forced smile. "Guess we're, uh, going to some cabin together and it's way cold up there?" He smiled all normal but raised his eyebrows, signaling something odd was going on.

"Uh, yeah. Hi. Mrs. . . ." I looked at his mom.

"Come on. Call me Nancy. I've told you that's fine."

"Okay." I sat down in front of her. No one said another word until Dad handed in his boarding pass outside and came onto the small commuter plane.

"What are *they* doing here?" I feared displeasing him more than anything because he was gone at sea so much, but his inviting my secret crush on our special birthday trip without asking me felt unfair.

"You know," he'd answered, not looking my way as he struggled to find the worn-out seat belt all tangled in the metal beneath his seat. "Nancy and I just planned it last week since they were going to be up here visiting family. We thought it would be a fun surprise."

Just call me Nancy, she had said. The betrayal squared itself in that moment. I wanted to cry, but I also didn't want Dad to see how scared and mad I was, not on behalf of my mother on the other side of the border, but for crushing my illusions that he was a good husband, the kind I would want to marry someday. I looked at his profile and tried to gauge whether his excitement was for the ice fishing with his buddies who were already up there or for the woman sitting behind me, because somehow I knew the answer and felt left out.

James grabbed my shoulder on the side near the window where no one could see and leaned forward to whisper into my left ear, out of Dad's earshot. "Buck up. He's on one of his rolls. There's no stopping him now."

"I hope so," I whispered back. "I just don't get why you two are here."

"Look on the bright side, then," he said as I turned my head to see his eyes. "You won't be alone when you freeze your butt off on the icy lake."

SOMEONE KNOCKED ON the wood of the table top hard. "Hey. Helloooo? I asked you to answer one small question, please," Tommy said. "You just totally spaced out there for a minute. What happened to James and his mom?"

"James's mom. My dad. They died. James and I lived. Okay?" I forced a laugh to break the tension. With my sweater sleeve, I covered up the one ugly scar from that night located on the top of my wrist . . . a spot conveniently located that I had to look at one thousand times a day.

"I could tell you about my messed-up script instead of all this?"

"Fire away, Tommy." I settled into my chair. And then, "Can we go someplace for a drink?" I interrupted a mere three minutes into his synopsis. "I need a glass of wine," I said.

"My script really is that bad, isn't it?" He laughed.

"No. I'm just a little, I don't know." I smiled at his eager face. "I just want some wine. I need to have a drink if I want to keep concentrating, as strange as that sounds."

"Doesn't sound strange, sounds good."

Yes, I was following his screenplay. Yes, he had heard the bare outlines of mine. Yes, we had been deep in conversation a bunch of times before about all the dead ends in scripts we could create for ourselves. But one phrase kept running through my brain and it went something like this: *What the hell are you doing?*

"I know the perfect place," he said and practically lifted me out of my chair and onto the street.

Tommy and I walked in silence to a French bistro around the corner. He held the door open, and I walked inside to a dark room with mirrors behind bronze rods lining the top of the velvet banquettes. As hard as I tried to gloss over what was really going on, even I couldn't convince myself that Tommy was simply a smart guy from class who helped me to open up about my feelings or my writing. Yet I willingly chose to stay here and not bolt to the next taxi on duty. We stayed a two-foot distance apart until we got settled at the bar, our legs magnetically inching toward each other.

Tommy peppered me with more questions. “If you’re writing about lost loves, girl loses boy, that longing that can be so powerful, are you channeling this guy James? Fuck, you went through a lot with him.”

“Yes, in a way.” I tried not to slug my chardonnay. “I mean, I’m trying to, and finding in writing, the longing is much more poignant than the actual scene of them finally hooking up.”

“Speaking of channeling things, for so many girls, their love stories are so intertwined with the daddy thing.”

I looked down at his hand millimeters away from my leg and pulled my knees together. “I’m not going to tell you about the accident.”

“I’m not asking you to. It’s just that writing it down might exorcise it somehow.” And then he couldn’t resist: “That plane crash had to screw with your head when it came to guys, right?”

I closed my eyes, and replied, “You really want to know how much?”

14

Danger Zone

Tommy looked at me like he was measuring me up against the size of his bed. "You and James ever actually hook up or did you just torture yourselves?"

I took a sip and cracked the back of my neck. More late drinkers and people on dates came into the cozy bar so I didn't feel quite so alone with Tommy. "Okay, I'm going to indulge you this once," I answered, feeling game to open up in a way I rarely did. "Here's the true headline: I don't know if it was because James entered my life in the years before my father died and witnessed the whole damn thing, but despite my feelings for him, I still could never, ever really let him in in that deep, intimate, romantic way. He was a willing player in the game of push and pull. I mean, we went through so much so it's hard to figure out the seesaw of emotions I always have with him, but it was like I always had to preserve something. This deprivation thing that felt safer. You know about that?"

"I understand, but I think I'm the opposite, more of a love addict of sorts," he answered. "This is going to help your writing, I promise; when was the first hookup? Tell me about the scene when you knew this was your soul mate guy."

"The summer we were thirteen and fourteen, a group of us were playing Marco Polo, jumping into a lake off a tire rope . . . It was nearly sunset when James rode his bike up, pretending like he was looking to hang out with the guys. But both of us knew he was there to see me, and that thrill caused a new ache in my core. He was much more developed than the rest of the guys. And his dirty blond hair curled all over the place." Tommy tried to ruffle up his own short hair, but it didn't work. I smiled and bit my lower lip. "To this day, he's the guy who never cares what people think or see, and he's always been pretty gruff and clueless on the emotional front. But there was also a seriousness that attracted me to him." I glanced up at Tommy's blue eyes. The dim lights of the bar glowed amber. "There was this small swarm of mosquitoes circling his head like a halo. It caught my breath."

I coughed and swung my legs around to the front panel of the bar as his had touched mine and stayed there for a longer beat than is normal for two people *not on a date*. "At first James treaded water just next to our group, but then he came right over to me and pulled me onto his shoulders to chicken fight with another couple of kids. I kept falling down his back and having to hold on to him piggyback, all wet in my bathing suit, slipping up and down. My newly curvy body filled with so much excitement, it ached." My blush had turned into a permanent flush.

"Did you let him know somehow?"

"Almost, but my dad showed up, right there to survey my first real intimate and very sexual contact with a guy, yelling at me from the road." I imitated him: "'Allie! You're late. Your mother's going to kill me if I don't get you in this car right away. It's her party!' He was sweaty and dirty from the docks."

Tommy asked, "Did he see for sure you slithering on James's back?"

"No question he saw us; I watched him watch us. I suddenly felt naked and ashamed. Weird. When we walked up the bank, Dad grabbed me on one side and had James walk on the other, and he suddenly said to James, 'You're George Whitman's son. Jesus, you look like him. And his wife, Nancy.' It was a bizarre thing to say. James answered, 'Yes. They are my parents,' which echoed how weird Dad sounded."

"What was so weird about it?" Tommy asked, his face looming ever closer to mine.

"I don't know exactly." When we were a little older, like seventeen, James and I decided that his mom and my dad definitely had an affair, otherwise why were they on the plane so secretly last minute like that? And there were other clues we figured out later, but I wasn't about to add that to my list of confessions to Tommy.

"I do remember my father stiffening at the sight of us with bathing suits half falling off and saying, 'Don't you kids have towels?' and he looked really uncomfortable. Even after all that happened and all that I would understand many years later, I still remember that detail distinctly: *Don't you kids have towels?*

He was always the cool-dude dad. I'd never seen him rattled the way he was just then, trying to cover us up."

"He knew James was the one. Protecting his little girl, obviously."

"I guess. Anyway, James threw his bike on the rack in the back of Dad's Jeep and jumped into the back, holding the roll bar. It was so hot outside that our bodies dried off quickly and I felt sticky from the dirt in the lake. As Dad hurtled his Jeep up the rocky path to the road, James instinctively put his hand around my lower hip to make sure I didn't fall. I looked at him, a little shocked that he was touching me, and that he kept his hand there. He whispered deeply into my ear, 'You okay?' I could only nod; the touch was so intense. 'Good,' he said, a buzzing sensation by my cheek. 'Real good.' "

Tommy was spellbound in front of me. "You wrote this all down, right? I mean, this is in your script? This brush with first love?"

"Not that scene in particular."

"Well, that's the scene where everything started, right? You falling for someone, your dad's watchful eye, both paternal and Oedipal. Then you lose both of them? This is what it's all about. This is your hero's journey, to get back the love you lost, or find it elsewhere. You have got to write this all down. It's real stuff that works."

I knew that Tommy was right: my life was all about what began that night. It was that night, under the elms, with a peek of moonlight shining through the maroon maple leaves, that I first understood what love must be like. Something you can't help but feel. Something I would spend decades trying to run from, or desperately searching for in places it didn't exist. And ever since the accident in all that billowing and hateful snow, it'd been a mad dash, groping toward an illusion of intimacy, only to be left empty-handed.

"I think I need to get home," I said, pulling on my coat. "I want to get writing on this while it's still fresh."

Tommy buttoned my coat close around my neck and cocked an eyebrow. "You need a ride?"

Before I knew it, I was hanging on to Tommy's hard body as we sped up Eighth Avenue on his beat-up motorcycle. All I could think was, *This is really, really dumb.* He wrapped his fingers in mine at a stoplight near my apartment on West Twenty-Third Street and Tenth Avenue and I tried to free them, but he just clamped on them harder. By the time we pulled up a block away from my building, I was shaking. He took his helmet off and rolled the bike onto its kickstand.

"You can't come up," I blurted out.

"I wasn't asking to." He took a step closer to me. "But you could come to my apartment instead."

"I'm married," I blurted further.

"No shit," he answered, his hand on my arm, his head tilting to the left. "We'd have fun. I promise you you'd have a great time."

"I mean, I'm not in the greatest relationship."

"What a surprise." He smiled within inches of my lips.

"But it's not, I mean, I've never . . . this isn't what . . . I just wanted to talk about writing . . . I didn't mean to get this so far down the line and give you the impression you were coming up or that I was going to run to your apartment or was ready in any way to . . ."

"Stop worrying. This isn't about that."

Tommy cupped my cheek in his large rough hand and kissed me so hard and feverishly that he had to hold the back of my neck with the other hand so I wouldn't crash backward.

15

Spin Cycle

With my head caught in a spin cycle, I quietly slipped into the apartment. That was the only time I'd kissed anyone else since I married Wade.

Of course it was.

I wasn't like Wade. I didn't sample other people or get tempted or drawn into secret situations. When I got into bed at night with him, I would never want to have been with someone else. My nerves couldn't handle it. I think I would blurt it out within twenty seconds that I'd cheated and I was sorry.

Now my nerves had to handle it. Now was different: I told myself that Tommy *was not* retaliation, but that he was put before me just then to help me see things. Of course in a moment of honesty I knew that forbidden kiss was tit for tat on some level. Many things were too blurry just then, so I held fast to my base belief that Tommy's encouragement with my writing was going to lead me somewhere good.

It was well past one A.M. Wade and the kids were sprawled in a tangle on the couch with the television still on and Häagen-Dazs chocolate ice cream bar wrappers strewn all around them. The light-headedness that Tommy had kissed into me crashed to a stop as I took in how Wade had managed to trash the apartment in just four hours alone with the kids. As incensed as I was about the mess, the blue light gleaming on their dirty faces told me how much fun they must have had during their sloppy, rules-breaking night without their bad cop.

Always the irrepressible clown around them, always the irresponsible parent taking their side in a ridiculous debate with me over bedtime, unhealthy food, or an inappropriate movie—all this still made me profoundly enamored of Wade and his sloppy, boundless love for our children. How could I not still love him somehow, the father in him who was my partner in making our kids, watching him there with them? While Wade never volunteered for the tough stuff of parenting—narcissists don't take to personal discomfort—he was the best overgrown puppy any child could want around.

It was painfully obvious that Wade was capable of living like this forever, Peter Panning his way through a second childhood alongside Lucy and Blake, and then angling for the next round with our grandchildren. No wonder he'd been so excited each time I turned up pregnant. He was making playmates.

I watched them lying there in a messy clump, six legs intertwined, and felt the heartbreak of the inevitable flow. How was

I going to stay with a cheater and how was I going to ever move on when he and I both loved our kids so much?

Even if what Jackie Malone had told me at the bar weren't 100 percent true—that Wade had a finger in a larger scandal—I had a deeper suspicion that she was onto something, maybe even something unsafe.

I lifted up Lucy silently and carried her to her room, letting the boys figure out their own sleeping arrangements should they stir. The entire apartment looked like a herd of rhinos had trampled through it; drawers were opened, the contents of Wade's closet were strewn all over our floor, and his desk and office area were upended. I sighed. It was going to be a long night of restoring order instead of writing. There was no way I could focus on my screenplay, let alone get that perfect Tommy tongue out of my mind, with this level of chaos around me.

After changing my rag-doll daughter into her pajamas, I took her filthy clothes into the laundry room. I gathered an armful of towels, and a toy clattered to the floor. Bending down to snag a little headless Polly Pocket before she caused yet another clogged drain and a $400 visit from the plumber, I saw something behind her missing head. It looked like a matchbook sticking out of the crack between the wall and the dryer. I pulled a small screwdriver from the tool shelf and pried the piece of plastic free.

It was a flash drive, the kind of thing that would have fallen out of a sport coat pocket. The mess in our home that night took on enlarged meaning: Jackie might have been right; Wade had misplaced something that she was trying to find in his jacket in the laundry room. I fondled the flash drive with my fingers and wondered something: Would the flash drive, coupled with my screenplay, be the ticket out of my crazy life and into a completely new chapter where I could leave the ass-kissing of the PR world behind me? One where I concentrated on two things: mothering my children intensely well and writing better than I ever had.

I slipped Wade's secret flash drive into my laptop as if it were my getaway car. I scanned a dizzying twelve-page Excel sheet with code words at the top of the columns reading Project Black, Project Red, Project Green, and so on. I couldn't decipher it. I decided I should copy the material quickly on both my laptop and a second flash drive and return the original flash drive to the safekeeping of my jeans pocket. With Wade still asleep in his study area curled up with Blake, I tiptoed back to the kitchen for tea and returned to our bedroom, door slightly ajar. I puttered around, trying to understand what on earth color-named projects had to do with something illegal.

I opened my computer to distract myself and to try to write a scene about that day by the lake that Tommy had sucked out of me. Kiss or no forbidden kiss, Tommy was there to help me, damnit. From the first day of class, he and I had had so much to say to each other. The easy intimacy we shared might help me purge painful and poignant scenes from deep inside. He was a convenient crutch, a logical and harmless crutch, one designed to help me write and find the truth. I didn't need to fear him.

I also didn't need to kiss him back like it was our final good-bye on a sinking ocean liner.

WITH A CANDLE sparkling nearby and my computer screen blank, I was thankful when my phone rang and I recognized James's number. Of all people to reach me now. My mind ricocheted from Tommy to the man across the Atlantic. James would call at all hours in Paris, or maybe he was now calling surreptitiously while his Clementine was sleeping. In any case, I was more unhinged than I'd realized and I was grateful James would help me think clearly.

"Hey, need to talk, perfect timing," I said, letting out a huge breath, hoping to expel some madness and heartbreak along with it.

After a moment of silence, we both spoke at once.

"How's Paris?" And "How's that husband of yours?"

"In general Paris is fine" and "Wade's fine. Same as always."

I paused to let him speak next. "Well, that doesn't sound like a ringing endorsement," James finally said.

"You know. It's okay," I murmured. "Maybe we could talk a little now and I'll walk you through the latest. It's not good. In fact, it's bad."

"Why is it bad?"

"I don't know. If you want me to simplify it, it's like he isn't who I thought he was."

"Maybe he was always like this, and you didn't see it or *listen to me clearly when I tried to explain it to you before you got hitched,*" he nudged.

I laughed a little to show him I heard his point. "I prefer to think he changed."

"Well, you could come visit Paris this summer and we could spend some real time on this."

"How would Clementine feel about that?" I asked with a hint of bitterness I just couldn't help.

"She'd be fine; she's all into her stuff at UNESCO, you know, helping students all over," James said, giving no hint of movement on their front. "You could bring the kids. We could show them around. You and I could have dinner and talk. Clem's great with kids."

"Maybe," I said, cooling on the idea of a Paris get-together. "Maybe not such a good idea." We were at a silent impasse, into which the shriek of an ambulance simultaneously howled outside my window and on the phone.

"Holy shit," I said, almost dropping the phone. "You're not in Paris."

"No, I'm not," he answered. "Busted."

"Were you calling to tell me?" My cheeks were on fire, but whether it was lingering anger or the thrill he was here now I had no clue. "You didn't even mention you were coming to New York."

"Jesus, relax, Allie. You launched right into your crisis with the man I told you would put you in constant crisis if you married him. I'm crashing at Jerry's for a bit. Down the block."

"You're what?" I thought I'd heard wrong.

James laughed at my girlish excitement he knew too well. "I only landed in New York about three hours ago; my plane was very late from Europe, and I feel bad I didn't warn you earlier I was coming. I took a nap, a little shower. I'm leaving at dawn to go up to Massachusetts because my dad's sick for the hundredth time. I was planning to call you from there. I should be in and out of the city though, if you want to do something for real."

Yes, I wanted to do something for real.

Call it man whiplash, call it tit for tat, call it longing from forever way back, but there were a lot of things I wanted to do right then and there with James.

16

Confrontation Catalyst

Wade pushed open the bedroom door that same night, which startled me so much that I knocked over a glass of water on my jewelry tray. I'd hung up after the James call a mere thirty seconds before.

"Damnit, Wade. Can you give me some warning?" I felt like I'd cheated on him with two men in two hours and I was very jumpy.

"Last I checked, this was my bedroom too. I'm just getting my pajamas before I go back to the study alcove. Do you have a problem with that that I should know about?" He walked into the bathroom and tore his boxers off and threw them into the corner basket in a huff.

"You look too thin, Wade." His skin was sagging.

"I'm on a new health kick they say will decrease free radical damage, boost antioxidants and omegas . . ."

"Wade. A goop fasting cleanse is for women who want to look like Gwyneth Paltrow. A forty-four-year-old man cannot exist on parsley juice for a week."

"Parsley juice and a little cheating with a Häagen-Dazs bar. I feel like a million bucks. Psycho energy."

"Well, you have a pathological level of energy when you aren't on a goop cleanse, so let's rethink this. I'm glad you feel so good, but you don't look well when you don't eat. And why does the entire apartment look like a pigsty?" I asked coolly. "I leave you alone one night with the kids and the whole place goes to shit?"

While brushing his teeth, he mumbled back, "I lost something I need very much."

The flash drive.

"Like what?" I had him, I just knew it. It made me think that perhaps Jackie wasn't lying.

The brushing stopped, but the water just poured out loudly into the basin for a while. In the reflection of the door's full-length mirror, I could see him hanging his head down and steadying himself on the end of the sink before standing in the doorway and looking at me. "I'm sorry, Allie. I really am. I'm sorry about everything." He then wiped the toothpaste off his mouth and threw the towel on the floor. "I hate to do this . . ."

"You hate to do what?" I had no idea what was coming. I thought he might admit he was in love with someone else, or might ask for a separation, or might just be asking for a simple wifely favor, like could I please get a loose hem restitched at the cleaners. I braced myself for everything. And I considered telling him I wanted out because he lied and cheated on me with Jackie Malone and always would.

He squinted at me as if in discomfort, so I knew he wasn't going to be talking about a dry cleaner. "I hate to bring up the unfortunate incident at the party. It's just that as I was grilling that young woman, I lost something important and I had to tear the apartment up to find it and I don't know what day the cleaning lady comes and maybe she put it someplace and . . ."

"Laundry Room Escapades for $600, Alex."

"Allie. Stop. This is serious. I need this thing and I can't find it and I'm getting extremely upset trying to figure out where on earth . . ."

I pulled the object out of my pocket. "And the answer is: What is a flash drive?"

"OH MY GOD!" Wade was so relieved, he crumpled down on the edge of our bed and put his head in his hands to regain some kind of composure. He mumbled through his fingers, "Where did you find it?"

"Thousand-dollar Polly was trying to abscond with it. What's on it, Wade?"

"I'm sorry for all the drama, Allie. It's for a film project that's linked to one of our magazine pieces. I couldn't explain it if I tried. Please just excuse me this one time." He looked up at me like a Hallmark puppy who had just peed on the carpet. What did it matter if I gave it to him? I had a copy on my computer and on another flash drive.

I wasn't at all sure if life would take me there, but I thought I could someday break out from my marriage and experience something new: liberation. I breathed in deeply to familiarize myself with what that might feel like. No more mendacity from a husband brushing his teeth or putting his head in his hands so he didn't have to look me in the eye. No more analyzing half-truths. (*The flash drive with account numbers on it has to do with a film project linked to a magazine piece? How lame an answer was that?*) No longer would I have to pretend that everything was so damn okay with the man I loved. Yes, I loved him, or at least parts of him, but everything was not okay. Those truths can live in full-blown, blossoming tandem.

"Wade. Take the flash drive." I tossed it in the air and he jumped up to catch it, scampering back to the study alcove like a boy who had just stolen a load of cookies from the kitchen jar.

I felt a sliver of something shoot down my body that I'd someday recognize as rock-solid strength. It took intense will to walk from that plane, to live without my father so young, and, yes, to smile through my husband's "distractions." But that didn't mean I had to put up with Wade going forward if I didn't want to—that part was my choice, and understanding that equation made me feel pretty damn good suddenly. Sure the pain followed me around like a lapdog, but maybe, just maybe, all this time the strength inside lingered just as closely.

I SAT ON our bed and thought, *Not so fast.*

I marched after him and found him furiously poking the flash drive into his computer. "Allie, I can't get this damn thing to work; will you just tell me how to—"

"I've got a better idea," I answered, no longer able to stick with the non-confrontation-about-Jackie-Malone plan.

He looked up, unfamiliar with my new tone of voice and visibly startled by it. I barely recognized my own speech. That brief notion of liberation did feel so good, I almost considered donning Wonder Woman-blue hot pants and a superhero shield. "What's your better idea?"

No answer.

"What, Allie?" He looked terrified and guilty.

"One question: What 'unfortunate incident at the party'?"

He closed his eyes and started to scrub his face with both hands as if he could clean his mess up right then and there with his bare hands.

Hallmark puppy look again. I wasn't buying it this time either.

"What *unfortunate incident,* Wade?"

"It wasn't like that," he answered.

"It wasn't like Jessica, the horny photo assistant who threw herself at you while I was breast-feeding your infant? It wasn't like that this time?" I cocked my head in feigned confusion. "Then what was it like? Elucidate, if you will. You threw yourself at *her*?"

"I didn't!" he insisted frantically.

"You didn't what? You didn't sleep with that girl at the party who went back to the kitchen with you? You mean you didn't sleep with her at the party, or you didn't have sex with her ever?"

"I didn't!"

I crossed my arms. "Well, I think you did, numerous times.

Maybe you even loved her at one point."

"I DIDN'T!" He yelled it this time, but tried to come over and hug me when he saw my pooling eyes beneath my bravado. He spoke softly. "That woman was rifling through my stuff and . . ."

I managed to say, eking out the last reservoir of fortitude inside, "That woman? Which woman, Wade?"

"The woman at the party; I found her in the kitchen. I was getting a drink and she just appeared back there."

"Um, I don't think so." I shook my head from side to side and swallowed hard so I could get some words out. Anger must prevail over heartbreak. "I think I watched you follow her back there. Caitlin saw it too."

"That girl was simply searching my stuff, and I had to get her to leave. Plus I did have to help her with some information and, yes, we stupidly went into the laundry . . ." I knew he'd never admit it; that's why I needed the goods from Jackie or this confrontation would be fruitless. He might even claim she was there for a *film project linked to a magazine piece*.

"Then why were you in the room with her for so long?"

"I don't know. I had to ask her what she was doing, I guess."

My newfound, bold persona was drifting away rapidly, but before I lost it in front of him, I pushed him out the bedroom door and threw his pajamas after him. He at least wouldn't get the satisfaction of witnessing my reserves of strength go from one million to zero before his very eyes. The betrayal hurt, plain and simple.

17

Torn in All Directions

Somehow I made it through my next workday in one piece. Standing in the hallway outside my apartment door at 5:30 P.M., heels in hand, I bit my lip, and then clenched my teeth as I carefully turned our large brass doorknob. No way the kids would detect the slight noise of the spring lock being pulled back into the casing. I pushed the door open very slowly and peeked my nose through to survey the hall before I would tiptoe, delicately as Tinker Bell, into the living room to get on a call that Murray had just ordered up.

The pressurized volcano erupted in all its glory.

"Where *werrrre* you?!" Blake hollered at me, throwing his arms around my waist and knocking my shoes to the floor.

"Mommy! Mommy!" yelled the more docile, yet equally indignant, Lucy.

"Jesus, I love you guys," I whispered under my breath. I hugged both of them tightly and for a lot longer than I normally did. If I couldn't show them love between husband and wife, I needed to start showing them possibility: a sturdy, determined mother, and two parents who adored them no matter what life brought.

I knelt down to focus on Lucy and Blake at their level. "You guys. I really missed you so much all day, but I have to make one quick . . ."

Blake groaned. "C'mooooon, Mom. Can't you do that at work? Why now? I had the worst day at school ever."

My phone rang before my coat was off. As my kids clung to me, I acrobatically grabbed my Bluetooth headpiece from my purse and saddled it onto the back of my ear.

"You better be ready, because I've got a fuckin' government agency twenty feet up my asshole and—"

"Mommy, Mommy, my tooth is loose!" Lucy shrieked, hanging around my waist. "We need to leave it for the Tooth Fairy!"

Blake chimed in, "The Tooth Fairy isn't even—"

"Stop." I put my hand on his mouth before he destroyed Lucy's total obsession with a real live fairy buzzing around her room.

"Jesus, Allie," Murray bellowed in my ear. "I give you flex-time, now do you think you could return the favor by locking those kids up during a conference—"

I pushed mute on my phone to squelch out Lucy's primal scream as Blake took a swing at her for no particular reason.

I released the mute button long enough to say, "Murray. You have two young boys. I know Eri does all the heavy lifting and I'm not saying you're not a modern dad, but don't tell me they are not disappointed if you come home and get on the phone right away." But the sobbing was so loud that I had to yell over Lucy's complaints. "My children have missed me all day. They just saw me come home, but I will now move into a room and lock the door on my babies so you can talk."

I hated him for making me unable to tend to their needs, especially Blake's. He was still shut out of his group again by that mean kid Jeremy who thrived on dividing and conquering. Explaining to my nine-year-old that Jeremy was power hungry wasn't working because Blake's feelings were constantly bruised during playtime on his school street every day.

"You're a hero mom, but you need to spend some of that money I give you on decent help."

"My sitter is better than decent, but Stacey has her own life, Murray." I put the phone back on mute and shepherded the kids into the kitchen where Stacey already had her coat on. I mouthed to her, *Five more minutes? Pleeeease?* The kids would have none of it.

"Then tell that cheapskate Wade I think you should have married better!" Murray cracked up, not understanding I was beginning to agree with that statement.

"I'll be sure to tell him." I wiped the tears off Lucy's face and reached in the freezer for ice pops—handing one to each child—which instantly stopped her crying. My heart ached to hold her and give her all my love and attention. I held both kids tight again against me while they unwrapped their Popsicles behind my head.

"Look, the next shit storm is Max Rowland. Not easy to

come out of prison and get things back to normal when you're running an empire that crumbled in the downturn. Everyone's on Max Rowland's ass, and we need some good press to rehabilitate his image. The *New York Post* is running a piece in the morning called 'How the Great Max Lost His Groove.'"

"Murray, how am I to get a puff piece published about someone who destroyed his own company? He is a tax-evading, money-laundering convicted criminal whose company has had a forty percent market share drop. It was more his greedy moves than the economy that caused so many of his people to lose their jobs." I muted and unmuted as best I could as the children started squabbling about the flavor of their ice pops. I tried to walk down the hall away from them as I unmuted. "I mean he's kind of a major pig, Murray." Mute. "Lucy, get a grape one. Blake doesn't like those." Unmute. "I could write him a good speech for some charitable work that we might get covered. Some of those inner-city schools he and every hedge-fund guy sponsors." Mute. "Blake, please stop grabbing at her. You hate grape. You're just taking that one to . . ." Unmute. "You know, Max Rowland caring about poor kids." Mute. "Just go in the kitchen for five more minutes and I'm all yours. I love you, please!" Unmute. "But it's just so disingenuous, Murray. The Rowlands never had kids because they don't like children, so why are they helping inner-city kids anyway? His magnanimity isn't the easiest point to prove when he just fired two thousand people, lost forty percent of his stockholders' money—all due to his own greed. It makes me sick."

Murray ignored my clipped speech. "Rowland and poor kids.

I like that. I can work with that. Get on that. Maybe a photo on a Harlem stoop, with kids around him, make him look like a fuckin' *Sesame Street* regular. And for the film festival, I want you to produce some splashy panels, something Max could sit on and be informative to the crowd."

I fished a Tootsie Roll out of my bag and raised an eyebrow at Blake. He took it and put his arm around Lucy, shepherding her back to the kitchen for ice-pop replacement. I exhaled and unmuted. "You do know that the first screening is tomorrow, right?"

"After each film, I want a moderated panel that explores some issue in the film—with experts, actors, or directors. I know we have a few scheduled already, but I want more. As for the audience, I don't want some boring New York cross section of starstruck filmgoers. We need opinion makers in the audience. I want Max tomorrow night with a hard-on on his way in *and* on his way out of our first film. You got me, Allie?"

"Murray," I said smoothly, trying to draw him out from the little fantasy world he was creating. There was no way I was ignoring my kids tonight to make sure we had hard-on-inducing *opinion makers* in the audience. "You're in one of your moods."

"Well, then you know I'm a momma's boy who needs to be indulged. And I can't survive until I get what I want."

"I'm not your mother, Murray."

"Goddamn right, you're not my fuckin' mother. She'd tear the whole production to bits. She'd see there's not enough buzz on the festival for it to make it worth Max's while and we're the ones who convinced him to invest in it!"

"Some say you have a great business mind, Murray. Maybe you can amortize some of the hundred grand you spend a year on your shrink to remember that you're getting all panicky because you might not be achieving one specific little thing—but you're achieving many things at once, and very well," I said. I felt a poke at my forearm and looked down. Lucy. I took her down the hallway.

"Allie! You're not my fuckin' shrink, either. Fuck my mother. Fuck my shrink. Just let's get this done."

I considered Murray's understanding of the word *Let's* as I went back to the kitchen and whispered to Stacey, "I'm sorry, I can't get off the phone."

She smiled and lured Lucy into the back of the kitchen with the promise of a book she loved coloring. God only knows what had happened to Blake, but the muffled sound of a video game from the general direction of the TV area suddenly gave me the answer. I pushed mute to unmute again, I hoped for the final time. "I'm so sorry to tell you this, boss, but you're going to have to suffer with your impatience for a little. I can't pull off any new events for tomorrow night. Not enough time to book the important people you want for these. You're going to have to give me a break and be reasonable."

Murray screamed. "Damnit, Allie, pay attention. If it's that film with radiation in the seas near Japan, we need some corporate pro-nuclear-power asshole on a panel to say he doesn't know what they're whining about with a twenty-four-billion-mile-square mass of water covering the planet. You got me, Allie?"

"You want controversy, Murray. I will give you controversy, just not tomorrow night."

"I want fireworks on that stage after each film, and get Caitlin to deal with the party afterward; she's ready for that. You concentrate on content." Murray roared on. "I want people to say I educated them. I want everyone saying we blew this thing out of the fuckin' park. I want hard-ons, Allie."

I stifled a laugh. "Hard-ons. That has always been the plan."

"You know who I want, Allie?" Murray yelled so hard I had to pull the phone back from my ear. Here we go again. "No more ass-kissing celebrities. Been there, done that. I want a fuckin' criminal on that stage. Someone everyone loves to hate. Remember that British Petroleum CEO prick from the oil spill in the Gulf off Louisiana? The guy from BP who said he wanted his life back when his company's negligence had just killed eleven men on his rig and fifty thousand fuckin' pelicans? Let's get him to say there's no problem in the waters off Japan."

Big shots always had big ideas. But many of those ideas were bumbling and unrealistic, or worse, offensive.

"Murray, you're off base. The British Petroleum CEO got hammered to a pulp by the press; he's not going to—"

"I don't give a shit. Tell him we'll pay for a first-class ticket and give him a spa package at the hotel. Might even work out a happy ending for the guy!" Murray laughed out loud. "And you, this Friday. I want to see all the contracts for the films next week. Prepare a report of what we can do for panels in a week's time. Pull it all together so it makes some goddamn sense, okay? I want poster boards in the old-fashioned way I like. Make it pretty."

"But I can't possibly . . ."

"You can. That's why I hired you."

ONCE THE CALL with Murray was over, I was able to concentrate fully on my kids in the hope of having a somewhat normal end to the day. I wanted to pour my love all over my children and to allow their innocence to heal me as it always did.

Just then my phone pinged.

JACKIE: *I am going to the screening tomorrow night. It's going down tomorrow.*

ME: *What kind of stuff? Something really bad? YOU MUST TELL ME THAT!*

I worried that Wade would lose his job, or that something I'd done by innocently helping someone's PR was going to be linked to something bad.

JACKIE: *Not your personal safety but your livelihood is in danger. Keep your eyes open and you'll see that everything I've said is going to come true. It's time to trust me a little more. I need that flash drive.*

ME: *Clues PLEEEEEASE.* I CAN'T DO THIS!

JACKIE: *I don't know much more than I've told you; it's all unraveling tonight. Keep watching how everyone interacts—your boss will be blowing more steam than usual. And remember, I never lie.*

I threw my phone on the bed and decided tomorrow would be one of those days of reckoning my screenwriting professor lectured about. Maybe I'd finally see things I didn't want to see.

This night, of all nights, the kids were winding each other up, so much so that Lucy threw up her dinner all over my bedroom carpet after Blake sent his hundredth verbal missive her way, including whispering in her ear that the Tooth Fairy wasn't coming because she wasn't . . . I stopped him again just in time. So much for their joyful innocence healing me; they almost put me under that night.

As I placed the dirty laundry in the hamper in the kids' room, with my back to Lucy just six feet behind me, my tears flowed. Especially at night when I was tired, when I let myself slide down the "I'm scared to be on my own" side of the slope rather than the "I will make it through this" side, the fall felt impossibly treacherous. No hot pants or shield would make any difference once the descent began, and I could feel myself slipping the moment I hugged my kids that night.

Lucy was too intuitive to let me hide my red eyes. "Mommy. Why are you sad? Where's Daddy?"

Did my five-year-old just say "Where's Daddy?" because she was looking for another adult to help me, because it's unsettling to see a grown-up cry? Or because she instinctively knew that Daddy was the reason for the tears?

"It's allergies, honey."

"What's that?"

"It's something itchy in the air that makes people's eyes water."

"It's in the air?"

"Yes, honey. It's called pollen." I couldn't even finish the word without my voice sounding weak and unconvincing.

"Mommy. Why does the pollen make you so sad?"

I was so anxious, I could hear my heart pounding in my ears. How was I ever to leave my cheating, lying husband, find a new home, pay for that home, and, during it all, keep strong enough for Lucy and Blake? I lay down in the bottom bunk next to her.

"Mommy, why are you crying?" Lucy wasn't buying the pollen story.

"Honey." I had to stop this. I had to pull it together for her. "Mommy just feels frustrated. Like you do when your day isn't working out the way you want. Like when Samantha canceled her play date last week and you were looking forward to it."

She nodded. Getting her engaged in a miniconversation stemmed my tears and fears for a moment.

"You remember when we had all the ingredients out for your new ice cream maker?"

"Yes. The strawberries and milk."

"Yes, honey. And the cream and the gelatin and everything the instructions said all laid out on the table and she didn't even call to say she couldn't come? And you so much wanted to do it with her and you were so stubborn and waited and waited and wouldn't let me just go ahead and make it with you?"

The fury and frustration of that day flooded back into her little psyche.

"Well, that's how I feel, because I was counting on not being sick with pollen and I have so much to do that I feel frustrated and angry like that. Just like you, the whole plan isn't going to work out, so Mommy's a little sad."

Try *obliterated.*

She lay back and stared at the ceiling. I thought maybe for the first time in her life she was considering the outrageous, far-off possibility that her mother wasn't just a dispenser of food and fun and warmth and hearth, but that maybe she was a person with her own feelings. She kept concentrating and squinting her eyes and nodding.

"You are that upset?"

"Maybe not as bad, but close, honey."

"Wow. That's a lot. Why aren't you crying more then?"

"Because I have to be strong for you, honey. That's what mommies are for. To take care of their children, which I will always do."

She nodded and took this in. She squinted again as if to help her concentrate. But this time her upper and lower lids were so close together that they simply couldn't resist the pull to touch each other and stay stuck closed. She was fully out in twenty seconds. I could have tripped over a table with a complete tea service that went crashing to the floor and she wouldn't have budged.

Blake wasn't so easy. He was curled up in a ball on my bed with his huge brown bear, worn out from three years of being his favorite stuffed animal, lodged between his legs.

I wiped the smudged mascara from under my eyes with my fingertips before I lay beside him, flat on my back, hands clasped together on my stomach. These days, Blake often wouldn't let me snuggle him until after a little conversation had warmed him up. But his impending slumber increased his need for his mom's caresses.

"Why was it the worst day of school?"

"The kids played dodgeball and Jeremy told them all not to pick me. And it's like everyone follows what he says."

"Everyone is that scared of him?"

"Yeah, everyone but William. William just wants to play soccer with the girls and two other boys."

"Well, can you just join them for this week? Then Jeremy will see you don't care about his rules. If he can't bully you, then it takes his power away."

"I don't know."

I smoothed down his hair. "Try for me, honey. Please. Do it for me."

"I just want to play football. No one wants to play football." Then he turned his body on his side facing the other way and I curled up behind him.

"I know it's so hard, honey. Can you go to sleep?"

"Where's Dad?" he asked, as if he'd been holding the question in.

"He's at a dinner," I lied. I didn't even know where he was.

"Why is he out all the time?" Blake asked softly.

"Um, I don't know, honey. I think, as we have talked about, the economy is really bad so companies are suffering still so the advertisers aren't willing to give him ads. Daddy has explained this. When he is out at night, he is usually taking out people who work at the Vitamin Water company or the Gap to get them to place ads in *Meter*. After he takes them out to dinner, it's easier for him to ask them if they want some ad space. Unfortunately, he has to do that more now because people aren't spending as much . . ."

"Are you getting divorced?"

"What?" I sat up faster than a jack-in-the-box and grabbed his little shoulders, then pinned them down on the bed. "What did you say?"

"Nothing."

"Oh no. You said something. You asked me a question, Blake, and I want to talk about everything with you." I had absolutely no idea how he'd gotten to that question. Wade and I rarely fought in front of the kids, and there were no signs we could have possibly left that would lead our son to deduce this.

"Why did Daddy sleep on the couch for two nights last week in his study? Right after Christopher's dad slept on the couch, his parents got divorced."

Okay. Maybe we did leave signs.

I didn't know how to answer this question so I tried the truth.

"Because Daddy and I got into a big fight, and it took us a few days to make up."

"Are you made up?"

That was a harder question than the first one. "Your daddy and I sometimes argue about things. He and I are very different. Sometimes it takes us a few days to work it out. Just like with your friends." I started massaging Blake's forehead to get him to pass out and hopefully cut short this line of questioning.

"How come Dad isn't around as much? He used to rush home after work."

I felt relieved to be focusing on this tangent. "I tried to explain, honey. Everyone is saving money. We skipped our Florida trip last Christmas and stayed here in New York; just last week we talked about having dinners at home and not wasting money going out. Everyone in this country is spending less than they did. Now remember, we are so lucky to be doing much better than many people, and a lot of families are having a terrible, terrible time suffering with this economy, much worse than us.

"But no doubt Daddy has to work harder than before to convince people to buy advertisements because all those companies have less money because people are spending less. His clients don't have as much money as they used to, so he has to take them out and really be nice to them to try to get them to see how great his magazine is."

"So is that where he is tonight?"

"Yes, honey."

We lay quietly together for a little while. I buried my eyes in the crook of my arm and bit my lower lip so I wouldn't lose it again. If I started crying, Blake would instantly know that it had to do with his line of questioning. I couldn't believe things were this bad, that my home life had spiraled to the point where my kids were wondering about divorce. Blake would never drill me the way Lucy could, even though she was four years younger. He could wander from Eli Manning to the latest Xbox FIFA game to mean Jeremy to divorce without focusing more on one or the other. Little boys' messy brains were like that.

Blake's eyes fluttered a few times before shutting, and while I waited for his breathing to even out, I held him tight. This whole week had rattled me in a way that only holding my children could cure. I turned the light out and lay there, still, alongside my son, gaining strength just from my pact to protect them.

18

Guests at the Masquerade

"Goddamn it, Allie!" Murray let off steam behind a rope that cordoned off the gaggle of reporters in a chic downtown gallery space. They were covering the premiere of *The Lost Boys of Sudan,* a documentary for the Fulton Film Festival. "How many times did I tell you I want the reporters to say hello to Eri and take her photo? I can't be the one to do that, it looks self-serving."

Did Murray not know that every action he ever took in life was self-serving?

"My wife wants her photo in the society pages. She's gorgeous; why can't they just do that for us? It's not like we don't feed these reporters good leads every day; it's the least they could do. Instead they keep asking me about Max Rowland."

I pressed my hand against my forehead. "My BlackBerry has been blowing up with news alerts all day about Max Rowland's potential takeover of Luxor." Of course it didn't escape me that the computer company Luxor's annual report had been hidden in my husband's desk, but I had so much work for tonight I couldn't focus fully on that noncoincidence. "Murray, Max is known as a criminal. Everyone knows you're advising him on his comeback, so they're going to go after you till he gets here."

I'd learned long ago to tell Murray the truth or he'd step all over me. "I'm sorry, Murray, you have to be realistic. We've gone through a very serious economic downturn in this country. Wall Street is up, but people's jobs are still on the line. This whole event tonight is supposed to be focused on helping lost young souls in the world's most brutalizing war zone, and you're sending the opposite message. A criminal banker is fresh out of prison and the first thing he does is consider planting a stake in a hot, growing company. And when he says this, the stock climbs to record heights." I pressed him. "Did you even know about the potential Luxor position?"

"Of course I didn't." He twitched uncomfortably and scratched his cheek. "I would have told you last night so we could prepare for it. He hasn't taken the company over yet; he's just considering it."

He was lying, and at that moment, I started, just a little, to trust Jackie, the woman who slept with my husband, more than I did my boss of ten years.

"Well, it looks like Max Rowland is up to his old tricks: somehow the public will suffer and he'll keep gaining. You are seen as his enabler, like it or not, because you're paid to go out there and defend and protect him."

"That's just great, Allie, hoist me onto my own fucking

petard, and make sure the press witnesses the execution. You're a great help." He sneered and looked at his watch.

I ripped my sweater off to cool myself down before I spoke. "Murray, Delsie Arceneaux was on CNBB all afternoon blowing it up as if it might be the biggest takeover so far this year. She was so proud she'd broken the story—you could see it all over her face. She was so smug, it wasn't normal."

Murray started scratching his face like a dog with fleas, something he did when he was piling on the world-class level of BS to clients. "Delsie is so fuckin' pleased with herself all day no matter what she does. I just want my wife taken care of with the society reporters right now or she's going to kill me."

People were now fully packed into the front lobby of the Paul Kasmin Gallery on Tenth Avenue in the mid-Twenties for a quick glass of bubbly before tonight's Fulton Film Festival screening next door. At the bottom of the red carpet, Max Rowland and his wife, Camilla, finally arrived. They stepped out of their Mercedes, he in a dapper bespoke suit with a kelly-green-striped tie and coordinating green paisley pochette and she in a bubble-gum-pink St. John dress with matching pink pumps, as usual channeling more Vegas than New York. She looked like she had run through a cloud of cotton candy and was just emerging out the other side.

Camilla held her Texan husband's arm proudly as they walked the red carpet gauntlet up to the huge gallery front space: their first public outing into New York social life, photographers present, since his incarceration. "*Max, Max!*" they yelled under the stars of a warm May New York night. "*Tell us about Luxor! Are you trying to be the new King of the Street?*"

It's pretty easy to get cynical and assume all Max's money kept Camilla loyal to him, especially since she was sporting diamond studs in her ears the size of headlights. But observing the way she held his elbow as he lumbered his weathered, but manly, frame up to the entrance, I chose to believe she loved him when he was poor and had a little idea for a parking garage in downtown Dallas right out of college, and that she still loved him the same when he began to run every major garage, hangar, and terminal across the land. You didn't park anything with wheels in this country without Max Rowland taking a cut. And now it seemed he'd be taking a slice of Luxor, one of the hottest computer networking companies in the land as well.

We watched the madness from the cordoned-off area in a side tent. The invited guests got their passes from beautiful young things sitting at tables with the letters of the alphabet displayed on cards reading A-I, J-Q, R-Z.

A few well-known New York socialites posed on the red carpet for photos to show how engaged they were in policy issues facing the African continent. But they jumped right back into their waiting cars without any pretense of actually attending our Sudan screening once the society photographers were done clicking.

Murray turned to a dogged reporter who had jumped the rope. "No comment," he said, throwing the woman a charming, kinglike smile before turning to me and snarling.

Jackie's text came back into my thoughts: whatever he was

about to lose, Murray did seem more anxious than during his "normal" big-baby freak-outs. I looked everywhere for Jackie to no avail.

I checked my phone and saw a text.

TOMMY: *You wanna work out a few of your issues later?*

I felt a bright, guilty smile appear on my face and hoped no one was looking my way. This Tommy guy could cheer me up from anything, even a three-hundred-pound toadlike man hopping around in a rampage. I bit my lip and texted back.

ME: *You don't have that kind of time.*

My phone pinged again.

TOMMY: *I definitely have that kind of time.*

"Hey, babe."

I looked up from my crush to find Wade standing over me with his vodka and cranberry half finished, all chipper amid all the potential social dragons he could slay. He was like the old Wade that night, but playing with an anachronistic full deck from the boom time, all glossy paper 1990s. Facing me, he massaged the back of my neck with one hand.

"Whoa." He massaged more. "Reeeeelax."

I swatted his hand. "Wade! Oh, God. Stop!"

"What's your deal?"

"Sometimes, especially if I am running an event with two hundred fifty people, I *want* to be on edge. It keeps me on my game. The adrenaline makes me more on point."

"Chill, honey. It's just a film screening." Wade grabbed both my arms and looked deep into my eyes and said to me, like I was a kindergarten friend of Lucy's, "Your client's going to do fine, honey. No biggie."

I spied a way out across the room and pasted on a smile. "Of course you're right. Hey—there's Bruce Cutter smoking in the corner. Didn't you say you wanted him for a cover?" Bruce was standing in the shadow of a small terrace, chain-smoking, and not uttering a word. In Hollywood this meant he was a genius.

Wade turned and fled toward the Ryan Gosling wannabe before the rest of the words were out of my mouth. I wanted to smack Wade for obscuring everything, or trying to. He had no doubt betrayed "us" again in some form or fashion because things were going on around me that he was lying about. He would do that in the future. I would either smile through or ignore the signs in the future. I would feel angry and lost and alone in the future. I would tear up photos again in the future that represented romantic ideals.

I suddenly felt crowding around me a sea of whining VIPs, like cartoon toddlers with tears sprouting from their eyes, in full-blown panic over the impending grown-up game of New York movie premiere musical chairs. They also wanted to suck every last thing out of me they could.

"Allie! Do I or do I not have a seat?" An ad executive named Jimmy Marton howled at me like I was his nursemaid.

"There are three hundred seats in the theater, Mr. Marton. You will find one, no problem." Cushy seats, in fact, which rocked a little for extra comfort. "You can take your drink in there with you. I promise you'll find . . ."

"Do I have a *reserved* seat?"

Caitlin pushed her little gymnast body between us. "It takes starring in a movie, or being a subject of a documentary, or being a sponsor of the festival. I'm sorry, Mr. Marton, I wasn't aware that you were . . ."

"Neither. I got it. I just figured with my . . . never mind," Jimmy said with a huff and turned to face the throngs.

"Nothing changes," I told Caitlin. "Seventh-grade cafeteria theory. I can't stay for this all night, by the way; I've got way too much work to do back at the office. You've got it under control, right? Or I would never leave . . ."

"I got it handled," Caitlin confirmed.

I was surprised I hadn't seen Jackie yet. "Great. You can also deal with the last-minute stragglers." I started to stuff my screening file in a purse that was already overloaded, adding, "I've got a bull's-eye on my chest saying, 'Come to me with your petty problems, I'll fix them.' And that's just pissing me off the more I do it. Part of the problem is, I'm awful good at fixing petty issues and they know it. Thrilled my writing degree has paid off in the form of babysitting billionaires."

I watched as an entire theater of eyes bounced back and forth from Max Rowland to Murray Hillsinger as if they were at a tennis match—everyone trying to figure out if Max was going to take over Luxor and if Murray's PR spinning would save him.

Ten feet to my right, my husband was holding court like he was Scarlett O'Hara at the barbecue. Caitlin listened intently inches away from him, which of course annoyed me more than slightly. "So we're doing a huge cover piece on Blake Lively and Ryan Reynolds," Wade told his fawning audience, as unaware of his obsolescence as he was. "And they actually tell me they are trying to be the next Brangelina and they want me to come have dinner with them to show them some famine projects that might help . . ."

I needed intravenous Klonopin at this point, as Camilla Rowland was now fuming and running toward me with a major bee up her ass.

"I don't want Max sitting on the side aisles," she growled at me. "*Especially* given what he's been through. You know damn well he deserves better, Allie."

"He's got a nice seat, Camilla, one on the aisle where he can get in and out easily if he—" I said, restraining myself from saying something worse.

Camilla sharpened her gaze. "Nice doesn't cut it. Are you calling us nobodies, Allie? After all we've done for your husband?"

I met her eyes and suddenly saw an unexpected opportunity. Exactly what had she and Max done for Wade? Had Wade insider-invested in Luxor before the stock rose? Maybe I could verify Jackie's warnings on my own. "Of course not, Camilla. Let me get Caitlin to fix this. You're absolutely right, you're absolutely right, your reserved seat isn't the right reserved seat."

"Caitlin," I called out, annoyed at her shrill laughter directed in my not-so-funny husband's direction. "Will you please just put signs on two seats in the center section for Camilla and Max and mark them Rowland?"

I was about to let Camilla know the good news—we found your seats!—when I spied Jackie Malone standing at the side entrance of the theater looking like a ghost. She curled her index finger, beckoning me over. I managed to work my way through the crowd and up the aisle with more purpose than a blitzing linebacker.

"What the hell, Jackie?" I whispered. "What happened?"

"Everything's blowing up right in front of your eyes, and you can't even see it. I'm telling you, I have put the pieces together now and the completed puzzle is lying before you." The normally calm Jackie looked a little crazed as she pulled me farther behind the curtain. Her neck tendons were popping out in a long, clear, stressed-out line.

"Okay, here's the deal: I will trust you and tell you the whole damn story now and you do your part and start to believe me and keep looking for that flash drive."

"I may do that. I may, but this I understand only. Now the Luxor price is up so high, Max is screwed and can't afford it."

"You really believe that's what's happening? None of the dots we talked about are connecting for you? Look how high the stock is now on this news that Max Rowland might take over the company. Can you see there's a scenario where this could be good news for him?" she asked. "Do you understand your boss is fully capable of lying to you and putting you out front to make false claims for him? Did he tell you to tell the reporters that it wasn't supposed to leak?"

"Yes, he did, Jackie, but he didn't want it to leak, right?"

Jackie exhaled and pulled her hair back tightly from her forehead before letting it fall in a fragrant wave. "Okay, I'm going to inch out on a limb and connect the dots for you so you understand I'm onto something. *This is all a ruse.* Let me make this very clear to you:

One: *Murray is pretending to be upset that a potential takeover of Luxor got leaked.*

Two: *Murray is pretending Max will not be able to buy it with the price suddenly so high.*

Three: *Murray is asking you to tell that to the press to make sure his story is out.*

And most important, four: *Max Rowland wants the Luxor stock to go up because he already owns a ton of it through an unnamed entity in Liechtenstein.*

"They have boosted the price through trumped-up media rumors of him taking it over. Now the stock he secretly bought a few weeks ago has doubled on just the news of the rumor. Think, Allie: *media rumors.* Who do you know very well who is a big media guy?"

"Is Wade investing in this deal and not telling me?" I asked.

"No! For a smart woman, you can be so blind! He's in control of the media rumors. Can't you see that's his gift? Swirling up gossip and rumors that make investors react? And react in a way that certain individuals could benefit from if they were betting on the stock going up? Wade gets it online in those brokerage news services and persuades Delsie to put it on CNBB that someone who looks and acts a lot like Max Rowland is about to orchestrate a takeover of Luxor. He gets a reporter to tell another reporter. Guess what? The stock climbs sky high because investors think that's good news for the future of Luxor. That's all Wade has to do," she concluded coldly. "Watch everything, think about the power of information and the mechanics of the media and how they can be used to manipulate stock prices."

"It's not insider trading then?"

"Well, ask the SEC that, but it's manipulation of rumors to make stocks move. Easy to do when you've got a media Oz like Wade swirling the dial. He's sold out more fully than you could ever know."

I did not want to believe my husband started out in journalism to get the bad guys and somehow became one of them in the process. "It wasn't *Meter* that published the news," I said plaintively. "It was Delsie at CNBB."

"You think I don't know that?" she answered. "And you think Delsie and Wade aren't close? You're telling me you never noticed her throwing her sherbet-colored scarves around the Tudor Room and winking at him?"

"He bought that for her?"

"He didn't buy it for her, but he is creating situations where she can buy stuff like that on her own is all I'm going to say."

"You sure?"

"I think they all made a ton of money tonight. I'm pretty sure of that."

"Allie!" Camilla Rowland roared up to me again—a lioness protecting her ailing Max—followed by a festival assistant whose headset was flying behind her. Jackie squeezed my arm and then effortlessly slipped behind a decorative drape next to the door, avoiding Camilla.

"Don't think I don't understand what you had your girl do," Camilla said. "Those were fake reserved seats." Camilla was now on the verge of real tears. "And why is a tacky newswoman who sluts around army tanks given a reserved seat that is better than ours?"

I punted. "I think Murray wanted Delsie to cover the event up close—that's how the press likes to work."

"Is it because Max is a convicted felon? Is that it? Bad enough he was living in prison with real criminals for nine months at Allenwood but now that he's out, he can't be treated normally? You have to snub him too and give him B-list seats? Well, he's out of the tax evasion business. So he had his banker set up a little account for us all in Liechtenstein. It's just to get a little privacy. Ever since the Swiss got rid of bank secrecy . . . as if it wasn't enough they bankrolled Hitler's machine!" She snorted and then moved so close to me that I could smell the spearmint Altoids on her breath. "And now your Wade is protected too."

Jackie poked my hip from behind the curtain, and I straightened my back, coughing a little signal back to her. Camilla wasn't done. She whispered, "If you don't think he's given Wade a cut overseas on certain matters that all of us have benefited from . . ."

I had to get more out of her, but didn't have the slightest clue how. "But what happened with the accounts overseas is all okay, right? I mean, you know it better than me, in the sense that . . ." She ignored my lead.

"Whoa, darlin'. Stop. I don't want to cause trouble. Allie's a good girl; she's just doin' her job," said Max, who'd finally caught up to his wife. "We are gonna have to move on. One day at a—"

"Camilla, darling." Wade swooped in and gave her a double air kiss. "Of course a society belle like you needs . . ." He could charm anyone out of any situation, and my confused and hurt angst abated a little watching him make her anger melt away. I was forever attracted to this side of him: the cheerful side, the smooth side, the side that would pull us all out of the daily doldrums that life sucked us into.

He said in an aside to me, "I'm going to make everything up to you. I'm sorry I've been so distracted. I love you. I love the kids. I love what we have. Don't forget that. I've just got to work on getting you to remember that. And I will." His sudden directness and honesty surprised me. The more I watched him with Camilla, the more I saw Camilla succumb to his velvet touch, and the more my heart ached.

Jackie's snakeskin shoes were visible behind the velvet curtain. Wade had his back to her, not knowing she was inches from him, but perhaps catching a whiff of her signature spicy perfume. I wondered for a moment if I should pull the curtain back just to confront them both and see Wade squirm. I could see Jackie inching along the wall and then toward the exit.

"You look stunning, Max, my old man," Wade insisted. "I knew you'd get out better than you were before. Good to see you out and about at a big event. You look strong and rested, ready to take over the world again."

I heard the exit door slam shut. Jackie had managed to slip away.

"Let me work on this one." Wade grabbed Mr. and Mrs. Max Rowland, locking elbows with one on either side, and sat between them in perfectly good seats two rows from the front. Of course, that magnanimous gesture wasn't only to save me; perhaps he was also kissing the ass of someone who might well have a sizable chunk of our retirement money.

I ran outside the theater after the woman who had the answers for how I got here, why I got here, and how I'd get out of that very unsettled place called "here." As I watched Jackie run away, I noticed a black SUV roll down the street after her, maintaining a careful, one-hundred-foot distance. I tried to catch up with her to no avail; I could hear only the sound of running heels clacking on the pavement bricks against the balmy spring nighttime air.

19

Focused and Frustrated

"I can't believe you're not going to your own party." Caitlin plowed into our office a few minutes walk from the gallery with a tray of Starbucks. "Here, this should keep you solid for the next few hours, one caramel Frappuccino for your fat ass and one triple espresso macchiato for your veins."

I looked up from the white leather desk chair, where I'd sat for the past two hours, having left the theater as soon as the screening began. I hoped to pull together as much of Murray's panel demands as possible before turning to my own screenplay work, both of which were due at noon the next day—a marathon night lay ahead of me. My glass desk was piled with markers and festival plans. I had to get my work done and shut out the real possibility that my boss, my husband, and a parking lot mogul were trying to manipulate the stock market together.

Everything Jackie said made more and more sense—Max and Murray secretly buy stocks in some foreign name, they have

Wade Crawford the media maestro pass out rumors like hot hors d'oeuvres to unsuspecting journalist friends that something is possibly happening with a company that would make its stock go up, and then stock they already own does indeed go up. They then sell instantly for a profit while the rumors have new investors jumping in.

Even if the rumor were false, their stock would still go up in time for them to sell. I wasn't even sure if it was illegal for Wade to lie to the press to get them to spread an untrue rumor; it just smacked of horrible ethics and cheating. I hated to have to believe Jackie, but it wasn't the kind of thing someone would just invent as a story.

"Allie! I'm talking to you, and I'm handing you a hot drink that's about to spill; snap out of it."

"Thanks, Caitlin. Every inch of my body appreciates it."

She placed a white paper bag on my desk. "And some lemon squares for your thighs."

The phone rang and I picked it up, wondering who on earth would call me at the office so late. I heard only a hang-up and made a mental note that I'd heard a few clicks like this in the past few days from a private number. If this ever happened again, I'd start to wonder about that SUV I'd just seen.

"That's strange. No one on the line." I took a quick, scalding sip, trying to decide if I was being paranoid or prudent. "How was daycare for the grown-up toddlers after the film started?"

As she picked her own coffee out of the cardboard holder, Caitlin answered, "Well, everyone was so busy gawking at Murray and then at Max with his potential Luxor move that the room was just crazed with electricity. Don't think one person actually watched the film."

"That sounds like fun."

"It was a nightmare! Completely overshadowed the importance of the film." Caitlin pulled up my guest chair and tried to look me in the eye. "What is going on with you, Allie? Everything okay with you and Wade? You and Murray?"

She shifted next to the desk and started reorganizing piles of information on the shiny white floor. Task barely begun, she sat back. "You know, the whole Tribeca loft decor in this room is off. I remember at the beginning when we moved in here it was all clean lines and chic and spare. One glass desk. One bouquet of red flowers. Nothing on the desk except a pristine metal penholder and a metal Apple computer. Now it looks like something from those reality shows on people who hoard."

"Just leave it and go to your after party for the documentary. Try to get the press interested in the film, and not the surrounding business gossip, okay? It's a possible award winner, damnit. Get the press concentrating back on the Sudan, rather than how Max is only getting richer after prison."

"We have so many people there working the press already, I don't mind staying here," she responded.

"This is all stuff I need to do myself. Go."

"You mean it?" Caitlin practically jumped to her feet. "Seriously, I should stay. What can I do to help now?"

The phone rang and she picked it up. "Hello?" She laughed a little and then handed me the receiver with a stern look, like she suddenly despised the caller. "It's Wade. For you."

I put my hand over the receiver. "I thought you hated Wade. Stop laughing at his jokes. Go back to the party and be young and have fun."

"You sure?"

"Just go already!" I threw a pencil at her as she slid out the door, and then I turned to the phone. "Looks like I'm not coming home until very very late. Can you relieve Stacey when you're done with the party?"

"What time was she expecting you?" Wade asked.

I shook my head. "I don't know, Wade. What time was she expecting you?"

"How come you're so pissy?" he said.

"Like you don't know?"

A long beat of silence passed while he considered his answer. "What should I know, Allie?"

Oh God. Where could I start? I swiveled my chair around to look out the floor-to-ceiling industrial windows of our big loft office. A tugboat was yanking a barge of garbage down the eerily dark Hudson River.

I shook my head. "Well, I have a lot of work, Wade. I have to prepare a presentation on our panels for next week's screenings and somehow in between find the time to write a good beginning of a screenplay by tomorrow to e-mail to the class. Remember when we met, I was hoping to actually write fiction and make a living from it? Not write fictional press releases for assholes and criminals."

"I know you're working hard." Wade was trying to be patient, but I could sense the tension in his jaw through the phone lines.

"But do you know what I am working on?" I asked, stalling. I couldn't play this game anymore. I could barely focus on any work without wondering who actually was the person I'd married. Then I steeled myself. "Tell me, Wade, for real. Are you screwing someone else right now, tonight even?"

"Oh, please. I don't even know where you're coming from."

"You're not cheating on me right now with some young thing?"

"Allie. Listen to yourself."

"Yes or no? Simple question. Deserves a simple answer, Wade."

"I'm not with a young thing."

"Are you with a woman?"

"Right this minute?"

I exhaled. "I'm not an idiot."

Finally he said softly. "I was and it's over, but I wasn't sure if you knew."

I waited a long time. I felt relieved and horrified and kicked in the stomach all at once. Part of me felt better because it was somehow comforting to have confirmation of what I knew to be true. The tension of not being 100 percent sure felt worse than the pain of knowing. At least in that moment. "Well, I did fucking know, Wade!" I yelled into the receiver. "And I already asked you in our bedroom and you had the nerve to deny it. It's actually easier if you just tell me the goddamn truth! Yes, do that, even if you know it hurts just as much as last time."

"I didn't do anything to hurt you, Allie. I'm just . . . living my life. It has nothing to do with . . ."

There was a very long pause on the line.

I then stated clearly, "Well, did you consider that it would hurt me, and that you promised you wouldn't ever again do it? I mean, we have a family and I know you love that family. But it's like you're totally psychotic and have a whole other life that you are quote, unquote *living*. I don't understand how you can do this again."

"It's not another whole life. It was just one night, and it just kind of happened. It doesn't mean . . ."

"Doesn't mean what? That you don't love me? Are you sure? You sleep with another girl, knowing it destroyed me once, and now you do it again? What am I to think, Wade? Did I really marry one of those guys who just can't help himself?"

"It's not like that, it's not me, a pervasive thing. It was just a onetime thing with maybe one . . ."

"One, Wade? I count two right now."

"Okay, you're right . . . two girls," he admitted.

"And how do you explain yourself? Really, I'd like to hear."

"Life for men is a slide show and for women it's a movie," he answered firmly. "For me it's all a slide show, a quick unrelated thing with each. You are turning this into a whole narrative movie linking this action with that tendency. I swear, it just happened with her one night and . . ."

"I'm not creating narrative female drama, so don't try to lay that or any paranoia on me here. And it's honestly just not the girls. It's real, Wade, what I'm feeling and seeing. It's the constant lying, the constant covering up shit you think I don't know about."

"Covering up what?" he asked.

"Covering up whatever you are covering up on every level. It's such a slam on 'us.' Remember that notion of 'us' . . . everything we always promised each other?"

"I do love 'us.' "

"That's just it, Wade. You love the convenience that *us* brings you. But what about me? And speaking of me, what do you bring to me by lying to me again and again? I know you have shifty things going on and I know you aren't telling me."

Long pause. "I'm going to skip the party," he said. "Take your time." He sounded both defeated and annoyed—as though I'd somehow been the one to ruin his fun night out.

"I may not come home," I said, my voice now devoid of emotion. "Not sure yet, but I may sleep on the couch here. You'll have to send Stacey home in a taxi; it's getting very late. If I'm not there in the morning, give the kids some form of protein for breakfast, please; tell them my report was due and that I'm at the office. Don't forget we agreed you would pick up the kids at noon tomorrow. It's a half day, and Stacey has an exam so she can't come. Remember?" It was bizarre how quickly his admission had plunged me into parenting logistics. Split-up rule number one: focus on the kids, so you don't feel the burn.

"I got it," he said. "Allie—"

I held my breath.

"I'm really sorry. I didn't mean it the way you are taking it," he said, sounding defeated and confused. "I'll see you tomorrow. I don't know where we go from here." In that moment, I wished he'd said something else, something that reaffirmed our family life or his willingness to keep trying, or anything.

I gently cradled the receiver, all my preparation for this moment leaving me limp. And I hadn't even pushed him about the illegal web Jackie had him spinning. "Neither do I, Wade, not right now, but I might know more soon."

"What the hell more are you going to know?" he asked innocently.

"I have to focus on my work or the bills won't get paid and I can't get into this; it's ten P.M. I'll call you tomorrow. Unless there's something else you want to say—like you're in love with someone else, but you're giving me the apartment."

"Allie, stop. It's not at that point."

"Well, what point has your slide show brought us to exactly, Wade?"

"I don't know. I just do my thing sometimes, I guess. It doesn't really mean . . ."

"It doesn't mean what, Wade?"

He didn't answer my last question; I just heard his rattled breathing on the other end of the line. I looked around at the mess in front of me. How the hell was I supposed to finish my work with this bizarre, awkward, unfinished, hurtful conversation looping in my head?

"Wade," I said. "I can't do this now."

I hung up and suddenly I was back in that mangled plane, in the snow, desperate for a protector. Was Wade just giving more of the same unsafe feeling I'd wanted to flee from? And it hit me that I hadn't so much forged a new life in marrying Wade, I'd simply come full circle. Strange how we seek what we hope to escape.

20

Playing the Procrastinator

After thirty minutes of gritty, hard work, thirty minutes in tears on the toilet, and another thirty fuming on my office couch, it was almost midnight. I felt so many things at once—hurt, anger, failure—I couldn't keep track. Existing in the blur had its advantages; namely, I could walk around acting like everything was okay. That strategy had expired since Jackie Malone entered my life. I reached into my bag and checked a text on my cell phone.

> TOMMY: *Stop procrastinating by checking your phone. You should be writing!*

I dialed him immediately. "It's the procrastinator."

"Why aren't you writing?" he asked. "You've got to send us your pages tomorrow so we have time to read them before class next week. Hope you have something in mind, because he said noon Friday."

"Hold on." I went and lay down on the sofa and exhaled everything out of me. "It's been sort of a long day. I had to work on this event tonight, and there was a tough phone call I won't go into, but I'm finally done with my real job work, and I'm going to start writing here at the office."

"Your writing is your real job, you idiot. You want to tell me about it, about what you're writing?"

"I don't know what to write tonight," I admitted, pushing away thoughts of jumping him. "Heller said hand in a big scene, and I tried putting some things down for half an hour, but I don't think I have one in me."

"Write your own story," Tommy said. "Write the thing that resonates the most for you. Not passing stuff, not events that are transitory or that popped in and out of your life by chance. Write what defines you, what you couldn't live without, the stuff that sustains you."

What is sustaining me right now is talking to you. I tried to think about writing topics we had discussed. "Well, there was that guy James from the real-life scene by the lake . . ." I offered, squirming, rationalizing that I could turn my supposedly previous romantic obsessions into productive work.

"Did you ever get into a situation where you were skirting something, just maybe, like maybe you're a world-class avoider?" Tommy said the last sentence with a sarcastic laugh. "I don't know, call me crazy, but maybe you get into a situation you think you want, but then just when you are about to get it, *so good you don't even know,* you push the guy away, don't go back to his apartment, and bolt upstairs for no clear reason?"

"Tommy. It's not going to happen between us, so stop teasing me about it," I said loudly. "Honestly, I don't know where to start because I want to write a completely new scene, maybe even ditch my old script."

"It's late," he answered. "But I think I can help. Give me half an hour to put some clothes on and get downtown?"

"You want to come to my office?" This was not probably a good idea, but I was in no shape to deny myself. I went from exhilaration to despair, remembering the trauma of Wade's admission. I wanted to forget the blow I'd just confirmed, but it lingered like fog around me.

"Gimme the address now."

"Uh, 553 West Nineteenth, right on the river, next to the IAC Building."

"I'll bring my laptop. We can write together, and I'll push you to do things you never thought you could do."

"Would you please stop with the cheesy sexual innuendo? I HAVE TO WRITE TONIGHT."

"You're gonna write like a friggin' genius once I get you sailing in the proper direction and you stop avoiding the obvious. It's right there in your head. Bad cycles. Shit that holds you back. Write it down. That's the problem in your script. You got me? Then the Act III, chasing after the shark, crushing the Galactic Empire, for you means chasing after whatever the fuck is going to get you out of that messed-up cycle. You're not the first person on the planet with regrets that fuck with their head. It'll be a great movie because people will say, 'Oh God, I do that all day.' I'll be there in twenty minutes, going to race down the West Side Highway on my motorcycle."

"Don't kill yourself," I pleaded.

"I think you're in more imminent danger of that." He hung up.

THE FOG LIFTED just a little. Work has a way of conquering depression. I was trying to do just what Tommy said, write what sustains me, when the guard called up from the lobby. Next I heard Tommy's voice echoing from the elevator. How was I not to fall for a guy who understood me quicker than I understood myself?

"Allie? Where you at in this cavern?"

"Oh, yeah, in here," I yelled from my desk, trying to act nonchalant, like I wasn't really that interested in him.

Tommy stuck his head in the doorway with his helmet cradled in the crook of his elbow, smiling a devilish grin.

"You ready to stop bullshitting yourself?" He walked toward me like he meant business.

"That sounds painful."

He reached into his backpack and threw a bunch of Twizzlers, mini Milky Way bars, and grape bubble gum on my desk. "Serious work needs serious sugar. In my book, anyway."

He then walked around my desk to my large white leather chair and plunked his backpack and helmet down on the floor. "Can you stand up, please? I need to sit in your chair."

"Why, what are you . . ."

"Just do what I say, Allie. Trust me."

I blew out a big breath and stood six inches in front of him. He sat down and grabbed my hips and pulled me toward him. His tongue first licked my belly button and then very slowly just under the top flap of my jeans. I was covering my face with both hands wondering how long I could act like I wasn't interested. Yes, Wade had done this infidelity thing numerous times, but that didn't mean I could or should. "Are you trying to get me in touch with what I want or something?" I pushed him back, not at all ready to indulge in anything crazily sexual with him. It felt so good, but it also felt like unhealthy payback at Wade.

"Nope." Tommy pulled me down so I was sitting on his lap and yanked my legs over the chair arms so he could hold me close. Maybe a little closeness couldn't hurt, maybe being drawn to someone who supported what I needed to do, what I always wanted to do—write for real—wasn't the worst thing I could do. As he kissed me slowly, his hands reached inside the back of my pants so he could grind up against me. He was fully hard beneath his jeans.

"I guess it's pretty clear what you want," I said, trying to yank myself off him by pushing down on the arms of my chair with my elbows. He put my arms instead around the back of his head and kissed me harder while he explored my ass.

Just as I became so turned on that I felt I might not be able to say no to something I wasn't at all ready for, he held my head in his hands. "Now. We are going to stop, if that's okay."

Even though that was the right thing to do, I had glided over to the dark side and wasn't so sure stopping was a good idea just then.

"The reason we are stopping is simple: sugar and sexual tension will give you a combined punch to write well." He got up, methodically, and pushed me back down into the same chair, pulled my keyboard in front of me, and made a nice neat little line of candy to the right side.

He went over and lay on the sofa as he casually rearranged his bulging hard-on. "This ain't easy for me either. But it's going to help you, I promise. We have all the time in the world ahead of us to do what we want, when we want. This is your office and your script pages are due in the morning. You're spending too much time writing about the plot from six years ago. An infertile couple meets their surrogate. Hell breaks loose. It was a fun fresh idea before Sarah Jessica Parker used one for those twins. Problem is: it doesn't relate to your own life, so it will be dull on the page."

My cheeks burned from his critique. "Great. So I'm at square one? Thanks for coming by and blowing up years of work."

He grinned. "For tomorrow's assignment, just write about James and see where it takes you. Write scenes that mean something, and then we'll sew them together. I'll help you. Now that you're so turned on, let's hear about the absolute worst time you almost slept with James but didn't. What happened?"

"Jesus, Tommy. I don't know. That was the MO for our entire relationship until we grew up and made our choices. The best times were always the worst times in a weird way. There was a really bad scene in San Francisco."

"Okay. For now, we're after the longing: the tingling, painful, tangible longing that will produce scenes of great regret and then intense passion. Remember we said the longing is better than the doing. Give me some of that."

I raised an eyebrow as I rearranged my underwear back in place from the rear of my jeans. "I'm not so sure of that anymore."

"Nope. That's just more procrastination," he said. "How about this: gimme an example, the worst one. Did you ever storm out on a guy, even though you wanted to fuck the guy so bad you couldn't breathe? But your anger or fury or fear or whatever got you spooked? Think about the five senses. That's what they told me the first day in another writing class, and it sounds corny, but it does help—get your mind working on the feel, the sight, the sounds, the smell. Let's start with that: What did it smell like when you were at your worst, dying to get laid but, as is your MO, walked instead? In a stinky city? In a forest with the smell of pine?"

"That's easy. It smelled like trans fats."

A delicious deep laugh exploded over from the sofa where Tommy was lying with his messy motorcycle boots propped up on my pristine white pillow. "What the hell? Trans fats?"

"Yep."

"From where?"

"A Jack in the Box restaurant in Berkeley."

"Okay. Then we're starting your fucking screenplay there." He was so excited. "Interior: Girl in a Jack in the Box. Sipping a strawberry shake, greasy french fry and chicken tenders trans fats wafting in the air, lost in thought as she watches kids play outside in the parking lot playground on those weird-colored habitrails for children."

"Yep. Been there. Was there." I felt better. Maybe I could do a bunch of things I wasn't sure I could do. Like write better. Like screw the brains out of this emotionally available, generous guy on my couch. But not now.

"Okay. Now let's go back a little. How did you end up there?"

"I went to Berkeley to visit James at college in his tiny one-bedroom apartment just outside of town."

"What did his place look like?"

"It was a rickety little blue house with white trim. When I got there, he was sitting on the steps with that dry California sun in his messy hair, like he'd been waiting all week for me."

"Okay. Nice crisp sunny flashback. Then what?"

"James gave me a big hug and said, 'Too long. Waaaaay too long.' Then he kissed my forehead, and I knew things were going to get weird. He loved to act like we were friends all the time, no problem, but then this undercurrent would occasionally come barreling through."

"How come?"

"I don't know, some kind of unfinished business lingering between us."

"Get back to San Francisco, please."

"Okay. Back from the present to the past: I thought he might drag me into his house and have sex with me right then and there."

"But he didn't."

"Nope. Instead he said he had a surprise, what he called the single coolest thing ever. So I locked my car and hopped into the Jeep with him. His body had filled out, and his hair was so sexy and messy under his Yankees hat."

"I'm waiting . . ." Tommy said, as he made a continue motion with his hand, and then laid an arm over his eyes.

"I didn't love that James could change so much in the three months since summer. His legs were more powerful and his shoulders were wider. I didn't know that would happen, that he'd turn into a man. It made me feel so far away, even sitting right next to him. The blondish stubble on his face caught the sunlight as he turned onto the freeway. He looked like he was getting laid a lot."

"That's good. That's so true," Tommy said from under his arm. "Certain people just have a look when they are getting laid a lot. You have to put that in somehow, although a script is just dialogue so it won't be easy, but we'll find a way."

"Yeah. Well, he had that well-fucked glow, and I didn't like it one bit."

"Then what?"

"We cruised straight onto the Bay Bridge, through San Francisco, and over the Golden Gate toward Highway 1. I checked the Jeep for evidence of another woman. I found a girlie, strawberry-flavored ChapStick in the little ashtray that seemed suspect, especially when he took it from me and slipped it into his pocket. It felt like an admission of guilt."

"Nice detail," Tommy said dreamily. "Great way to convey gotcha without words. Easy to use that."

"Thanks." I unwrapped a Milky Way and took a bite. "When we pulled into a lot marked Stinson Beach Parking, and I saw people pulling on wet suits and taking surfboards off the roofs of their cars, I was instantly furious. I hadn't surfed since my dad died, and I told him so. He grabbed my arm and shouted, 'You think I don't know that? You think you're the only person who lost a parent that day?' "

Tommy sat up. I stopped talking for a second, unsure if I wanted to get into the pain that James's words had inflicted. "Go on, this is good," Tommy said.

"Okay." I took a deep breath. "James grabbed my arm and shouted, 'You think I didn't know your dad loved to surf with his boat buddies and fish and be in the water, or that he was made for the outdoors, but got stuck in some claustrophobic situation in his small fishing town? My mom did the same thing: married a guy in a nice little lonely town who quashed her dreams. You think I don't know everything about you and your fucking history at this point? My mom, your dad chasing the rainbow, escaping the prison they put themselves in and, then, getting killed in the process? Why the fuck do you think we're out here?' His eyes were wet, and I know it was all about that crash."

"Well, that's pretty heavy," Tommy said. "The two of you chasing some joy out there that eluded your dead parents?"

"I guess so; he was so adamant we get out there in the waves doing something my dad loved."

"What about sex?" Tommy asked. "Did you still feel like things were weird?"

"Yes, massive sexual tension in the car. It was a heady mixture of the familiar and the new. He reassured me, 'Once you get into that wave, I promise there's no better feeling. Well, maybe one better feeling but it's pretty damn close.' We got out there, he tried to tandem me on the waves, both of us on the board at the same time, but we ended up falling over and over again, and it felt like the inside of a Maytag washing machine."

"So no salty kiss?"

I shook my head sadly. "No, that pretty much capsized my romantic notions. I sort of hit my head, and we had to pack it in."

"What happened when you got back to the house?"

I closed my eyes and began a trancelike monologue about one of the worst scenes in my memory.

"James made fun of me all the way back. 'You're so graceful, Allie. Really, a natural out there.' He laughed as he yanked the board off the back of the Jeep when we finally found parking a block from his house. A beach towel hung around his shirtless neck and I could see his windswept face and nest of wet tousled hair through the rearview mirror of my visor. I sat in the Jeep for a moment, smiling to myself about the warmth of the day. It was a stark contrast to the harsh months of winter when we had had hot sex in the same Jeep."

"Why didn't San Francisco make it easy?" Tommy said, retreating to lie back down on the couch and staining all my pillows with grimy boots. "Sounds like you were already sloshing all over each other in the ocean? That's as sexual as it comes."

"Because things got twisted around. First, I made a reference to dying out there together, which wasn't really funny, since we both almost died together on the plane with our parents. Something sarcastic like 'Yep, it was just like you promised, James. What a *feeling*. Total rush to almost die out there with my best friend.' He shot me a strange look. It just came out like that, but the real problem was I turned and practically tripped over *her* on the steps."

"Who?"

"Samantha. His girlfriend. He yelped, a jogging pace behind me, all out of breath. He must have spotted her from the curb. Everything came to a stop except my head, which promptly began to spin. I looked at James, but his face was empty.

"'Allie, Samantha.' He held his hand toward her. He said, 'Hey, Sam, I didn't think you were going to be back in time to meet Allie.'

"She turned her full-wattage California sunburned beauty on me and cooed, 'I hope you liked my board.' I could barely mutter a thank-you. Then she stood up and her sickeningly shapely legs towered over me. She looked right at me and said, 'Did he tandem you? He *loves* to do that.' Oh my God, Tommy, I was so pissed off, you have no idea." She had worn rows of cool, hippie bead bracelets that chimed together as she walked toward James.

"Was she hot?" Tommy asked. When I closed my eyes and shook my head and didn't answer, he added, "Let me rephrase that: How smokin' hot was she?"

"Put it this way: she was a Southern California blond chick who looked like the hottest bohemian bikini model out there. White-blond thin long hair, torn-up jean cutoffs, a tank top that practically slinked off her braless breasts."

"Of course she was. Blake Lively can play her when you sell the script."

"Thanks a lot; now I have both the image of Samantha *and* the hot body of Blake Lively planted in my head." I threw a Milky Way at Tommy. "Anyway, after the three of us had a horrible quick taco dinner, the last thing we all needed was to try to converse more, so the second we got through his door, James and I both said on cue, 'So tired.' After a painful round of good nights, James pointed me toward the bedroom and said, 'We'll just sleep out here on the futon.' "

"Awkward," Tommy said, laughing as he ate his Twizzler in a way that made me want to eat the other end of it at the same time.

"Totally. I went into the bedroom and piled up my clothes and placed them on a tiny chair that I recognized from James's childhood bedroom. I fought back some serious tears as I yelled out, 'You two, I'm just fine in here!' But I wasn't, so I stuck my head back into the living room. They were sitting on the couch.

" 'You two, just, you know.' I couldn't even look at him. 'You do your thing in here. Whatever.' I banged my index fingers together. I think I meant to convey two bodies lying next to each other in the fold-out futon, but because of the banging, it seemed like, well, exactly that. I closed the door, but when Samantha's shower turned on, James walked into the bedroom in his sweatpants and rumpled T-shirt. He sat on the edge of the bed and put his head in his hands."

"The prick," Tommy said. "Did he want a three-way?"

"No. He whispered, 'If you had said to her "That's so great, sooooo great" one more time, I was going to kill you. And please *stop* acting so fake,' he begged.

"I was so attached and drawn to him at that moment. I had this firm idea in my head that we were officially better in love than as best friends, but he wasn't on board. I just hugged an Indian print pillow that smelled like cats and focused on a crack in the ceiling. He said, 'I'm really sorry, Allie. I was so happy you were coming for a few days, and I missed you.' He mimicked my index fingers banging together. 'You're telling me you want us to do "our thing"? First of all, beyond weird and awkward thing to say.' "

Tommy sat up. "This is going to work really well. I like this; it's like *When Harry Met Sally,* only they don't end up together: more real, actually, and less Hollywood-y happy ending. Friendships between men and women get sexual and fucked up and awkward all the time. That's the truth. People get possessive and jealous over their friend's boyfriend or girlfriend having more power and figure their jealousy is actually love, but then it isn't always. You can explore that in the script."

"Well, I was definitely feeling possessive that night. Of course I didn't want him to screw someone ten feet from my head; I wanted him to tell her to go home and then make love to *me*. My intense feelings for him scared the daylights out of me."

"No shit!" Tommy yelled from the couch, listening with his eyes closed, brownie crumbs littering his wide chest and getting ground up on my white sofa under him. "But do please go on."

"James as usual then put me on the spot, saying, 'What's your deal, Allie?' Conveniently for him, he asked me instead of saying something meaningful himself."

"Did you tell him?"

"Well, I punted, saying 'You know what, we have all day tomorrow to talk about this without a naked girl in your shower.' Then I gave him a false smile."

"That must have worked."

My office phone rang again. It was past midnight. I didn't want to talk to Wade in front of Tommy, but I picked it up, saying "What?!" in a bitchy tone. I heard only another hang-up.

"Who was that? Anything wrong?" Tommy asked.

"Wrong number. Let me get back to the story." I tried to dive back in but felt disturbed by the clicks now on two calls: now and from earlier after I saw the SUV. "So, anyway, James in his messy college apartment bedroom patted my leg and stood up, saying, 'I have one class at noon, but yeah, I guess we'll have time to talk.' He let out a huge, depressing, defeated sigh. Neither of us seemed too keen about a rushed groping session the next day in bright sunlight between his class and the time she might knock on the door and surprise us again. Before I went to San Francisco to visit James, I was definitely imagining no Samantha at all in the picture, candles, complete privacy, and all the time in the world."

"You're such a romantic," Tommy added.

I ignored that and went on. "'You're the culprit,' James finally said. 'You're the one who's been'—and he slammed his index fingers together—'with every lowlife in Massachusetts.' I told him not everyone and that he was exaggerating."

I waited for Tommy to analyze that one, which he promptly did: "Okay, so you fucked random guys right and left to get the pain out of your system, only making it worse. Screwed-up strategy, but hardly uncommon. I can't believe you and James manage to have a somewhat normal friendship now after all this dysfunction in your history. Then what?"

"James walked over to the bed and placed both his hands on my shoulders, then sat down and cradled my head in his arms. And he said, 'I need a signal. Okay?' "

"Thank fucking God for James!" Tommy yelled.

"The bathroom door opened and closed very loudly. I was terrified, so I smiled and said, 'I think she's clean.' "

"Brutal," said Tommy.

"Yeah, brutal. I couldn't sleep at all, listening to first their muffled conversation, then what sounded like a fight, followed by her making little mewing noises like she was trying to seduce him. Maybe she did. It didn't matter; I couldn't bear to face either of them again. I remember lying in his big bed alone that night and wanting him so badly my entire torso ached.

"The next morning I bolted town before they got up and cried over my greasy egg sandwich at a Jack in the Box down the highway, the smell of trans fats permeating the air."

I looked at Tommy who was no longer lying down. He was sitting, rapt, with his elbows on his knees. He stood up, walked up to my desk, and kissed me slowly with his tongue circling my mouth, and one hand inside my bra, one inching down my zipper.

After about two minutes, he came up for air, still holding my face with one hand. "I'm going to leave now," he said, leaving me only wanting him to delve deeper beneath my clothes. "You take everything you just told me and you write that whole scene down. Don't leave out one second of it."

THREE HOURS LATER, I pushed the SAVE button on a scene I had to admit I liked. Agitated by the sexual tension between Tommy and me, the come-to-Jesus conversation with Wade, the clicks on the line, and caffeine, I curled up on my couch and put my face deeply into the pillow that still smelled of Tommy's woodsy shampoo and drifted into a dreamless sleep.

21

Under His Spell

The next afternoon, after I'd pushed SEND on my screenplay scene for class, then written in the final film festival panel outline with pink, orange, and purple markers just like Murray had asked, I texted Jackie to set up a meeting once I knew Georges and the chieftains of industry would be gone. I was beginning to believe some of what she was saying to me and even wondering about *her* safety—if she knew about the SUV following her down the street. I didn't know if the hang-ups on my phone line were linked to any of this, but I would ask her that too.

WITH TREMBLING HANDS, I paid the taxi driver outside the Tudor Room. My heart throbbed with a bizarre mania, and my legs propelled me up the stairs into the restaurant I had no business being in the middle of the afternoon. Those voices, the kind that admonish the listener to rethink the plan, whispered in my head. But nothing could prepare me for what I saw.

As I waited in the entryway, a few busboys set the tables in the distance.

"You looking for me?" A woman's voice traveled across from the bar to my right. "Glad you wanted to come."

Jackie. As usual, she was sipping her coffee as if she were lolling around a little bungalow on the Mediterranean. She smiled. "What would you like?"

"Just a cup of tea." I sat down and tried to get comfortable so that I could have another conversation with a woman who told me in no uncertain terms that she'd slept with my husband.

As she swiveled around to me, I snuck a look at her tight waist Wade must have grabbed. A good-sized part of me seriously contemplated how to find a little cyanide for her coffee. But first I needed some more information . . . and her stories were becoming more credible by the day.

"You starting to understand the connections here? You have questions? Still doubts when I look you in the eye and say I will never lie to you?"

It was possible she hadn't actually lied to me. I asked, "Are we in an unsafe situation or a shady situation? I really must know this."

She shook her head and smiled kindly. "No. I assure you."

"Well, I watched you leave the event last night after you poked my rib and bolted."

"I just wanted to signal to you that Camilla and Max and Wade are doing stuff together. And Camilla was thinking you knew all the details of the overseas accounts when she was talking to you. Doesn't that show you—"

"Jackie. I watched you leave. A big SUV followed you down the street."

"It's nothing. I promise you." She seemed so confident it made me feel slightly better. And just as she said that, my eyes scanned the room, and I noticed the back of a man I was starting to know all too well. It couldn't be. "Uh, Jackie. Excuse me." I stood up and started to walk, trancelike, in his direction.

A man with a beefy frame was organizing wine bottles into a wood-panelled cellar near the maître d' podium. At first I wasn't sure, but as he picked up some heavy cases of wine, those thighs were unmistakable. I tapped his shoulder.

Tommy turned around and laughed out loud. "What are you doing here? You should be sleeping after all that work."

"No, what are you doing here?"

"This is one of the places I consult on buying good wine at auctions. You look so spooked—what, you don't think I work at restaurants as nice as this?"

"I just thought, I don't know, not necessarily here with the business guys who . . ."

"You're acting like such a snob; you think I can't . . ."

"No, no, it wasn't that. Just here is so different from the type of place I had imagined you . . ."

"Well, I actually assist the main sommelier wine expert with good deals he might not have found otherwise. I've just yesterday found some great bottles at auctions for them because, believe it or not, these days, even this place is looking for great prices." He stood up and brushed my cheek with the back of his hand and then fondled the back of my ear with his fingertips.

I pushed his hand away. "You didn't tell me it was here! You never once said, 'Oh, I consult for the *Tudor Room*!'"

"What the hell is wrong with you, Allie? Just because I worked in my uncle's liquor store in Rockaway doesn't mean I don't know wine. I do know wine pretty well, and my uncle taught me a lot."

"I didn't mean to insult your wine knowledge, what I meant was . . ."

"Well, it sounded like that. You got a particular problem with this place?"

As a matter of fact, I did have a big problem with Tommy being here, starting with the fact that Wade had charged his lunch here to the *Meter* magazine expense account at least once a week for the past twenty years. Tommy never asked about my husband and silence on the topic seemed an unspoken deal in our relationship since that first kiss—I had never even mentioned Wade's name to him. I shifted back while he continued to pull me toward him. "Question is, Allie, what are *you* doing here?"

I snapped my hands out of his. "I, uh, had to check on something."

"Check on what? Nobody's here for dinner for a few hours."

"Well, I was here and I had to meet, sometimes we book meetings in the private rooms, I mean I left something . . ."

"Nobody's here, Allie." Tommy looked furtively over his shoulder. "In fact, why don't you come inside here behind the cases so I can say good afternoon properly?" He grabbed my hand, which I instantly pulled back. "What's with you? And why are you so nervous?"

"I just didn't think I'd see you here; it's out of place."

"Nothing's out of place for me except seeing *you* here," he whispered in my ear. "I'm done in an hour; let's go celebrate the scene that you handed in." I jerked my head back, knowing Jackie was watching. "Will you be in the neighborhood? I have to get back downstairs to do some inventory. I'm going to text you later; I need to do a little more exploration work inside those jeans of yours."

"Uh, I guess, maybe, sure," I answered, still in shock as he bolted down the stairs.

I walked back to Jackie in a stronger daze.

She chuckled. "So you know Tommy?"

"Please don't tell me you know him?" I said to her.

"I know he's the cute part-time wine guy with a light around him everyone wants to bathe in."

I tried to minimize our relationship as best I could. "Yeah, it's just so strange; he is in a class I'm in, and we work together on writing sometimes, but I barely know him *at all* and . . ."

"And he's got you under his spell."

"What do you mean by that?"

"Just looked like it. That brush of his hand on your cheek is going to tell me just as much as if he'd ripped your bra off."

"Nonsense!" I sat down and tried way too hard to convince her otherwise, motor-mouthing a million miles an hour back at her. "*Total nonsense.* I mean, I just know him from the screenwriting class, and it's helping both of us with these messed-up screenplays and . . ."

"Don't sweat it. I just put two and two together." She rolled her eyes. "That guy falls in love every week. He's very intense."

"I know," I answered. She had me. She saw him touch me, not just my cheek, but pull my hands toward him. God, how I wanted to fall into him but held myself back. I thought a lot about the conversations Tommy and I'd been having and I realized I cared a lot about what he thought about work and me. But, of course, I had to play it cool with the world-class seductress in front of me. "I mean, I know the intense part. From help he's given me in a screenwriting class is all."

"Are you really interested in him?"

I wanted to say, *He might just be a lifeboat for me if I ever get up the strength to jump off the Wade juggernaut*. But I didn't. I held firm to my as yet unaccomplished mission of figuring out just why Jackie had bulldozed her way into my life. "This isn't about me or Tommy. That's really not why I'm here," I said, switching to a businesslike tone.

Jackie answered, "You've got one hell of a client roster and an impossible, self-destructive, self-obsessed boss, and you should be focusing on your screenplay in whatever spare time you have right now, not Tommy, the likes of whom come a dime a dozen if you're in the market for it."

She didn't know Tommy. She had no way of understanding how well he understood me. I had to change topics. "How do you know so much about Murray? Did you have a thing with him?"

She rolled her head back at that. "Wow. Definitely not. I'm

determined to figure his piece in all this. I want him to come clean about things he doesn't even know."

"Why? About what? Murray's the most transparent person I know," I told her, now more concerned about my job and my livelihood than ever before.

I pulled my purse discreetly closer into me, with my one last piece of power inside—the second flash drive I'd copied everything onto—and tried to switch subjects. I of course didn't trust her enough to imagine handing it over. "Can we talk about you for a minute? I get that you love to hate many of the people in here who are drunk off their own power. Believe me, so do I: I didn't come from this world either—they act like aliens if you ask me—but why does this all matter to you so much? And why were you at the screening? What did you know ahead of time and how?" The questions came tumbling out almost faster than my mouth could form them.

"I have explained almost every bit of it to you. In time you will understand why I can't tell you one thing right now until I figure it out for sure. But I will add this: I knew they had a ton of Luxor stock and hoped it would go up. A few simple media stories about a fake potential takeover caused all the sudden upward movement in that stock. Nice thing if you secretly own a ton of it. I'm sure this isn't the first time they've done it, this merry little group. In fact, I know they're planning another false media story to make another stock climb even higher, and they're going to make serious bucks off that one. Luxor was just practice, kids' play, for what they have in the pipeline."

I listened carefully but I still had to argue hard for my

family's sake. "Since the very first night I met Wade he used to talk about taking the bad guys down all the time. It's in his blood; that's why he likes journalism, like it's a vigilante calling or something. He's got a very irreverent spirit that rebels against authority. I just still have a lot of trouble believing this."

She stopped me by placing her hand on my arm. "The rebel in him may be waning. Your husband's a little desperate and more than a little sold out, for your information." My husband's ex-mistress then took a sip of her cappuccino. "Just trying to wake up the wife here."

"How do you know all this?" I asked. "Other than searching these men's laundry rooms, that is."

I glanced in Tommy's direction to make sure he was still downstairs and out of view of this conversation.

"What are you looking for?" she asked.

"Nothing, I was just . . ."

She narrowed her eyes. "Are you *boy crazy*?"

"Well, I wanted to make sure he was leaving . . ."

Her head shook slowly as she tried not to laugh. "We're talking about much more important stuff here."

I smiled a little at her catching me. So did she. "You got me."

"Don't tell me you're one of these women who can take on the world, but you let the men take over your life? Wade and his childish behavior? Murray? May I add the seductive Tommy to the list?"

"I don't let men . . ."

"You sure look and act like you do," she answered, with a big, kind, forgiving smile.

"I don't think it's that easy," I answered, but then I couldn't help adding, "Not many women I know, myself included, are able to be hard-core on cue like you seem to be. Men are sometimes an unhealthy obsession . . ."

"Oh, Jesus, just fuck those men." She took a slow sip of her coffee while keeping her glare on me.

"Well, ignoring them is easier said than done . . ."

"That's not what I'm saying," she answered, her gorgeous face very close to mine. "I mean, literally, *just fuck them*. Why all the torture over Tommy? Why are you resisting? Just get it over with."

I put my hand to my forehead. "I need Tommy to help me write, but I have no intention of sleeping with him."

"That's so charmingly Edwardian. You give him that spark; I just saw him yank you into the closet like he wanted to attack you. You need to just fuck the guy and find out if there's any *there* there for *you*."

That did sound appealing on more than one level. "Well, I'm married, last I checked."

"How can you be so prudish when you're still in your prime?" She licked the froth of her cappuccino.

"Jackie, if you want to talk, girl to girl, and you want me to trust you, then I'm going to really consider it, though no promises. Let's hear your story," I said, drinking a few sips of lukewarm tea between questions. "Do you have a boyfriend that makes it easy for you to act all hard-core about everything on cue? Do you even let any guy into your life? Didn't any man ever obsess you, cast a spell on you, control *you*?"

She closed her eyes and shook her head. "Not really."

"That doesn't sound definitive."

"Well, there's someone I met who is a little different, very different and special in fact, but I haven't taken the plunge there yet. . . . As for the rest of them"—she smirked and took a sip of her drink—"I like sex and I like it no strings attached."

"Well, I certainly had a few men I slept with in high school and college," I answered, defending my ability to have sex for fun. "Slutting around in my own way."

"Listen to yourself." She cocked her head in disdain. "You weren't slutting around; you were sampling the merchandise, figuring out what you wanted."

"No, I don't think I cared much about the quality of the merchandise." Truth was, I didn't even look at the merchandise, much less check for a sell-by date.

"Well, why can't you do that now?" she asked, as if she were suggesting I try on a new pair of shoes.

"Maybe I want to set a better example for Lucy." I think I must have looked at her in that condescending way mothers do to those women without kids. It didn't make even a tiny dent.

"So you prefer this needy state you're in now with Tommy where you're so fearful of your own shadow and your own desires you can't even figure out what you want?" Clearly it was her turn to condescend. "Besides, your husband is doing it, so why can't you?"

"Well, his wrong doesn't mean I am okay with my doing it," I answered, raising my pitch. I felt a bit uncomfortable opening up to her, but I did like hearing her take on things—more independent than anything I was capable of. Except for Caitlin and a few sweet moms at school on rare occasions, I didn't like to let people know how I felt deep inside, which meant I didn't naturally open up to many girlfriends. Besides, James had an understanding of me that no one else ever would. And that sufficed.

She waved my concerns away with her hand in the air. "Sex is what you make it. It's just a release if you want it to be. Ask any man."

"You may think it's freedom, but I'm not so sure . . ."

"It doesn't mean anything to me, if I don't want it to mean anything to me." Jackie shook her head at my simplification. "And it means the world to me, if I'm in love. I'll take the freedom to make that choice any day. Are you following what you want or what society wants you to want? Make sure you don't walk around town with the scarlet letter pasted on your chest, Bovary's arsenic, all that creepy 'punish the woman' bullshit."

"Those novels are more than a hundred years old."

She tied her straw in a heart-shaped knot and tossed it in front of me. "My point exactly. You are following ancient dictates." She sipped the last drop of her cappuccino and slipped her small laptop into her bag. "Just fuck him, if that's what you want. We're not in Saudi Arabia." She leaned close to my ear. "Whatever you decide, don't let society put you in a box."

I looked into her velvet brown eyes, her pupils enormous in the low light. My opinion of her swayed; I went from thinking this woman was out of her mind and someone I just had to hate (or poison) to thinking she might actually be making some good points. "I don't think I'm going to do anything, and I certainly wouldn't be broadcasting it to you if I did, but I'm going to think about what you say. I'll give you that."

"Well, think about it; and if you indulge, watch those guys in the thirty-and-under crowd. I know Tommy passes the thirtyish bar, he's what . . ."

"Thirty-two."

"Well, from the looks of him, he's a wild card."

"Watch what exactly?"

She licked her lips and stood to go. "Oh, you know . . ."

"I'm not exactly a virgin, nor was I before I met Wade," I answered.

"I think you can peg men by the decade. I can, anyway." Jackie responded like the expert she apparently was. "Guys in their fifties are all desperate to show they've still got their mojo. They try to show off uncomfortable positions they themselves don't even like."

I thought about Wade, heading into middle age, imagining him acting like a total fool in bed with Jackie, some bucking bronco positions I couldn't even fathom. Part of me was humiliated to be linked to him. "Go on."

"Thirties and forties are pretty much the same; they know how to please a woman and they know what they like. Pretty straightforward. They like the woman to be turned on, and they understand turning her on actually makes it better for both. You know, normal, pleasurable sex as if, strange enough, that's the goal."

"And the under thirties?"

"That's the wild card decade right now, I'm finding."

"You're finding or your friends are telling you . . ." I had to ask.

"Well, a combination of direct, in-the-field research and what I hear, let's say. But the under thirties are Internet porn obsessed for sure; they watch it like a tutorial. That's how they learned to do it, not like the old days where guys learned from the hot sitter down the block teaching them the moves that a woman really likes. They jerk off to it, copy it, emulate it, and they don't know there's another way. They'll slap your ass out of the blue, get a little too rough by holding you down; basically they fuck like they're a porn star the entire time, and they expect you to do the same."

"Jesus, that sounds horrible. Is that it or is there more?"

"Much more, but I'm late and have to go." She threw her bag over her shoulder and whispered to me, as she got ready to leave, "Truth is, they all want to replicate the money shot and they're too stupid and immature to understand that the money shot is just for viewers, not real people actually doing it."

"And by money shot you mean . . ." I sounded like the fishing town girl I was.

"They like to get their jollies on you rather than in you. They forget there are no viewers waiting for the finale. And if you don't get my drift, I mean get out a handkerchief for your face. Put it that way. Or rub it in; it's supposed to be good for your skin."

"Uh, well," I huffed loudly. "Thanks for the advice, on all fronts."

Her sudden smile lit up the bar. "Don't thank me yet. For all

I know, despite all his intensity and passion, maybe Tommy sucks in bed. Wouldn't that be ironic?"

"Yeah." I laughed awkwardly and reluctantly. "That would be hilarious."

Jackie gave me a long, sideways glance as she laid a hand on her purse and kissed me softly on the cheek. "And I'm sure you can get it the way you want in anyone's bed, regardless of their age, but think about what I said about the men in your life having too much power over you. I meant it."

22

Blasting Heat

The entire day at my office, I couldn't help but contemplate Jackie's man-by-the-decade theory. As for her ideas on the morals of sleeping around, part of me wanted to kill her for doing just that with the man I married (and for looking so good while doing it), but I had to admit to myself I liked hearing a woman talk like a man. At least she didn't love Wade back and just considered him a quick, middle-aged-guy-trying-to-prove-something lay. The clock hit one P.M. and my phone rang.

"Allie." Murray started in without saying hello. He sounded a little out of breath, even for a guy whose breathing was always loud, rattly, and labored, like he might go into cardiac arrest at any moment. "Do what I say."

"I always do what you say, Murray."

"Yeah, I know, I know. But this time, don't fuck it up and improvise with some of your own input. Do *exactly* as I say," he instructed.

"Okay, first of all, you sound like your mother, which is pretty much not who you want to be in life, and second, I don't mess things up." I was concerned something serious was going on, but I didn't want to let on to Murray how much I knew.

"You don't. I'm just used to having to say that to every-fucking-one. I'm sorry, just do what I say, you hear me?"

"Yes," I answered. "I think we've established that."

"I need to see your reports, but I want everything in person now. In Southampton. Today."

This seemed ominous. Why couldn't I fax or e-mail them? "Today? You want me out there? We talked about doing it on the videoconference."

"Nope, I need something else as well. A man is going to come to you from a bank. He'll arrive downstairs in approximately three minutes. Let the guard know he can come upstairs. He is going to personally deliver an envelope with some documents to your office door. Not a messenger, but a banker. No one may look at the documents. Not you. Not the guy delivering them. You got it? There's going to be tape bonding the envelope closed. Make sure it isn't ripped anywhere."

"What am I supposed to do with this envelope?" I asked with great trepidation.

"Get your ass on the Long Island Expressway and bring the envelope to me. And if you get into a car wreck, and the car's about to blow up, grab my papers and let your fuckin' purse burn."

A FEW MINUTES later, a guy looking like a humorless Swiss banker in a suit appeared in my doorway after having been cleared by the guard. He was upstairs for all of forty seconds before he left again, not saying a single word.

I placed the envelope—closed up with red tape that read CONFIDENTIAL—in my bag. I wondered what was in it, but I knew I couldn't open it and find out. I then gathered all my own papers, rushing out the door and bumping into Caitlin bringing me a fresh Frappuccino for my thighs. My phone rang.

Wade.

"What?" I practically yelled.

"Oh, thank God I caught you."

"What?" I yelled again.

"I'm downstairs with the kids."

"Downstairs where?"

"Your office building."

"Okay, well, I'm working a full day as we discussed, and we also discussed that you would take them for the half day, remember? And I'm suddenly on my way out to Murray's in any case so I can't take them now." I winked thank you to Caitlin and grabbed the cold plastic cup.

"Great." And then he turned his voice away from the receiver. "They'd love to take a ride out, wouldn't you, kids?"

I closed my eyes, trying not to say motherfucker out loud. "Wade, we discussed how much work I have. How often do I save you from kids when you're overwhelmed? How often do I say I have to work instead of being the main caregiver? *Never.* Today is different. My turn to be overwhelmed. I can't take the kids today all the way out to Southampton; that's nuts." I mouthed *Motherfucker* to Caitlin and pointed to my cell phone.

"I know, I know, but something's come up, and I need to play a round of golf with Max Rowland this afternoon. We have to discuss a film in the festival that he's now sponsoring; it's not going to launch so well, and I can help with some much-needed buzz, so . . ."

"What do you have to talk to Max about? The prereviews are already out there. You can't bring them back."

"He wants to discuss international distribution so he can double down on his investment here and overseas. His car is waiting to take me to Bayonne Country Club right now."

"Motherfucker! Wade, really? Golf? That's your excuse for screwing up my presentation?"

"I promise to make it up to you . . ."

"Make what up to me? Your cheating throughout our marriage or ditching the kids with me on my big report day for my boss?" Caitlin's eyebrows were raised to the heavens at that one, though she quickly occupied herself with neatening up my files and charts in the bag on the ground.

Wade didn't answer for a long time and then finally offered, "Allie. I'm sorry. Jesus, we're in a bad place right now. I, I . . ."

"Yes, Wade, you are making up what exactly?"

"I was referring to today's unfortunate planning snafu. Making that up to you, I mean."

"You can't make that up either, Wade." And I hung up.

"Wowza," said Caitlin. "So by cheating, you mean the girl at the party or just from way before when Lucy was born?"

"I'm not answering that."

She stared into my eyes, standing on her tiptoes a little to do so. "You have to. I need to know."

I tried to push by her on my way out of my office. "And why do you need to know?"

"Because I want to give you good girlfriend advice, and you're so clammed up, we can't figure this out."

I plunked my sorry body down on the sofa in the hallway before the elevator bank and placed my head in my hands.

Caitlin rubbed my back. "Where are you guys? Where are you in all this?"

I shook my head. "If you fall in love with someone who turns out to be a liar and you still love something about him and you have kids on top of that, then you're fucked. It's like Lucy and Blake form this concrete block that trips me up. They deserve the family I never got. I'm telling you, I'm so lost in this mess."

"Well, maybe Wade just isn't quite the man he seemed when you . . ."

"Wade is just a big kid. He wants it all and he wants it now. And he's exciting in so many ways, but his flaws are very, very real. And they cause acute pain, because a lying mate doesn't mean the connection turns off like a faucet. It just means confusion reigns and, in my case, a prickly and constant state of *what the hell do I do now?*"

"Well, how long can you hold out?" Caitlin asked, like it affected her somehow. "Are you going to try despite his, I don't know, his ways?"

"I wouldn't be the only woman in America who'd

overlooked that issue." My heart hurt and I felt a rush of anxiety wash over me because I had no idea what I wanted or how to fix this.

"Look at Jackie O," Caitlin said, sounding dejected.

I shook my head and stared at the horribly creased shirt I'd slept in. "Nothing about me is like Jackie O."

"Look at Hillary Clinton!" Caitlin offered next. "She might be president someday; then we can say the leader of the goddamn free world overlooked a womanizer!"

Yeah, but maybe I just couldn't overlook it, and maybe I couldn't find the right answer either. A happy me didn't exactly shine on either side of the coin. I had two choices: leave him and be alone with the kids and face God knows what hell or stay and feel like I wasn't meant for any of what had come of my marriage.

I stood up straight like a good soldier and stabbed the elevator button. I had a report to present to my boss, a confidential package to deliver to him, and two tired children downstairs in the lobby on a steaming hot, disgusting, muggy New York day. No way around it but to take them to the meeting and feed them enough cool ice cream to keep them as happy as possible. Hugely depressing thoughts were creeping through every inch of my body, but I closed my eyes and willed them buried for now.

THERE'S AN UNWRITTEN rule in Manhattan that says "on summer Fridays, leave for the Hamptons before two o'clock or after seven o'clock." Never in between. By the time I got the kids into the car and a movie playing on the drop-down screens, it was one thirty.

This time, the unwritten rule was wrong by thirty minutes, which only amped up those depressing thoughts. Two hours later, I sat on the Long Island Expressway, caught up in a perfect storm of pre-rush-hour, middle-island business, and rich Hampton weekender traffic around exit 50, twenty long, slow exits before the off-ramp to the Hamptons.

We were at a standstill on a four-lane highway, and the air conditioner on my old Volvo wagon huffed and puffed. At least the kids had both passed out after the first hour of nonstop poking and teasing and whining. I looked back at them all passed out, finally, and they looked like little rolled-up cherubs. *At least I had them, and no one could change that ever.*

My phone rang—Tommy's number on the screen—and I clicked on my Bluetooth earpiece quickly before it woke them. At least a little ray of light in an otherwise taxing morning.

"How's the presentation?" he asked.

"Mashed potatoes at best. My boss will point out every shortcoming."

"Well, fuck your job. Stick to the writing."

"When's yours due?" I asked.

"I got a week."

"I'll be on your ass next week then," I promised.

"That sounds nice, you on my ass. We could maybe try that before then to practice a little . . ."

I coughed. "I'm undecided on that front, you know that," I said, while making sure the kids were out cold in back.

"I can help you with that decision. Why don't you just chill out, come to my apartment and rip off my clothes, and you take charge; have your way with me . . ."

"How about instead I help you with your writing?" I asked, hoping to even the score, and cool him off.

"It just so happens I am having this one problem with my main character. There's this nice girl he likes, but he wants to cheat on her with this hot, totally destructive chick, and I'm concerned it's making the audience hate him. How do I do that and make women want to go to this movie, and, on some level, like him?"

"Well, that's not easy, but you should thank God it's the guy you're trying to make likable. Audiences hate it when a woman cheats, especially a mother, so much puritanical backlash baggage about all that. If a married woman actually cheats, then the writer has to have her jump on the train tracks so the audience can go home happy . . . oh, shit." I slapped my forehead with the palm of my hand.

"Allie?" Tommy said, clearly alarmed. "You there?"

"Yeah, I'm here." I shook my head as my anger resurfaced. "But I gotta do something. I'll call you later."

"Okay, do that. And put your ass on me next time it's convenient."

I heard rumblings in the backseat as Blake stirred and asked for a drink, his eyes still closed.

"Honey, there's your favorite strawberry Capri Sun drinks in the cooler; take a sip of something and go back to sleep. When you are both awake, while I'm working at my meeting, you can turn on *Toy Story 3*."

Next I anxiously called lobby security.

"Good afternoon, 553 West Nineteenth Street."

"Hi, Lorenzo, it's Allie Crawford from the Hillsinger offices. I have a quick question."

"Shoot."

"Do you remember I came down to greet my husband and children?"

"Yes. Always remember the children. Can't say that about the husbands."

"Okay, Lorenzo," I pleaded. "Please please please try to remember, just before that, you sent a messenger upstairs. A Mr. Prissert?"

"Okay, yes, I see it. Mrs. Crawford, it's like Grand Central Station here, I don't remember every face I sign in."

"Did you happen to see my husband talking to that man, Mr. Prissert, the guy who came up with the envelope?" I was gripping the wheel like a crazy person, with all my knuckles turning white. It hit me like an electric shock. If Wade and Mr. Prissert were talking in the lobby, then Wade and Murray were in some kind of financial dealings together for sure and I just might believe everything Jackie was telling me. Maybe I would even hand her the flash drive.

"Honestly, Mrs. Crawford, I'd really like to help you, but I just don't remember. I remember your kids running in when you came down and thinking you must be an awful nice mom, seeing how you treat me nice all the time. I remember that. And I remember you going outside to someone; I mean the kids wouldn't have been there alone, I guess."

"Can you find any security tapes?"

"Yes. But I'm not supposed to . . ."

"Please, Lorenzo. Look at the tapes. And also tell me if there's an SUV, a black one, outside that was with the guy who brought up my package."

"Okay. Give me an hour."

I just needed a link between Wade and the envelope Murray wanted so badly from some bank and then I'd be pretty close to believing everything Jackie said—why the hell else would my husband pray to Jesus in thanks on the floor when I handed him a missing flash drive? The pieces were too easy to ignore: Max Rowland, a.k.a. Texas Takeover King, looking to get even richer; my husband manipulating media stories; Delsie broadcasting fake news on CNBB to earn some more cash for her Easter-egg-colored Valentino suits; and Murray spinning more tales with the help of media mover Wade Crawford to protect them all. A nice little circle of crime that went round and round . . .

Jackie said this crew was up to another deal that would be even bigger. I had to find the missing link before that happened. Problem was I didn't understand all the codes and numbers on the flash drive. Though I could tell that the Projects Red, Green, and Blue had bank account information linked to them, I didn't know what they meant. I was still worried that they implicated Wade in a way that would harm him, and us, and because of that, I kept a firm grip on the flash drive. I would not be handing it to Jackie just yet.

23

Landed Gentry

At 4:40 P.M. that steamy day, I rolled my car through Murray's automatic gate, which dramatically revealed his stucco Southampton château. The pebbles on his circular driveway were raked to an even perfection like frosting on a cake. An enormous elm tree that was new to the yard loomed over the driveway.

On the lawn in front, I spied Murray with a Wiffle ball and bat in his hand at home plate. He was clad in pinstripe seersucker shorts held up by probably the longest needlepoint belt known to exist—his initials "HH" sewn in pink and green squares every three inches, with crisscrossed golf clubs in between. He wore bright orange Tod's driving shoes that looked like they were about to explode on his puffy feet.

Murray's sinewy wife, Eri, quite elegant at last night's screening in a Dennis Basso gown with the jewels and the chignon, was looking decidedly out of place on a makeshift athletic field. She wore white leggings on her drainpipe legs, a fuchsia Polo shirt, and $1000 snakeskin Lanvin "sneakers" on her feet. Her bright blue contact lenses made her dark Asian eyes ethereal in a deeply creepy way.

I drove the car a little bit around the circle and watched the Hillsinger family from my front seat as I pretended to be on a call. I couldn't bear to walk out into the bright, blistering sun just yet.

Murray was playing ball with his two sons, Benjamin, aged six, and Noah, aged four, with Eri supposedly playing catcher: one of those insta-families created by older rich men who've left their long-loyal wives for all the hopes and promises younger flesh seemed to offer. The boys wore little colored twill shirts tucked into khaki shorts that reached their knees. Benjamin, skin bulging over the top of his socks like his dad, walked up to the pitcher's spot that Murray occupied and whined, "I hate team sports. Why do we have to play this stupid game?"

"Murray! The kid needs to take a break. Take it easy on him," a matronly woman yelled from the shade of the front porch.

"No, Ma! The kid needs to learn to play ball. You think you were easy on me?"

"You weren't nothing like Benjamin. You couldn't do anything right. You needed to work hard just to get even with everyone." Mrs. Hillsinger lumbered up from her chair and walked down the steps of the front porch while her enormous breasts swung to and fro. "Benji's already a star. Come heyah, my Benji. Come to Nana for some love."

"Ma! Stop!" Murray smacked the top of Benjamin's head,

knocking his cap off, and told him, "This is only finished when one team reaches twelve points. You got that?"

I pulled the car behind the garage and got out into the intense heat, leaving the engine and AC on, and walked right over to the game, hoping my own kids would remain hypnotized by the wonders of Pixar.

Murray yelled over, "Give me ten minutes, Allie. You got the envelope, right?"

I smacked my bag and held it tight. "Yes, I do. Unburned."

"Murray!" Mrs. Hillsinger yelled again. "Don't you go working and ignoring my boys. Allie's got your life in control. You've got all afternoon to do your work!"

I walked up to the steps to the house and kissed the formidable Toni Hillsinger hello. She grabbed some flesh on my arm. "Allie, darling. You're lookin' too thin. What's with you city girls? Eri over there is so skinny she looks like Popeye's girlfriend. A Japanese Olive Oyl!" As she laughed, her enormous Murray-like stomach shook.

"Well, Eri is quite elegant actually." I was trying.

"If you like that kind of thing." She added in a loud whisper Eri could hear. "*Not my type! That's for sure!*" As she walked back to the stairs, she continued on her charming rant, no longer with any pretense of discretion. "And look at my Murray, what's with the fey needlepoint belt and orange girls' moccasins on his feet? He forgot where he came from. Just because he buys a house on a bay with pretty flowers doesn't mean he's a gentile."

"I can hear you, Ma," Murray bellowed. "Allie, go ask Eduardo for some *gentile* iced tea. Or he'll bring you one on the back porch. Go sit, Allie," he barked, as if I were his lapdog, which I guess wasn't far off.

"Sure thing." I went back to check on the kids to see if they wanted to come into the television room or watch the game outside.

Just then, a beat-up 1986 Ford F-150 pickup rolled around the driveway. In it, I spied an older woman behind the wheel, and a passenger I couldn't see properly. The truck stopped short of the walkway near Murray, and the messy-haired woman in her late fifties waved a hearty hello from the driver's seat. A BARBARA'S ORGANIC GREEN THUMB sign was painted on the side of her truck.

"Barbara, what are you spoiling us with today?" Murray stopped his game and walked over to the car.

"Everything. Looks like you could use some fruit in your diet. No pies for you today." Barbara cracked up in a raspy voice that sounded like it was caused by far too many Kool Menthols—I noticed three used packages lining the filthy dashboard. She grabbed a small basket of strawberries from behind the passenger seat and held an especially plump one up to the sky. "Look at these babies. Rubies from the heavens."

She was a handsome woman with a stocky middle and long legs, curly grayish-blond hair, and deep brown eyes, looking for sure like she was born and bred on the salty East End of Long Island. Barbara pulled down the creaky and heavy back door of her truck, which had long ago lost its springs, and pulled out a cardboard box bursting at the seams from the weight of the fresh berries, peas, and lettuces. She unloaded more boxes of heavy produce as if they were filled with cotton balls.

"What about me?" yelled Eri, feigning disappointment and jealousy. "Don't I matter, Barbara? Didn't you bring anything for me?"

"Now *you* pay the bills?" Toni Hillsinger said from the porch. Eri shot her a cool look, while Barbara piled on.

"I've known Murray a lot longer than he's even known you," Barbara yelled back. "Maybe before you were born, sweetheart!" More laughter cracked out from both older ladies staking out territory. Barbara stomped her strong build through the back door and toward the pantry.

"See, Ma? See how a woman treats me nice? Could you try that once? I send you to Boca on the East Coast, to the Bacara on the West, not to mention possibly the Cip in Venice—you could act a little appreciative."

"You know Pop and I worked hard to make you good at everything so you could make all that money and have all this. And I don't even get any thanks for it. Ah, the hell with you. I'm takin' my nap." Mama Hillsinger walked through the front door without saying another word as she let it slam behind her.

Quite unexpectedly, out of the passenger seat of the beat-up truck pranced a sexy thing in hot shorts, tangerine orange in color, who murmured to the older woman, "Hold on, I'll give you a hand, I didn't realize there was more . . ." The shorts were hiked up so that the back of her bottom ever so slightly bounced out with each little provocative step. A high ponytail of streaked blond curls sticking out of a New York Yankees hat was all I noticed at first. Pert little breasts in a tight turquoise cotton camisole next. Then that unmistakable face.

No. It couldn't be.

It was. Jackie Malone. Here in Southampton. *What on earth? Was she stalking me?*

As she approached, I watched Murray's eyes bulge out at this candy-colored confection of a girl.

I barely recognized Jackie. This wasn't the lip-smacking sophisticate who was slithering around my parties and the Tudor Room; it was the spritely, down-home, country singer, Barbie version.

"I'll get it," Jackie said. Wow. The weatherworn lady driving the pickup must have been her mother, and Jackie's story about a mom in financial straits started to take on more meaning.

I studied Murray's expression. Something about this Jackie woman terrified him. I was sure he'd witnessed her around New York and at the Tudor Room, but seeing her in this setting was seismic for him in a way I couldn't decipher. I could tell because his face wasn't just red, it was full-on purple, just like the fresh beets Barbara had yanked out of the earth.

Jackie arched an eyebrow and rounded the truck, which caused Murray to blink wildly from the amount of perspiration dripping down his forehead and cascading down the divots in his pockmarked face. When he saw her twirl around the corner of the Ford F-150, as if to help her hardworking mother in such a selfless way, I thought he might just melt into a round puddle of sweat like a cartoon character.

"Murray. Try to be a little cool." I nudged him. I was watching Eri watch Murray watching Jackie and couldn't quite figure out the dynamics of the trio.

"Who is that woman?" he asked me.

"Have you seen her before, Murray? I think I have somewhere."

"I-I don't know. I just can't figure out who she is, doesn't matter at all." And he turned to face his boys on the field.

"I'm not sure. Looks like she's just helping the lady," I answered just to screw around with him.

It took me a moment to realize that Blake was standing at my side, prepubescent mouth equally agape. I turned him back toward the car, dropping my carefully collated package of charts in the process. Jackie strode over and reached for the envelope marked CONFIDENTIAL.

"Let me help you with that," she said as she bent her knees into an elegant squat next to me.

24

The Guard Saw All

Jackie lifted the confidential envelope off the driveway pebbles, wiped some dirt away, and deftly slid it into her saddlebag.

"Not so fast, Jackie. Drop it." I held her arm tightly and surprised myself by digging my nails into her smooth skin, all the while watching Murray try to waddle across his sprawling lawn to get a fly ball that he of course missed by ten yards. "Give it back before I cause a scene."

Jackie stared me down. "I'm protecting you. I'm going to get into the car, scan what's in here, and slip it right back to you. My mother will take twenty minutes to get her stuff settled inside; she arranges some wildflowers in his—"

"How much crack have you been smoking exactly?" I asked her. "I don't care if your mother relandscapes the entire estate while we're waiting. You are NOT taking this envelope. *Give it back to me or I'll call him over here and—*"

"Mom. It's soooo hot." Lucy draped her limp body across my bent back and wrapped her arms tightly around my neck.

I tried to loosen Lucy's grasp even as I held tightly to Jackie. "Lucy. Please get off me, sweetie. I'm sorry it's so hot. Go wait in the car where the AC is blasting and I'll see if they have some lemonade."

The horn in my car honked for three full seconds. Blake. I looked toward the car, behind the garage and out of view of the Wiffle ball game.

"Blake! Stop that right now!"

"Mooooommmmm. C'mooooooon." He stuck his head out of the window of the car with his tongue hanging out, panting like a dog.

I held on to Jackie, fearing she would run with the company package. "Do you know Murray?"

"I can't answer that question right now." This was all she was going to give me.

Lucy started crying and tried to pull me by the waist into a standing position.

"Lucy. Please, it's way too hot for you to lie on top of me and pull me like that. Mommy's working." I pried her sticky body away. "I promise we will get ice cream after we're done here."

"You promise?" Lucy sniffed in her tears and finally retreated to the car.

I nodded and turned back to Jackie. "Okay, well, then answer this: Is Wade involved in this envelope somehow?"

"I'm sure he is. That, among other things, is why I need to look it over. It's for the next scheme they're planning, and there might be some key information about it. That's all I need. I know the flash drive has the account numbers that will nail them for sure and the account names, but you said you can't find it anywhere, so what is in this envelope might be very fruitful."

"Allie!" bellowed Murray. "Come back over here! What the hell are your kids doing here? We might as well make them useful while you're getting your work together. Get them to teach my kids how to throw a damn ball. Hell, we can all play, family against family for ten minutes. What do you say, kids? Winner gets the new Mercedes GT3!" Of course, more gut-bouncing laughter at his idiotic joke. Lucy and Blake, freed from their isolation chamber, ran happily over to join the game.

"Let go of my arm." Jackie spoke sternly through her teeth and pulled me behind a very Hamptons, indigo-blue hydrangea bush. "Let me look at the papers before he realizes we know each other. Leave your bag in your car. Help with the Wiffle ball game. I'll look like I'm helping Mom. Then I'll slip it back in your bag."

"It's sealed."

She opened her bag. "And the pièce de résistance." She pulled open an inside pocket holding a roll of the exact same red tape marked CONFIDENTIAL that had sealed the envelope.

I looked into her elusive eyes. "How do you know all this, Jackie? How do you know all this about these guys?"

"Because I used to fuck your husband."

I blinked hard.

Jackie continued, "Sorry to say it like that, but it's the correct answer to your question. And I know where he hides his information. And the guy at the coat check at the Tudor Room lets me go through his briefcase. I've been through Murray's bags and files too. You've got to listen to me on festival business; I can help you turn it around. The indies used to count on a robust DVD market, but now they don't have that. Your business plan is so outdated—the Fulton film *channel*. I'm telling you. Get Max to pay for that and you'll be rich on your own and you won't need these guys' nonsense."

"How come I didn't see any of their nonsense myself if you're so sure . . ."

"How can you *not* know, Allie? It's all right in front of you, if you'll only get those blinders off and look around a little. I'm telling you, this group is planning another big splash soon; mark my words and watch for it. You are playing the fool. You're telling the press on the day of your screening that Max isn't orchestrating a takeover of a hot new company on the horizon, Luxor, but, in reality, he already owns a ton of it. Not exactly a sin on your part, but if you're not careful, you could get snagged in all this." Jackie stamped her sneakered foot so that the charms attached to the laces jingled.

"Stop being so damn loyal to the men around you and open your eyes. Get a grip. Stop avoiding the truth. Or at the very least, figure out the truth and then act on it."

When she swung the garage screen door shut, dust flew like sparkles in the late-afternoon sun.

MURRAY YELLED, "ALLIE, pick up your crap and get your ass over here. Your kids are waiting!"

Minutes later, I was rounding third base, gunning for the Mercedes convertible, far sweatier than this kiddie game or even the heat warranted, when my cell phone buzzed in my pocket. After I made it to home base, I checked the screen.

The caller ID read: *Guard Station*. Lorenzo. I broke into a second layer of fresh sweat.

"I'll be right there, everyone," I said in an overly cheerful way, pretending as if I really cared about this stupid Wiffle ball game. "Blake is up. Go team!"

"Mrs. Crawford, it's Lorenzo."

"Yes?" My face was locked into a huge fake smile. "Go, Team Crawford!"

"I just took my coffee break."

"Yes?"

"C'mon, Mom!" Lucy yelled. "Blake's out. We're in the field."

"Well, seeing as you're all nice all the time, I—"

"Please, Lorenzo," I said calmly, like a cop speaking to someone about to leap out a forty-story window. "Just give me the news."

"Well, there's no security screens at my desk, they're all in the back room so I had to leave to see . . ."

"Yes?" My entire bra was soaked at this point.

"Hey, Allie." Murray was now next to me, yelling in my other ear. "Get your ass on the pitcher's mound." I tried to keep up my smile, even as Murray started poking me in the arm like a child.

I held up a finger, and Murray huffed toward home plate. "Now!"

"Well, from the look of the security tape," Lorenzo continued in his painfully meticulous manner, "the man who brought your kids to the building, I don't know if that's Mr. Crawford, but he got out of the driver's seat with the kids and took them to you."

"Yes. My husband. What about him? Did you see a black SUV?"

"Allie. Off that fuckin' phone!!!" I knew that tone, and I knew his limits. Murray was seriously pissed off.

"Well, yes, an SUV was behind both men, but neither got out of it. But it's all clear on the tape: your husband was with the kids, and then he was the one who gave that envelope to the man who went upstairs to see you. He even smacked him hard on the back after he whispered some joke in his ear."

25

Texan Rage

"Yes or no?" Wade yelled at me down the hallway outside our apartment. I was sending Lucy and Blake with the sitter, Stacey, into the elevator with their little backpacks and sleeping bags. They were headed for a sleepover with their aunt Alice, Wade's unmarried, overworked half sister. We hardly ever saw her, but she adored taking our children for special nights.

"Give me two minutes, Wade." I kissed each of the children's foreheads hard as I cradled their heads in my hands. "Good-bye, honeys. I hate having you away, even for a night when you have no school tomorrow." I winked at them. "I'm sure you're going to consume zero candy and no milkshakes tonight." This made them giggle as the door slid closed.

"Yes or no what?" I yelled back to Wade and let our front door slam hard behind me. I walked back into our bedroom and watched him prepare for his *Meter* cocktail party that night to honor Svetlana Gudinskaya. The party aimed to celebrate her

Belle de Jour II, The Temptations Continue. She graced the next week's cover of *Meter* magazine in a sunny yellow dress with her blond ponytail pulled tight back from her porcelain complexion in a shot meant to mimic Catherine Deneuve's Chanel No. 5 ads of the '70s. I wondered which came first in Wade's head: the sunny yellow napkins working in his home or the cover dress working on the girl.

His movements were so much like my father's just then, especially the way he continued to arrange his just-showered wet hair. Where our marriage stood was irrelevant to him: something that possessed me almost every moment of every day was apparently something that he could just ignore and float around.

While intently cuffing his dark jeans so the bright splash of his magenta socks could be seen, Wade asked again, "It's a simple yes or no question. Did you look at the guest list of Svetlana's people or not?"

I threw my shoe on the floor in disgust. "I actually have a simple yes or no question that I'd actually like answered first, Wade. Are you a serial liar? I need to know that because over the past few weeks I'm not quite sure who I married."

He untied his tie and started over again, evening out the ends with great concentration, obviously trying hard to craft an appropriate response.

"Well, I'm not. You know that," he said to his reflection in the mirror, and not to me.

"Wade, you can't even look at me when you say that? I don't even feel like you are my friend anymore, let alone my partner. What the hell?" How was I to cajole him into coming clean?

He put his head down and ripped his tie out of his collar in defeat. He then walked over to me and wrapped the tie around my back and pulled me toward his body. I didn't know if this was going to be one of the last times we hugged or whether we could somehow dig ourselves out of the thick, horrible slog we were now in. "Life gets messy, Allie. I'm sorry. I'm feeling very uncentered in this new world we live in. I'm feeling like I'm about to lose everything . . . my livelihood, my magazine that just doesn't translate well online; my whole industry is changing in a way I don't see I can survive. It's affecting me at home. I know, it's rubbing off on us and the way I treat you. But I've got a gas tank at zero tonight. I can barely get it up for about a hundred people, many of them advertising clients about to cancel their ads in the magazine. So if we are going to make a living and pay for the children and the home, I think our main priority now is covering our bills and our asses in this economy, not focusing on an unimportant, meaningless . . ."

"Meaningless to you, Wade!"

He said softly, "I didn't mean to you, I meant to me. Absolutely meaningless."

"Wade, first of all, what does an ad recession have to do with other women? I can't trust you if you are sleeping around and doing shit at work I don't understand and . . ."

"I . . . can't do this right now. Allie, I just can't. I'm sorry if I'm not being a good friend or lover or husband, but I'm cracking on the job front and I need you by my side, and you need to be by my side tonight for the kids' sake."

He may have been doing a master manipulation job on me

just then, but he was also desperate in a way I'd never seen since I met the great Sun King. I closed my eyes, relented, and prepared to do what my husband needed that night. So thrilled to be a member of the sisterhood branch that carries the softy disease. It's the way most caretaking women are, even though they deserve better.

"Come stand with me and help me focus on the clients and ad execs about to barge through our doors. You have no idea of the tension I'm dealing with on that front." He threw the tie on the ground and smudged a nick off his vintage Gucci loafers he'd just bought off eBay and headed out of the room into the party he'd organized for Svetlana, his favorite Russian supermodel with zero talent.

Before I acted the happy hostess, I sat on the bed and contemplated my options. Should I try to get him to fess up to everything and work on our marriage? Was this the absolute worst rough spot and would we get through it for the sake of Blake and Lucy? I didn't honestly feel I could. I didn't see how I could live with a man I didn't believe.

Regardless of whether I was *possibly maybe* leaving him, I wanted to come up with a version of Wade's actions that I could stomach. (I had willingly married the guy without a gun to my head as I remember.) So I told myself this rather far-fetched story line: maybe the clueless Wade was so used to drawing people toward him like bugs to a porch light that he didn't understand the one time he was being played.

Wade had gotten in over his head with Murray and Max as a way to compensate for his impotency in the Internet age. It couldn't have been easy this past decade to be dethroned by a bunch of Silicon Valley youngsters who turned his glossy pages into yesterday's news. Maybe the tips Wade gave reporters were valid somehow, or maybe Murray and Max didn't clue him in entirely, and maybe Wade didn't fully understand they were all profiting from false media rumors he was actively planting.

Yes, he had had a "thing" with Jackie, but perhaps there was a chance I could look at it as a onetime middle-age crisis and not a long-term coping mechanism he would surely repeat. (Only problem with that pathetic rationalization was that this was the second time, at the least the second time I knew about.)

Wade walked back down the hall to get his speech out of his bag as if everything was just normal between us. "And you remember the *Meter* people I have coming, from the book and magazine division?"

"I can't remember every face. I try," I answered as I yanked the small buckle closed on my high-heeled sandal with more than a hint of anger. "But they change jobs often, especially with the advertising recession, and of course they're all sucking up to the boss's wife, so they know me, and . . ." I couldn't shake this feeling of dread.

"Regardless of our issues, please remember Svet's people. It's all I ask."

I sighed and walked down the hall three strides behind Wade, mashing earring posts into holes that I couldn't somehow locate. "Okay, I'll go over her list," I promised. "It's her producer, PR lady . . ."

"Yes, all them. But Max is the most crucial guest we have."

Wade looked unusually stressed, like all this posturing and posing wasn't at all easy for him anymore. I flashed back to how Wade had sucked up to Max Rowland at the Sudan premiere and remembered that he had ditched his own children to play golf with him. "Max's happiness here is most important, I assure you."

I leveled my gaze. "Yeah. I know Max. He's the criminal who just got out of prison who may be on his way back in."

"Yes. Yes. Of course," Wade said distractedly, not hearing me, as he sped toward the front door to welcome the first arrivals with a breathy, "Oh, thank *God* you're here and the festivities can begin."

TWENTY MINUTES LATER, young Internet entrepreneurs in sweatshirt hoodies and bohemian indie movie executives littered my living room. Instead of diving into the party, I sipped a vodka tonic and studied the tactics of the next generation from the windowsill: beautiful and self-important women and men hoping to cozy up to one of the great accomplishers in the room.

There was Delsie Arceneaux with her sexy news anchor glasses, chatting up Wade at the bar. As I watched, she went up on tiptoe to whisper in his ear. I studied the look that passed between them. Was it a "we're in cahoots" look? A "we're fucking too" look? I couldn't quite tell. Maybe there's no difference when the wife is left out. My humiliation was boiling again. I closed my eyes and willed myself to cast aside that *why me?* feeling stewing inside.

In the corner, on a zebra ottoman, a Somali artist named

Maleki, another one of those women without a last name, was sitting with her benefactor, Murray, who had cornered the market in her work by buying up every piece he could. Wade had feted her the previous month with a six-page profile, coining her as the art world's new "It" girl. I watched Murray talking to the very dramatic Maleki, both of them clearly using each other for their own gain: she needed his cash flow, and he needed her black cool. I studied her exotic look: her stretched-out dancer's neck, Cleopatra-esque eyes heavily lined, and her thick mane slicked back halfway along the top of her head, then fanning out fabulous and wild behind her gold-beaded headband. Murray kept inching closer to her, gazing into her eyes, almost in her lap now like a child bewitched by Santa.

Thing is, women often read their office husbands better than they read their own. As I observed Maleki looking at her benefactor like she was preparing to screw him from here to kingdom come, I saw the dots suddenly connect. That wasn't Murray's *please blow me on my plane* happy face, it was Murray's *I'm getting cash out of this* happy face. After ten years watching him interact with thousands of females, I knew the difference.

I thought about that: she the artist, he the PR wizard spinning her story all over Manhattan while he secretly owned most of her work and had gotten it at cut-rate prices. The man who'd gotten rich people to buy over two dozen of her confounding paintings when she was a virtual nobody. Maleki's paintings in turn sold at Art Basel Miami Beach the next year for close to a million dollars apiece. At least. Wealthy art ignoramuses put her bold, graffiti-filled canvases in their living rooms alongside their emerald-green Scalamandré silk curtains to pretend how edgy they are underneath all that pomp.

In a global economic downturn and magazine recession, my husband had spent thousands of *Meter* dollars to send a reporter and photographic team to Somalia for her fashion spread that appeared inside the magazine—rarely did he ever spend that on a cover. Was that Somalia shoot being used to boost Maleki's public profile for Murray's financial benefit?

If I remembered correctly, Delsie Arceneaux had graced that cover, propped up on her elbows on an army tank in a Tweetie-Pie yellow jacket that made her dark skin glow like butter. I turned back to the artist, who was hand-feeding Murray a cheese puff. I'd thought Murray was a visionary for finding her, and it was lucky that my husband was promoting her. Now I'd call Maleki's rise deliberate and purposeful and preplanned and well executed, and nothing to do with luck. They were manufacturing her rising star for their bottom lines—buying up her art, then manipulating the press to make her look like the next Damien Hirst. Perhaps they were having sex with her too, but at this point in the shit show that my life had become, that seemed secondary.

And then I thought this: *I'm an outright idiot.* I didn't need Jackie to sew these fragments together; they were lined up clear as day on my stolen-from-a-photo-shoot zebra ottoman. This was the kind of link Jackie meant. Wade puts stuff out there and Murray cashes in with his or Max's funds, and then funnels money back to Wade. It was so simple. Wade was able to engineer the press in favor of this artist to economically benefit Murray.

At least I'd found the game, independently and without Jackie's help, and a link between them that made sense. I thought about Max, about the sudden introduction of his possible SUV henchmen into my life, and I started to worry that we were in actual danger. What kind of money were they taking from Max, if this game was all real? And if there was another big scheme on the way, as Jackie had warned when she studied the contents of that envelope, what kind of trouble were we all in?

I spied Svetlana, standing next to a businessman who looked like he'd just cornered the world's gold market. Determined to figure out her role in this high-stakes game, I pretended to check the booze levels while I eavesdropped. Call me paranoid, but suddenly everyone in the room was casting an ominous shadow over my life and future.

"Tell me about your vork," Svetlana asked Mr. Hedge Fund, obviously a pro at seducing rich men. I didn't know his name, but I knew he was loaded, one of those "2 and 20" guys who took home 2 percent of his five-billion-dollar fund whether he performed or not, then 20 percent of the profits if he did.

"Forget my job, let's discuss you," Mr. Hedge Fund said to Svetlana. "Let me give you some advice: Sundance. It's much bigger than the Fulton Film Festival. You should really consider that next year."

Screw him and the amount of food and drink he was consuming from my home while insulting ten years of PR work I'd done to put the festival on the map!

He continued, "You know, I'd be happy to take you and some girlfriends out to Utah next year on my plane; it's very comfortable. The man who designed my apartment also did the interior of the plane, so it's very cozy. I could definitely introduce you to the right people." I saw him brush his elbow across her right breast as he reached for a handful of nuts. She chuckled and pushed him away, and he looked me over, discerning quickly that I wasn't hot enough for him—as he asked the bartender for two more shots of tequila.

While his back was turned, Svetlana made a beeline for the powder room. Mr. Hedge Funder turned with his drinks. "So, really, I'm serious, you should come to Sundance . . ." Only to find his Russian beauty was gone.

Murray's M-E-R-I-T-O-C-R-A-C-Y speech during our lunch at the Tudor Room—*it's not about the money in this room*—echoed through my head. This douche bag could be loaded to the gills, but he'd never get a table in the Tudor Room, because this guy wasn't a player. Even Svetlana figured that out within five sentences and one cheap feel-up.

The gathering quickly turned into a crowded party, and I pushed through several groupings to look for Max, nowhere to be found. Out the window, I saw that same black SUV idling outside, and I wondered if that was Max's car, why wasn't he up here yet?

Someone from the *Meter* staff dropped a glass on the wooden floor next to the bar. As I knelt down to help pick up the pieces, I noticed the most outrageously sexy pair of shoes I'd ever seen:

strappy green ostrich on the top and what looked like real feathers dipped in gold on the heels. I reached over to touch the heel to see if the feathers were actually fluffy or if it was somehow a design illusion. On my knees, with my bottom in the air, I then looked up to the most toned, moisturized racehorse legs in the history of womankind. Jackie smiled down at me and nodded.

I whispered to her, "Did Wade invite you?"

"Nope, I came with a hedge-fund asshole."

"I think I know the one."

"Yeah, well, I wanted to warn you in person," she answered, "that something bad went down today with a stock called Novolon. Just found that out. And your husband's in deep shit." Then she slipped away into the crowd.

Clink clink. "Svetlana, a toast for you." That very husband was busy getting everyone together, oblivious.

The bleached-out Svetlana strode up to Wade, parting the crowd as she did so, with her stick-pin legs, bouncy little breasts, and straight ponytail pulled so painfully tight off her forehead that her eyebrows looked stretched back like a face-lift gone haywire. Her corn-silk hair brushed the top of her hips as she stepped like a giraffe up to my beyond-horny husband. He reached his arm around her impossibly small waist, cinched even tighter in her rose-petal-pink chiffon minidress: long sleeves, no cleavage, giving the illusion of conservative, but with a pornographically short skirt that barely dusted the bottom of her butt cheeks.

"I've come up with a little top ten list of pitfalls for

Svetlana to avoid as she roars up the path to Hollywood superstardom." Wade snapped his fingers twice in the air. "Come here, beautiful." Then, with a studied pause, he corrected himself, "*Belle*."

Oh God, spare me, was he doing her too? My imagination went straight to the most insane positions he could fold her into. I stared at her tight waist and cursed the muffin top pinching the back of my pants. Was it purely physical with these women? Or did he love them? Did he love them so much more than the proverbial "us"? This was not the "family" I had referred to when I thought I'd keep us together for Lucy and Blake's sake. No one should make herself stay for this.

Despite my dour mood, there was a festive, upbeat vibe in the room in part because Wade had invited lots of young *Meter* staffers to fill the place at the last minute, and a few less dreary Masters of the Universe like Mr. Hedge Fund.

All that cheer dampened rather quickly when Max Rowland suddenly stormed in the front door like a raging bull with a freshly branded ass.

Murray left his gorgeous Somali cash machine by the wayside and waddled up to the front hall and tried to stop the huge Texan, with his arms spread out front, grounding himself with his not insignificant weight, his heels digging divots into my wood floor.

"Max. Please. You know we couldn't have fuckin' predicted . . ."

Jackie parted the crowd and mouthed to me, *I told you so.*

I said a silent prayer to myself in gratitude at this point that my children were chomping on their fourth package of

Starbursts at Aunt Alice's and not here to witness this madness.

Two bodyguards in black suits chest-bumped Murray, who flew out of Max's way like a huge airborne beanbag chair with legs, smashing the silver-leaf legs off the zebra ottoman into bits beneath him.

Wade reached into his pocket for his toast, thinking he was the cleverest soul ever to stalk the planet, and started in on his Letterman Top Ten List. "Number Ten: How does a foreign ingénue with talent like this . . ."

Wade had no idea that at this point in his toast, Max Rowland, on the other side of the ring, was on the warpath, and moving rapidly in his direction.

"Number Nine: When a Catherine Deneuve look-alike . . ."

"Wade! Stop!" I screamed.

Wade then grabbed Svetlana's bony hip even tighter.

Finally, Max, taking a cue from dustups in the prison yard, made it to the front of the pack of Svetlana's well-wishers and Wade's pliant sycophants. As he breached the final row of revelers—champagne flutes and vodka tumblers in hand—Max stretched his arms out to part the crowd, some of whom tumbled back onto each other like drunken human dominoes.

Wade threw his arms in the air, as if a dozen gangsters had rifles pointed at his chest. "Max! Wait! I can explain everything!"

Max had no time or patience for East Coast, city-boy pansies. He grabbed Wade by the silken green paisley tie and through clenched teeth said, "How does one person fuhuhck everythin' up at once?"

Wade shook his head back and forth. "I, I had nothing to do with . . ."

Before Wade could finish his sentence, Max threw a hard right hook across his left cheek, and two of my husband's teeth went flying in a perfect ten-foot arch across our green lacquered alcove.

26

How to Keep It Clean Now?

"If there is an element of surprise in your plot, a dramatic shift," Professor Heller explained, "then you need to make sure you're holding your audience's hand properly. On the other hand, it's exciting to peek into the dark unknown. Just make sure the unknown is a place you the writer understand. If you're going to write, you have to love."

I shot Tommy a look and whispered, "This should be good."

"You have to fall on your face, swim against the tide, make terrible mistakes, and pay the price; you have to tune in, turn on, drop out, drop back in, fight, cry, lose, win."

I hit my head with the eraser end of my pencil and tried hard to focus on something other than the Texas craziness that had gone on in my living room.

"Above all, don't get too comfortable. Go out there and get your heart broken. You won't be able to write until you do." My script should sell for a million bucks in that case.

I couldn't begin to follow and absorb Heller's dictums with all my worries colliding at once. To make matters worse, from under the little desk attached to my chair, Tommy started outlining the inner seam of my jeans with one of his goddamn ubiquitous Twizzlers. My nervous system was crackling with the wrong kind of energy, my skin was on fire, and I felt itchy all over. Having a real affair, with all the beautiful and the ugly elements, was just not something I could handle at this point, though another part of my body wanted it so badly I could scream.

A voice inside calmly spoke to me: *You don't need to do this. Keep it clean, make things simple in your own head, come to some resolution of the problems with your husband before you do anything—including the frauds on the business front and the frauds on the home front—and stop getting distracted by Twizzlers of all things!*

I tried to take longer breaths, but the air only made it halfway. Tommy squeezed my thigh and chuckled. He was thinking he was turning me on so much I couldn't inhale properly.

"Let's work first with Mr. Foster's script," Professor Heller said. "Then we will work on Allie Braden's scene." I scanned every line of his face for clues: My brilliant scene filled with tension and pathos? My jumbled mess of a scene?

Rather than focus on Heller's instructions, I kept trying to make sense of all the scenes going on at the cocktail party: Max's brutality, Wade's arm around Svetlana's waist, Delsie's sultry whisper a little too close to his ear, Jackie foretelling all of it, and Wade's shattered side teeth.

"Fuck, my dentist's away, and he doesn't leave a fucking replacement guy," Wade had yelled at me as he wiped blood off his cheek in our bathroom after the guests fled the party. "Who the fuck do we know?" Wade wasn't scared. He was furious, humiliation a foreign emotion to him.

He kept barking orders at me. "Call Dr. Brownstein, ask him who the fuck dentist he knows who will go into his office at nine o'clock at night."

"I'm not making any calls until you tell me what is going on with Max Rowland, with everything," I had answered calmly, my arms crossed, leaning against the doorway of our bathroom. "And I don't mean your friend Svetlana."

He blinked wildly, but ignored my third mention this month of the women in his life. But at this point, fully into Act II, Svetlana seemed like a minor plot line compared to getting his teeth punched out by a Texan parking lot magnate with the anger of a diminishing fortune fueling him.

"Wade," I demanded, "why did he hit you?" Then I decided to throw another question into the conversation to see how he squirmed. "Why was Murray all over Maleki at the party? Why was everyone all over Max Rowland at the screening? *Almost like you guys were in business with him.*"

Wade winced at the pain of talking and put a Ziploc bag full of ice tenderly against his cheek. "What are you talking about? I barely spoke to Max; it made me uncomfortable just to watch him with that former stewardess wife of his trying too hard to claim her stake back in society after the disgrace of prison. Pathetic." He pushed past me into the bedroom, searching for a clean shirt.

"I don't know." I followed him, helping to undo his tie so that he could keep the ice pack in place, and so that I could look him in the eye. "It just seemed to me at the screening that you, Max, and Murray had a lot of whispering going on." I tried that out for size and stared at his every action and reaction, looking for blinking, twitches, stuttering, but Wade was a cool player unless it came to cheating and girls. Then he blinked. But now I wasn't sure I could honestly read him at all.

Wade looked at me, not sure if I was buying any of his bullshit. His eyes went slightly buggy. "I don't even remember seeing Max at the screening, to be honest."

"You're friends with Delsie, don't deny that. You and the anchorwoman seemed awfully cozy. She was practically rubbing her breasts along your back as she whispered in your ear tonight." I stomped after him.

He turned to me. "So the fuck what."

"Well, I saw a Luxor report in your desk, odd I thought, that's what the fuck what."

"You were in my desk?"

"I needed the checkbook," I answered. "Just seems weird is all."

"We don't own any Luxor stock, Allie." He was practically running out of the room as he said that.

"You control information, that's all I'm saying. And that control might be worth a lot to someone who, say, buys and sells stocks."

"I, I . . ." He looked at me, but his face was impossible to read.

I pressed on. "What about the Somali art princess with no talent? Do we own any *stock* in her?"

"Maleki's got talent." He blinked wildly. Jesus.

"No, she doesn't."

Wade pinched the bridge of his nose as though it were about to bleed. "You're fucking nuts. You know that? Maleki was shown at the Guggenheim Museum before we got anywhere near her. Do you even know she was already in *Art in America*?"

"Yes, I'm sure you did a very nice spread on her, but this was glam you could help a friend profit from. Murray bought up all her art just before your spread came out."

"Stop complaining about a job that pays the bills. You're not exactly writing poetry these days yourself." Did splitting up mean we launched into mutually assured destruction first?

He went on, "Stop making absurd connections between things you don't comprehend." He yanked off his bloody shirt, threw it in the trash, and managed to get a T-shirt over his head without my help.

"I understand more than you know, Wade."

"Then understand this, Allie: I need a fucking dentist. I have this doctor's card somewhere who lives a block away and told me I could call him anytime. Maybe he knows a dentist nearby."

"Wade. You're being immature to assume you don't need to explain this. Max slugged you." I followed him down the hall and watched as he searched his pile of business cards. "He *assaulted* you. You know this, right?" I asked. "Are you pressing charges? Didn't that aggression violate his parole rules or something?"

"Did you see the size of his bodyguards?"

Stuck in my head through this argument: the image of Svetlana pleading with Max to stop before he delivered that blow to Wade. I watched her clutch Wade's arm as Max plowed past the guests toward him. The way she rubbed her chin up against my husband's shoulder, the way he grabbed her hip told me everything.

I asked calmly again, "You know, I'm awfully sorry to be pressing you with that ice pack up against your swollen cheek, but did you do something to offend him, maybe print some pieces somewhere he didn't like?" I tried that out for size.

"I don't do business pieces, Allie. You're so far off the mark, you . . ."

"You could have someone do a business piece with one phone call with news that could help any of your friends."

Wade looked at me stone-cold. I knew I had him. I also knew he would lie and lie and lie to wriggle out of this. He only offered this: "Max is a grizzly bear with a big brow that could headbutt itself through a brick wall. How the hell else do you think he commandeered half the country's concrete plants?"

"I know he's a bully," I answered. "Jesus, Wade, I know who he is, and unfortunately what he is capable of, but why did he hurt you? And are you in bed with that teenage blond actress Svetlana whose hip you were grabbing for dear life?"

"What are you talking about?" He pulled his coat on his shoulders. "I am not touching that girl. And she's not a teenager, she's twenty-two and a half! It's been a year and a half since she can drink in New York; she's not a child! Don't blow this girl thing out of proportion." Wade came over to me, his nose an inch from mine, and said, "Please don't ask again."

This was the moment I should have walked out the door.

"No," I countered. "I'm saying this. If you don't clue me in to whatever the hell is going on with you and the Texan mobster . . ."

"He's a businessman. He's not in the mob; for God's sake, don't you understand anything?"

"Parking lots and all that concrete to build them is not mob . . . ?"

"No. Allie. He's not the mob," Wade said with an obnoxious high-pitched tone, mocking my female voice, swinging his head to and fro. He pointed his finger at my nose. "You know why?"

I thought one thing only: *I hate this man.* "Educate me, Wade."

"Because when you own half the buildings in the country, you shit on the mob." He turned his coat collar up dramatically and walked to the door, dialing a number from a card in his hand and summoning the elevator.

"So what the hell did he mean, you 'fucked everything up'? Are you betting on stocks with him? Don't think I don't see things."

Wade looked at me like he had no idea how I could have put these pieces together. And then his entire face fell flat. All the tension and will to fight me simply bled out of his face. A long twenty seconds passed silently before he admitted, "Allie. My magazine life is vanishing before my eyes. That's my entire world. Everything. Don't ever forget that."

I grabbed my coat from the foyer. "I'm going with you. Please."

"No, you're not. I need to make some calls. You actually need to stay here." He flew out the front door. So there it was. The marriage had rolled out of the ICU with a white sheet on top and was officially flatlined.

27

Can't Climax Yet

"This class is confusing me more than it's helping," I told Tommy as we walked down the hall during the break. What with that image of my marriage on a hospital gurney moving toward the morgue, a Texan punching out my husband, and bright red Twizzlers up my thigh, I hadn't been listening to anything the professor was telling us. I was tuned in enough to hear him regaling the class with his epic, surely exaggerated stories of working with people called Marty and Francis. I couldn't possibly talk to Tommy about any of this; he always maintained, as he did the first night we met, that he didn't want to know about my husband. That meant he still didn't even know that I was married to Wade Crawford and *Meter.* Instead I kept the conversation neutral and focused on the class. "I don't know how much to follow Heller's rules and how much to ignore them."

"You'll see, everything he says will sink in; you need to have some structure within which to write," Tommy answered sympathetically. "Then you can go off and break all the rules."

"Then what's the point of taking this class, if poetic license ultimately drives what I'm going to end up with?" The inherent contradiction of screenwriting rules was getting to me. "I'm writing very well this week. Scenes are coming out of me, senses blazing like you said, and I'm putting them in some kind of order, I guess."

"Well, you're learning from my fuckups at least." He laughed a little and pinched the back of my hip as he pushed me along. "This is the cathartic year you realize you were barking up the wrong tree, because you weren't writing what you know. Now that you're writing a great, unrequited love story, filled with longing and desire like your fucked-up story with James, it's going to be a mad dash to the finish. Only remember this: killing the shark means you are going to have to figure out if they get together.

"Maybe they don't. Maybe your protagonist has this image of what she wants him to be, and she's holding on to that, but it isn't something that's real. So think about that one. Everyone does that; key is to figure out if the love is real or an illusion or an idea of something we want. Let's get you a coffee, and a little sweet treat." His grabbed my ass way too fiercely as he said that.

As we turned the corner on the second-floor landing, we saw a janitor rolling a huge rubber garbage can with mops, sprays, rags, and garbage bags hanging off his cart away from the closet where the cart was kept.

"I think you and I need some time alone to discuss your

plot." Now Tommy was kissing my neck openly against the wall just around the corner. "Oh, yeah, also add to that"—more mauling the skin on my neck—"your characters. They need work too."

"Tommy. Stop." I started rubbing the red out of my neck. "It's so bright out here. With everyone . . ."

"The two of us and a janitor is everyone?" He started up again, this time with his hand halfway up the back of my shirt.

"No, I mean it." I was laughing now as he tried to put his fingers underneath the front of my bra. "You have to be more discreet. We can't do this. Really."

"Oh, really," he replied playfully, mocking my serious tone. "I don't think so . . ."

As soon as the janitor had pushed his loaded cart into a vacant classroom, Tommy grabbed my arm tightly, pulled me into the dark cleaning closet, and wrapped his body around mine. "God, you are so sexy tonight," he said, slipping one hand down the back of my pants and one down the front in the ammonia-filled darkness.

Before he got anywhere, I yanked his arms out, but I couldn't help but smile. "Not now. Not here."

"C'mon. It'll be fun. You won't be sorry, I promise." He stopped pushing and kissed me deeply instead. I wondered about what Jackie said about the thirtysomething-and-under generation and if he'd watched a porn movie about a sexy janitor lady in a university cleaning closet.

As he got more intent on having his way, by holding my arms tight against the wall as his tongue explored every inch of my mouth, all the sexy nonsense was not working for me. Not one bit.

I was way too distracted: I was horrified about Max hitting my husband, and my marriage falling apart terrified me even more. I didn't make enough money to support anything like our current life. My mind raced to places I could move. Of course we couldn't afford our apartment and a second one. Could I rent a tiny apartment in a good enough neighborhood to ensure a good public school for the kids?

"Tommy, hold off. It's not exactly conducive to . . ."

"I think it's hot." He started at me again.

If I was going to do this for real, it had to be *out there,* not *in here* in a closet.

"What's with you?" Tommy asked. "Lemme just . . ." His tongue went at my breasts.

I couldn't enjoy his touch. *Especially now.* Wade would blow a gasket once he found out about Tommy, which would just complicate a separation agreement. I didn't need *she was having an affair* added to my family curriculum vitae.

I let out a little confused moan. None of this was working; I didn't want Wade in my head while I was trying to *not* get off with Tommy.

"Come on, baby, that's right," Tommy purred, mistaking my anguish for ardor.

I pushed him away a little. "Class is starting. C'mon. We can't do this."

"Yes, we can," he said, kissing my neck and reinserting his

hand at the top of my jeans, inching down. "I want you to go all the way. Here. Now."

I momentarily relented a few inches, but the ticktock of my insane life kept swirling in my head.

"We . . . have . . . to . . . stop . . ." It took all my strength to pull Tommy's hands up and out of my pants. Even if Wade strayed from time to time, I still felt sick about my own infidelity, which I was definitely experiencing in Technicolor now. My unconsummated affair with Tommy felt like a crime.

"I know you want this," he whispered.

Morality aside, this was ridiculous. I was not going to climax, standing up, in the dark, in a strange place at New York University, amid the smell of institutional ammonia in a dank closet.

"You're so hot," he whispered again.

I was feeling anything but.

"I'm sorry. It's the ammonia."

"We got all the time in the world, you know." Tommy finally relented. "But when you do find yourself ready, you're going to get seriously mauled."

I opened the door of the janitor closet slowly; the last thing I needed was to get caught by a student in our class. Most of them were milling around the door of our classroom down the hall.

"Tommy, let me leave; you get us coffee."

Instead he started at me again.

I pecked his forehead in the most chaste manner I could. "Let me leave first and get everyone facing the other direction, then you look down the hall and leave when it's clear, okay?"

"Yes, ma'am." His blue eyes sparkled at me as he fixed the worn-out collar of his flannel shirt and tucked the tail into his jeans. He was combing down his ruffled-up hair as I snuck out of the closet.

"DRIVE FAST, BUT safely," I whispered to Tommy on the way uptown from class.

He parked the motorcycle outside a Walgreens pharmacy on Twenty-Seventh Street and Tenth Avenue, four blocks north of my apartment. I would walk the rest of the way. There wasn't much chance anyone I knew would see me in west Chelsea after the dinner hour, but I still wanted to play it safe.

"See you tomorrow?" I asked. We'd planned to spend some time on his script. The bright fluorescent lights from the drugstore were shining in my eyes and killing the nonexistent romance.

He looked up at the skyscrapers lighting the city sky. "I have a busy week. We might have to wait until the next class."

The next class was simply too far away. Before this, I hadn't wanted Tommy touching me. Now all my mental and physical desire seesawed in his direction, like a turbocharged bipolar mood swing.

"You sure?" I pleaded. "You helped me so much with my script. I owe you."

"Yeah. Positive." It was clearly no big deal to him not to see me until class. He slammed his foot down on the pavement, braced the kickstand, and flipped his visor up. It was almost a challenge. His body was saying, *You gotta problem with that?*

Yes, as a matter of fact, I did. First he couldn't get enough of me fast enough and now he wasn't even interested? I know he was pissed that I wouldn't close the deal but maybe just some people are more okay with cheating and some aren't. I felt he should be patient with me.

"You sure you're sure?" I teased, with a note of desperation. He understood me so well; he was so intimate with my past and stories, and he should just know I couldn't rush into things but I needed him.

Rationality was not ruling my emotions here. It didn't make sense to me he was backing off only because I selfishly didn't want him to back off. I, like Wade, was close to zero fuel, and in no position to fully understand where and how Tommy had hit his limit with my rejections. "I could really help with your script, and we can talk things through, about everything . . ."

"I get it. I got it loud and clear. And I'm not ready for script help."

This man had spent so much energy pulling me into him. Now he was definitely pulling away. I could feel my eyes burn, but I wouldn't let him know that or see any tears. "But you've helped me so much. Listen to what the class said, and so much of it is thanks to you. They really like it, and Heller told me to keep going on the same track," I said. "Like we planned, I just want to pay you back and focus on your script this time. Can't we just . . ."

My heart ached as if Tommy were the love of my life and I'd just this very instant lost him—neither of which was remotely true. However, a woman in a failing marriage who is hanging on to the idea of some secondary guy, and what he will do to save her, feels crazy enough to flail herself all over the nearest train tracks Anna Karenina style. Believe me, I know. That's exactly where I was that night.

"Jesus, Allie. Chill. I've got so much work to do, on my own. That's all." Usually he joked about how much he wanted to steal time with me. No way was I waiting a full week for more of this. Right then and there, in front of the Chelsea Walgreens at ten minutes past ten, I realized the fulcrum of this relationship had tipped into unbalanced territory. He looked down the avenue. "I'll text you."

Which only meant one goddamn thing: I was going to put myself in a position to get hurt. Love junkie reporting for duty.

28

Simmering Situations

For my presence under the bright lights of the Tudor Room the next day, I had only to blame the following: a semi-to-fully-self-destructive side rearing its ugly but exciting head. That morning, Wade had demanded we meet at the Tudor Room to discount the stories in the *New York Post*'s Page Six gossip page that Wade was badly hurt by Max's powerful fist, the headline reading TEXAN TWO-PUNCH. A *Post* reporter always hovered at the bar of the new hot place to check out who was seated where in the room and with whom.

"It must be the Tudor Room," Wade had demanded. "Because we must keep up appearances and I need to show everyone I'm just fine thank you. Why is this so important? Because I'm fucked, that's why. Totally fucked right now." I knew this lunch had nothing to do with our marriage ending or his dalliances. No budging Wade on the locale, and needless to say it was impossible to explain to him that I didn't want to bump into Tommy O'Malley organizing the wine cellar during our lunch and why that might prove awkward.

As though I were preparing for battles to be waged on every front, I'd carefully chosen some good fashion armor: a tight skirt, black suede platform pumps, a go-to lacy Tory Burch blouse with a long black cardigan cinched by a four-inch-thick belt with a silver buckle. I conjured up a little "I'm important too" attitude to get me from door to table. Walking in, I knew I looked all right, even though everything went very all wrong.

Just as I walked into the restaurant trying hard to act like I was feeling just fabulous, my phone rang. Seeing the number, I froze for a second: James. I spun around and found a small leather chair by the high windows, away from the bar, away from the lunch area, and away from the cloying maître d', Georges.

I sat down and clicked on my phone.

"Hey. How's your father? How are you?"

"I'm okay, Allie. It's just a waiting game. Definitely not a fun time. You know he and I were never close and he was such an ass to me my whole . . ."

"Don't say that now, James. I know better than anyone what a cold guy he could be, but just let's keep it neutral while he's in the hospital. It's bad karma. When can I come help? What can I do?"

"I was hoping to come into Manhattan to see you. I'm sorry I haven't called, because I'm worried about how you sounded last time we talked. Your marriage certainly sounded like it sucks."

"I'm fine." I pressed him. "Your dad's dying. This is about you, not me."

"Well, I've been seeing everyone from high school and just sitting in this depressing family area at the end of the hall for a big long waiting game."

My eyes wandered up the paned glass windows that framed the restaurant and I wondered if everyone inside felt like they were in a fishbowl. I did. It seemed wrong that I was sitting here in this pressurized New York restaurant and not sitting with James up in Massachusetts in the hospital waiting room. Georges came over to tell me that Wade's office had called and he was still in a meeting. While James talked about people who were visiting, I laid my head back against the hard, cold glass behind me, remembering the moment a dozen years ago in our early twenties when I'd told James that I'd met this editor named Wade. It was the moment I clearly made the choice to move from James, my real love, to Wade, the husband and father replacement I psychologically lusted after.

"SO, ALLIE, WHO'S the lucky big-city guy these days?" James had demanded across the beer bottles all those years back.

"Well, we've barely started anything, but he's something to contend with, put it that way."

He let out a gust of air and wiggled his eyebrows at me, telegraphing *have fun selling out,* before tipping a long draw of beer into his mouth.

"I'm not *selling out,*" I hemmed. "I'm not," I said again, in case he didn't hear me.

James shook his head and laughed. "You said that, not me. Tell me about this *guy*."

"I don't know where it's going exactly, James. He's just some editor guy. I don't know. He takes me to a lot of parties. Do we have to . . ."

James set his beer down on the table so hard that it foamed up and spilled out the top. "That's just great, Allie. I'm so happy that you found someone *important* to share your life with." He looked off toward the bar and signaled the waiter for the check.

"What is your problem?" I slapped him on the arm. "You're the one crisscrossing the globe, sleeping with God knows what. I can't even have a potential boyfriend?"

"You've always had boyfriends, Allie. Busloads of boyfriends." He looked me straight in the eye. "This one just seems . . ."

I turned my hands up, empty of excuses. "It's a whole situ-fucking-ation, if you want to know the truth." I was starting to get a little angry myself. If James wanted me as more than a friend, it was his job to express that, but it wasn't fair to belittle the life I was trying to piece together.

"You know what? Forget it, I'm only here for two days before I head overseas; it's not . . ." He had stopped talking as the waiter dropped the check.

By the time we'd left the restaurant, James had found ways to lighten the situ-fucking-ation by poking fun at my description of Wade, and it made me feel like we were simply two pals who knew each other better than anyone. Sexual tension pervaded the evening; he'd paid the bill, held my coat, and opened doors (without swinging them pranklike in my face for once in our lives) as if we were on a real date. When we were back in my exposed brick, little studio on West Eighty-Third Street, I decided to get a couple more beers. But as I reached my kitchen area, the refrain was pounding throughout my body. *If not now, when?* We had to do it again, it had been so long since that night in the Jeep. I was, after all, a grown-up now. And I was about to get serious with another man, for Christ's sake.

"Allie," James had said suddenly in a very sexual tone. "What are you doing? Come over here."

Hands firm on the side of the kitchen sink, arms rigidly holding my shaking body up, eyes closed tight, I broke into a huge smile because I didn't even need to look at him to read him. This time I really wanted it to happen and knew it would. One big problem: the fluorescent light above was so bright it was practically buzzing. We were about to make love in a room lit for surgery.

I turned and walked across the room and snapped off the light, and then back to the sink, where I began to feel my knees shaking. I bit down hard on my lower lip as I sensed James moving silently, closing the space between us until I could feel his breath on my neck.

With my eyes closed, and holding steady for fear of crumbling to the floor . . .

"Oh God," I whispered, "I swear I don't know how to make love."

"I swear you do," he said. "We already did it once, so I know you do."

"That was so long ago, it wasn't like . . ."

He just answered, "It was to me."

He pushed his body close behind me and reached around my hips, placing both his hands between my legs. With each hand on the inside he gently pulled my legs apart and grabbed onto my inner thighs as he pushed himself up against my back. I braced my hands against the sink and let my head roll to one side as he began to kiss my neck.

"Oh, no," I whispered.

His fingers were now inching down the zipper on my pants as he carefully and slowly opened the top of my jeans. I put my hands on his as he ventured farther inside, half holding him back, half guiding him along.

"Don't you dare stop me," he said into my ear and then licked it.

I arched against his chest. "I'm not, I'm just a little . . ."

"What? You don't want this?" He wet his finger and slid it down my pants, slowly outlining me.

"This is just . . ." I took a deep breath in. At least he was behind me, and I didn't have to look him in the eye. ". . . a little crazy."

"I'm about to make you a lot crazier."

Minutes later we were on the floor, and he was on his knees yanking my jeans off. I lay back feeling everything all at once: relief that we were doing this, fear that we were doing this, total excitement that we were doing this. As I listened to his exquisite moans, I knew how much I really wanted this. I'd waited so long since that time in the cold Jeep with the swirling snow illuminated outside by the parking lot lights.

The smell of sex was then weighing heavily in the air around us, with James's sweat dripping down the sides of his naked body, and the two of us rolling around in a frenzy on my dusty, hard wood, walk-up floor . . .

"ALLIE? YOU THERE?" James's voice bellowed from the phone in the corner of the Tudor Room. "Did you hear what I said about running into Neal and Charlie?"

"I did. So weird." I hadn't focused on one word, I was so lost in that moment years before on my sweat-drenched floor and why I hadn't taken that path. *Fuck. Why hadn't I taken that path? Why was I so impatient to get married with James off and gone just after we did make love for real?* I quickly asked, "Can I come up for a day to sit in the waiting room with you? Would that be helpful?"

"Not right now, especially since Clementine couldn't come. That just wouldn't . . ."

Clementine wasn't with him so I wondered why an old friend couldn't support an old friend. "James. Why the hell can't I be there? It's me talking. I'm just trying to be there for you and . . ." *And maybe rekindle something in your hour of need . . .*

"No, it's too much here. I'm so happy to talk to you and focus on how you are. But with my family here, I just want to focus on them, so it will just frustrate me . . . Anyway, Allie, I gotta go. Just checking in." And he hung up.

ONCE HE SAW me over on the chair behind his podium, Georges the maître d' threw his arms in the air as if I were the Queen of

Sheba. "Oh, Mrs. Crawford, you look divine." He ran over to me and pulled me up. "Why your husband would keep a woman like you waiting is beyond explanation." He glanced at his table chart on the lit lectern he presided over. "Let's see, with this beautiful woman here, that changes things . . ." He tapped his pen on his forehead. It took me a minute to focus as I was reeling a bit from the James call and the choices I made that maybe weren't the right ones.

"Georges." I read the table chart upside down. "Changes things how? Are you giving Wade a nicer table because his wife is here or a less important table because he's not dining with a CEO?"

"Are you kidding? You come here and I arrange the room around *you*."

This guy was such a pretentious, disingenuous fool—acting like I was so important when he had enabled Wade's affair with Jackie, I assumed, among others. At the corner banquette, a B/B+ table, Murray swiveled his head and spotted his prey.

"Allie!" he barked. "I've been meaning to call you all morning."

"What's up, boss?" I said as I scanned the room. No Tommy.

"Svetlana. You know her."

I thought about my husband's hand way too intimately grabbing her hip bone. "Yes, I know Svetlana."

"Well, there's a problem," Murray said.

I thought about my husband's two teeth flying across my living room.

"You know what, Murray? I sensed there was a problem. Call me a genius but . . ."

"We need to do something with her film; the preopening reviews are just going to kill her and sink her. It makes the festival look lame when such a high-profile model tanks. We need to showcase it a little more."

"But, Murray, her film sucks. We are all about *quality not glitz,* remember you saying that?"

"Yeah, yeah, whatever." He didn't give a hoot that I'd nailed him. "Showcase the girl. Okay? Ask Delsie Arceneaux's people to do it on CNBB? It'll make a long list of things move a lot smoother. I promise you. I don't need Max Rowland breathing fire up my asshole."

"I think we just witnessed in my living room that that isn't a safe idea."

Murray focused his gaze across the room in Delsie's direction. She was wearing a springtime violet Valentino jacket with a see-through blouse underneath, having an extremely intense conversation with the secretary general of the UN and, from what I could see, about to crawl on the table on all fours.

As I stood up to leave, Murray motioned for me to sit down again. "And do me a favor, between us."

"What, Murray?"

"Stop asking your husband all those questions about Max Rowland. It's no good for you. Just stay out of it."

He whisked me off with a flick of his hand. Well, that was revealing: one more dot to connect. He and Wade were talking about the fact that I was asking difficult questions. I was a party to these jerks getting their way for long enough. With Wade now twenty minutes late, I perused the room and stewed over the fact that the Vulgarians in this place made their cash on the backs of actual workers like me. And with a salary ratio of a million to one. A simmering rage began to work its way up the back of my neck as I walked away from Murray.

Now Max Rowland, at the regular table next to mine, was right back in the thick of questionable activity, lecturing some rapt investors with a little Texas twang. "If y'all consider how energy intensive your businesses are, you should really be hedgin' more. I have close relationships with people close to the leader of Kazakhstan and I could give you some very confidential information on that pipeline." Recidivism rates probably aren't recorded for the likes of Max, but they say it's common for all criminals to return to a life of crime.

And then . . . stage left, two swans entered where before there was only one. Jackie Malone slinked in behind the bar so no one could see her with an equally statuesque redhead. It was the first time I'd ever seen her with another woman. A couture-decked twentysomething was one thing. But two of them? Since when do mistresses hang out together? Or maybe this new girl was just a friend in town for the week and Jackie brought her by to show off her power haunt? And yet . . . it was rare to see anyone their age at the Tudor Room.

Jackie's friend was wildly sexual beneath her deceivingly prim outfit. She had straight red hair in a perfect shoulder-length cut, slightly longer in the front. She was wearing a tight, smoky gray linen dress that I guessed was Dolce & Gabbana from the bold silver zipper going down her back.

Jackie stared right at me, clearly wanting to ask me something. She pointed her finger to the seat next to mine, asking if I was expecting Wade.

I shrugged, indicating I had no idea where he was. Then she motioned for me to meet her down the wine hall. Great. Bump into Tommy with Jackie.

She walked past and winked in my direction as she moved toward the ladies' room. I followed her, leaving my cardigan on the banquette so Wade would know I'd arrived.

I walked down a long corridor lined with locked glass doors with small spotlights showcasing wines from every major wine region. Dangerous images of Tommy groping me in closets and elevators, groping me down romantic wine hallways, started to make me feel sick. I began running down the hallway to the ladies' room.

"In here. Hurry!" Jackie whispered.

The upstairs restrooms at the Tudor Room were more like small chic ebony drawing rooms. Every twelve inches, white tulips in crystal vases punctuated a glass shelf that lined the perimeter of the room. A woman, silent, but privy to New York's greatest secrets, obsessively wiped clean every surface and folded and refolded the stiff linen hand towels stitched with a discreet brown T.R. in the corner.

"We need to talk!" Jackie again whispered loudly from one of the toilets. There were no actual stalls at the Tudor Room, but rather four separate little rooms with shiny black lacquer sinks.

The attendant busied herself with slightly more frenzied wiping of already pristine counters.

"We can sit out . . ." I offered.

"Nope. In here. I know why Max punched your husband." She yanked me into her little room and shut the door. "Max was right. And you were right. Wade doesn't know what the hell he's doing, and he *definitely* fucked everything up with the media spin on that Novolon stock. They bet everything on that going up. Wade tried to boost the rumors of Novolon's superior technology by planting some puff piece articles and getting Delsie to sing Novolon's praises on her business stock show. But then the story just didn't hold."

"He can't control every opinion out there, there must have been naysayers," I added.

"Yes!" she whispered. "He's not the Wizard of Oz that he thinks he is. He played his hand too big with these guys and Max bet huge on Novolon going up and it didn't. Everything I told you is true. Now that you know everything, please recognize we are in this together. That flash drive will be our best proof of their hiding profits and shifting cash overseas. It has the account numbers of where Max Rowland is stashing the money. We will have no way of knowing if it's Liechtenstein or Switzerland if we don't have banks and account numbers for their shell companies."

"What the hell do you mean, 'we'?"

"I mean me."

"Well, I don't want to get my husband in trouble; we are still a family. But I do want to know all this; how do I know you won't do something to hurt him?"

She grabbed the sides of my arms. "They want Murray and Max. I promise you. Wade is a two-bit player. The flash drive will be the linchpin and you've got to get it to me."

"Who is *they*?"

"Just trust me. Get me the flash drive."

29

Please Don't Let This Happen

"So sorry; I got a little caught up." Wade rushed over to my table. He struggled across to his side of the banquette.

"You're thirty-five minutes late," I said, wanting him on the defensive. "Do you keep anyone waiting this long as a regular practice? I hope not."

He ordered his usual Red Zinger iced tea and checked out the room—his eyes fluttering ever so slightly as they passed the bar area with Jackie and her new friend by her side—before he focused on me. And then he focused on himself. "I'm so sorry. I've got to say hello to Maude Pauley."

Before I knew it, Wade was actually inching out of our booth in order to table-hop and say something oh-so-fascinating to the aging female CEO of a cosmetics behemoth she'd created from a door-to-door business almost fifty years ago. He glad-handed his way past Murray's booth, whispered something, at which they both laughed heartily.

Was it a show for the room or had they recovered from Max's shock and awe? More likely, the former. Now every single person in the restaurant seemed to be acting shady, taking down the country and possibly me in the process.

"Now," Wade said, scooting back into the booth, holding my hand and lowering his voice. "Allie, I've been short with you, and I apologize for that, but it all has to do with the same thing." He clasped his hands carefully for full effect.

"It's the financials at *Meter,* Allie," he said, sighing at my rolling eyes. "We're on the brink of implosion." He looked around to see if anyone might be within earshot and dropped his voice even lower while smiling his Wade Crawford signature grin. The effect was creepy.

"The financials are far worse than my projections, and I may have gotten myself in a real shit storm at work over this. There are those who want me out, but I won't allow that to happen."

I matched my smile to his, but nothing about this conversation was making me happy. "What are you going to do? And I need to know what this has to do with Max Rowland."

"He's part of a longer story. Let me stick with *Meter.*"

"Wade." I put my hand on his arm. "An angry Texan who may wear a suit but who just got out of prison is a little more important than your magazine, especially an angry Texan who knocks your teeth out. You can always find another job if they fire you."

"Find another job? *Meter* isn't just a *job,* Allie; it's something I created twenty years ago—it's my entire career. It was nothing before I got my hands on it. But I don't really expect you to ever understand that I'm, in turn, nothing without it. *Nothing.*" He looked genuinely pained by the thought. "I've already taken steps to ensure that we'll survive this lingering advertising recession."

"What steps?" Finally, there was a glimmer of the old Wade, making plans to keep our family safe. I gave him one last shred of a chance to convince me.

"We had to eviscerate the ad rate base, for starters. I can't even say the figure out loud. Let's just say it's less than a Whopper with Cheese."

"Oh," I said, and sat back in the booth with my hands folded in my lap. His "we" was different from *my* "we."

He squinted at me, as if he was about to tell me that he'd successfully laundered millions of dollars through the Caymans. "I wanted you to hear before the press jumps on it."

"How thoughtful." I returned his squint.

"What on God's earth is wrong with you?" He was livid. "We are in *deep shit*. This up-and-down economy has me by the balls. It was supposed to smooth out by now, damnit, but instead it's far worse than I could have projected." He took a bite of bread and grabbed his left cheek where Max had punched him. Putting a napkin over his mouth, he then mashed his new tooth caps back into place. "Damnit, my smile is forever ruined by that dickhead." He spoke softer so no one could hear. "And taking *Meter* online only is not an option. I want to touch and feel the print version. Many of our readers still want those glossy photos in their hands."

"I know how you feel." I tried to sound sympathetic. "Our

donations are also way down for some of the charities we're working with pro bono. No one wants to pay for important films that help people when—"

"We're talking about *Meter* here, not your little film projects."

"My what?"

"Come on, stop being so sensitive." He used a napkin to dab at his slightly sweaty brow. "What you are missing is that with *Meter* I am talking *millions and millions* of dollars *out the window* for a major company. All under *my* watch. They're going to say I ran this thing into the ground."

"Is this really the only problem right now? Isn't there much more to the story?"

"Yes, there is," he answered. "There is more to the story. But I have a plan, and I need you by my side. If I can get *Meter* out from under its corporate ownership and run it independently, I can get past this problem. I may have some outside investors who will buy the thing and let me run it. I just can't let it get out how far under we are."

He sat back and gave a little wave to someone across the room as my heart sank right into my knees. I wasn't just married to a philanderer; I was married to a gambler. "We have to be a united front. If it gets out how bad things are, we're going to have to do everything we can to contain it. I talked to Max Rowland's CFO and got some ideas about pushing our costs like printing and postal to a later quarter and advancing our ad revenue to dress up our financial picture. It might get us past the investors' smell test."

"And then what, Wade? You get Max's teams to invest in something absurd and they bust your kneecaps the next time they don't make the money you promised? Or you promise him you can fix things in the media for his benefit?"

He looked at me like he was trying to decipher how globally I was talking and how much I knew. "You mean, then what what? I'll still have complete control over the *Meter* brand."

"That's not what I mean. What kind of shady business do you have going on with Max? Whatever you are doing with him is worse than *Meter* failing. More dangerous, I mean."

Wade looked up and grinned as Georges approached. "Today we are offering a beautiful piece of Chilean sea bass in a green tomato coulis with caramelized leeks and baby purple fingerlings drizzled with a miso acai glaze."

Wade tapped his fingers nervously on the table, waiting for Georges's litany of choices to end while I stared at the small, tight bouquet of white flowers in the silver vase until it got blurry. "We have a lovely roast loin of lamb with mascarpone polenta topped with light strands of frizzled chanterelles and a medley of summer vegetables . . ."

I hated to think just what kind of stupid idea Wade was about to execute and with whom. I knew he would never admit it to me now, and he'd never even care to explain why Max punched him out. One thing I knew for certain: I no longer could afford to delay my decision making. If he went down, he would certainly take Blake, Lucy, and me with him.

I watched Wade wave to people and check his e-mails on his phone ferociously, oblivious to every thought going on in my head and every feeling pounding in my heart. Life is so hard to wrestle down: we think we're making the best decisions and then a confluence of events takes place and we don't know whether we made the wrong decision or stuff happened out of our control that turned "good" decisions into "bad" ones.

Growing up, from that time on the lake that late summer day, through the plane crash to my twenties, I thought James and I would end up together. How could we not? Through that billowing snow when the rescue workers pulled him out and he gripped my hand on the tarmac later, I never thought on any level we'd let go. And then something just happened. Life flung him overseas just as I wanted to set my feet on the ground. I wanted stability. I wanted kids. I wanted to be with someone who would replace all I'd lost.

When I was twenty-five, I'd thought this man beside me would give me the life that was taken from me, that he would replace my father's electric sparkle that had been so violently extinguished in the crash. James wasn't that person, but he was my best friend and soul mate. How would life have turned out if I'd married my soul mate rather than the New York thrill ride next to me? Probably easier, more settled; I'd have felt more secure, more loved, sure of myself. If that's what I wanted and needed, why did I push that away and replace it with this Wade who was such a struggle to pin down?

Looking at Wade now, trying to sharpen my understanding of him, trying to remember how fun he was, how good with the kids—trying desperately to salvage those feelings I had and to justify the life path I chose—I couldn't help but remain in shock he wasn't looking at me just now. *He didn't get it.* Was that electric sparkle ever once in our marriage focused on *me* the way I needed?

Or was he another New York media type in this room: a man fueled by a toxic combination of self-aggrandizement and self-loathing?

"So, Madame Crawford, let's start with you," Georges said, ever the loyal servant, while bossing his patrons around. "You'll break my heart if you don't try the sea bass."

"As you wish." I couldn't bear an argument.

"Excellent choice. And you, Mr. Crawford?"

My eyes wandered around the room while Wade teased Georges about his ridiculously high margins. "Don't rob me with your usual prices because I want a baked potato with onions and broccoli on top. Enough of your fancy-ass food. I'm not in the mood today."

Georges said, "We'll give you our version of onions and melted cheese: caramelized shallots with some mascarpone. I've got an idea for that mascarpone. I'm going to serve you the best glass of wine we have open. Free. That should harm my margins more than a measly potato! I'll fetch Mr. O'Malley, the real wine expert around here. He's always got great ideas of pairings that . . ."

"That's okay," I said, clutching Georges's arm. "We don't need wine. Just an iced tea for me, please."

"Allie, don't be rude," Wade scolded. "Thank you, Georges, we would love to talk to him."

"Very well, Mr. Crawford," Georges said as he moved my hand from his arm and strode off to the next table. I started the

Lamaze breathing that I'd learned, but never used, during childbirth. It didn't work this time either.

Wade smiled at me and said through his gritted teeth, "Look, as I was saying, when we get through this period and I'm firmly in charge of *Meter,* it's very important we appear united. Once the magazine is on a steady path, I want to really talk about us, and how we find a way forward—even if that means, well . . ."

"I'm not sure I do know, Wade." I wondered if he'd say the word *split,* but at that moment I spied Tommy halfway across the room, which seemed like a far larger problem just then.

My entire torso became as damp as my palms already were. I decided to quickly scoot out to the ladies' room before Tommy could reach our table. In doing so, I jerked the table and knocked my water glass onto the banquette. With no other recourse but to hide in plain sight, I let my hair fall over my face as I pretended to wipe up the liquid beading on the velvet bench with my napkin, prompting Tommy to come to my aid.

This was not happening, I told myself.

"Allie, for God's sake. Let Tommy handle the mess; it's only water."

Wade knew his name? What kind of crazy three-way did we have going on here?

I persisted in my charade, pulling all my hair over the top of my head on the left side to obstruct my face. There are a lot of Allies in the world. Leaning lower, my head was now in a position that looked like I was delivering oral sex.

"May I take that from you?" Tommy asked, reaching his hand into the space between Wade and me. I surrendered, shook my head, and looked him straight in the eye.

Tommy narrowed his eyes at me in an obvious and deliberate fashion, but he didn't flinch. I couldn't tell if he was embarrassed to be helping me and putting on a brave, tough face, or so surprised he didn't know how to feel.

"May I recommend a wine, *Madame,*" he said, leveling his gaze right on me.

"I, um, don't think I drink in the middle of the day," was all I could muster.

"Well, then, Mr. Crawford, would you care for a glass of red or white? I believe Georges wanted . . ."

"Tom," Wade answered. "I'll have what we had when we brought the Estée Lauder people here last week, the one, you remember, with the light, I think you said, cranberry and licorice mélange of some kind?"

"The 1996 Domaine Armand Rousseau Chambertin?"

"Yes, just the thing. And just one glass; my wife will stick with her iced tea. Thanks."

"Your wife?" Now Tommy turned slightly ashen, his tough-guy veneer crumbling. "I, uh, hadn't . . ."

"Ah, I guess you never met her. Allie Crawford, Tommy O'Malley."

"Allie *Crawford.* Never met *your wife* before."

"I'm Allie Braden," I offered, like a token of peace. "I, uh, use Braden professionally, I uh . . ."

"Since when?" asked Wade, looking at me like I'd lost my mind.

"I do," I shot back.

"Not at your job you don't. What other profession do you have?"

"I mean, sometimes when I meet . . ." My voice just trailed off.

"So, Domaine Armand. Very well, sir." Tommy turned neatly on his heel and strode away from the table, trying hard to act unfazed. I was highly fazed.

Wade grabbed my elbow in a viselike grip. "Allie," he grin-whispered. "I don't care if you're already switching to your maiden name. I get it."

"That's not what I meant." My face was burning now. Never a mention of divorce and yet here we were, practically discussing the terms.

"I want to know every single goddamn thing about your relationship with Max Rowland."

Wade's face was glistening with the exertion of lying to me. "I have to go wash my hands." Clearly his shark-infested waters were more dangerous than even I had understood.

As Wade worked his way through the room and to the stairs, I was not one bit surprised when Jackie's friend from the bar in the tight dress slung her bag over her shoulder and sashayed down the stairs right in front of my husband. It was a good ten minutes before either of them returned.

30

Rare Moment of Maturity

I exited the Tudor Room, jacket half on, scarf trailing behind me and catching in my heels, as if I were running for my life. Wade had left a few minutes ahead of me, sexy redhead with the severe blunt cut now on his coattails. I'd thought about surreptitiously following them to their lair, but I decided that at this point in my life, I simply couldn't control who Wade was screwing or where. I ran around the corner full speed for no apparent reason, full of regret at the way I'd treated Tommy, full of angst over why I'd married Wade in the first place. I rested against a telephone pole and considered throwing up Georges's $48 sea bass into a trash can in the middle of the day in Midtown Manhattan.

Just then, Jackie tapped my arm with her forefinger. "I saw the whole thing go down. I was dying. There was nothing I could do."

"Oh, Jesus. It was awful, Jackie. I like Tommy so much, and

I swear almost nothing has gone on yet between us. I wanted to write with him, help him with his script as he's helped me with mine. I don't know, having a partner of some kind while I do work that scares me to death. He's never cared about my husband, but now I'm sure he does."

"Can I give you some advice?" she offered, her mere twenty-five years of life experience only emboldening her further. "Because it looks like you need a little."

"Yeah."

"Affairs aren't for pussies."

"What are you talking about?" I asked, amazed she'd pegged me so well.

"Believe me, I know. Remember affairs are a dark and dirty game, only for the toughest of the tough."

"But you told me to just screw anyone like you do," I reminded her.

She looked down. "I'm pretty sure you don't roll like that. I'm getting to know you a little. You get hooked and then you let them reel you in."

"I know exactly what I'm doing," I answered sternly. "It's just a screenplay thing."

That lame explanation fell flat, and she rolled her eyes at me. "C'mon, there's a false bottom underneath every affair that's designed to give way just when you think you've hit rock bottom. If you only think you can handle it, you definitely can't."

I was feeling like I'd hit rock bottom, and I hadn't even officially started the affair. I told her, "He just came over to our table out of the blue; it's not like I'm going to be destroyed. I'm not even . . ."

"Thing is, you look like you do care, a lot. Just beware." She smiled. "Affairs are like gambling is all I'm saying. You have to fold the split second you're ahead. You'll want that one more pull of the lever. One more spin of the wheel. The jackpot of all jackpot turn-ons might be just one little turn around one more little corner and your obsession will take over all the reasoning powers you have."

I was surprised by her astute advice, but Jackie was right: just when I got hooked on Tommy O'Malley with the magic tongue, the ground gave way, and all the confidence I'd artificially gained from his affections went tumbling after.

My cell phone rang.

"What the fuck, Allie *Crawford*?"

Long pause. I looked at Jackie and mouthed, *Tommy,* and pointed to the phone. She caressed my shoulder, turned, and sped back into the restaurant.

"You sound mad," I replied, trying not to sound weak or too upset. "And if you're mad, that's just not fair, and I'm not going to take any shit from you and we're done, if that's your position." I was distraught, and I didn't even remotely mean what I said. It was all false bluster on my part and hardly his fault we'd bumped into each other.

"You think I sound mad? Allie Braden? I googled you and nothing came up."

"My husband is not part of the deal, you said so yourself. We agreed never to discuss him." I paused. No answer on the other end. "I get that you're a little shocked, but if you're pissed, that's not fair. You kept details about your life from me too."

There was silence on the line. I felt uncomfortable having this conversation over the bleating of horns and screech of brakes, but there was no stopping it now.

Tommy finally answered, a controlled calm in his voice. "You told me your husband works in the magazine business. You come off like a normal woman, working at a PR firm of some kind, party planning, like no big deal."

"I don't have a big-deal job. I told you the truth about all that."

He sighed. "There's a difference between giving me the barest outline of things and telling me the real deal."

"Stop being like that," I countered. "We're in an undefined relationship. You specifically told me not to bore you with my real life. You never wanted to know who he was or what he did. That's what you do when an affair is on the horizon—you ignore the real world."

"You do know that if we were having an affair we would actually be fucking, right? And besides, there's a difference between nondisclosure and deception, Allie Braden, or should I say *Crawford*." His voice seemed less angry, a little hurt, even. "Look, we talk about everything. He's not just some guy, you know. I happen to serve him his pinot noir three days a week. If I'm banging his wife, or close to it, I'd like to know that so I can either spit in the pinot or get someone else to serve him."

I spun on my heel. With Tommy still at the restaurant, maybe I could patch things up a little in person.

"You're right," I answered quietly.

"And so what if I'm good at saying, 'Oh, Mr. Big Swinging Dick Wade Crawford. Yes, that candied black raspberry aroma with a little smoky kick you enjoyed with your Chilean sea bass last week? It was the 1994 . . .' That doesn't merit a whole explanation, Allie. It isn't a *deception* because I didn't tell you exactly which restaurants I consult for."

"It wasn't a deception on my part either," I said. "It was discretion. Big difference."

"Right. Discretion. Potato, potahto."

Let's call the whole thing off? Was that what he was saying?

I went on. "You're right. We both kept things from each other. For reasons only each of us might understand that the other doesn't. Can we just accept that and not play guessing games that lead to God knows where or try to nail each other on some point just for the sake of it? Can we please just move forward?"

Silence. He was considering my proposal, one that shocked even me in its maturity, especially in my current whacked-out state of mind.

"I have to think about all this," he said after a few moments.

Maybe the Wade Crawford news was a game changer. Maybe Tommy was intimidated by Wade's success. Or maybe Tommy didn't like that he actually knew the husband in the flesh. That does, I suppose, make a difference. I felt sick inside. I debated whether to tell him so.

"I feel sick inside," I said.

"Me too," he answered gently.

I stayed silent. Listened to him breathe. *Affairs aren't for pussies,* I recalled Jackie saying.

After a long pause, I asked him, "If we both feel sick, maybe we should consider for a minute how unusual it is that we feel this bonded in so short a time."

"Agreed."

"Well, what now?"

"I don't know, Allie. I just don't. We have to reconsider."

"Okay. Look. Can we talk tonight? I've got to get back to work." Of course I didn't want to be the one who called. I wanted him to call me and say, "This was all so silly." No reason to stop the fun now, and we had script work to do. "You've been so generous with my writing, I do want to return the favor. It's your turn, you know."

"Sure. I'll text you."

As I slipped the phone into my pocket and crossed Fifty-Fourth Street, the wind whipped up the side of the building and practically threw me against the person next to me. Two strides back, no wind; here a virtual tornado. I kept my eyes closed, praying that Tommy wouldn't run for the hills.

THAT NIGHT AT SIX P.M., my phone pinged and I saw his number texting me. I leaped for the phone.

It read:

WE R DONE.

31

Life in Boxes

Something very *base* took hold of me during this time, and I felt its pulse slamming against a deep cavern inside: the fear of being alone.

I'd wake up in a lonely and desperate box, clouded with a fog of insecurity. In that box, it wasn't only self-doubt that enveloped the walls around me; it was a total inability to see that I could pull myself away from the mess I'd become.

That alone fear had the power to make me irrational. It convinced me I'd chosen door number two when I should have chosen door number one; so when I woke at four A.M., I'd plot every way to get James back on this side of the Atlantic. Or, when James didn't fill that hole, I would seek someone else to. I'd sit at my desk sitting on my hands not to text Tommy to ask for a second chance, feeling so adamant that his adorable everything would just plain save me. Save me from what exactly? Why did I need to fill the hole with another man the second I considered purging myself of my husband?

Sometimes, mercifully, that alone fear wouldn't ride me so hard. I would then say to myself that I could survive with the kids on my own; Wade would simply get a little studio down the block and have fun with whichever naked woman he wanted on his kitchen counters there. Oh, the glory of no lying husband in my house! He'd live nearby! We'd get along! I wouldn't care about his photo assistant girl or his Jackie dalliance and their perfectly toned arms! Life would be like a permanent spa vacation in Tahiti with no husband and no male-servicing duties.

I'd walk around the city and feel all neat and packaged up in the strong, confident, I-can-do-this box, perhaps channeling Jackie more than I thought I could. *I don't need anyone. I'm not a total mess.* But that bravado would be fleeting . . .

To get through this, I told myself most women contemplating divorce for real must react like I did. It was okay to give in to both feelings—to experience the momentary highs of independence and the fears of soul-wrenching loneliness. So what if I was strong 10 percent of the time and fearful the other 90 percent? If I felt tough all the time and ignored the painful part of my reality, then my supposed strength would be no more than a mere brittle façade. That's the self-help speech I gave myself anyway.

Three mornings after the breakup text from Tommy and after seventy-two hours of dark glum inability to see how I would ever feel that 10 percent of strength again, I experienced the physics of rebound.

I yanked open the curtains to let the early morning light shine in, while I forced myself to start working on my screenplay.

I thought about something Helen Gurley Brown, the founder of *Cosmopolitan,* who looked fabulous into her eighties, once said: *The greatest love in your life should be your work, not your man.*

I decided I would do exactly that: strive for intellectual passions to feel good about myself rather than obsess over men who hurt me or who I'd let get away.

It was Saturday morning, and Wade as usual had the kids on this day for pancakes and special daddy time. I was going to work in bed and let him handle kid duties. I liked this plan: my brain passions would save me! At that point in the turmoil, I grasped at anything to act as elusive *savior,* whether it be a man or a work concept.

I pulled the laptop off my side table and started making notes in my script. I mapped out up to page 115, thinking about how the problem would be set up in the first act, how the reckoning would have to begin happening in the third act. My own reckoning was moving like a locomotive, but I sensed speed bumps ahead with no surefire man to hold me tight as I flew over them.

Two hours later, I was deep into writing a successful scene where the new love interest dumps the heroine, making her hit rock bottom before they even started—writing what I knew, in other words—when Wade opened the door. The kids appeared with a wobbly breakfast tray they'd all put together in the kitchen—his first of many peace offerings that weekend to atone for his other women sins.

"You kids!" I said with a scratchy morning voice. "Thank you so much!"

Blake carried the tray, Lucy held a small bouquet of tulips

bought from the corner Korean market, and Wade walked carefully alongside them, his hand supporting the heavy tray carrying orange juice and eggs that was swaying precariously to and fro in my son's arms. "You slept so late, Mommy," Lucy said. "Daddy took us to get you these." She placed the flowers next to my bed.

"I'm going to take the kids out all day so you can relax," Wade said, edging toward the door. "We left you some gifts outside. You're the best mom in the world and we wanted you to know."

"Thank you, guys, this means the world to me," I answered, getting out of bed to hug my children. Having Wade say that only brought me down; he knew how good I was to him, so how did he let this all happen?

Blake whispered in my ear, "Thanks for giving me the best advice ever on Jeremy. I wanted to write you a card like Dad said I should, but I didn't have time."

"Well, what would you have said, honey?"

"What I said to Dad. That you are a good mom because you told me if I ignored him and played with William, Jeremy would stop being mean."

"You can make all the right decisions on your own; I just wanted to remind you not to let a bully see you react. That's all they want. Why don't you each pick out something yummy from the candy bag in my closet?" They cheered and ran out of the room. I paced between the bed and the door, slipping on jeans and trying on three different shirts before settling on one I liked, all the while waiting for Wade to talk. I did yoga breaths to try to summon some deep strength I wasn't sure I possessed at all. Wade stood by his dresser, frozen like a child.

I finally stepped in front of him. "Do you have something to say?"

"I do," he answered in a low and humble voice. "I'm sorry about everything. Really I am. You're the most caring woman in the world. You deserve better."

I turned to the man I married. "I know you fall hard when you fall for someone. Did that happen?"

Silence.

I went on. "Let me put it to you this way: Has that happened several times in the past two years?"

He just put his head down like a little boy.

"So you still want to maintain that each of these instances—some major, some minor—are just some fucking *slide show* that you, as a male, have lived? Not a *narrative* movie? Not connected in any way to each other? I don't know, call me crazy but I think I see a pattern here: lots of women behind my back, some you fall for. I don't think there are just isolated instances anymore. You can't lie to yourself or to me and maintain that."

He tried to answer, "They were individual, separate . . . I don't know, Allie. It's hard to explain. I care about you. I don't know why I did it when I knew it would hurt. And I don't want to have to go through . . ."

"You know what?" I said, trying to control my voice. "I don't need details; the big *narrative* picture has come through loud and clear."

"You deserve better, Allie," was all that he could muster.

"Well, you're not the only one who thinks that. I'm considering my options."

I had to choose my words carefully or risk Wade covering his tracks. "Is there anything about your business or our finances I should know about before I speak to a lawyer?"

"I can't tell you about business right now, and I'd really appreciate it if you would wait a bit before making any rash decisions," Wade pleaded. "Besides, it was only this one time."

My pulse skipped a beat. We were clearly entering divorce waters, and I was pretty sure that neither of us had a paddle, much less a boat. "You're already lying. There was the photo assistant when Lucy was three months old! But I don't care about the girls, Wade; I care about our kids."

"So do I. Which is why you have to believe me when I tell you that there is nothing you need to worry about."

"I am worried, Wade. Desperately worried," I answered, tears in my eyes. "How did we get here? How did *you* get us here?"

"I've got it under control," he replied, wiping under my eyes and then pulling me toward him.

I rested my head on his shoulder, and he put his arms around me. "Well, it certainly doesn't feel that way. On any front."

"I can't make you feel better, but know I'm trying, Allie."

Just as quickly as he'd barged into the bedroom, he turned around and left. I could hear him getting the children all excited about their big day with magic Daddy. By the time I followed him out of our bedroom, good-bye hugs were already being offered up.

Wade hurriedly gave me a peck on the forehead. "We're on the same team, Allie. Remember that."

32

Fear of the Unknown

A few nights later, I'd come home early from work and played board games with the children for a few hours. Then I started to get ready for screenwriting class and the first post-*WE R DONE* Tommy sighting. Playing with Blake and Lucy felt curative. Maybe we were a unit that could survive happily on our own. I felt better, stronger. But when I got into the shower to get ready for my screenwriting class, I crashed.

I thought about facing Tommy that night in class, my only cute, fun hope for a lifeboat if I left my marriage, and I slithered back into the sad and lonely box. Jackie would chastise me for caring so much about Tommy's breakup text, for wanting to replace one man with another right away.

I couldn't help it.

Once the kids were settled into watching a television show, I figured that showering might help my decline: maybe I could physically scrub away my tears and fears. I let my head drop and the water pound on the back of my neck. Watching the soapy water gather around my toes, I went into a Tommy trance. Everything that popped into my head sounded ridiculously sophomoric:

I want you back.

I need you.

Wade is gone to me.

I can't write without you pushing me along with good advice.

And what if I just lied to him?

I'm fine without you.

I don't need it.

We can just be friends.

AT 8:05 P.M., I walked into class with damp hair. I could tell my shoulders were slumped.

I didn't even need to look up to see if Tommy was aware of my arrival; I felt him watching me. There were about fifteen chairs around the circle in the brightly lit classroom. I moved to the side farthest from the door, right next to the professor. Usually Tommy and I sat near the door, the cool kids who needed a quick getaway plan—but not tonight. Tonight I'd be sitting like a chaste little kiss-ass next to the professor to glean all the insights I could for my future as a screenwriter, a future I now had to bank on.

I think I felt better about myself when Nicky Chace broke up with me four months after my dad died and I had to walk past him and his Goth friends in the cafeteria. As I studiously avoided Tommy, I kept telling myself: *You're a grown woman, you have a flourishing career, a great screenplay in the works; you have beautiful, healthy children. Tommy is a blip on the radar. Hold your head high, woman.* Nice try, but none of that worked that night. I was in a newfound low.

As I sat down and stared at my bag, I spied Tommy's muscular legs and worn Nike sneakers about fifteen feet across the floor. I also saw that the seat next to his was empty. I could not look up; instead, I turned in the direction of the professor, placed my elbow on the little desk attached to my chair, and my hand across my forehead as if blocking sunlight from my eyes.

"Have you read Mr. O'Malley's scene, Ms. Braden?" How could I have forgotten that this was his big night? I could have sworn I'd never gotten a class e-mail with an attachment from Tommy. I glanced at Tommy, who met my look with one of real disappointment before he looked away. I desperately wanted to tell him that if I'd known it was his turn, I'd have devoured his screenplay. Not only had I been a cock tease, I'd been a really bad friend. No wonder he wasn't texting or sexting me.

"A lot is going on in Mr. O'Malley's scene, Ms. Braden, wouldn't you agree?"

"Oh, yes," I lied.

Heller went on, "It's an interesting piece of social satire that I found amusing, if a bit far-fetched. Of course the protagonist needs a bit more rounding out." He walked to the whiteboard and wrote out the following: "Is it the girl he wants? Or is he after the guy? Maybe you don't know. You know why? You've got to be present in your life!" Heller started slamming on desktops, on one of his rolls again. He positioned his face three inches from mine and I yanked my neck back. "Allie! How do you brush your teeth? Top or bottom row? Do you brush in little circles like you're supposed to?"

"I, uh, I'm not sure."

"Well, that's a bullshit way to live, Allie!" *Excuse me? This guy was nuts.* "Pay attention to every detail! Be a reporter. See what you can dig up!" Heller was now acting out his words, brushing his teeth, arms in the air and beating his chest. "If you're writing the worst, most villainous baby-seal-killer of a character, find something of yourself in him. There's a beating heart somewhere in that chest, blood running through those veins. If you can't find the humanity in your characters, they're nothing but statues in a museum!"

While I struggled to understand what brushing my teeth had to do with the murdering of fuzzy, white seals, Tommy raised his hand and spoke to the class.

"Well, I've been working on the scene for the last forty-eight hours pretty much night and day." He looked at me as if that provided an explanation for his radio silence, and I took it as a tiny olive branch. "It's a departure from my young crew script, just a scene that popped into my head, and I wanted to do exactly what you said, find myself in it, and write it down for practice. I was having trouble, but then I just decided to inject some truth into the situation." He looked at me hard.

"Why wouldn't you inject truth into every line, Thomas?" asked the professor. "That's when you'll have your audience by the balls and have them captive: when they recognize what they know to be true. A play within a play. Is it just me, or is it kind of funny that Hamlet stages a play about regicide to catch his father's killer? Feed them the truth, Tommy."

"I wasn't thinking about the actors; I was protecting people I know in real life, I guess," Tommy told the class. "Just for fun, I took a break from the slog of my script to write about this restaurant I consult for. I wanted to write something that had just happened to me to get the juices churning. There's some pretty unbelievable stuff that goes on in this place, and at first I didn't want to 'out' people, but then the scene went limp on me. So I took some time to tell it like it is, and write what I know. I broke through somehow."

"You don't have to 'out' people to get to the truth in fiction," Heller interjected. "That's not what I'm talking about. But you do have to tell it as you think it really is. It's a subtle distinction, but I hope you understand the difference."

"In this case, I had to tell it the way it went down. Out people or not, I don't give a shit." Tommy stared me down. Other class members looked my way, and my face started to burn.

By now a sharp pain was pounding inside my head. What the hell was he saying? That he was writing about us in his screenplay? That one of the things that happened was based on our own dustup? I was starting to understand why Tommy hadn't sent me the script before the class: he didn't want me reading it.

Tommy went on, "Writers write what they know and that's

the only way I could tell it. You know that line, 'you can't make this stuff up.'" Tommy's voice was getting higher; the way men's voices do when angry. "The real stuff was better than my sugar-coating it and protecting people."

Tommy got up and slammed his scene down on my school desk.

```
INT. Restaurant—Lunchtime
  WAYNE CRAWLEY, the editor of a society magazine
called The Grid, sits at a side table designated
to midlevel power players in the hot new Tudor
Room. (Other tables go to men and women at the
helm of more major corporations or investment
banks.) He nods discreetly to a few "associates"
around the room. He knows everyone in New York
City, of course, but chooses to acknowledge only
those who would be of use to him that week before
he is served an expensive glass of red wine. He
shakes his longish hair out of his face as he first
sniffs and swirls the bouquet, then sips from his
favorite wine, a 1996 Domaine Armand Rousseau
Chambertin. As he smacks his lips with a sense of
loving familiarity, he reaches into his pocket and
winks at the MAÎTRE D'.
  CRAWLEY pulls a $2,500 casino chip out of his
pocket and slides it into the hand of the MAÎTRE
D' as if he were passing him a gram of coke.
```

MAÎTRE D'

[placing chip discreetly in his pocket]

"The usual? Is that your preference today, sir?"

CRAWLEY

"Yes. Always. Genevieve. 4 P.M. The Willingham Hotel. Room 1602."

THE JUNIOR EDITOR at a nearby table sees what is happening and tries to interrupt his boss, Mr. Crawley.

JUNIOR EDITOR

[whispering]

"Don't you see? She'll get your money and make it look as though it was your idea."

CRAWLEY

"Nonsense, Tom. I know what I'm doing. She's safe."

MAÎTRE D'

[ignoring the young associate's admonitions]

"You gave me an expensive chip; you looking for a real workout, sir?"

CRAWLEY

"Yeah, I want to fall in love,
if you know what I mean."

MAÎTRE D'

"I shall make sure the lady
receives the message."

They both look over to the bar, where GENEVIEVE McGREGOR, a stunning blond-streaked beauty dressed to the nines in the latest, sexiest fashion, peruses an econ textbook.

Suddenly the whole picture came into focus so fast that my entire neck hurt from whiplash. All the anguish on Tommy's face across the room suddenly made perfect sense. He was writing what he knew in every sense, and in the process he'd outed my husband and the game playing he'd seen at the Tudor Room. Not only were some of the guys breaking the law on the investing front, but Jackie Malone was in cahoots with them. And she was a goddamn whore.

33

Percolating Problems

The manager of the Moonstruck Diner on Eighteenth Street and Tenth Avenue barked "Scrambled, whiskey down, side a bacon!" at the short-order cooks. Metal spatulas slid against the griddle, and coffee brewed in giant silver urns. I walked past a sea of impatient New Yorkers, all anxious to get to work, waiting for their take-out bags, and found a quiet table in the back.

Four hours earlier, I'd rolled over to see 5:07 A.M. illuminated on the bedside table and noticed this text from Wade:

I'm working so late on closing this issue, I'll be pushing straight through and sleeping at the office, if I'm lucky. Kiss the kids.

No way to know if he was telling the truth or not. 5:09 A.M. Two full hours before a show of composure was required to prepare the little ones for their day. Two full hours of slumber might allow me to make it through my own day, wake up in the strong, happy box without a pounding headache. Two full hours before I'd have to ask Jackie what the hell was going on. I closed my eyes.

Then I opened them wide. One single line in Tommy's script echoed through my mind at this early hour: *Don't you see? She'll get your money and make it look as though it was your idea.* It was that raw time of the early morning when my anxieties tend to explode with possibility. Had I fallen for the oldest con in the world: empathize with the wife, then gaslight her into giving you all the banking information, so you can grab the spoils? I scrambled out of bed and into the den, grateful that I'd at least had the sense not to give her the flash drive. Jackie had enough information from the files she'd yanked from me in Murray's Southampton driveway to figure out who owned what anyway.

Then another harsh predawn reality hit me: I'd never paid too much attention to our larger investment accounts. I paid the bills online and carefully made sure we had enough going in and out properly, and Wade put money into checking at the first of the month to cover our expenses. He and Danny Jenson, a smart, slick money guy, would meet every quarter to go over our expenses, taxes, and investments. There wasn't much money to play around with, especially toward the end of the year, but we had some savings that we had both worked hard to accumulate. This was our kids' college fund, our nest egg, the untouchable money that we treated as sacrosanct. It wasn't something I would check often.

Searching Wade's desk for our accountant's annual review, I remembered that in April, Wade had met with Danny while I was traveling. He'd been meaning to tell me what Danny had said, how we'd managed to weather the latest downturn without the staggering losses many people had experienced.

We kept a Chase banking card with a fifteen-digit code on it in order to access the nest egg investment account online, and this was what I could not find in its usual place by 5:14 A.M. Had Wade hidden it from me?

The doorbell rang. Maybe Wade lost his key? Now I could ask him.

I pulled on a robe and shuffled to the front door in my slippers. The superintendent of the building was standing there with a slightly dazed look in his eyes.

"Yes, Joe, what's up? Is everything okay?"

"Yes, Mrs. Crawford. I just have a note that she wanted hand delivered. Sorry to wake you, but she told me to send it right up."

"She?" As if I didn't know.

"Yes. A young woman. She was downstairs, but she didn't want me to call up on the house phone. I didn't entirely understand, but she said it was very important that you get this note."

"Thank you, Joe." I stared at the heavens. What could Jackie possibly want from me now?

I ripped open the envelope.

Don't call or e-mail or text me about the shady dealings of these men. You and I need to stay clean about this right now. You can only send texts about other mundane topics. Why is Wade so freaked out? I hope you didn't tell him anything. Meet me at the Moonstruck Diner near your house at nine.

Hope I didn't tell him anything? What right did she have . . . why hadn't *she* told me she was a *hooker*?

Within seven seconds, my head was covered in a sea of cashmere blazers in Wade's overstuffed closet. After twenty sweaty minutes checking every single outside and inside pocket of every suit and jacket, and then, in case my memory was mistaken, every coat in the hall closet, I came up with no Chase bank card.

I made a cup of green tea and lay back in bed in my sweatpants. And then I looked in between the mattress and bed base for a mahogany box that held his Borgata casino chips that weren't in the back of his underwear drawer anymore.

My hunch was correct: lodged in between the mattress and box spring, I found three $2,500 chips and that Chase Manhattan bank card with the fifteen-digit code. We used the same password, Penny, the name of Wade's first dog when he was a child, on every single online account in our home: banks, Amazon, PayPal, Barnes & Noble, the lot. There was a second layer of online security in our bank account. First the "Penny" password, then there was the fifteen-digit number on the bank card.

Once, earlier this year, when I'd wanted to check the accounts, I couldn't find the Chase bank card and asked Wade, thinking nothing of the fact that it was missing. Wade's answer now echoed in my head with far more resonance: *Just let Danny handle all the investment stuff, Allie. These days it's all so volatile because of the ups and downs of the markets, it's going to make you upset. But over ten years it'll have gone up about 10 percent a year, or so they say. So just let him handle it. I've lost that Chase bank card. But I'll get another one. Soon.*

Of course he never lost the bank card; he was only hiding the one we had. Despite my anger at Wade, I couldn't help but wonder if he'd been played, that his childish inability to focus had gotten him into a whole heap of trouble he hadn't even understood. I logged on and pulled up our investment account and put in the Penny password, only to be rejected. He must have changed it. I closed my eyes and tried typing our kids' names, my maiden name, Braden, and then, finally, Jackie. It worked. Motherfucker. Then I entered the code from the Chase bank card.

I stared at my new economic reality on the screen. Everything we worked for—gone. I felt my throat convulse and didn't quite make it to the toilet.

34

Girl Loses Girl?

With a dented metal spoon, I swirled a hefty amount of sugar into my coffee. As it dissolved, so did my uncertainties. Jackie Malone had a hold on Wade's dick and his cash. Somehow she'd played him—played *me*. Somehow she'd gotten him into something treacherous and benefited from it herself. I was absolutely positive that only a woman could get this much out of Wade, a world-class manipulator in his own right.

The crowd up front thinned out in the diner as the clock ticked to nine. Out the window by my lonely table in the back, people rushed by to get to their jobs, narrowly missing each other on the sidewalk, like the rush in a high school hallway to get to class before the bell.

Did the casino chips in my husband's drawer really come from his jaunts to Atlantic City with Murray and Max? I'd seen Georges the conniving maître d' pass Jackie a chip; he could have easily been asking for the full monty for one of the powerful men dining at the Tudor Room. I had figured it out—or Tommy had figured it out for me to see. That's how Jackie was paying off her loans—if there even were any loans. She was a high-class hooker, plain and simple, her currency untraceable casino chips. No checks, no bank transfers that could be traced, and none of her clients had to sully their hands with a dirty cash transaction. She got paid with casino chips she could cash in anywhere in Atlantic City any time she wanted for cold hard cash. I'll bet she had businessmen clients out there too.

If only I'd just trusted my instincts in the first place. First Jackie sucked their dicks, and then she sucked information out of their briefcases and BlackBerrys. Then she found the unhappy wife to help her get access to more of that money, conning all of us all the way to the bank. For all I knew, the account in Liechtenstein was all her idea gleaned from some class in Philadelphia. If there even were an account over there. Or a business school.

I have to admit, when Jackie waltzed through the front door at 9:09, turning heads the entire way, I was shocked. I really didn't think she was going to show. She sat down opposite me.

"Oh, Jesus, thank God you're here." Jackie kept up the pretense of actually trying to help me. "Sorry to be late. I do have some really really important questions for you. Why is . . ."

"I only have one question for you: Did you take all my money?" I half screamed, half whispered.

For the first time in my relationship with Jackie, she looked utterly shaken and I did not have any idea how she would answer.

She sat there in silence, staring first at the table and then up at me, softly. She actually looked wounded. "How could you?"

"How could I . . ."

"After all we've gone through, me admitting the thing with your husband the first time you asked?" she pleaded. "And us talking about your life and men and me with my mom, and everything we're working on here, I feel like we were such a fast, unlikely pair in some weird but important way, you know." She paused a long time. "I did sleep with your husband, so that was big of you even to talk to me, but how could you think I'd take your money? You really think that is what this is all about?"

"I don't know what to think. My bank account is in ruins and you—"

"And I what?" she interrupted, sounding unbelievably hurt by the accusation.

"You expect me to take everything at face value in this whole deal when all my money is gone?" Sweat dripped down my neck, and I pushed the menu back down on the table. "You're grabbing and looking through confidential folders in Murray's driveway in Southampton, you tell me the information is all there, but then it isn't, you say, I assume it's some bank account linked to Wade and . . ."

"You still don't trust me. Amazing." She studied the breakfast choices with a deep sigh. "I told you there were no bank accounts in those files in Southampton. I told you I still need that flash drive." Her voice cracked and she rubbed the corner of her eye.

I fired the questions at her. "I can tell you're upset. Really I can. But this isn't about your hurt feelings at this point. I'm sorry, but I have to know this: Where is my money, Jackie?"

She folded the menu and flagged a waiter. "Your husband took it, to invest, and then he fuhuhcked up, as Max Rowland himself put it in your own living room."

"How do I know you didn't take it?" I answered. "Prove it to me now."

A large waiter wearing a white apron approached our table. "Whataya want?"

Jackie continued to look at me, then calmly turned to the sweaty waiter. "A Greek omelet, please. Dry rye toast on the side."

"You want home fries? You wanna the omelet egg white only?" he asked.

"Neither, thanks." She smiled at him.

"I'm fine," I answered without looking up from my steaming cup of coffee.

"Don't you just hate egg whites?" Jackie said. "So rubbery. Don't know how women diet like that."

"Jackie! We are not talking about our egg preferences. We are talking about how I could trust you. I think you lied to me!"

"I have never lied to you once," she reassured me. "Just please try to focus on Wade. I need to know what you told him and why he's so upset that you know everything. Not everything is as it appears. The money is elsewhere, and he's added to it. Then he lost it. But now, it's actually back. You won't have access to your money for a while, but you will at some point very soon."

"I have two children. 'Very soon' doesn't work," I answered

tersely, wondering how on earth I was going to nail her. "And by the way, how do you know? Are you an expert in money laundering and overseas transactions as well?"

She pulled out some sheets from her bag. "You had about two hundred and seventy-five thousand dollars, right? I mean in all your retirement accounts and savings and everything."

"How on earth did you know that number, Jackie?"

"Well, look at this sheet. Project Green is Wade, see that? The envelope I took from you had some good information in it about various people's financial dealings but no account numbers to nail them for sure. That's what's on the flash drive. See that amount? It's all just transferring from them and back to Wade. Don't worry, it's all there. That green column is Wade's. See how it went way up here . . . and now it's just where it was when he started this thing . . . he won a lot on his bets and then he lost a lot."

"How do I know Project Green is our money and we will get it back?"

She took a deep breath. "Because the authorities are on it now, Allie. That woman you saw me with at the bar, the redhead with the blunt cut in the gray linen dress that day with Wade? She works for the FBI. How else could I possibly know all this? They approached me when they figured out I was following the same people they were. I couldn't lie, and I didn't see any reason not to help them determine who was breaking the law."

"You're working with the FBI? Is Wade in huge trouble?"

"Nope, he's not who they're after at all. If he talks, he'll get full immunity. You and I just need to stay quiet for the next two days. That's why I sent you that note about no obvious texts."

The waiter slammed Jackie's greasy omelet on the table and filled up my coffee, splashing a little on the saucer.

"Excuse me," she yelled at him over the clanging of the busy coffee shop. "Some ketchup, please?" She picked up a pepper shaker and vigorously dusted the omelet.

I hit the table to keep her on topic. "I want to talk right now about you, Jackie. Your motives."

She speared a huge piece of omelet with her fork and poured ketchup on it before devouring it, almost Murray-like. Then she said, "You sure you didn't say anything to anyone or do anything else?"

I flinched at her unladylike eating habits. "What did I do? What did I do?" And then I quietly rummaged through my purse. I took a bunch of casino chips and spread them across the table. "Of course you can tell me you know what men are like in the hay from every age decade. *That's because you sleep with everyone.* Only you get *paid* for it. Did you leave that part out on purpose or were you going to tell me, *girl to girl*?"

Jackie took an even larger bite of omelet and chewed as she glared at me, swallowing hard and taking a sip of water before she spoke. "It's not like it seems, Allie."

"What's not like it seems? Tommy works in the Tudor Room. He watches you operate, and it makes him go nuts. He watches you screw Wade, and he can't stand Wade. Believe me, now I get why he hates my husband. First, I thought it was me, but it's because of this." I pointed at the chips. "He watches you sell yourself to the guys, Wade, Max, God knows who else. And, by the way, you know what Tommy just did?"

Ms. Cool Cucumber dabbed the corners of her mouth with her napkin, in a sudden display of table manners, then crossed her arms and raised her well-tended eyebrows. "What did Tommy do?" she asked.

"He outed you. He wrote a scene in our class about an Ivy League call girl in a powerful lunch spot."

"Oh no." She rolled her eyes.

"You don't care that people know that you have sex for money? How did your mother think you were getting all the money to help her pay off the loans?"

"My mother is clueless, one reason she's trusted the wrong people all her life. She thinks I got all my money from my summer jobs at banks and she's grateful. Period. I leave it at that with her. As for others around here, I genuinely don't care what people think."

35

Cash Call

"You don't care people know you're fucking for cash?"

Jackie pushed her omelet away and leaned over the red-flecked linoleum diner table. "What we are really talking about is this: I fuck for a lot of things, Allie. For a lot of reasons that will all become clear to you. And yes, if you want me to be truthful, I did some fucking for cash."

"You wanna refill?" the waiter asked as he cleared her plate and tried to linger over this conversation a bit longer.

"I heard," I answered.

"I got customers waiting, lady." He started to add up our bill.

"I'll have a blueberry muffin and a tea, please." I turned to Jackie. "Go on, please explain how you did some fucking for cash."

The waiter tried to hear until she glared at him to leave.

"It was very simple, really, on so many counts."

"Doesn't sound simple."

She pulled her hair behind her ears. "I wanted my mom to

have her house down payment now, not later. It took me like four months to collect that. A five-grand casino chip for a few hours. To tell you the God's honest truth, it was just so efficient, I couldn't resist. Someone important I worked for at a summer analyst position wanted sex, and I told him he'd have to pony up big-time first. It was really that simple, just a transaction. And then there were more."

"A few hours of pure hell!" I exclaimed.

"Well, yes, on some level it was pretty unsatisfactory, but I knew them all and they were perfectly gentlemanly and businesslike. It was about four guys over the past few years, and my mom's settled where she should be. I know it may seem strange, but some girls get gifts; I got large amounts of casino chips."

"Cash isn't the same as gifts. Gifts usually mean you're in a relationship of some kind, not a cold transaction that—"

"Well, for reasons that benefited me, I decided to take the cold transaction . . . and by the way, think a little about what you are insinuating here. I know it's not exactly a common thing for a business school grad to be doing, but I think I'm just more realistic than most about how stuff goes."

"Can I give you some advice for once?"

"I'm listening." She poured some cream in her coffee and raised an eyebrow.

"Could you just quit with the ruthless expediency of it all? I mean, it's going to catch up with you. It's going to destroy a part of you or screw with your head somehow."

"Allie. When there are people you love whom you have to take care of, you'll do anything." Her voice almost cracked.

"You didn't have to use your body."

She looked down and her lip twisted a little. "You're right. I didn't. But if you could learn to give people a break, you might see I was getting my family out of a desperate financial situation as fast as I could. I used my business acumen and my body to get there. My summer associate money wasn't going to get my mom on track fast enough."

"What do you mean? Whoring is more realistic? You don't find it debasing?"

"Really, Allie? What exactly is whoring?" She cocked an eyebrow. "Half the women in this city should take a look in the mirror."

I pulled back against my seat to hear the coming onslaught. The waiter delivered my muffin and slapped the check down next to it.

Jackie placed her elbows on the table and stared at me. "Would it be more honest if I'd taken all the school loans, married some rich banker that I liked well enough, and then once he'd paid off my debt, divorced him and taken him for twice as much once I *came to my senses*?" At this she made little quotation marks with her fingers and went on.

"Many women do that, get comfortable until they can't take it anymore, and take half the man's fortune, having never loved him from the beginning. I bet you don't judge them. That could work too, I guess. But if the wife stops loving him, and the husband is making all the money, isn't she fucking for money too?"

I answered quickly. "Most people love each other in a marriage at some point."

"Bullshit. I've known my share of girls at school who are looking for one thing: the rock. They could care less about the cock, but if they have to suck on it a little until they get what they're after, then they lower themselves to the job." She sneered. "I actually like sex. I guess that's what makes me truly different."

"Jackie, I get you think this is normal."

She shook her head. "Fuck normal. I just said it was more honest than most people can admit. And in that sense, it has more integrity. But that casino chip business is over now. I don't need to do it anymore."

"And Wade, how did he figure in exactly?"

"Max would throw him a few chips on Atlantic City trips, and he saved a few for me. It was like a couple of times with him, but he got hooked. That's when I stopped and said he's all yours."

"You sure you're not doing any sex for cash anymore?"

"Yes, I'm done. The house down payment is made, and Mom and I can earn the rest with 'normal' jobs, as you say." She threw her dirty paper napkin on the table. "Do you understand my motives better now? And, more important, how did you leave it with Tommy?"

"I don't want to talk about Tommy."

She touched my arm. "Allie, whether you like it or not, we're in this together now. Tell me what happened with him."

"Nothing. No big deal." And then two nanoseconds later, "He left after class without talking to me!"

"That's called a man's baby routine. He just wants some attention—if you want to give it to him, he's back eating out of your hands."

"He's not interested in even having a friendship with me," I said, throwing a ten-dollar bill on top of her money on the check and sweeping the casino chips back into my bag.

"Well, maybe yes, he's hurt because he didn't know you were married to the great Wade Crawford, but he'll get over being pissed at you if you just give him a little female attention."

"I will tell you I have to fight an intense urge to text him, but it's just not a good time to start with him. I do know that. And, honestly, I don't think he wants me back. Now, forget Tommy and me for a minute. What else do you or the authorities know about Wade? Do you know where he is at the moment on all this? Let's start there, now that I have the whole picture, which"—I paused—"which I'm choosing to believe." I broke into a wry little smile.

"Well, good thing and good timing. Wade did technically fall for me, but he's licking his wounds now with others. That's something I just found out with help from the people who are following him. I learned about it last night and now you need to know."

"Others?"

She pulled out a room key. "Go to the Willingham Hotel right now. Penthouse 1602. It's where all the guys from the Tudor Room go for the utmost discretion. They're so weird, they all are competitive over who gets this one room with automatic shades that go up to enhance their viewing pleasure during whatever other pleasure they are experiencing in the groin area. Go find your husband and ask him yourself."

She gave me the key. Now I figured I owed her. And, this

being the entry into Act III, I might as well just get to some tipping point in this madness. And so, in the depths of a filthy, cluttered side pocket of my purse, I stuck my finger through a little hole that had ripped in the lining and dexterously pulled out a little flash drive and set it on the table.

Jackie closed her eyes and placed her palms in prayer position, resting her head on the tips of her fingers like she'd just witnessed the Second Coming.

She then calmly took out her laptop, slipped in the flash drive, waited two minutes while the information downloaded, and said, "Thank you, Allie. This is exactly what we needed." She bit her bottom lip as she nodded up and down, up and down, as she carefully perused the columns of Projects Red, Green, and Blue. "Wade'll get full immunity. Don't worry."

I tried to look over the top of her computer. "What is it?"

"Give me twenty-four hours."

I grabbed the key from the table. "You want me to go to the Willingham Hotel now?" I asked.

"I can't say I really want you to go there, but I do want you to believe two things: one, I have never lied to you, not once, ever. And two, I want you to trust me always, because the feds don't care about Wade and he's cooperating now anyway for immunity. And I'm sure of where the bodies are buried and I'm so very close to finding them."

She picked up the check to take it to the front counter and added, "Oh, yeah, one more thing to remember when you get to the Willingham Hotel: your husband's the whore, not me."

36

Afternoon Feast

The taxi driver slowly inched up Sixth Avenue, all the corporate headquarters with their imposing gray glass façades on either side. He then took me through the park at Fifty-Ninth Street and up to the more residential and tree-lined Sixty-Third Street and Madison where the intimate and chic Willingham Hotel awaited.

The hotel key in my shaking hands featured a thick, blood-colored silk tassel with a heavy gold metal Roman-style coin, with the number 1602 embossed on it. Was I really going to walk in on Svetlana, the supermodel who was pretending she could act, or maybe Delsie Arceneaux, or some other siren, and my husband? I wasn't sure which woman I'd find, but I did know approximately four minutes from now, I'd creep into an ornate penthouse hotel room and discover something unsavory.

I paid the taxi driver, wondering what exact sex position I'd encounter. Delsie's thick thighs V-shaped in the air as Wade serviced her every desire? Naw. More likely Svetlana's bony ass in the air servicing Wade and welcoming me.

A white glove opened my taxi door, while another reached out for my hand. "Checking in, Madame? Do you have luggage I can help with?"

"No, I'm fine." I felt like a cat burglar about to break and enter. My hands were shaking. Actually, everything was shaking: my breath, my fingers, my knees, even the flab on the back of my hips.

"A reservation in the café perhaps?"

"I'll be fine. Thank you."

Past the revolving doors, another white-gloved doorman with a cap asked if he could be of assistance. "The café is on the right."

I shook my key at him.

"Ah yes, he's upstairs waiting for you." He escorted me to the elevator and reached inside to turn a security lock to allow me access to the penthouse. The Willingham Hotel had an old-world feeling and a nineteenth-century decor to match: the lobby had high ceilings with ornate plaster moldings, slightly worn Oriental rugs, and high, dark brown leather wingtip chairs in each corner.

Why did the doorman already know he was waiting for me? I strode in and hesitantly pushed the button for the sixteenth floor. Was the whole plan ruined? Had I gotten here too early?

Was Wade waiting for his midday hooker, or his paramour, and I'd beaten her to the punch?

I panicked and pushed fourteen, then practically leaped out of the elevator to catch my breath and figure out my next step. Nothing else to do but text Jackie.

ME: *The porter downstairs says Wade's expecting me. What the hell is going on? Did I get here before whatever woman got here?*

It took about four seconds before she responded.

JACKIE: *Nope. You're fine. Go ahead.*
ME: *Are you setting me up for some weird situation?*
JACKIE: *I can't promise it won't be weird, but he's 100% not expecting you.*

Jackie was right about that one, too.

I got my behind back in that elevator and used the small security card on the key chain to once again get access to the sixteenth floor. The ping announcing the elevator's arrival startled me so much, I jumped.

Weaving the silken tassel between my fingers, I walked down a hallway with walls covered in oil paintings of horse races and portraits of British war heroes from God knows which war a hundred years ago, to room 1602, which stood in its own vestibule at the end of a long hallway. It took me a second or two to untangle my fingers from the key's tassel. Listening at the door and hearing nothing, I slid the key into the lock very slowly and turned it ever so slightly until it clicked open. The noise was loud enough that someone inside might turn his head, but soft enough that if he was preoccupied with something, he wouldn't notice.

I put my nose through the door of the hotel suite. The living room seemed pristine enough. No champagne, no bra hanging off the chandelier, no trail of just-ripped-off clothing leading to the bedroom. My breath quickened, as I stood like a statue in the front alcove, unable to move. Before me, a carved marble fireplace mantel, dark wood floors, and two yellow chintz sofas facing each other. Huge maroon drapes festooned with silk tiebacks framed the oversized windows. To my left, another room.

Oh God, just do it. Biting my lip, I tiptoed in the direction of a distant grunt and made it all the way to the slightly ajar door of the bedroom. Another sound. This time, a woman, saying "yes, yes" in a muffled voice against the sheets. For the briefest second, I thought I recognized that raspy, energetic voice. Couldn't be. But if it was, I had to find out.

I pushed the door and it swung open silently about twelve inches, enough to give me a full view of what was taking place on the crumpled sheets. Wade was bent over on his knees, his slightly hairy ass before me, head down low to the bed and body before him, obviously enjoying some kind of delectable treat below.

Since Wade was clearly preoccupied, I decided to get his attention by taking in a loud breath through my nose. It worked. He turned around like a cheetah on all fours, his face ashen, and threw the sheets over his paramour.

"Shit, Allie. I didn't . . . it's not . . . how did you get in . . ."

I just crossed my arms and pressed my lips tightly together. It took every ounce of restraint not to cry.

Wade scrambled off the bed, ran over to his boxers, and hopped on one foot as he tried to jam a leg through them.

"I've seen you naked before," I told him.

He threw the entire king-size comforter on the bed over the woman's body and then sat on the corner with his head in his hands.

After about forty-five painful seconds, the body under the sheets still frozen in the spread-eagle position I'd walked in on, Wade looked up. "Look, you got me. I think it would be easier on us if you could meet me downstairs in the bar."

"Nope," I answered.

"If you could just let me get dressed, let me handle the situation here with as much grace as possible, I'll be down there in ten minutes and you can have whatever you want."

"Nope."

"If you would just do that for me, Allie, you can have—"

"Where is our money, Wade? That's what I really came to ask. It's not the girl at this point. It's our money, my future, our kids' future. Tell me where it is. Is it overseas in an account? You tell me and I'll leave the room because I don't give a damn who you've got under the sheets at this point." That was not exactly the truth, but crying was thankfully now out of the question as my anger took hold and I found my voice.

I felt like it wasn't even me standing there on this bizarre hotel stage. Since I'd just at that very moment in my mind finally jettisoned Wade 100 percent out of our marriage, I had to hold it together for myself more than anything else. Everything was clear, right before me: a future *on* my own, a future *of* my own. A husband whom I could never trust, who would never grow up, who would never put me or the kids first. A man I had to leave.

"I've got a handle on everything, Allie." He attempted to smooth down his scarecrow hairdo as he caught a glimpse of himself in the mirror on the wall. "You don't need to worry about—"

"Oh, I'm worried all right. All our money is gone. Two answers and I leave the room—one: how did our money get out of our accounts? Two: where is it?"

"Allie. This is private. Please."

"Okay, you know what, Wade? Fine. You're right. I'll sit on the couch in the living room. Put your pants on and answer those two questions outside."

"In the lobby?" he asked, looking hopeful.

I shook my head, my voice still resolute, as I walked out of the bedroom. "I was very clear the first time: in the living room of this very suite."

He appeared ninety seconds later.

"I want a divorce," I said calmly. I didn't necessarily feel calm, but I did feel resigned to say what I needed to say and resigned to do what I needed to do for the kids and me. "And half the value of the apartment and half of our cash. Where is it?"

"It's in an account overseas for safekeeping. You see, I lost a lot of it with something that—"

"With something you '*fuhuhcked up*' as Max so delicately put it?"

"Yes, that thing, but I made some of it back now, and if you can give me some time, it'll be more than we had before, but you have to help me keep up appearances here."

"Let me get this straight," I said to my soon-to-be ex-husband. "You want me to help you keep up appearances, because you're working so hard to keep up appearances by screwing another hooker at eleven in the morning?"

"It's not what you think," he answered.

"You weren't screwing her?" I asked.

"I mean, the girl, it's not what you think; you know, Allie, we haven't been getting along so well; it's just a little . . ."

"I'm calling my lawyer once you give me those answers."

"Don't do that, Allie, please. There are too many tentacles now to get a lawyer in on this. Please, I beg you, let me just clean up the mess I have made."

I shifted back into the couch and my back hit something hard. I pulled the pillow away. Wade lunged to try to hide it, but it was too late.

I spied a pink computer case, like one I'd given as a gift to Caitlin. Wade straightened out his shoulders and looked straight at me. "I care about her, Allie."

A deep laugh brewed in my midsection as it all came into focus. I stormed toward the bedroom and flung open the door so hard it chipped a piece of the bureau along the wall.

"Allie, please don't . . ." Wade mumbled like the pathetic coward he was.

There she was: Brutus with a short bob hairstyle on the bed, in the form of a tight little gymnast zipping up her boots.

37

Girls Can Hurt More Than Boys

I ran sixteen flights down the exit stairway of the Willingham Hotel and bolted into the bright day outside on East Sixty-Third Street. It took a few minutes for my eyes to adjust to the harsh light. "Allie! Allie!" I heard someone calling my name through the bleating of horns, but I ran down the block, farther and farther away from that voice, not wanting to hear a lame defense from Caitlin. I kept on going and the voice kept trailing me, but as I looked back, I didn't see anyone on the sidewalk whom I knew.

Finally, a black car screeched alongside the curb next to me. Jackie stuck her gorgeous head out the window, looking like a young Sharon Stone. "Would you stop ignoring me? I wanted to be here for you when you came out and you don't even know my voice at this point?"

"I didn't know the voice was yours. I thought it was Caitlin, apologizing."

"She's going to need more time to gear up for an apology,

that one." She shook her head and opened the door. "I'm sorry, Allie, I may be ruthless, but I wouldn't betray a friend like that. Come on in."

I groped around inside my bag for my sunglasses to hide my tears. Jackie softened her voice at the sight of my shaking hands trying to open the case. I felt like Wade had punched me in the stomach and then Caitlin had kicked me to the ground. "Listen, a girlfriend betraying you can strike harder than a guy. I'm sorry, I'm really sorry, but I felt you should know, and since you didn't seem to believe me, it seemed the best way for you to find out."

"Well, I did find them right in the act," I answered.

"Caitlin is lost on so many fronts. She doesn't even realize that's the hotel room all the Tudor Room men go to for their high-class fuckfests. Wade probably tells her he cares so much about her up there. I've been in that suite myself, so I know how it's used and how the doormen are the most discreet in town."

"I think he may have some feelings for her."

"You know what, Allie? Your husband is out for himself. When you're fucking a girl, you tell her you have feelings for her. You start to believe that. Wade is just groping around at anything because he feels desperate. He's getting older and his thick, glossy, expensive-to-produce magazine doesn't matter to anyone who owns an iPad." She put her hand firmly on my arm. "And I also gave you the key so that you could know to believe me. One thing to remember: if you leave him, you're going to be just fine on your own."

I could barely hear her kind advice now that so many images

of Caitlin and Wade were spinning in my head—and not in slide show form, but in hazy movie scenes that linked together to form a clear narrative plotline. I remembered how she always giggled like a schoolgirl at his jokes, how concerned she was to know about other dalliances. Was I stupid not to see it? Or was it all so nuts that I never could have known? I could barely concentrate on what Jackie was telling me, but I had to gird myself to hear her out. "I don't understand how you know about Wade's every movement." I had no one to trust but her right now.

"The authorities tell me," she whispered in my ear. "The situation is getting more tense by the hour. That's why I gave you the key. I wanted you to be armed with that information when you're asked some questions."

I sat up straight from my slumped position. "Who is going to ask me questions? What the hell do I know besides what you've told me?"

She looked down and whispered very, very softly, "Well, there are some things you don't fully know. I wasn't allowed to tell you."

"Please tell me now; I mean, I'm so raw, you might as well." This woman before me felt like all I had in the world just then. While I had no choice but to forge out on my own now, that alone fear still throbbed inside me.

"Driver, could you pull over by that park bench for a minute? We need some fresh air." She grabbed my arm and pulled me out of the car. "Wade's being followed by the authorities twenty-four-seven now. And the feds are driving me around until the investigation is done. That's why I wasn't concerned about the

SUV following me around. I knew exactly who it was. I was helping them figure out some of the final pieces to the puzzle. But that's finished now that we have the flash drive."

"Is Wade going to jail?" I was terrified.

"Never. I promised you he's getting full immunity. They want Max Rowland and some shady characters he invests with."

"How do you know?"

"I know." And she started to cry.

"Jesus, Jackie." This is something I thought I'd never see. She looked shaken.

"I just found out something."

"Well," I answered softly, "I know how you feel. I just found out my best friend at work was screwing my husband." I handed her a Kleenex.

"I promise, Allie, I wouldn't have done that with Wade if we were friends, and when we weren't even friends, I told you right away. We don't belong with these people. One more problem: I never told you one thing that you're going to hate me for not telling you."

"Are you crazy? There's more?"

"In a few more days, I'll be able to tell you absolutely everything. But I've got to go now before I lose it." Jackie jumped into the car in her vertiginous heels and then sped down the avenue, her car weaving out of sight.

38

Hold on Tight

Six hours after I left the Willingham Hotel, I saw Caitlin across the room at the Fulton Film Festival panel she had produced for *Belle de Jour II.* She avoided my eyes. My mind had been bouncing back and forth between scenes of Wade and Caitlin in love and Jackie in tears over something I couldn't even begin to decipher. I had no idea when I would figure out the cause of Jackie's crying, but I sensed it would finally explain her role in this whole drama.

Murray grabbed my shoulder. "Why is the room so fuckin' empty?"

I turned back to him. "Don't forget the buzz on *Belle de Jour II* is horrendous. The critics have been brutal, no other word for it. People are discounting it even before it opens."

"If the critics knew anything, they'd be making movies. They're the fuckin' gym teachers of the entertainment world.

Where's Caitlin?" He looked around. "You never should have let her . . ."

I spun around, my nose inches from his. "You know what, Murray? Let me put this to you in terms you can understand: Svetlana's a blond stick insect with nothing in her brain. That's why no one's here. No matter what you and Wade have done to try to prop up this film, the girl has no career and the film is a piece-of-shit remake you all engineered to keep Max happy. Not even Hillsinger Consulting can turn this one around."

Murray was silenced for once, with no comeback. Next Caitlin slinked up to us. But Murray sulked away as if his mommy had just screamed at him.

"I don't need you to defend me, Allie," she said.

"That's good, because I wasn't."

"I don't know what to say, Allie." Her lips were pressed so tightly together I could see a white line around her gloss.

"Spare me, please." I saw the whole thing in my mind's eye. Wade couldn't help himself from grabbing the cookie jar and a nice little tight athletic ass. Guys never paid attention to Caitlin, so she was a willing sucker. Simple as that.

"Well," she added, "you said he wasn't your soul mate. I knew you didn't fully love him. So I—"

"So you what?" I crossed my arms.

"It's been awful, every bit of it. And even more so, because now I've lost—"

"You screwed my husband right in front of me. End of story." I turned to walk, but then decided I needed to give the knife one tiny twist. "By the way, everything you know is about to come crashing down around you. Hold on tight."

"TELL ME, SVETLANA," Delsie Arceneaux asked onstage in front of a few audience members, as she yanked on the seam of her kelly-green suit skirt from atop an uncomfortable-looking barstool. Loops and loops of Lanvin, thick pearl and grosgrain bow necklaces, cascaded down her chest. She pushed her sexy, bold librarian glasses she didn't need up the bridge of her nose and went for one of her trademark and, therefore, searing lines of questioning: "Is this your big break?"

"Allie," said a voice in the dark from behind where I was standing. "Allie. Come here."

I whipped my head around. At the sight of him, I cracked my neck to loosen the tension, and it sounded like twenty chopsticks breaking in two.

"I've been watching you," James finally said.

"For how long?"

"Long time. Back here in the dark. And you didn't even sense me." From the cushy maroon velvet theater seat, he clasped his fingers behind his always messy, dirty blond hair. I felt so relieved to see him there that every muscle in my body suddenly relaxed with a big, internal, physical *aaahhhhh*. His strong arms and elbows pointed out behind him, and he leaned back in his chair in a way that New Yorkers just didn't sit. He placed his ankle on his knee and put his black sweater in his lap. He looked like he was readying himself in his Super Bowl lounger to view the game rather than about to watch a precious little snobby New York screening. His scruffy stubble crawled up the side of his strong jaw. I could see a slight change in his eyes.

"Is it over?" I asked. "With your dad?"

"Took a few more days, but yes. Both parents are gone: just me now."

"Okay," I answered. "I'm sorry."

"Thanks, but I'm actually relieved." He stood up and grabbed my arm to draw me toward him in the dark. I tried to pull away, but he held on and said, "Don't even think of resisting, Allie. Let's go grab a drink."

"There isn't a drink in Manhattan big enough to handle me at this point. Plus I kind of have to stay . . ."

"Yeah, 'kind of' being the operative phrase," he whispered boldly. "You don't have to stay. These people are boring. This is all foreign to me, but don't tell me you don't know exactly how long this panel lasts; you did this stuff in your sleep when you were in your twenties." He grabbed the program. "It says right here. Discussion: forty-five minutes. Film clips: one hour and thirty minutes. We'll slip you back in five minutes before the lights go back on. We're getting you a drink the size of Manhattan then. You don't really have a choice anyway. Let's go."

"I'M FINE," I said, my voice cracking as I gave in and we headed outside.

"Don't tell me you're fine when you're not fine."

It felt like a huge cord was twisting inside my chest. "Are you still here alone?"

He exhaled through his nose. "Yeah, Clementine couldn't come over for the funeral."

That fear of life alone started settling in and gripping me . . . "Oh, well, that's okay; she couldn't come over. I mean, fine. I would have come to the funeral, you know."

"You know, it was just like three of us spreading his ashes in his favorite part of the shore; we didn't want to do anything much."

I so wanted to be there for him even if he felt he didn't need me. I would have *shown* him he needed me there, *especially* if Clementine wasn't there. "I don't know where we can go," I said, quickstepping to keep up with his loping pace.

All I knew for sure was this: everything felt surreal because I kept feeling inside that James was the answer even though he wasn't acting like the answer. He was acting like we were close old pals, not, as I decided in my raw state, the two most emotionally connected people in our galaxy. We were walking down Gansevoort Street in the West Village at eight o'clock at night, and he looked more like a lumberjack than a native.

It was quiet on the barren cobblestone street. The stores had closed for the day. Beautifully lit mannequins in the windows were posed as if they were frozen in the act of doing something important. On their way to a party. Checking out a guy about to ask for a date. A still frame of players caught up in the immediacy of the city. I was so on edge that the mannequins almost scared me. It felt like a *Twilight Zone* episode where they would come alive, walk out of their stores in the darkness, and say something to me like: "*Allie. The reckoning is here.*"

"Look." James pointed to a bistro on the corner. There were about twelve small round tables outside, all empty but one.

"We're getting some food right now; I'm making that unilateral decision. You look like you need something solid. We can be back by the time the film is over." He put his arm around me and squeezed me tight against him. "C'mon, kid. Lighten up. You got the weight of the world on your shoulders." He turned to me and loosened up my shoulders by rolling them around in opposite directions, then started doing quick karate chops on my back. "Jesus, Allie, you're a mess."

Karate chops, like an older brother would give his sister, were not what I wanted. I needed caresses like he'd suddenly decided I was the one he should have been with all along, especially since his girlfriend was so far away. France was almost another planet, after all. We started walking again with his arm tight around me. "You're the new orphan," I told him as I rested my head on him.

"It's been forty-eight hours and I've already moved on. He's at peace."

I turned and searched his face. "You seem like you have; really, you do."

"You know what?" James said softly. "I have. He was who he was, plain and simple, and now he's gone. I need to live my own life now."

"Sounds better than when we talked last week when you were calling him an ass on his deathbed. You seem really okay and healthy now. Not common forty-eight hours after the death of a parent, but good. Really good."

He looked at me hard as we stood inside a building alcove

and placed a hand on my cheek. "Yeah, you could use a dose of healthy, too. You are too tough on yourself, Allie." He grabbed my hand and made a small outline of the scar on my wrist. I pulled my hand back. "It's been almost twenty years since your dad passed."

I shot him a look. "What the hell is that supposed to mean?"

"It's supposed to mean move on and grab your precious life by the balls." He held on to my arms as if that would help him connect to me more. "Live a little on your own terms. Hell, live a little on your own!"

Not what I wanted to hear. I was not at that moment in the happy, confident, I-can-do-this box by any stretch. I took a deep breath and then said, "I'm doing what I need to do; I'm ending my marriage." I tried not to sound defensive.

"For real, it's over for good with that prick?"

I rolled my eyes at James. "Stop." His insulting Wade felt like he was insulting me for marrying him and I didn't need that piled on. "It's serious what's going on. And yes, it's seriously over. And it's tragic to end a marriage and complicated, so please don't be joking about what a prick he is, even if he is." I let out a small smile for the first time in weeks. "It makes me feel like I should have known better, even if you did warn me over a few beers a dozen years ago."

"Well, I salute this move, but what are you doing for you that makes you—"

"I'm writing all the time, diving into work, thinking about some new strategies to make the Fulton Festival make me some money. That's handling my life on my own terms."

"That's the scaffolding. I'm talking way inside, those swirling emotions I see on your face. You know, when I see you less often and we talk about everything like it was yesterday, you're still frozen in that Daddy's little girl mode. I wonder if you forget your dad died in that plane crash, not you."

"That's ridiculous. I'm a grown woman."

"It isn't ridiculous." And then in a quieter tone he added, "Jesus, it's good to see you. I need an old friend tonight."

I smiled back at him. "Me too, you have no idea." I needed a little more than a friend but that didn't seem to register with him.

I sat down on a metal staircase, trying to move a bit closer to him.

"C'mon . . . no choice . . . we're going to get you some dinner," he said, tweaking my nose, not exactly a sexual move on his part. I figured I should maybe lean into him again. I put my hand on his thigh and rubbed the inside a little in a way a friend wouldn't. He very quickly pointed to the restaurant terrace and pulled me up. "Look at that far table. No one will hear us. You can tell me every fucked-up thing about your fucked-up life."

"I'll be cold." And I sat back down. He sat next to me and thank God pulled me tight to him. Maybe he was getting it. With Clementine gone, this could really work. Timing is everything and Fate was finally on my side.

He took off his thick black sweater and put it around my shoulders. A garbage truck lumbered by us creaking side to side on the uneven cobblestones. Two men standing on the rear of the truck stared at us, the only other people on the street.

James turned to me and said, "You know, I was looking

through photos of Dad last week and I found so many of you and me from way back."

"And . . . ?" *So we were meant to be?*

"It really got me thinking how close we were."

"What the hell? So now we aren't close?" My eyes filled with tears. I suddenly felt like I was losing everything: James, Tommy, Caitlin, and my prickish husband to the authorities.

James shook his head. "Of course we're still close, Allie, but you have that look like you think I'm going to solve everything for you when that's just impossible. I mean, you're in this horrendous storm now for sure, but you're the only one who can navigate yourself out of it." He took my hand and folded my fingers one by one into a fist. I didn't hear anything he said as I moved my face closer to his. Unfortunately, I didn't take note of his craning his neck back. "Sometimes, I wrap myself in the mythology of us too and I even get lost in this idea I have of 'us' as eternal soul mates. You have me, Allie. You'll always have me. I don't mean to say I'm not here for you." His voice was a door slamming far off in the distance.

"I need to know my old friends are there. I can't do this divorce alone," I said, about to lose my last bit of strength. "It's not the orphan talking . . ."

"You sure?" he asked. "Because from where I'm standing, I think you're going to be okay with or without me."

My anger flared, remembering Jackie telling me the same thing, that I needed some time on my own. "Why does everyone keep saying that? Isn't it possible that I don't *want* to do the impossible alone? Why do I have to be okay? Why can't I want the crutch I want to get through this?" Full slide backward now. "I promise you, I can't do it. Any of it. Of course I'm going to take care of the kids, but the rest I don't know if I can do and I'm so scared and I . . ." I started sobbing those horrible wails where I couldn't breathe or catch my breath. I felt like a full-on crazy woman in need of a horse tranquilizer.

The world went still.

Then he gripped my shoulders and pinned my arms. "Allie. Stop. I know your life sucks right now. But—"

"I *mean* it, James."

And then I did the unthinkable. I kissed him way too hard. I held his cheeks like he was the long-gone love of my life. He grabbed my hands and kind of kissed me back, but I wouldn't call it a passionate reckoning on his part. More like a what-the-fuck-is-this-woman's-problem kind of reaction.

"Allie. You're losing it."

I shook his hands off and clutched them back in my own again. "I know I messed everything up by rushing into marriage with Wade, but I was nervous, and I thought he would solve everything. And I did love him. I did. I mean, I think I did, in the sense that I loved the man I hoped he'd be, the idea of him. Problem is, I'm not sure he ever became what I had imagined him to be. On top of that, I'm devastated he didn't love me back in the loyal way I thought he would, like the vision never became the reality." I looked up at him, hoping honesty and directness might prevail, as all else wasn't exactly working as I had wished. "I know you are thinking it's really fucked up we just kissed, but I swear it isn't."

He actually looked at me stone-cold like I was out of my mind.

I carried on, "Maybe we would have been better together. Maybe I made the wrong choice back then and didn't wait for you, and fucked up everything, and now it's too late, and you have your life overseas and I . . . well, with her gone now, maybe you'll just reconsider a little and—"

James put his hand across my mouth, and I lost it again. I couldn't breathe. I collapsed against him. It was misty outside, which made me feel cold even though it was balmy.

A group of teenagers walked by briskly, and I began to shiver. James cradled the back of my head in his right hand and then held me tightly along my back with the other. He smelled like he always did: sweet and warm. He rocked me back and forth until my pathetic shuddering stopped.

"We tried," he said. "A few times. And despite the fact that I'm far away, I still adore you. But you can't go kissing me like that just because you're freaking out like a little girl."

"I'm not. I'm just . . . you didn't want me to kiss you, did you?"

He laughed a little. "Look, I'll take any kiss from any pretty girl, but it's not who we are right now." He wiped my nose and smoothed down my hair. "Look at you! You're just a mess!" I muffled a laugh and he went on. "It's much better like this, us as friends forever, you know that. You're going to be all right, Allie," he whispered into my hair. "I promise. You're going to do what you need to do right here."

I didn't like that response in any way. "I don't know if I can."

"Allie," he started, and then shook his head and looked at his feet. "You are going to be fine. You have it stuck in your head that some far-fetched notion of 'us' is going to solve all your issues, but it can't . . . *I* can't. There are telephones. Call me anytime about all the screwed-up things that happened in your marriage and we can go over what went wrong and when. But it's not that complicated because guess what? He was a lot of fun, maybe even a good dad, but he's also a selfish dick who's out for himself and cheats on you. It's not that difficult to analyze. It's good you're moving on."

I decided to try. "You sure?"

"Positive. But I have something really important to tell you." He paused. "I actually came into town to tell you this in person: Clementine is five months pregnant, and I'm really happy about it."

"Wow," I croaked, stunned. "I guess that's why she couldn't fly here, huh?"

"It's a boy." James was happy. He'd said he was at peace. And he meant it.

Something to aspire to.

So this was finally it. I could practically hear the final boarding call for the next flight to Paris. That moment I either stood up and relinquished his hold on me or threw myself on some pyre of pity. I snapped out of my hysteria, and that reckoning I'd been looking for slammed solidly into my head. And the nice thing: that elusive happy, confident box suddenly, weirdly didn't feel so hard to climb over and get into.

39

Surprise in the SUV

With the idea of James as salvation off the table, and Tommy no longer my quick-fix crutch, maybe I was finally ready. No longer could I depend on Wade for anything except being a fun-loving dad—I had to understand that once and for all. The kids would always get my love and tons of it, but I'd have to work on feeling better inside if I were going to mother them like they deserved and I wanted.

The healthiest first step would be to march into work and call a divorce lawyer and get the separation ball rolling. The new me would execute all that without a blip. The new me would finish the final draft of the new me's screenplay without needing Tommy to paint-by-numbers me through it.

But all that Oprah magazine self-help stuff would have to wait.

AS I WALKED about fifty yards down the block from my apartment building to work, sunglasses hiding my puffy eyes, I noticed an SUV with dark windows rolling down the sidewalk at the same speed as my steps. Quickening my gait, I tried to figure out if I was out-of-my-mind paranoid: a man on the corner in mirrored aviator glasses looked away quickly, as if he'd been watching me. I was sure he must be a Max Rowland acolyte and that this was the same black SUV I'd seen a few times before, maybe not the FBI one trailing Jackie, maybe an SUV of a bad person. I ran into the Korean market two doors down and went straight to the back wall lined with glass refrigerator doors. But as I opened the glass case door to reach for a soda, a large man came to a stop inches away from me.

"Please come with me, Mrs. Crawford," he said in a spooky, authoritative voice.

"Oh my God, you scared me. Who are you?" I pulled away.

"You're perfectly safe." He showed me a badge I couldn't read. I figured it was a fake. He took another step toward me. "Please, just do as I say."

I ran to the front door where I bumped into another man blocking the entrance. "It's okay, Mrs. Crawford. We're with the FBI. Let's not make a scene. Just follow us. Please, we're going to explain everything to you."

"I don't need anything explained, and I won't say a word to you all until I get a lawyer." I tried to barrel past him, but with the security cameras watching and the manic Asian owner at the cash register holding court with the hordes of New Yorkers in line to order their morning coffee, I wasn't at all convinced that would help.

"Really, I'm definitely not interested in talking to you, either of you, right now. I'll just go to work and you can call me there." I went straight for the tea and coffee bar and started making myself a cup of tea, figuring I'd come up with an alternative.

The two agents were not in the mood to waltz around the deli with me. They pressed in from both sides, trapping me next to the coffee bar, and the first one whispered, "Mrs. Crawford, don't worry." Then he whipped out his badge again. "We don't want to make a big deal of this, but we're instructed to bring you in and we're following orders." I looked around for Jackie, half hoping she'd solve this somehow.

"What do you want?" I dropped the empty paper cup. "Why can't we talk on the street outside? No one will see us."

"I think it's better for you to walk quietly out of the store with us and to our vehicle, as if it was part of your morning routine. Just walk right up to that black Suburban, and get inside right now, please."

I did as I was told and we drove down to the FBI office at the tip of Manhattan, me sitting in silence next to Agent #1 in the backseat while Agent #2 drove. I didn't want to say anything that might get me into trouble. Let them tell *me* something I didn't already know.

As we pulled up in front of a brown brick building, I announced to the agents, "I will be calling my lawyer."

"That's fine, ma'am," said Agent #1 next to me as he got out of the SUV and offered me a hand down. "We'll be taking you up to our boss now."

One problem churning in my head: my lawyer was Wade's lawyer, and he'd probably helped him siphon all our cash to

Murray and Max Rowland. I realized I should probably find a new one in the next ten minutes.

At the end of a long, gray linoleum hallway, I was led to the closed door of an office marked SECURITIES UNIT, UNITED STATES ATTORNEY'S OFFICE FOR THE SOUTHERN DISTRICT OF NEW YORK.

Agent #1 with the mirrored aviators and a G.I. Joe jaw reached in front of me to open the door, and on the other side of the room, a well-dressed man with an air of authority walked around his desk to greet me. "Mrs. Crawford. I'm Assistant U.S. Attorney Tom Witherspoon," he said, handing me his card. He smiled at me with kind eyes and combed back his short, brown hair with his fingers. A handsome thirtysomething, he looked like a young legal whiz kid who had snagged the top job. He then escorted me to a soft side chair next to his sofa. "These FBI agents have been detailed to the U.S. Attorney's Office to work with me on major securities fraud cases overseas. Why don't I get you a cup of coffee? We're going to be in here for a long while."

"I think I need a lawyer," I answered, crossing my arms and not in any mood to sit down.

"We're not charging you with anything."

"You're not charging me with anything, but you obviously want information from me. And I have a right to a lawyer and a right to remain silent so I don't say anything that would be incriminating. There's a law about that, you know. It's kind of a famous one. Aren't you supposed to be telling me that, not me telling you that?"

"Mrs. Crawford, we are not reading you your Miranda rights

because you're not under arrest. You can sit here in silence and listen. You can ask us any questions you want, and we will answer them as truthfully as we can." He handed me a Styrofoam cup of lukewarm coffee that smelled like it had been brewed three days before.

"I still want a lawyer," I answered. I walked over to the window, where, beneath us, stood the square fountain memorial at Ground Zero.

"That's fine," Witherspoon said. "It's too late for that, I assure you. But if you want to call your lawyer, you can. But I wouldn't try your office."

"What is this?" I asked around the room, stiffening my body more. "Why can't I call my office? Where exactly is Murray? What's happened with him?"

Witherspoon chuckled and sat on the sofa arm with his hands clasped in his lap. "Why don't you get comfortable, Mrs. Crawford? I've got a long story to tell you that I know you'll be interested in hearing."

40

Courtesy Call

I tried not to laugh at Witherspoon's plan. "Sir, you cannot take one of the great narcissists and attention seekers of our era and put him in witness protection. It won't work in a million years." The cheap brown leather squeaked as I plunked myself down in the armchair. "Your usual plan of action just won't function well with Wade Crawford."

"He has no choice," Witherspoon answered matter-of-factly.

"Believe me: if you send Wade Crawford to a witness protection program, he'll spill the beans to the first grocery clerk he sees." I took a deep breath and eyed the glass awards and framed honors that lay haphazardly along the dusty windowsill. "The guy lives on recognition and notoriety," I said, amused at the mere concept of Wade assuming a different name. "Ward Cranford. Hah." I shook my head in mock laughter, but I could sense that it was already a done deal.

Witherspoon rested his elbows on his knees and delivered the following fact. "Your husband has admitted to his involvement in a corrupt investing scheme with absolutely no prodding from us, and now we need to protect him until we have the real offenders under wraps."

I laughed. "I'm telling you: witness protection won't work for more than twenty minutes."

"Many women have the same reaction you're having now. It can be hard on families, but we need to close in on every one of the characters involved in an international ring holding millions of dollars in these overseas accounts. We just want three months for your husband to take a little break. You can visit him with the children. We are there for you in every way, Mrs. Crawford, but he needs to be in witness protection for six months; there is no getting around that."

"How would he live?" I asked, imagining a cargo-short-clad, Teva-sandal-wearing Wade in his rented ranch house in Topeka, with a maroon Prius parked in the driveway. "You really think his ego will take not being able to run his little media empire for three months? I find it hard to believe he agreed to that."

"Witness protection is an important part of the arsenal in our investigations. It's much more prevalent than you know. People take sabbaticals from work all the time or care for a loved one. It's actually quite simple."

"It's nuts. I'm telling you." I nodded and pushed my lips together tightly. These guys would not get one more word out of me.

"The most important thing for you to know is your husband is going to be protected. He was involved as an accomplice, but his cooperation will allow him to remain uncharged and free from prosecution."

"Does he know this?" I asked.

"Yes."

"Do you know we're divorcing?"

"That is none of my business, ma'am, but, yes, I've heard."

"Is this what they do with mob wives? Get the case in order, criminals charged, then inform the wife calmly as a courtesy call when it's all over?"

"I'm not going to comment on our activities, Mrs. Crawford, and this situation is unique."

"Okay, then please inform me on just how unique." I wondered where the Jackie piece fit and when I'd be hearing that one thing she couldn't tell me that made her cry on that bench.

"We know you're aware of some of the dealings that have been going on," Agent Witherspoon answered.

"I am, kind of, but . . ."

Witherspoon went on, "First: your boss, Murray Hillsinger, is broke."

"He orders fifty-eight-dollar entrees every day, sir. And then asks the waiter to double it. I'm not sure broke is really the right term. Or else it's relative. Donald Trump was broke in the 1990s for a minute and a half."

"Mrs. Crawford," Witherspoon said, tapping Murray's file in front of him. "Murray Hillsinger is broke and in debt. Men who find themselves in this situation can get desperate. They need cash quickly, or their empire will tumble. He gambled too big on investments he knew nothing about to keep his PR firm afloat. He went long on stocks like he was at the craps table, thinking every media rumor your husband could spin would work like solid gold and boost stock prices. This did work for a time, but then the big one didn't—it's always like that; they get too greedy and then the big one takes them down." He shook his head. "We see this all the time with important figures who are low on cash. Sometimes they break the rules around the edges to get that cash back quickly. Since you were doing PR for the Fulton Film Festival, you should know they actually laundered a good deal of cash through a movie called"—he glanced at his notes—"*Belle de Jour II.*"

"Belle de Jour?"

"Yes, you see, the bigger you make a movie seem, the easier it is to juggle the profits and losses."

The panels, the *Meter* magazine cover, closing the festival with *Belle,* all to hype a film they knew was horrible.

Witherspoon closed a file. "Their real crime was trying to screw with the stock market by using the media to their advantage. You can ask your lawyer or me as many questions as you like. We have no reason to charge you. We're positive you had nothing to do with this. We did some checking." His kind eyes crinkled as he grinned a little.

"What do you mean, checking?"

"We have our methods, Mrs. Crawford. Max Rowland has been making shady deals ever since he left prison. He's one of the big ones we wanted, and we got him. We just have to nail those around him." Poor Camilla in her pink-bubble-gum St. John dress. Back to Allenwood for family visiting hours every Saturday.

"Any newscasters in the mix on this?" I wondered where Delsie figured.

"If you're talking Delsie Arceneaux, she's back at work and she just got herself a raise. That one knows how to take care of herself, but she wasn't worth the trouble if you really want to know the truth."

I suppressed a smile, thinking about how Delsie drove our entire company crazy with her requests. Apparently the FBI agreed: they found her so impossible and taxing, she'd scared them off from even trying to get anything out of her. "So what do I do now?" I asked.

"You take a deep breath." He placed a Chase bank card with a fifteen-digit code on the desk between us. "And I believe this is yours."

I shook my head. "Someone cleaned out that account, I assume Wade."

"Well, this is a new account." Witherspoon then barked at the guy with the aviator glasses. "Get Agent Egan in here, please."

The sexy woman who'd sat next to Jackie at the bar of the Tudor Room walked through the door with her straight red hair swaying back from her shoulders. As she introduced herself, I noticed her tight suit fit her behind as snugly as the Dolce & Gabbana number I'd seen her wearing when she followed Wade.

She told me, "Jackie made them put all your money back in another account and rename it yours alone now."

"Wade agreed to this?"

"He didn't have a choice, frankly. We even extracted a waiver from your husband yesterday," Witherspoon answered. "But he didn't seem too attached to the money, he was so concerned about the legal aspects of it all, and keeping his name clean."

This actually made sense because I knew Wade never cared about the cash; it was attention and the excitement of playing with the big boys that he sought. I palmed the bank card, thankful my kids and I were whole.

Agent Egan walked over to the seating area. "I was assigned to Ms. Jackie Malone. She said that the money in the account was yours, and you did nothing that should cause you to lose it, so you should have it. We won't be freezing the account."

"You sure?" I asked. "You sure it's all back in there?"

"Yes. Ms. Malone made sure of that," Agent Egan replied.

"We had one smart cookie on the inside who helped us crack this case," Witherspoon added. "Once she got a sense of what was really going on, she became obsessed with finding the answers. She thought someone ought to take them down. Never seen a woman so determined. I like that in a woman!" This guy was clearly smitten with Jackie. He went on to explain more. "And I hear Murray Hillsinger wants you to run the film festival without him. Max Rowland basically bought it with all their cash so Murray's company owns it and someone has to handle it now."

"He wants me to . . . you mean, run it?" I covered my face so they couldn't see me smile. Going from promoting films to actually choosing them was just the kind of independent life plan I needed at this point. "How's Murray going to fare in all this?"

"Well, Mrs. Crawford." Witherspoon got closer to me. "Murray is going to put his PR business on hold for a while and move away somewhere quiet too, like your husband, until we round everyone up. He's free from prosecution for now because he's cooperating, but he is not allowed to engage in business dealings of any kind, so yes, he is fine with your leaving the PR department to run the film festival. But . . ."

"But what?" I looked around. "There is something you aren't telling me."

Just then, the door swung open with the force of a hurricane. A flustered secretary appeared, apologizing to her boss for letting Murray Hillsinger in without warning. Witherspoon winked, signaling to her that he understood there was no stopping the beast.

"Oh, Jesus, I didn't want you to hear this whole thing from them. I'm just so sorry, kid."

I felt so uncomfortable. "Murray."

"You're going to be better off without me messing it all up." He slumped down on the sofa and put his head in his hands. Murray looked at me softly. Did I see his eyes watering? What the hell? "There's something bigger for me than all the business mess, much bigger, that's got me—"

"What?" I looked around. "There is something you all aren't telling me."

"I can't even begin . . ." Murray started shaking a little. Silenced for once in his life.

Witherspoon took over. "Well, let's start with the fact that Murray's fine with bringing Jackie Malone into the festival too.

He actually likes that idea, that if you were okay with it, Mrs. Crawford, that Jackie might be great at the spreadsheets, business angles; she's got a handle on the entertainment industry as she majored in that, right, Murray? For many reasons, it's important to you that Jackie land on her feet, right, Murray?"

"How well do you know Jackie?" I asked my former boss.

He didn't answer, like he was ashamed.

I went on. "I remember how shocked you were to see her at your house with her mom." Pause. No answer. His sausage fingers still covering his eyes. "It's fine, Murray; what about you don't I know at this point? I don't care, you can tell me. Were you one of her clients? The ones that pay with casino chips?"

Murray straightened up, disgusted at the thought. "Absolutely not!"

"Well, then, how do you know her?"

Everyone in the room looked at each other like they knew something that I clearly didn't. This was the one thing Jackie couldn't tell me yet. I knew it was.

"How do you know about her? I mean, I know you know her mom from way back." I slapped Murray's shoulder. "Murray, we're this far in; you've got to come clean. What the hell is going on between you and Jackie?"

Agent Egan walked over to me and looked into my eyes. "Jackie was doing a lot of investigating, and she kind of had him nailed. And once she had him nailed, she asked Murray for something, right, Murray?"

"What?" I didn't understand anything they were saying. "I

mean, why did she have to get Murray nailed so badly first? I don't understand."

Silence in the room.

Egan went on where the men wouldn't. "She wanted Murray to take a paternity test."

It was as if someone knocked me out cold.

Once I came to, about thirty long seconds later, I answered very slowly, "A paternity test for Murray Hillsinger, as Jackie's dad?"

Nods all around the room. Murray couldn't look at me.

"You're Jackie's dad?" I had to think about it for a minute. "From a thing with her mom, out in Southampton, way back?"

He nodded. I took that in for a very, very long time while the events starting clicking together in my head. I never could grasp Jackie's motives until now. Her aggressive pursuit going after Murray and uncovering the scam was so . . . primal.

That's why Jackie wouldn't give up. "She told me she needed to help me figure this out, because she didn't want to see another woman get screwed financially, which was only the excuse she was giving me. I now know that was only a secondary reason, but did you screw her financially, Murray?"

He heaved a few huge breaths out. "Her mom, Barbara, and I had a thing, when I had a little house and not so much money, way long ago. She used to tend to the garden. I was married to my first wife at the time, and Barbara was a lot of fun, and somehow she got pregnant. I didn't want anything to do with it and though we thought it was mine, we were never one hundred percent sure. She just wanted a kid so bad and said fine, she'd never expect anything. Then she started working for me about fifteen years later because I felt bad. She needed cash and she didn't want just a handout. I gave her as much business as I could, but I just didn't want to know about the kid. That's the deal we made way back when. She's a proud woman, never would have asked me for anything since we made a deal. I made a big mistake; I should have found my daughter, not made her seek me out like this. My mom's gonna kill me for being such a piece of shit."

Murray put his head in his arms and sobbed, his gelatinous body shaking like, well, a huge bowl of Jell-O.

"Where's Jackie now?" I asked everyone.

"As I said, you can find her, but you better hurry." Witherspoon looked at his watch. "She's graduating in two hours."

Agent #1 Aviator man from the SUV abduction stood at attention. "I'll be happy to drive her, sir."

Witherspoon grabbed his coat and me as we flew out the door. "Wouldn't think of it, Frank!" He seemed awfully eager to see that Jackie Malone.

Epilogue

Philadelphia's preppiest stores whooshed by the windows so fast I could hardly make them out—J.Crew, Talbots, the Christmas Store, Tiffany—as the assistant D.A. sped us through Philadelphia's downtown traffic.

I leaned into the front seat and yelled at Witherspoon, "You know, we're going to make it before the graduation ceremony; no need to kill someone the day they finally get their studies over with."

"I'm aiming to get you there quick, and get you there in one piece. The main green of the Wharton Business School is through those gates. Right off Jon M. Huntsman Hall." Something told me this speedy delivery service wasn't just for my sake. He slammed on the brakes, and with all the quick starts and dodging of cars and humans, I almost lost my breakfast. "I'll park and run right over."

From the left side of the car, I heard a crowd cheer, and my heart sank. "I think we just missed it—literally we just missed the whole graduation. Look."

Before us, through pink dogwood trees and federal architecture that lined the university side of the street, thousands of graduation caps flew up in the air, remained suspended for the briefest of seconds at the peak of their flight, then fell back to the ground, never to find the hands that launched them.

"Damn, I'll never know where she is now." I raced out of the SUV and into the maelstrom of celebratory students and teachers and parents, hugging one another in that sloppy way people do when they're relieved it's finally all over. I can't say my own emotions were so different.

After ten minutes of frenzied searching through a throng of families on the UPenn graduate school lawn, I located Jackie's mother, Barbara. She was marching around in a bright peach-colored dress and matching Easter hat, her messy gray hair framing her beaming smile.

"Allie, so nice of you to come. Jackie told me all you've done to help her out. It's been quite a spring for her." Her glowing face and strong build made her come off as tough on the outside, but her kind eyes belied that. I wondered how she felt about Jackie's discovery that Murray was the father all along.

"I'm sure a lot of her determination meant it was quite a spring for you as well."

She put her hand on my arm. "I think it's safe to say whether it's another big diploma or anything that girl needs to know, she's going to do whatever it takes till she gets there." She shook her head. "She was always the most stubborn child in the sandbox and had tantrums you couldn't imagine."

That characteristic must have come from her father; only he never outgrew the sandbox behavior.

Jackie strolled up next to her mother as if she'd just conquered the world. "Mom, gimme a minute with Allie. Girl talk." Only Jackie could make a graduation robe look sexy and adorable: she'd belted it and had a silk ruffled blouse underneath that opened up perfectly to reveal just a touch of her cleavage.

"Sure, hon." Barbara winked as she went over to a group of Jackie's professors.

"Jackie. I get it now," I told her softly.

"You sure? All of it?" she asked. "They found you?"

"Yes, some of your acquaintances came to take me to their lovely offices downtown."

"Yeah, lovely and clean and so fresh smelling. I know them well. They told me they were going to do that any day. Hope they didn't scare you. I wasn't allowed to call you, so I couldn't have done anything to warn you."

"And they explained that you were right on everything. I mean, you were telling me the truth." I took off my glasses to look her in the eye. "And that you were, as you said, helping me, watching out for me, all the while, I guess, also figuring out some bigger things for yourself." My voice cracked and she hugged me tight.

"Yeah," Jackie whispered in my ear. "I wasn't going to give up on the men screwing everyone over for their own gain. And once I had Murray by the balls, I knew I could get the proof with a DNA test. I just had to know. And the whole time the feds promised me it wasn't Wade or Murray they cared about, so I just kept pushing."

We broke the embrace but stood inches from each other. "Murray seems overwhelmed by finally finding you. Pretty shook up, but in a good way. Hopefully, it'll change him somehow."

"You think Murray Hillsinger will change ever? You don't think that big personality is set in stone?" she asked, incredulous I could even suggest such a thing.

"Put it this way," I countered. "I think he's visibly humbled. We'll see where that takes him."

Jackie took me over to an iron bench, sitting down and crossing her beautiful legs. She sat so close to me, our knees touched, and she told me, "I always suspected something between him and my mom, but once I had the evidence I could finally confront her with the goods. She said she was too proud to make him pony up when they had agreed she'd keep me and not involve him. In her world, women take care of problems by themselves."

"Until you made it difficult for him to ignore the so-called problem, I guess."

"Until I felt old enough and strong enough to take matters into my own hands."

"Thank you for watching out for me in the process, Jackie—you clearly had bigger things to deal with."

"You're welcome." She smiled, as if it were the most natural way to have behaved through this mess.

"What are you going to do with Murray now?" I asked.

She played with the tassels on her graduation cap in her lap and thought for a moment. "I don't know. I guess we start fresh. I mean, he doesn't have money to give us, and neither my mom nor I really want it. I just wanted to know. And he's going away for a few months so I have some time to figure out if I want any relationship at all."

"You might, you know. Now that I think about it, you're kind of like each other."

"How?" This intrigued her.

"Well, safe to say you're both pretty dogged and aggressive." I couldn't help but wonder if table manners might be genetic, too.

"Yeah, maybe we have some things in common, but I may not reach out. He's never been there, so I don't expect him to be now. It's just good to know is all." She bit her lip to hide an emotion she wasn't yet able to verbalize, then smacked her knees with both hands as if to help her snap out of it and added, "We've made it this far without him."

"Yeah, well, you might feel you need your dad now that you know who he is. Nothing bad about having a dad." My eyes stung at saying that.

"I know that. It's one day at a time for now." She gave me a short, but very warm hug, and then pushed me away suddenly in excitement. "Hey! We've got other things to talk about! What about the festival? Are you in?"

"Hate to admit it, Jackie, but it just might work. Right away when I heard the news I thought *how natural,* we could really make this happen. I think the writer in me will help me pick the best films that really touch people, and the smooth operator in you is going to make the right business decisions."

She touched my arm. "Yeah, at least Murray figured *that* out. It was his idea to put us together as a team, not that he had the choice."

"Jackie, I swear I'm done judging, but when you look back at this whole crazy experience, what do you think? Is there something you would have done differently to get yourself here?" I gestured toward the ivy-laced benches and brick buildings with white colonial trim around us. "It's remarkable you got this degree under these circumstances, so don't misunderstand. I admire so much about you. It was just, I don't know, it was an unusual path, let's say that."

She thought for a moment. "I was intent on taking care of my mom. And I could argue that all these men were using other people a lot more than they were using me. At least I called the shots and got highly compensated and found out everything I needed to know about my real father."

I thought about how young and old and male and female Jackie was at the same time. "You want to promise me something?" I asked her, putting my arm tight around her. "Be ruthless with the Excel sheets at the festival and make sure we're always solvent, but in your personal life, maybe be a little less ruthless. Call me nuts, but maybe you could just go out on a limb a little and find a real boyfriend or something."

She raised her eyebrows. "Allie Crawford is giving me relationship advice?"

"Well, I'm stating the obvious." I rolled my eyes over at Witherspoon, who was leaning against a tree about forty feet away, waiting for her to give him some attention; throwing any bone his way would have clearly made the guy's day. "You know I'm right."

She waved to Witherspoon, who gave her an overeager wave and smiled at her.

"He's kind of cute, that one," I went on. "He had nice things to say about you, couldn't stop praising you. I wondered about that."

"Well, I tried not to act too *boy crazy* during the investigation while I was chastising you for doing just that." She smiled a girlish grin back at him and then whispered to me, "You know, I just might sample that federal merchandise. But I want you to act on two bits of my advice for once."

"I'm listening, and I in fact always do what you say."

"I'd say you listen to me, but you don't act on it." She squinted at me, challenging me. "What about this: when you're not picking films, write like the wind."

"You already told me that, Jackie. And I was trying to do that, in the midst of a few other things going down."

She leaned into me. "You're at this turning point in your life, and it's definitely a story worth telling. You're going to bleed the truth now. Your screenplay is going to be fantastic."

"You think so?"

"I know so. You've been looking for a breakthrough, and the whole time your screenplay has been right in front of you. You don't need Tommy to help you anymore."

"You never know how life will bring people together, but I am going to try to just concentrate on my kids and my writing and that's it. Lord knows it all might just work, now that I'm shedding men right, left, and center." I looked at her. "You know Wade and I are going to split."

"I figured as much. Sorry if I made you see things that precipitated that."

"I needed to see things I didn't want to see before, and it's fine. I mean, it's not fine, but it is, if you know what I mean."

She laughed. "I know exactly what you mean."

I said, "What's the second thing?"

Jackie brushed the hair out of my eyes. "Pick films that *you* think matter to the world and write scenes based on what *you* want to write about. Stop looking for support classes and men to tell you it's okay and what to do next before you make a move. And while you're figuring out your new life, go it alone for now. It'll make you feel better."

"It sounds like maybe it just might, " I told her. "Like a huge relief not having to run to everyone else to prop me up."

"That alone thing will actually feel less alone once you try it. Go find your own answers. Trust that you can do it. Do you like the idea of that?"

I grinned and sighed with a level of comfort I hadn't felt in years. Now it wasn't just an idea; it was real.

"Yes, as a matter of fact, I think I finally do."

Acknowledgments

Writing a novel is great company. Fictional characters are in your head all the time just like the real characters in your life: an old boyfriend who called, a hot guy with trouble written across his forehead you wish you hadn't met, a child and her latest stumble, a boss with no concept of reality. For two years I walked, ran, showered, cooked, and mothered with Allie, Wade, Murray, James, Tommy, and that elusive but on-point Jackie in my head . . . all intriguing company. As I thought about how far Jackie would go to get what she was after, what basic truth Wade the narcissist couldn't grasp next, how Allie would actually feel if . . . I tested ideas on friends and colleagues.

Some of you read the manuscript in its embryonic state (forgive me David S. and Tom Y.), some read the entire book twice (Joel S.), some read only a chapter and got me thinking about a new way in, and one of you even left a presumably difficult version on the Hampton Jitney bus and forgot that you left it there . . . but to all of you who cared and gave me clarity on my convictions about life and love and women being okay on their own that made it to these pages, I am grateful.

Most of all, I am indebted to my agent, David Kuhn, and his deputy, Becky Sweren, who very generously guided me with their unique gifts of no-nonsense lucidity and precision. Tessa Woodward from William Morrow handled my manuscript like a best girlfriend—giving me firm counsel with just the right amount of distance and respect for my independence. Both Amy Scheibe and Susan Opie helped me sculpt early versions with immense patience and skill.

Also bottomless thank yous for sharing reactions and vital encouragement: Susanna Aaron, Eric Avram, Trisha Azcarate, Leslie Bennetts, Jessie Borkin, Kasia Bosne, Marie Brenner, Brenda Breslauer, Tina Brown, Ebs Burnough, Jess Cagle, JuJu Chang, Jean-Marie Condon, Courtney Dawson, John Durkin, Susan and David and Sam Edelstein, David Forrer, Jordana and Alissa Friedman, Emily Gerard, Kyle Gibson, Gary Ginsberg, Lynne Greenberg, Craig Hatkoff, Alexis Hurley, Karen Lawson, Katie Lee, Elizabeth Leeds, Jeffrey Leeds, Jennifer Maguire, Ray McGuire, Peter Manning, Albert and Carol Margaritis, Henry Margaritis, Crystal McCrary, Ashley and Jeff McDermott, Todd McElrath, Cynthia McFadden, Susan Mercandetti, Peter Meryash, Clementine and Lionel Steve-Miserolle, Todd Mitchell, Esther Newberg, Kathy O'Hearn, Glenn Petry, Richard and Lisa Plepler, Abby Pogrebin, Eli Richbourg, Seth Rosenberg, Bob Rylee, Fardad Sabzevari, Rick Saloman, David and Elizabeth Saltzman, Teddy and Jack Saltzman, Neal Shapiro,

Susie Stangland, Josh Steiner, Al Styron, Electra Toub, Heather Vincent, Darren Walker, Ali Wentworth, Betsy West, Sherrie Westin, Kim Witherspoon, Andrea Wong, Lee and Bob Woodruff, Andrew Wylie, and Tom Yellin.

And finally, to my insider family of sustenance: my parents Sally and Michael, and Pete and Joan, John Margaritis, my four brothers Johnny, Jim, David, and Michael, and their wives Patti, Wendy, and Tara, for putting up with me in general on every level, Joel Schumacher, Jay and Alice Peterson, ditto, and, most important, to my darling children, Chloe, Jack, and Eliza, for bestowing on me the joy of being their mom.

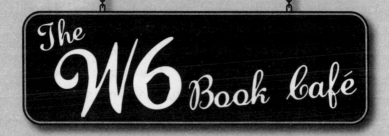